BIVALENT

BIVALENT

EVOLUTION OF CONTROL
BOOK 2

NAOMI M. WONG

Paperback ISBN: 978-1-7377275-3-8
Ebook ISBN: 978-1-7377275-4-5

Cover art by: www.fiverr.com/jannatulnisa
Credits for cover photo from istock:
"Eastern Newt" photo. This image was altered for the creation
of the book cover. Photo by: https://www.istockphoto.com/portfolio/epantha

Published by Naomi M. Wong

naomimwong.com

❀ Created with Vellum

To my family whose generosity and moral support enabled me to finish this book: Thank you for making this possible!

To the Love of my life, who is my beginning and end: Thank you for walking with me in the in-between!

To my writer friends: Thank you for the stimulating conversations that make me a better artist!

NOTES ON THE WORLD OF EVOLUTION OF CONTROL

Introduction

Readers have been asking me about how the world came to be the way that it is in the Evolution of Control series and about the specifics of how the racial classification system works. So, I decided to make available my notes on these subjects. I hope that, through them, readers will better understand the world that I am describing in Evolution of Control.

It may come as no surprise that I built this literary world through reflecting on my experience as a woman whose parents come from two different American racial minorities. As such, I have a unique perspective on race and racism, which I hope will prove a helpful contribution to the discourses currently in play. That said, readers will likely identify some aspects of this literary world as fundamentally racist. I write descriptively about racial hierarchy not because I believe that the idea has merit but because I perceive, all around me, evidence of internalized racial hierarchy in people's actions and words.

Moreover, my experience as a biracial person has opened my eyes to the fact that racism can take many different forms. I know with certainty that anybody and everybody can be racist, even if they do not mean to be. Sometimes, it is in our desire simply to have a place in the world, to seek the security and power of a distinct identity, that we perpetuate racist systems. In Evolution of Control, I challenge the ways that people claim that racial identity is—or should be—formed.

Let's face it: white supremacy introduced red, black, yellow, brown, and white categories in order to maintain power. Accepting these categories uncritically will *never* lead to offsetting this power dynamic, despite our best intentions. However, I also understand that dissolving racial categories would *not* be the answer to our current predicament. Race permeates American reality such that denying its existence would be unproductive. For a social construct, race has frighteningly concrete consequences that affect people's physical and emotional wellbeing. So, to instigate positive change, we will need to work with existing categories while remaining open to new ways of understanding them. Evolution of Control highlights the flaws in our current system of racial categorization in order that we might seriously reconsider how we conceptualize race and group identity.

I set this series in the late twenty-first century and early twenty-second century to provide some artistic speculation about the logical consequences of internalizing current racial categories. Such internalization occurs either through the acceptance of a hierarchy of race or, equally detrimentally, through the solidification of inherently hierarchical racial categories so that minority cultures may appear relevant or valid enough for dialogue with the majority culture. I hope that the following notes on the literary world of Evolution of Control and its racial classification system will be a helpful resource as you read this series.

The Origin and Rise of Neo-Eugenic Law

Neo-Eugenic law was first mentioned in a dissertation in the early 2030s. Its author was a doctoral student, whose name deserves to be lost to history. This person believed that they were writing a liberating manifesto of world peace. The student came from a majority culture background in the States and was sympathetic to the plight of minority cultures.

Neo-Eugenic law is based on the idea that everybody gets along when everybody knows who they are and how they should interact with each other. This necessitates strong understandings of group identity, which this student proposed should come from the essentialization of existing social categories that carried strong historical and cultural significance. The process of essentialization—the student believed—needed objective guiding factors or else social categories could morph, causing the system to malfunction. The student elected to call upon so-called science (a mangled form of genetics) and mathematics (simple arithmetic) to be the basis of and mechanism by which essentialization should operate.

According to the doctoral student, defined class categories would provide a framework within which each minority group could be understood as a valid, united body in the eyes of the majority culture. This could only work, however, as long as groups kept their blood pure—that is, they had to ensure that their genetic pools were distinct from those of other classes. Thus, the so-called "pureblooded" classes were formed, based on social categories that were salient in the view of the majority culture: white, yellow, brown, and black. Incentives to keep blood pure and measures to disincentivize blood tainting would need to be established in order to guarantee the proper functioning of the system. From these concepts, the idea of the Subclass would later emerge to take on an ugly life of its own.

The doctoral student never successfully defended their thesis. They dropped out of school and later submitted their thesis to an independent publishing house that agreed to publish it out of pity. A decade later, a public interest lawyer found the book at a used book sale. Reading it and being convinced of the truth of its message, this lawyer founded the group that would come to be known as the World Council of Eugenics.

By the time period of Evolution of Control, everyone is obsessed with the concept of blood purity. Although the idea defies science and transcends reason, it drives decisions on every level of society. Under Neo-Eugenic law, to taint blood is condemned; to have impure blood is to exist as a physical reminder of the wrong done; and to join with one of impure blood is to publicly condone what has been condemned as well as to taint one's own bloodline.

The World Council of Eugenics

The World Council of Eugenics (WCE) began as an American think tank and social mobility group. Their central tenets were based on interpretations of Neo-Eugenic law that were so extreme that the originator of the law denounced the group. While WCE members spoke loftily about the strengthening of communities and the fulfillment of personal identity, their primary motivations were fundamentally wealth and influence.

As the WCE gained more traction, especially among the American social elite, the council became more involved in business transactions. With the membership of leading political figures from around the country and around the globe, the nature of the WCE's business evolved and diversified. Thus, Neo-Eugenic law spread and morphed to take on new forms in different countries.

At the start of the Evolution of Control series, the WCE is active in the political life of the States as well as in covert operations of governmental and private importance. In addition to covert ops, it has sections in weapons development, research, and trade. Whatever the WCE appears to be doing in the public eye, it is certain that much more is happening beneath the surface.

Hierarchies of class and sex are very important to the organizational structure of the WCE, although much of the time these are kept in place mainly for the sake of appearances since everyone well knows that the best person for a task may be the person least expected by societal standards.

No one knows how many tenets the WCE has. The same tenet is rarely quoted twice, and the tenets always seem to give an authoritative air to an ignorant and opinionated speaker's utterance.

Geography After the Divisive Round

The Divisive Round was a two year long negotiation that was set in motion to formalize governmental restructuring as different regions of the States adopted or adapted Neo-Eugenic law in an official capacity. In the decades leading up to the Divisive Round, there were multiple waves of migration as people relocated to regions that better matched their sensibilities about interclass relations. People who were not affluent enough to relocate had to remain in place and adapt to new ways of life. The Round was both launched and completed in the 2090s.

While the eastern and western regions of the country had been diverging politically for decades, the Divisive Round formally divided the States into the Eastern and Western States—each of which developed its own federal government. During the time period of Evolution of Control, trade continues between these regions, and their military resources are shared.

The Meridian is a longitudinal line that separates the Eastern States from the Western States. The Eastern States comprises the Northeastern State and the Southeastern State while the Western States comprises the Northwestern, Southwestern, and Midwestern States. All of the states contain districts which can be home to boroughs, towns, villages, and urban centers. Typically, district identity is the most salient for inhabitants of these regions, although state membership does come into play with respect to trade and representation on a federal level. States also tend to set the tone for how their districts will adapt Neo-Eugenic law, although the specifics of this adaptation may vary.

To diverge from its parent state's adaptation of Neo-Eugenic law, a district may become exempt. This usually incurs some cost, as with Diablo which—because of its refusal to wholly adopt Neo-Eugenic law—is exempt from Western federal financial support and Southwestern State technology subsidies. A district may also be unaffiliated with the WCE, which can only occur if there are no members of the WCE who hold office there. In such districts, it is easier to pass laws in contradiction to the state's current views without needing to be officially exempt. Some have pointed out that the main difference between unaffiliated and exempt districts is the median salary since, due to a lack of resources and education, poorer districts are often unable to oust WCE-affiliated leadership.

The Classification System

The classification system is a system of racial categorization, which is based on the mythical four major biological races (classes). Proponents of the classification system believe that class is a biological phenomenon, and while there is little to no genetic evidence of this, they depend heavily upon stereotypes of bone structure, facial features, skin color, and hair texture to reinforce social understandings of class. Even at a glance, it is evident that this is a subjective science.

Purity of blood is important in the classification system, and this works on two levels. On the one hand, one maintains purity by associating with and procreating with members of one's own class. On the other hand, there is an assumed ontological purity that accompanies the possession of features that the majority culture once understood to be ideals. Despite ever-changing ideas of beauty, Neo-Eugenic law set in stone that the purest of the pure features include flaxen hair, blue eyes, and the least melanated skin possible. The combination of this phenotype with verifiable, untainted European lineage bestows upon the possessor the descriptor "wellborn."

The Four Registered Classes

Throughout time, people have classified the major world races according to their own experience with and exposure to people that they believed to be different from themselves. Thus, there have been various assertions regarding the identities of the major people groups from whom everyone in the world can be said to descend.

According to Neo-Eugenic law, the four registered classes are Classes 1, 2, 3, and 4, based on the very American understanding of white, yellow, brown, and black categories. By the time period of Evolution of Control, a special category—Class 4.14, pronounced "four-one-four"—has been created as well. The Subclass is a legally unregistered, hodgepodge group consisting of the offspring of inter-class relationships. All of these categories will be explained in more detail in the following sections.

It is important to remember that the classification system prioritizes purity as defined by Neo-Eugenic law. To be wellborn is to have a class designation of 1.0. Because Class 1 is best born, so to speak, Classes 2-4 are referred to as the "lesser" classes.

"Pureblood" is a term used to describe a member of any of the registered classes (Classes 1-4). Depending on the region, this term may also be used to describe an indigenous person, but it absolutely excludes any member of the Subclass.

Note: "pureblood" and "pureblooded" are equally appropriate for adjectival use.

While class hierarchy exists in both the Eastern and Western States, the East prides itself on creating more opportunities for the lesser pureblooded classes and has experimented with legislation to minimize harshness toward members of the Subclass. In the East, members of pureblooded classes are allowed to legally marry members of other classes, and they may retain their class designation—although their children are still subclass. In all Western districts except for Diablo, interclass marriage is illegal.

Class 1

Class 1 people are said to have their genetic roots mainly in Europe. They are stereotypically believed to have noses that are sharp, prominent, or both. They can have broad brows and deep-set eyes, but not always. They can have very thin lips, but not always. They can have a variety of skin colors ranging from alabaster to olive to tan, and their hair can come in a variety of colors and textures. Darker hair, curlier hair, and more melanated skin will result in a higher class designation which, according to Neo-Eugenic law, is less desirable.

Class 1 people were originally immigrants to the States, and through many ruthless actions they became the dominant majority culture. They have a troubled history of domineering and cruel behavior toward minority groups, a fact which was eventually widely acknowledged. A portion of the Class 1 population rallied to provide reparations for the worst of their ancestors' deeds and made substantial efforts to change cultural understandings of the class hierarchy. However, another portion of the Class 1 population resisted these efforts mainly because they believed that they were not responsible for the wrongs that their ancestors had enacted upon the lesser classes. Yet another portion of the Class 1 population advocated for the strengthening of hierarchical understandings of class because they believed that their ancestors had been *correct* in their treatment of the lesser classes. This clash of opinions in the Class 1 community was never resolved, although it lay dormant in some regions for a number of years.

A decade before the Divisive Round, the Class 1 community's clash of opinions reawakened in a bloody conflict. It was to be expected. Those at the top of any hierarchy are loath to relinquish their power. Equality and equity, to them, would mean the loss of power. And no one in their right mind, even the kindest and most honorable, *likes* to lose power. Because of this complicated history, Class 1 people—much like people of any other class—can have a variety of viewpoints and attitudes regarding class relations and hierarchy.

Slurs: paperwhite; thin skin

Class 2

Class 2 people are said to have their genetic roots mainly in East Asia or Southeast Asia. They are stereotypically believed to have noses that are broad or flat. They can have almond-shaped eyes, sometimes with monolids. Their lips can be thin, but not invisible. They can have a variety of skin colors ranging from pale beige to golden brown to the color of maple syrup, and their hair is typically dark brown or black and straight with a scrub brush texture. Their hair can sometimes be naturally curly, and there is often pressure within the group to artificially straighten curly hair. Darker hair, curlier hair, and more melanated skin will result in a higher class designation which, according to Neo-Eugenic law, is less desirable.

Not long after their entry into the American system as immigrants, Class 2s strove to be associated most with the American majority culture and to distance themselves from the oppressed of the land.

Such behavior perpetuated harmful prejudices toward the Class 4.14 community especially, but it also enabled the Class 2s to make a space for themselves on a new middle rung of the class hierarchy. Some Class 2s went so far as to seek, by means of the legal system, to be registered as Class 1s. They were denied Class 1 status. It was perhaps their desire to be most like the Class 1s that fueled their simultaneous hatred for and fascination with the dominant class.

Throughout American history, Class 2s tended to fare better than other lesser classes, but they were not exempt from mistreatment. For instance, they were exploited for cheap labor to build America's transcontinental railroad system; some were interned in camps during World Wars II and III; and as scapegoats for the pandemics of the mid-twenty-first century, they were subject to violent hate crimes. Sometimes, Class 2s of certain ethnicities were targeted over others, but this was not always the case. Class 2 ethnic labels, other than with respect to foreign affairs, became less and less salient to the majority culture. Thus, strong, public ethnic identification in the Class 2 group began to wane.

In the mid-twenty-first century, Class 2 identity superseded ethnic identity as the most prominent form of identification among members of this group—although within one's own family, ethnic identity remained well acknowledged and sometimes celebrated. By the time period of Evolution of Control, Class 2s are still known to be among the harshest critics of interclass relations in the States and have become purists within their own class. A 2.1, for instance, can be thought too wellborn for the likes of a 2.6, and families can split over that kind of situation.

Despite the dual role of Class 2s as oppressed oppressors in the history of the States, there were always members of the Class 2 community who acted in opposition to eugenist and purist social pressures. These brave people often paid for their actions through the loss of familial contact, social supports, and sometimes their lives.

Slurs: yellow belly; slanty; slurs carried over from American history

Class 3

Class 3 is likely the most ethnically diverse class in the world. Class 3 people are said to have their roots in Latin America, the Middle East, Southeast Asia, South Asia, Africa, or various islands in the Pacific. In the States, many Class 3s are immigrants or descended from immigrants. Ethnic identity is still very much alive in these groups, and Class

3 is mainly a designation used for official purposes or to identify oneself to a member of another class.

Class 3s can have flat or prominent noses. Their eyes can be any color and almond-shaped, round, or somewhere in between. They can have a variety of skin colors ranging from olive to copper to the various shades of coffee—inclusive of cream, but not always. They can have thin lips or full lips. Their hair can come in a variety of colors and textures. Darker hair, curlier hair, and more melanated skin will result in a higher class designation which, according to Neo-Eugenic law, is less desirable.

With as many ethnicities as are included in this category, there are as many complicated histories to consider with respect to their residence in the States. Throughout American history, Class 3 people have been subject to harassment and violent hate crimes. Generally, prejudice against 3s is rooted in the idea that they are foreigners, but difference of religion is also sometimes cited as a reason for their mistreatment.

Slurs: brownie; a variety of ethnically-based slurs

Class 4

Class 4 people are said to have their roots in Africa. In the States, they are sometimes mistaken for Class 4.14s (described in the next section), but the primary difference between the two groups is that the Class 4s and their ancestors arrived in the States as willing immigrants whereas the ancestors of Class 4.14s were brought to the country as enslaved people.

Ethnic identities remain strong within this class. Class 4s often retain—with pride—a solid connection to their ancestral cultures whether through language, cuisine, or other means. For some proponents of Neo-Eugenic law, these differences are enough to grant Class 4s a slightly more elevated status than 4.14s. However, for others, the similarity in physical appearance between the 4 and 4.14 groups makes 4s likely targets for the same hate crimes that may be directed at the 4.14 community.

Class 4s can have flat or prominent noses. Their eyes can be blue, green, hazel, brown, or black, and almond-shaped, round, or somewhere in between. They can have a variety of skin colors ranging from cream to copper to ebony to blue-black. They can have thin lips or full lips. Their hair can come in a variety of colors ranging from blond to brown to black, and it can also come in a variety of textures. Darker hair, curlier hair, and more melanated skin will result in a higher class designation which, according to Neo-Eugenic law, is less desirable.

Slurs: ethnic-specific slurs; when mistaken for 4.14s, a number of slurs carried over from American history

Class 4.14

The category 4.14 was created to account for the history of people who were descended from enslaved African Americans in the States. Because of this history, there has been tension between Class 4.14s and members of the other classes, most notably Class 1s whose ancestors were the original enslaving group. Although slavery ended centuries before Evolution of Control, violent hate crimes and anti-4.14 prejudice are alive and well. Consequently, the fight for civil rights and equity continues. A step in the right direction did occur, however, in the 2080s with the passing of the Value 4.14 Lives Act, which effectively reduced—but did not completely eliminate—police brutality toward members of the 4.14 community.

Often, Class 4.14s have a hodgepodge ancestry that can be traced primarily to African, European, and Indigenous American people groups. Reflecting on this can be painful, since this hybridity is due, in large part, to enslavers' abuse of the enslaved. Before the Subclass category was officially formed, there was a rule requiring every person with a 4.14 ancestor within five generations to be considered 4.14. Thus, membership in the group was flexible enough to include people with varying degrees of tainted blood, and the 4.14 community became home to a diversity of phenotypes.

4.14s can have flat or prominent noses. Their eyes can come in any color and can be almond-shaped, round, or somewhere in between. Their skin color can range from alabaster to russet to copper to ebony to blue-black. They can have thin lips or full lips or lips somewhere in between. Their hair can come in a variety of colors ranging from blond to red to brown to black, and it can also come in a variety of textures, generally with some curl but not always. Darker hair, curlier hair, and more melanated skin will result in a higher class designation which, according to Neo-Eugenic law, is less desirable.

While Class 4.14s won great social victories in gaining a more humane lifestyle and establishing the validity of their collective voice before the dominant culture, they had a sort of self-destructive revolution in the mid-twenty-first century in which they claimed that membership in the 4.14 community should no longer be extended to individuals who did not have two registered 4.14 biological parents. The community began cutting off not just those of impure blood but also those of impure associations—that is, members of the Class 4.14 community who procreated with members of another class. The community did this in order to preserve and protect what they believed to be the purity of the 4.14 class and to have legitimate grounds for dialogue with other pureblooded groups.

At the start of Evolution of Control, the range of phenotypes within this class is as wide as ever, but only the immediate offspring of two Class 4.14 people will be registered as Class 4.14.

Slurs: blam; slurs carried over from American history

The Subclass

Subclass people are descended from biological parents of differing classes. They can have their roots in any region and any people group. They are known to have a variety of phenotypes and can often have a similar physical appearance to members of any of the other classes, even if they are not descended from those classes.

Unlike purebloods, members of the Subclass are unregistered. This means that they can move across district boundaries with relative ease because no governing bodies within the States count subclass people in their percentage requirements. However, not being registered bars subclass people from a number of activities and opportunities, depending on the region. They and their families are often shunned, harassed, and sometimes harmed by proponents of Neo-Eugenic law who view the Subclass as a threat to the classification system on which so much of their social reality is based.

Subclass people, if they are fortunate enough to maintain some connection to their extended family, must keep a clear division in their mind between their family and the rest of their heritage communities. Even though their family might accept them, they cannot expect the privilege and security afforded to registered members of a pureblood class.

While members of each of the lesser pureblood classes can make a case for how class stratification puts them at a disadvantage, they often overlook the great advantage of being recognized as a registered member of one's own group for social and financial protection. Subclass people are often denied these protections. And although members of their heritage groups tend to assume that subclass people can approximate this kind of protection by blending in—or passing—

as a member of another class, this route is unreliable at best and, frankly, anathema to many members of the Subclass who harbor great love for their family and heritages.

Subclass people who are able to pass for one or the other of their parents' classes will sometimes do so in the hopes of receiving partial social protection. They will never be officially registered, so they will remain exempt from certain opportunities—especially those offered by the government. However, they may receive the social benefits that come with acceptance in one of their heritage communities.

In the Western States, the descendants of a subclass person will always be subclass. This is due to the belief that blood cannot be purified once it has been tainted. By the time of Evolution of Control, some districts in the Eastern States have come up with a plan to offer subclass individuals a chance to reenter their heritage communities: through marriage to a person of one of their parents' classes, as long as that parent is a pureblood.

Proper notation: A subclass person is a member of the Subclass, and they have a subclass designation.

Slurs: subber; slurs having to do with one's heritage communities

Indigenous People

Indigenous people are treated differently across districts and across the world. In the States, there is a tragic history of genocide and oppression of the indigenous people. Some districts make more substantial efforts than others to give reparations to the indigenous people, but those reparations may seem to do little in the face of repeated offenses including withholding of resources, taking of land, overlooked injustices, and a blatant lack of respect for human lives.

There are many groups registered under the label "Indigenous," even in the States alone. While it is commonly believed that the indigenous people in the States migrated across a land bridge from Asia long ago, their origins remain a mystery.

There is no single designated phenotype that reliably indicates descent from indigenous people groups. Indigenous people can have skin colors ranging from alabaster to tan to copper to blue-black. Their noses can be sharp or broad. Their lips can be thin or full. Their hair can range from blond to brown to red to black, and it can be straight or wavy or curly. Their eyes can be almond-shaped or rounder and can be blue, green, hazel, brown, or black.

In many areas of the States, people are so steeped in a four-class mindset that they do not give much thought to indigenous people at all. When this happens, an indigenous person is likely to be subject to the viewer's best estimation of class designation.

It could be said that Indigenous Americans are no strangers to eugenism. Blood quantum, a colonial imposition, was instituted centuries ago as a way to control and designate tribal membership. In this case, both estimated phenotypes and mathematics came into play as the dominant culture attempted to essentialize social categories. Similarly to those officially represented in the four-class system, indigenous communities may take different views of blood quantum as it may restrict or serve them, relatively speaking, in their quest for survival.

Slurs: landlord; slurs carried over from the past couple of centuries of indigenous peoples' history

Calculating Class Designation and Subclass Designation

It is easy to calculate one's class designation. One simply takes the average of their biological parents' class designations. For instance, if one has a parent with the designation Class 3.5 and a parent with the designation Class 3.3, then this person's class designation is Class 3.4. The parents, by marrying and/or procreating within their own class, are said to have "kept the average" (see motto below).

Calculating subclass designation is slightly more complicated. If one has a Class 1.0 father and a mother of some lesser class, that person must divide the mother's class designation by the father's to get their subclass designation. For instance, if one has a Class 1.0 father and a Class 3.5 mother, that person's subclass designation is Subclass 3.5.

If the father is not Class 1.0, the person's subclass designation is calculated by *adding* the class designations of the parents. For instance, if one has a Class 3.5 parent and a Class 4.2 parent, that person's subclass designation is Subclass 7.7.

This old motto is taught to children in State-sponsored schools to help them to understand the hierarchy and mechanics of the classification system:

> *Four is lower than three, than two, than one, since adding is subtraction*
> *So, we keep the peace with our division, dividing without fractions*
> *Everything divided by one is the same, and same divided by same is whole*
> *Keep the average, keep the peace, keep control!*

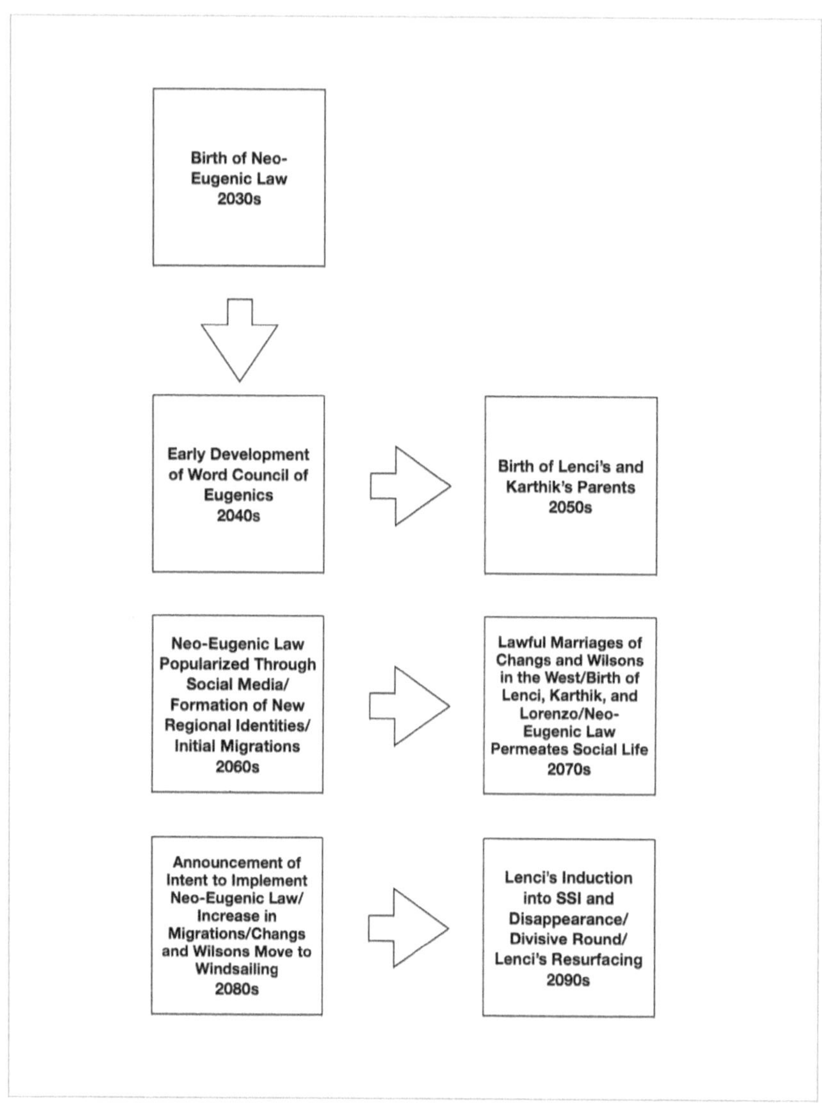

Timeline of the Rise of Neo-Eugenic Law in Relation to Evolution of Control

CHAPTER 1

WHAT IS NECESSARY MUST NEVER BE LAMENTED. THIS IS ALWAYS TRUE but never so starkly recognizable as when one is hurtling through the space between two buildings at ten stories up. Such was the case for the woman of copper-colored skin and large, muscular legs who sailed across the gap between the Central Bank and the Class 1 School for the Gifted. She was the Agent, known there in the southwestern district of Carmelita by the deceptively delicate name of 'Posy'.

The Agent named Posy was wearing a tank top, shorts with gray, cable-knit stockings, and a green backpack full of explosives. She tightly grasped a small package that contained a finger, which she had harvested from the recently deceased head of the district. She tried to cradle the package, but she landed with such force on the school's rooftop that it flew from her hands.

She skidded after the package, secured it just before it slid over the far edge of the building, and bounced up with bloodied forearms. She stuffed the package into her backpack, then turned to confront her pursuers.

"Gentlemen," she said, "you will find, after some investigation, that the district head's agency-issued cyanide tooth is empty. At 0300, Mitchell chose his own demise. So, can't we resolve this amicably?"

The men had only just landed on the roof themselves, and they seemed more winded and irritated than they had on the last two roofs across which they had chased her.

"Not a chance, Posy," said the one whom she had nicknamed Pat. "His wife wants you for questioning."

"You can tell Agnes I said it wasn't personal." Posy bit her lip. "On second thought, that won't help at all. Don't tell her that. Let me escape instead. What do you say, fellas?"

"You'll come with us alive, or we'll bring in your body," Pat responded.

Matt—her other pursuer—said, "Give up the finger, and we'll talk."

The men looked at each other as if they needed to take a timeout to discuss their plan of action. The Agent charged Pat and kicked him square in the abdomen. He caught air and landed beyond where the roof ran out.

Matt pulled an extendable steel baton out of a holder in his pant leg and swung at the Agent's head. She grabbed his wrist and broke it.

"Not my face, please," she said, relieving him of the baton.

Grimacing through the pain in his dominant wrist, Matt jabbed at her with the other hand and caught her on the cheek.

She then roundhouse-kicked him off of the roof.

"I told you, '*not my face*,'" she said.

Her eyes scanned the shadowy rooftop as if other pursuers would suddenly appear. But they did not. At length, she wiped her bloody arms on her shorts and chuckled.

"Down, girl. Consider the roaches squished."

"Roaches," she called them, for reasons of a past life. She rarely dwelt upon the details, but it had to do with their being necessary to crush—or something like that.

She turned and looked out at the entire district expanding before her in a sea of lights. The lights appeared to flicker because of the wind, but that was just an illusion. The wind was bending the light-waves, disrupting them. The false flickering reminded the Agent of how lives can start and end in a moment. And yet, the very idea of light in darkness—much like the miracle of life itself—so muddled the Agent's understanding of beginnings and ends that it seemed an invitation to persevere. There still remained one little light in her dark world, a light worth all of the trouble of perseverance.

It had been about a year since her child was kidnapped by Hinny, an operative of the World Council of Eugenics. Before Kiddo was born, the Agent had made the child a promise—that she would make sure that he or she was safe. Admittedly, Kiddo's abduction had been a setback, but the Agent had every intention of fulfilling her promise.

When she thought of Kiddo, she ached terribly. It was an excruciating and constant pain that was somehow both dull and sharp at the same time. She had spent months preparing for her child's arrival only to be left bereft and, doggedly, still expectant.

Somewhere, her child's earthly sojourn continued without her. How many of the little one's big moments had she missed already? Kiddo was probably learning to walk by now and, unfortunately, to fight—if the Assistant Vice had anything to do with it. All sorts of fears filled Posy's mind following that thought.

"Say it again," she whispered gruffly. And her fears subsided.

For months, the Agent had scoured the obscurest corners of the Western States, networking and exchanging her highly coveted skills for information. She had broken her share of bones, manipulated Carmelita's district head and his wife, and even extinguished a few lights of her own—all to get her to this place at this time.

Hinny was the principal at Carmelita's Class 1 School for the Gifted. While there were rumors that the WCE was actively recruiting Class 1 minors for a black ops program, Posy had observed that Hinny mainly used the school as an after-hours drop point for transactions with arms dealers. She apparently wore many hats at the WCE.

Ten floors down, there was a caravan of three armored cars pulling into the parking lot. If this evening was like any other, the dealers had already come and gone, taking the money that had been left for them in five duffle bags. And now, Hinny and her roaches were there to collect the weapons.

When the armored cars parked, six roaches hopped out. Five of them ran up the steps to the school, and one went around to the passenger's side of the lead car to open the door for Hinny. She stepped out, smoothing her bleached blond hair, and walked with purpose up to the door of the school. The middleman, who had overseen the drop, leaned out to greet her. Hinny and her roaches followed him inside.

Showtime. The Agent moved her backpack to the front of her body and did a roundoff over the side of the building. She caught footholds and handholds wherever she could, and there were many along the decorative exterior of the building.

The principal's office was on the third floor, and it had a window through which the Agent intended to enter. She paused her descent at the fourth floor and began to move laterally to position herself above the window. The wind whipped past her. It was messing up her already wild, curly hair, but she did not dare to take a hand off of the building to smooth it. Oddly, the height at the fourth story was more intimidating than it had been up on the roof. Keeping her head down, the Agent shuffled the rest of the way to the room above the principal's window.

From the displacement of the light coming from the office, it appeared that there were four people congregated near the window. The Agent figured this would be her best opportunity to make a fairly uncomplicated entrance.

She swung downward, propelled herself through the window, and landed on the middleman, who bumped his head on the desk and expired on the floor. Hinny and her two roaches aimed assault rifles at her. The Agent dismantled the weapons of the roaches—whom she named HorseFace and Ponytail—in time to wrestle with Hinny over hers.

HorseFace approached the Agent from behind with his slightly congested breathing. The Agent kicked him into Ponytail and used the downward force to rip the gun from Hinny's grip, dislocating the woman's trigger finger in the process.

She struck Hinny with the butt of the gun and asked, "Remember me?"

Crumpled on the floor, Hinny looked too dazed to remember anything at all. The Agent used Hinny's weapon, somewhat unconventionally, to prevent HorseFace and Ponytail from interfering with her mission—permanently. Their gurgling screams echoed in the hall, and in response, there came the tramping of booted feet. Hinny's other roaches were just down the hall from the principal's office, and they were approaching quickly.

"Come on, Kidnapper," the Agent said, dropping Hinny's gun and pulling her to her feet.

The WCE agent was weak in the knees, but she couldn't be left alone. So, the Agent dragged her to the door. Then, with the door closed and locked, she tied Hinny to a chair.

When her eyes refocused, Hinny smirked. "Come to think of it, I *do* remember that tragic face."

"Shut up," the Agent said.

By the light switch, there was a panic button enclosed in a glass box. The Agent broke the glass and pressed the button. A thick metal sheet descended from the doorframe. The floor and ceiling rumbled as the same happened somewhere beyond their stark, hospital-white surfaces. Only the windows facing the street, by which the Agent intended to escape, remained vulnerable. At one-second intervals, a buzzer sounded and white lights flashed around the room. There was a faint tapping on the other side of the door, likely the futile attempts of Hinny's roaches to blast it open with bullets.

"Alone, at last," the Agent said, setting her backpack on the floor.

"So, this is what it comes to?" Hinny said. "I tried to kill you, and now you've come to try to kill me? How trite."

The Agent burned with rage. Her motivation was anything but trite.

"I've been watching you for months," she said. "I could have killed you before."

"Then, why—"

"Because you have information I want. And once I have it, I'll be on my way."

Leaning forward with a sly expression, Hinny remarked, "Information only? You've lost your spark, *Fire!*"

"Don't call me that!" the Agent growled. "I left that name at Home."

"But it *is* your mark, is it not?"

The Agent leaned in to meet Hinny's gaze. "The only marks I have are the ones I created myself."

Hinny spat at her. The Agent leaned to the right, and a small blade shot past, narrowly missing her face.

"I wonder how many of those you can keep in your mouth at once," she said, grabbing Hinny by the jaw and forcing her mouth open.

After ensuring that there were no other sharp implements hidden in there, she asked, "Where's my kid?"

Hinny cackled until she choked on her own spit. "You spent a year tracking me down just to ask about that subclass chunk of tissue?"

The Agent kicked her in the tibia, and she yelped.

"No pain management," the Agent observed. "Just as I suspected."

Hinny cared for nothing and for no one, so physical pain was the only soft entry point through which the Agent could maneuver her into compliance. She stomped on Hinny's foot, extracting another cry of agony.

"The Assistant Vice ordered you to do it, fine," the Agent said. "Tell me where she sent my kid."

Hinny smiled sassily. "She sent a Phib for the drop. That was my only contact."

"Phib," short for Amphibian, was the WCE's official term for operatives of the Agent's cohort. They had been trained in isolation and knew little of each other, but the Agent had—about a year before—gained access to a master list of all of the Songs that were the tools of the Amphibians' handlers. She had committed the Songs to memory and destroyed their source files. She, therefore, had a roster of the whole Amphibian cohort and the means to control any Amphibian. Of course, she had been trained to forget such sensitive information until she needed to access it for survival's sake, but extracting a name from Hinny could make the information relevant and therefore available to her conscious mind.

"Which Phib?" she demanded.

Silence from Hinny.

"Don't test my resolve," the Agent said, striking Hinny's ribcage. "If I have to, I will break every single bone in your body."

The WCE agent's mouth opened and closed, but the words did not come fast enough. So, the Agent backhanded her, knocking her sideways in the chair.

On the floor, Hinny began to laugh hoarsely. "Grapevine says the Assistant Vice got what she wanted and she disposed of him. She's moving on to more profitable projects."

Concerned that one of Hinny's broken ribs might pierce her lungs and inhibit her ability to speak, the Agent turned her onto her back.

"I don't believe you," she said.

Hinny waggled her tongue in a way that sent chills up the Agent's spine. "And you're next. She's sending her best after you."

"*I'm* the best," the Agent told her.

Hinny's eyes focused momentarily. "Hubris—the universal soft entry point."

The words hurt.

"Time is running out, *Fire*." With a lightning-fast tongue waggle, Hinny popped the cap off of her WCE-issued cyanide tooth. At that angle, the pill easily slid out into her mouth.

"No, no, no!" the Agent cried, sticking her fingers into Hinny's mouth to keep her from swallowing. "Tell me where the Assistant Vice is keeping my kid!"

"Ticktock, ticktock," Hinny choked. Her smug face took on a bluish tinge, and she began to convulse. Then, just like that, she was beyond the efficacy of a pain-driven interrogation. She had won.

The principal's office was eerily still. At some point—the Agent could not recall exactly when—the beeping and flashing of the alarms had stopped, which meant that the door would soon become a vulnerable entry point once again. She pulled the explosives from her backpack, initiated the countdown to their timed detonation, and cast them like confetti around the office.

A loud rumbling indicated that the panic door was receding. Looking out of the window through which she had entered, the Agent noticed a street lamp only a few meters down. She dove out of the window, aimed for the arching pole of the lamp, and caught it. The downward force put enormous strain on her shoulders, and she thought she might have heard something snap. She swung her legs over the pole and hung upside down from her knees.

The explosion from the office was hot, bright, and loud. After the shower of window shards had settled, the street was cold, dark, and silent. The Agent exhaled deeply. Hinny had wanted her to believe that Kiddo was dead, that the Assistant Vice had disposed of him. But the Agent, who had personally escorted many to the darkness of eternal rest, believed it was possible to sense when an innocent life remained in the world against all odds.

"Him," Hinny had said.

"Kiddo's a boy," the Agent whispered with a smile. "My son."

It was disappointing that, after months of searching, she had only partially gained the information that she so desperately sought. However, there was still some kind of information on the chip that was embedded in the district head's finger. Although the Agent had gained her freedom from David Miller the Killer, his control over her remained in one form: the anti-tech conditioning. Despite this substantial vestige of her time with him, the Agent had a workaround. She knew someone who could help her to access the information on the chip.

* * *

Rackelle Wernicke was sitting at a worktable in her lab at the Cooperative FBI Headquarters. It was after working hours, but she had stayed at HQ to perform routine maintenance on her probes and

3-D programming tools. As she greased her probes, she had a holographic message playing on a loop. It was Samir Bourghin's last message to her, which he had recorded only hours before the event at SSI where he passed away. It was precious as such and also because Racky was fairly sure that there was more to the message than met the eye.

When the holoprojector timed out and clicked off, she restarted the recording from the beginning. Bourghin's image appeared in the middle of the room. He sat with his shoulders hunched and his hands folded.

Racky rubbed her greasy hands together and closed them carefully into fists before putting them on her hips. A flush crept into her creamy cheeks as she regarded the grainy three-dimensional hologram of her old mentor.

Hey, Racky. Samir shifted the camera, so it would face him more at an angle. *If you're seeing this, I've finally met my maker, and—more likely than not—Lenci is in the wind. I don't know who else to trust, so I'm invoking your agency commitment to serve and protect Lenci as your charge. I know this road can't be easy, but I want you to think about how you were when we first signed you.*

"I was a rapscallion, for sure!" She laughed, smoothing her voluminous, honey-colored curls. "And a hussy."

That same tenacity, that relentless optimism we had for you…

"That *you* had for me," she corrected.

That refusal to give up on a human being's divinely given potential—have that for Lenci. She needs you now, more than ever.

"I *will* find her, Sam."

He cleared his throat. *So, um, I guess I should get to it. The information I'm about to present to you is from bugged conversations at WCE facilities and WCE agents who were willing to exchange information for money. Since Lenci got back, I've been pulling out all the stops to get to the bottom of this. And let me tell you, if this stuff is true, we're all in a bigger mess than we know.*

"You got that right," Racky said, picking up her probes and her greasing cloth again.

Much of my research points to a link between Lenci and a group of agents called the Amphibians. There's almost no available information about the Amphibians, or Phibs—as they are sometimes called. All my sources can agree on is that the Phibs are a group of elite operatives that were poached from other agencies to further the WCE's efforts in the project known as "the Cull."

Some sort of substitution process occurred, resulting in a pool of agents half the size of the recruitment pool. No one has been able to tell me why roughly forty agents were recruited for the program or what happened to the twenty that weren't selected. I'd bet my life that our twenty missing agents from SSI were shunted into this program. The question is what the WCE wanted with subclass agents and ones from our agency in particular. It might have something to do with Beatriz—I fear that Miller has found some way to maintain control over her after all these years.

There was a rustling over by the lab's door. Racky didn't bother to turn around. It was probably Theresa coming to mock her about watching Bourghin's recording for the umpteenth time. Racky turned up the volume as a deterrent against any interruptions.

Anyway, one of my sources was—for a price—able to get me limited, supervised access to a homing chip. Every Phib handler has one implanted in their finger with slightly different coordinates, all within the boundaries of the compound where the Phibs were trained. The chips aren't only trackers; they're some kind of reminder. You know how the WCE is always inside of everyone's head. Anyways, I've written the coordinates in my green notebook, but I—

Samir looked at his watch. *I don't have time to travel there to investigate. Lenci is going to meet Beatriz this evening, and I aim to be there as well to, uh, mediate any discussion that may take place.*

When I first had a bad feeling about some of Beatriz's interactions with our subclass agents, I thought registering Lenci as a Class 3 would keep her from harm. It seems that I failed in that regard, but I'm going to try to make good on that tonight.

"Oh, Sam, I wish you had not," Racky said with tears welling up in her eyes. "Almost certain Lenci feels likewise."

Listen, Racky, none of my sources know exactly what the Phibs are trained for, but they all agree that they are intended to be some sort of human weapon. Even though the Phibs are considered a cohort, they were trained in isolation. They're rumored to have been subjected to mind control and brutal torture for the sake of compliance.

All that's to say: Lenci, if you find her, may not be anything like the girl you were primed to serve and protect. But she is still your charge.

Be careful, Racky, but you've got to find her. You've just got to find her.

"I have been tenacious in the search, Sam. I'm really doing my best, here." She wiped her eyes on the back of her wrist.

Samir ran a hand through his gray and apricot-colored hair. Racky smiled as he scratched his scruffy chin and turned his sad, gray eyes upward. He was fidgeting with something above his head, outside of the camera's scope.

Feeling strangely stirred, she paused the recording, stepped behind

Bourghin's image, and craned her neck to catch a glimpse of what he could possibly be looking at. She couldn't.

Pressing play, she watched as his arm moved like he was closing something, maybe a door or a drawer. Then the image flickered out.

Theresa's voice cut through the respectful silence. "You're still watching that old recording?"

She really had been standing by the door that whole time.

"Thank you for keeping your comments until the end," Racky said curtly. "I know I'm missing a big, chunky puzzle piece. I just can't figure out which one."

"If you say so." Theresa ran a hand through her silky black pony-tail and examined her split ends. "I just wanted to tell you this in person in case your buggy home security system is still filtering out my messages to your personal flake: Lee-Smith arranged for you and me to meet Wilson in Carmelita since Cormorant is only a district over from there."

Racky looked up from her tools, but before she could ask her question, Theresa was already answering it. "He'll debrief us on the Cormorant findings when we get back. Lee-Smith says time is of the essence. After our close call in the Milestone Desert, Wilson calculated Carmelita as Lenci's current hiding spot."

"I wouldn't call evidence of her being there two days prior a 'close call,'" Racky said.

"Close by the Coop's standards." Theresa shrugged. She looked at the bright red time display on the wall. "Anyway, I'm going to snag a nap in my car before we head out. Airstrip at 0600, Lee-Smith says."

"I'll be there," Racky said, turning to the holoprojector.

When she heard the door shut, she prompted the projector to play Bourghin's recording from the beginning and wrote down a plan in her calendar for Blair's approval. What she had seen at the end of the recording could have been nothing. But it *could* have been something. She hoped to visit Samir's widow, Esperanza, in Diablo as soon as possible.

CHAPTER 2

THE ASSISTANT VICE'S BEST... THE AGENT WONDERED WHETHER HINNY was among those who still believed that the Killer was at the top of the food chain at the WCE. Last the Agent had heard, David was still recovering from their bloody conversation the year before. It was unlikely that the agency had deployed him as a bounty hunter so soon, but the Agent didn't intend to stick around Carmelita long enough to find out.

Before leaving, however, she had urgent business to handle. She had managed to fish the chip out of Mitchell's finger and disposed of the digit in a toxic waste container at the corner of West and 16th. And now, she was on her way to visit her neighbor Crispin to enlist his help with accessing the chip's contents.

The Agent crossed the street to a dingy apartment building. She jogged up the nine flights of stairs, rolling her shoulders under the straps of her empty backpack. She had injured herself catching hold of that street lamp, but her natural range of motion would return shortly if everything inside of her was working correctly.

The couple in the apartment at the end of the hall was arguing again. Their voices carried through the paper-thin walls, and their poor kid—a skinny, blond girl with enormous blue eyes—sat outside their door, calmly waiting for things to quiet down.

"Folks still at it, huh?" The Agent smiled sympathetically.

The girl nodded.

"Hang in there," the Agent said. "I'll check on you in a bit."

The neighbor girl's peaceful adaptation to her parents' strife brought the Agent hope—hope that her son would adapt beyond the consequences of *his* parents' strife. She planned to make that possible by finding him and removing him from the WCE's custody, which was indirectly the reason that she needed to see Crispin.

She moved a couple of doors down to Apartment 9001. After picking up the package on the doormat, she pressed the doorbell. When there was no answer, she sighed and began to press the button repeatedly.

Eventually, the door opened to reveal an exhausted-looking man of latte-colored skin, green eyes, and a curly, auburn crewcut. Crispin stood at an enormous 2.22 meters and packed about 140 kilos of well-sculpted muscle. There were fading scars on each side of his head near his ears. Posy had never asked about them, but she supposed he had undergone a fairly serious surgery at some point. Anyway, the scars never seemed to bother him except when he was irritated. He gingerly rubbed the discolored areas by his ears in a circular motion.

Posy smiled at Crispin and pressed the doorbell again. The lights inside the apartment flickered twice. The man rubbed his eyes, then went back inside, leaving the door open for her. She followed him into the living room and sat next to him on the couch.

"It's 0430, Poseidon," he signed.

She liked the nickname, which he'd told her was most befitting a strong and awe-inspiring female such as herself. It was a welcome counterbalance to the more mild and palatably feminine name by which others in the district knew her.

"I'm sorry, Crispin," she signed back. "It's important."

"It's always important. What do you have for me this time?"

She placed the chip from Mitchell's finger on the cushion between them.

Crispin's eyes grew wide. "It's a media chip. That's beyond state-of-the-art technology in the Western States. You can't even *smuggle* these into Carmelita. Where did you get this?"

She dodged the question. "I think it might help me find someone I'm looking for. Think you can get into it?"

"Of course I can." He took the chip to his worktable.

"This package was on your doormat." She waved it at him.

"Doesn't excuse your waking me up at 0430." He took on a suggestive expression. "Unless you came to rough-and-tumble?"

It was an objective truth that Crispin was devilishly handsome, but tumbling with him would be extremely rough—the Agent was sure. His palms were the size of her face; his feet were one and a half times the length of her own; and his thighs were each thicker around than her torso. She had never been with a man so giant, and frankly, she was concerned that he might accidentally harm her. And it would be just that: an accident. Crispin was a gentle giant. Posy had never been afraid in his presence, but a woman in her line of work couldn't help considering all of the risks involved in such behavior.

And in any case, the Agent had never rough-and-tumbled for amusement before. She would not know quite what to make of that. So, she ignored his comment and placed the package on his worktable.

"Got a drink?" she asked.

"Whiskey's on top of the fridge. Pour me one, too?"

The Agent poured a generous glass for each of them. While her previous trainers had urged her to practice temperance in order to keep her reflexes top-notch, she had found that a drink with a friend could do the heart much good. This was especially true on the night when the woman who had taken her son had tried to convince her that he was dead. Her son. He was undoubtedly alive, but the Assistant Vice just wanted her to believe that he wasn't.

Posy admired the plethora of tools strewn about Crispin's work-space. He began to hum, which he always did when concentrating. He'd once told her that the vibrations inside of his head and chest centered him. Generally, he hummed only a series of five notes, but put together, they made a nice little song.

* * *

"You connected, Wilson?" Theresa's voice came in choppily through the car speakers, and the image of a school hallway showed up jumbled and pixelated on the front windshield. "We've got you linked on my flake."

She held her device at an angle that made her face appear long and thin. Behind her stood Racky and a man who appeared to be a member of local law enforcement.

"Sort of," Karthik replied, fiddling with the car's web connectivity buttons. "The car rental agency gave me this trashy vehicle because I made the reservation on such short n—notice."

He was traveling through Carmelita as quickly as he could because his team had been alerted to a messy crime scene that likely involved

WCE-sponsored arms traffickers. There was also an unidentified female body, which possibly belonged to one of the Cooperative FBI's persons of interest.

Racky's voice piped up. "But it *is* an auto-car, right, K.?"

"Semi-auto!" He grunted, yanking the steering wheel to switch into pedestrian watch-mode since he had just exited the highway. The car swerved and narrowly avoided hitting an elderly woman crossing the road against the traffic signal. "And I think it used to be a t—taxi. It still has all the markings and stuff, just n—no sign on top."

"That *is* trash," Racky said. "You should call that company—"

"Later," came the voice of Blair Lee-Smith, probably through Racky's flake. "Inspector Flanagan, can you just recap for Agent Wilson what happened there at the school? He was delayed at the border, but he's on his way to you as we speak."

"Chief Inspector of the Carmelita District Police, here," Flanagan said, not seeming to understand that Karthik was on a different device than Blair. He was still talking into Racky's flake. "This morning, cleaning staff found the classroom beneath the principal's office full of bodies. It had the look of bad blood between competing arms dealers, so we alerted the Western FBI. But they shunted the case to you because their office is overwhelmed with the investigation around the district head's untimely death. They said you were in the area searching for a female person of interest and figured you might find answers here."

"And you said that the alarms in the building had been going off for hours before your guys arrived?" Racky asked.

"Yeah, we never even got a ping on our end," Flanagan said, catching a glimpse of Karthik on Theresa's flake. "Remind me of your credentials and which office you work with again?"

A law enforcement team as diverse as theirs was a rare sight in the Western States, especially in a district like Carmelita, which was comfortably affiliated with the WCE.

"We're Special Agents from the Cooperative FBI, which only has one office, based in Corpus," Racky responded. "I'm Rackelle Wernicke, and this is Theresa Cravenly with K. Ethan-James Wilson on her flake. And this here on my flake is Blair Lee-Smith, our SSA. She's on desk duty at this time, but she will join us in the field after the holiday. She calls all the shots."

Racky held up her thin mobile communication device to Flanagan's face, and Blair nodded at him.

He huffed. Then, wrinkling his nose at Theresa's flake, he said, "So, they let *those* carry a badge in the Coop, hm? Would never happen in the *Western* FBI, that's for sure. They may have got reparations, but they've got no right to authority over the rest of us."

The inspector had made an assumption based on Karthik's red-brown skin and tightly coiled hair, and his assumption revealed a vicious anti-4.14 prejudice.

"You are wrong in so many ways, sir," Racky said indignantly. "First of all, he's subclass. So, if you're going to hate him, hate him right."

"N—now, Racky," Karthik started.

But she wasn't finished. "And I'll have you know that the director of the Cooperative FBI is Class 4.14 pureblood, and I myself am Subclass 4.14. So, if you have a problem—"

Blair's voice drowned her out. "I understand you have a body for us, Inspector Flanagan?"

Blair was subclass too—born of a Class 1 father and a Class 3 mother, who very well could have passed for Class 1—but one would not necessarily know it by looking at her. When Chief Flanagan saw her pale skin, round eyes, and wavy dark hair, he saw a Class 1 woman. Karthik noted that she made the most of this advantage to get the job done.

Flanagan motioned for Theresa and Racky to follow him. "Three bodies, actually. Looks like a hostage situation. Your person of interest, if it's her, barricaded herself in this office. Her pursuers tried to bust the door open with bullets. Before they could get in, she killed her two hostages and was herself apprehended by yet another party who likely had been waiting in the room for her. Torture and torch operation, after that."

Theresa and Racky brushed past Flanagan and stood, appalled, in the doorway of the office. They pointed their flakes down into the enormous hole in the floor through which everything in the room had fallen.

"The female body was over there at first, probably," Flanagan motioned to the right side of the room, "but everything fell into a sort of pile when the floor gave."

"Were you able t—to get an ID on the body?" Karthik asked.

"We got nothing from the DNA tests. My team is running the jaws against dental records."

"We're going to need copies of those," Blair said. "You can fax them directly to our office."

"Will do," Flanagan said. "Anything else I can do for you?"

"What happened to the ambusher?" Theresa asked.

"Ah, yes," Flanagan chuckled. "The window, we think. Guy set the charges around the room and then escaped down the side of the building."

Racky's gaze flickered toward Karthik, and he smiled at her. Maybe the body wasn't Lenci's after all.

The inspector continued, shaking his head, "With this act of violence and the death of our district head under uncertain circumstances, it was a rough night for Carmelita. Morale's been pretty low over at CDP."

"Yes, I saw about the district head on the news this morning," Blair said with practiced sympathy. "It *is* a lot all at once, but from my brief interactions with the Western FBI and with your officers, I'd say Carmelita is in the best hands."

"Kind words, Agent Lee-Smith," Flanagan said, putting a hand over his heart and nodding.

"Of course, and thank you for your help, Inspector," she replied. To her team, she said, "Guys, wrap this up and get back to HQ ASAP, so we can debrief Cormorant."

"Thank you for your time, Inspector Flanagan," Racky said. "We'll just be collecting some samples off of the body and some for the explosives, then we'll be on our way."

Flanagan did not respond verbally, but his facial expression seemed to say, *And good riddance.*

Karthik looked at the map display in his rental car. "I'm almost there, I think."

"Good," Blair said. "When you get there, go on in. Make sure we don't miss anything."

CHAPTER 3

He used a very fine-tipped tool to turn some kind of switch inside the tiny chip. There was a spark, and a holographic globe popped out. A red dot marked something important on the map, and the coordinates floated above it in green characters.

The red and green lights from the globe wormed their way through Posy's eye sockets into the dark recesses of her memory. She didn't want them there, but they pushed past her defenses, floating along like phantoms with a cruel purpose—namely to uncover long-forgotten graves in which failure had decayed into fear of exposure.

The Agent felt cold. She recognized the coordinates displayed on the globe. They were near a place that she used to call Home, the compound where all of the Amphibians had been trained. Specifically, they were near the burial site of the unfit ones. More than likely, the district head had trained an Amphibian whose counterpart was buried at those coordinates.

Sick of Mitchell to carry that around with him. But the WCE was like that: always doling out grim reminders of the reality behind the patched together story of a person's life. It was a strange coincidence that, while there were only nineteen surviving Phibs in the whole world, the Agent would cross paths with a Phib handler. She figured, though, that the concentration of such personnel must be higher in the Western States than anywhere else—simply due to the wide availability of WCE resources in that area.

The Agent covered the chip with a cloth, causing the fragile mechanism inside to click out of place. The image disappeared.

"Hey, what's the big idea?" Crispin signed.

"Sorry," Posy signed back. "I guess I thought it would be something more useful."

The package from Crispin's doormat was still sitting unopened on his worktable. He had piled a bunch of stuff on top of it, but it seemed a worthy distraction from the unhappy reminder of the coordinates in the chip.

"Aren't you going to open your package?" Posy asked. "It could be cookies."

"Poseidon, you have a one track mind." Crispin grinned. Then he shrugged. "It's probably just an attachment for my web apparatus. I'll open it when I get back from work this evening."

"I'd be very interested to watch you work on it." Posy smiled winsomely. "I've never been great with technology, but I do need to learn at some point."

Crispin yawned and stretched. "Well, I'm probably up for good now. Do you have any more of those raspberry tea cookies at your place?"

Posy nodded, then grabbed her empty backpack and headed out the door. She dropped off the backpack at her apartment and took her favorite cookies out of the cabinet. She lobbed a cookie to her little blond friend in the hallway. When she returned to 9001, Crispin was turning the package over and over in his hands. Then he put it on the worktable and stared at her perplexedly.

"Something wrong?" Posy asked.

"I feel like I've seen this before today," Crispin replied.

Suddenly having an inexplicable uneasiness about the package herself, she avoided looking at it and instead took a sip of whiskey.

Then she signed, "Well, all those online delivery houses are using the same weather-proof paper on their drone deliveries. It's probably that."

He nodded glumly and looked back toward the package. She held the cookies out to him, but he didn't notice. So, she stepped into his line of vision.

"I'll open it. No need to stress," she signed with a smile.

When she slid her fingers through the brown paper wrapping, she felt uneasy again. Pushing that feeling aside, she tore the paper from the box and ripped the panels off of one end. The contents of the box slid out onto the floor. Amid the white packing paper, there was a small, black and yellow object. The sight of it struck a cold dread into the Agent's bones. She did not need to examine the object very closely to know what it was. It was a dead fire salamander, gutted and limp, with a small metal chip affixed to its side.

The Agent picked up the salamander's cold, little body and turned it over in her hands. Although it had not been meant for her, this was a message that she could decipher. The question, though, was whether Crispin had already deciphered it—if the message was even for him. He appeared afraid and confused about the cause of his fear.

The Agent's heart pounded as Crispin took the salamander from her, but she forced herself to remain calm. It made no sense for her to initiate a fight or flight response until there was no other option. Crispin's gargantuan size would be of consequence in hand-to-hand combat and a foot chase alike, but his reflexes would be impaired due to his alcohol consumption. Of course, the Agent's reflexes would also be impaired. She hoped Crispin's slower reflexes would be slower than her slower reflexes because she honestly didn't know if she could best him.

A scan ray shot out from the chip in the salamander's side and moved across Crispin's face.

"Identity confirmed," a recorded voice said. "Commence message to Hellbender."

An image of the district head's smug, gaunt face popped up, and a deep, bass beat began to thrum through the room. It was so loud that the Agent could feel the vibrations in her chest and head. Then there came a simple, repetitive melody of five notes, accompanied by the words of a Song.

> *Hellbender, kill and end her*
> *Fire*
> *Salamander, full of slander*
> *Slip and slide*
> *Till she has died…*

"Damn it!" The Agent tossed the rest of her drink onto the dead salamander. Mitchell's ghastly face and loud, forceful chanting fizzled out.

If the Song on the chip was indeed Crispin's Song, the Agent would have to accept a string of terrible truths—foremost that she had not manipulated the district head and his wife. They had manipulated *her*, masterfully and efficiently, into complacency.

Crispin was fishing the chip out of the puddle of whiskey on his carpeted living room floor.

After examining it, he signed, "That Song—we've heard it before, haven't we?"

The Agent regarded him warily as he stood to his full 2.22 meters.

She asked, "How did you know it was music?"

"I could feel the vibrations," he responded.

There was something off about his face, a strange hardening. The Agent's eyes wandered to the scars by his ears. From the angle, she figured that they could have been self-inflicted. One couldn't be blamed for trying, at all costs, to avoid hearing one's Song.

"Crispin?"

"What?"

"How did you get those scars?"

"I can't remember." He grabbed a hammer off of the worktable and swung it at her.

The Agent dodged, grabbing the tool, and jammed her knee into the back of Crispin's elbow to try to break it. But because he was so large and sturdy, she did little more than hyperextend the joint. He whipped his arm backward, slamming the Agent into the table.

She went with the momentum and flipped herself over it. She thought herself accomplished for having gotten a piece of furniture between them, but she soon realized the error of her confidence. With one hand, Crispin overturned the table, sending tools and whiskey flying in all directions.

A long, thin probe hurtled by in the explosion of tools. The Agent caught it, knowing that her best chance of surviving this fight lay in maintaining some distance between her and Crispin. She had been wise to grab a weapon, but gaining it had cost her half a moment's attention.

When she identified the direction from which Crispin was swinging at her, she didn't have much time to dodge. She jerked to the side and the impact of Crispin's meaty fist caught her on the right hip, causing her to spin ninety degrees. She managed to regain her footing and jabbed the probe at his heart. He knocked it sideways, and it hit his upper arm. When it pierced his flesh, he barely seemed to notice. Apparently, he also had learned effective pain management.

He grabbed the probe from the Agent and broke it over his knee.

"Right," she breathed, backing away from him as the pieces of her weapon clattered to the floor.

Crispin was blocking the front door.

"Any chance I can squeeze by on your left?" she signed.

Her banter seemed to sour his mood. He snarled and began advancing toward her, slowly but with purpose.

She swore under her breath and fled down the hall to the bedroom. She locked the door behind her. There was one way out: the window. She was nine floors up, but there was plenty of ridging for a safe climb to ground.

Before she could get all the way out of the window, Crispin crashed through the wall. A pipe inside it burst, flooding the room with water. The Agent leapt, but Crispin snagged her by the ankle and dragged her back inside. His wet hand was like a muscled shackle, squeezing her ankle so tightly that she could feel a sprain developing right where he gripped her. The Agent found it a most undignified position, dangling upside down in his hand like a hunter's fresh catch.

Stupid whiskey. It was the only reason she hadn't jumped sooner. She cursed her affected reflexes as Crispin hurled her into the hall, where she slid across the hardwood floor and hit her head on the doorway to the common area. With heavy footfalls, he approached her, his breath rasping in his throat. Ignoring the throbbing in her head and the flashing spots blocking her vision, the Agent scrambled into the living room. She felt around frantically in the whiskey-soaked carpet by the overturned worktable for an object that would once more even up the fight.

None of the tools were long enough to offset Crispin's height advantage. As his footsteps thumped toward her, she found a meter-long metal file that was about three-quarters of a centimeter thick. It would not be the most effective weapon against an opponent so large, but the Agent had run out of time. Her hand closed around the file.

She held Crispin at bay with her feet, but she was unable to get off of her back. Long arms were his advantage in this instance as he was able to bypass her open guard and grab her by the neck. His hand was so huge that it went around her whole neck.

He lifted her to half a meter above the floor. From the way his hand tightened, however, she could tell that he was planning to suffocate her, not snap her neck. That was good news. She'd have to slow her heartbeat as near to a halt as possible to have a fighting chance.

Gasping theatrically, Posy grasped at his hand and kicked her legs progressively more slowly until she finally went limp. The file slipped from her hand onto the carpet with a *CLUNK*.

Crispin let out a deep breath. He released his grip and let the Agent fall, but before she hit the floor, she hooked his knees. As he pitched forward, she grabbed the file and drew it back for the kill.

It all happened so fast. One second, he was falling and the next, he was on the floor beside her with the file jammed through his throat. There was a lot of blood, too much blood—or the right amount, depending on how one thought of it.

Crispin's fingers fumbled with the hem of his shirt. Attentive to this hint, the Agent lifted the shirt to find a giant, burnt orange tattoo of a hellbender salamander on his abdomen. The tip of its snout and its tail touched the left and right sides of his waist respectively while the middle of the salamander's body curved in a U-shape below his navel.

The sight of Crispin's WCE-assigned mark chilled the Agent to the bone. Hinny's threat had been truthful. The WCE's best really were after her. The Amphibians had been commissioned to kill one of their own kind.

The Agent knelt beside Crispin and wiped the sweat from his face as he struggled to draw gurgling, blood-filled breaths. Even though he had been sent to kill her, she felt an unexpected kinship to this fellow member of the cohort because he had endured the same rigorous training and ritual abuse as she had.

She should have been more suspicious two months before when the suave, larger-than-life hunk just happened to move into the apartment next to hers. She should have known something was off when he just happened to reveal that he was a tech genius. He had helped her to monitor quite a bit of WCE communication, which she now knew must have been prearranged. She did not need to investigate how she had allowed this to happen. She had a soft spot for techies—for reasons of a past life—a soft spot that had been exploited this time around.

Even so, Posy thought about how Crispin hadn't followed up to confirm that she was dead, as any professional should have known to do. It seemed that he had been rather half-hearted in this attempted execution, and that was something she supposed was worth honoring.

"I know you didn't want to do it," she signed.

A single tear ran down his cheek as he gripped her hands. The pain was catching up with him; she could tell. As one controlled by any human being other than himself, his pain could be, at best, excruciating.

After a couple of laborious breaths, Crispin exhaled, and his tense body relaxed.

"Goodbye, friend," Posy said aloud, closing his eyes with a gentle hand. "I was glad to be Poseidon to you."

Crispin had found her and wormed his way into her life with ease. She wondered how many other Phibs could be out there ready to do the same. Her knowledge of the names and Songs of all the Amphibians now seemed an inadequate advantage since she still had to *know* that she was dealing with a Phib—and which Phib—in order to effectively weaponize a Song. But Phib handlers like Mitchell had probably received a file with her image, which they could share with their associated Phibs. Then they would be able to recognize her on sight, but she would be flying blind.

All other objectives had to be abandoned for the present. Survival was, after all, the name of the game. She would have to disappear and stay away from WCE circles until she could figure out a way forward with respect to the search for her son. She couldn't find him if she was dead; it was as simple as that.

The progress that Posy had made in her mission, the success and failure she had associated with finding Hinny, all of the good times that she had had with Crispin as well as the horrific end of their friendship—none of it mattered now. The feelings associated with the truth of these experiences waned until, at last, Posy's memories of her time in Carmelita were facts and facts alone. This was necessary for her to make a smoother transition, and she knew that what was necessary must never be lamented.

It was not Posy who left Apartment 9001. The Agent approached the little blond girl, who was still sitting on her parents' doormat, and knelt beside her.

"Hey listen, kid, I'm going out of town for a while," she said, handing over what was left of the box of raspberry tea cookies. "So, you take care of yourself, okay? Don't let the folks drive you too crazy."

The girl set down the box of cookies and rested her face against the Agent's. The Agent knew little of motherly affection, but she wondered if it was something like hoping that a child would be okay in the big wide world. If it was that, she had an abundant supply—even when her own drive to survive was looming large once again.

The Agent patted the girl on the head and said, "My Kiddo's a boy. I found out tonight, you know."

The girl smiled and then turned her attention to the box of

cookies. A wave of anxiety overcame the Agent as she turned away from the child. What had she to fear of the unknown? After all, the unknown was all she had ever really known.

"Say it again," she whispered. Then she fled down the stairs to seek survival in another life.

* * *

Karthik was two blocks from the school when his rental car died in the middle of the street. With a frustrated grunt, he slammed the steering wheel. That, of course, did nothing. He pressed a couple of buttons to run diagnostics, but they didn't even light up when he pressed them. The solar-powered vehicle had indicated that it was half charged when he picked it up, and he simply hadn't traveled far enough to use that much energy. The sun was only just peeking between the buildings that lined the street, so there remained at least another thirty minutes before he could get a natural charge.

He sighed and massaged his forehead. *First the loss of the kid in Cormorant and now this.*

"This day can—not get *any* worse," he muttered.

He was about to get out of the car to push it toward the curb when one of the back doors opened. Someone jumped into the back seat and slammed the door.

"Carmelita South, please," the young woman said in a polite but hurried tone.

Trying not to take out all of his frustration on an innocent stranger, Karthik took a deep breath. "Ma'am, this isn't a t—taxi. There was a mistake with my rental—"

Hearing a soft gasp, he met the woman's horrified gaze in the rearview mirror. Although her long, curly hair had been chemically lightened to a deep mahogany, Karthik recognized her immediately. He pressed the automatic door lock, but she was already busting the window with her feet.

"Lenci, wait!" Before he could even unbuckle his seatbelt, she was out of the window and sprinting down the street with her hair flowing behind her.

Cursing under his breath, Karthik pulled out his flake and pressed the speed dial as he ran. "Come on, Racky, pick up!"

Lenci ran in a straight line away from him, just as she always had since they were children, but she threw trashcans and other loose objects into his path to slow him down. She did not respond when he called her name, and when she got to a busy intersection she ran into the traffic without hesitation.

Racky's voicemail picked up just as Karthik got to the corner. He watched the cars swerve and pile up, just missing Lenci who leapt and slid across their hoods. She arrived safely on the other side of the street and continued her flight.

"Found her!" Karthik yelled into his flake, trying to keep an eye on the cars without losing track of his fleeing friend. "Headed southeast on 16th, probably t—toward Carmelita South Station. Pursuit on foot!"

He hung up and devoted all of his energy to closing the gap between him and Lenci. The sidewalk was crowded with morning commuters, which seemed to serve Lenci more than it served him. Although Lenci had always been a slow runner, she was agile and had fantastic body control. While Karthik bumped and excused his way through the bustling crowd, Lenci wove nimbly in and out of the bewildered passersby, swiveling on a dime whenever necessary.

"Lenci, get back here *right now!*" he called after her. "I'm warning you!"

He had closed the gap between them by half when something hooked his foot and he tripped. Someone in the crowd muttered a nasty word that historically had been used to demean Class 4.14 people. Despite the fact that Karthik was Subclass 7.65, ill-intentioned strangers had directed that word at him for as long as he could remember. His late mother had been Class 3.51, but to the uneducated eye, he seemed only to belong to his father's people. Anyway, it was a horrible word to say to anyone.

Ignoring his tightening throat, Karthik jumped to his feet and flashed his badge.

"Cooperative FBI!" he shouted. "Clear the way!"

Lenci looked back at him, apparently judgmental about the fact that he was invoking his authority as a member of law enforcement to truncate their chase. No one obeyed in much of a hurry, but a couple of people eventually stepped aside such that there was a clear path ahead of Karthik.

He pressed onward, having shaken off the physical effects of his fall. Shaking off the psychological effects, however, proved more difficult. It was like *that* word was stuck in time. It brought with it all the other times the word had been spoken over Karthik, certainly, and maybe even the times it had been spoken over other people throughout history. Thus infused with centuries' worth of hatred, the word more than demeaned him; it seemed intended to crush the life out of him.

"That just happened, Karthik," he whispered as he ran. "Push past the eugenism and assault on a federal officer. Eye on the prize, man!"

At the next corner, Lenci turned off of the main street and into an alleyway lined with apartment buildings. When Karthik rounded the corner, he found that the alley was quiet. About ten meters away from him, Lenci was emptying a pocketbook that she'd stolen off of an unsuspecting commuter. She stuffed a large wad of cash into her bra.

"Hey, wait up!" Karthik said, nearly having caught up with her.

At the sound of his voice, a rather angry sounding dog responded from behind a nearby apartment door. Both Karthik and Lenci flinched away from the door, but Karthik recovered quickly and took the opportunity to try to apprehend his friend. He sprang toward her, but she leapt onto a nearby dumpster. From there, she caught the low-hanging ladder of a fire escape. After a moment's hesitation, Karthik followed.

Lenci clattered up the fire escape two steps at a time. When she reached the top of the building, she paused and looked down at him with an odd expression. He stared back at her as he climbed.

It was only when he was pulling himself onto the roof that Lenci broke eye contact. She crouched down very low on the roof's edge, and just when Karthik approached her, she launched herself off of the roof.

"Lenci!" He grabbed after her but felt only the wind of her movement. He watched in horror as she sailed across the alley.

She had apparently miscalculated the distance to the next building but managed to catch the edge of the roof with her forearms. Her legs kicked a couple of times in a brief expression of frustration. Then she began to swing back and forth like a pendulum until she had enough momentum to swing her body onto the roof.

She shook out her arms and glanced back at Karthik before taking a running start and leaping onto the roof of the next building. Even if he were able to make the first jump, he couldn't chase his friend across the district that way. He stared after her, completely at a loss. All that time, Lenci had been luring him into a position where she knew he wouldn't be able to follow her.

His flake was vibrating.

He answered it. "Wilson."

"Where is she, K.?" Racky squawked.

"She got away," he replied.

She exhaled sharply. "Damn."

"Are you okay?" Blair asked, her voice garbled by the bad connection on the three-way call.

"Yeah," he said, "but we've got to get to the Carmelita South Station. She was going t—to try to escape by train, and I think she still will. But she'll be in a cargo car t—to throw us off."

"I'll request Carmelita's police department to get down there right away. Which direction?"

"I d—don't know," Karthik said.

"Well, they're not really enamored of us—quick to pull the jurisdictional trump card and all that. So, make your best calculation. Which way would Lenci go from here?"

He thought for a moment. "West, definitely. She's already been in the d—districts north and south of here. And just east is the border to the Eastern States, which she'll avoid because she'd be t—too traceable through their advanced technology. Shut d—down all westbound cargo trains."

"You got it," Blair said. "Now, I need you back near the school."

Karthik's brow furrowed. "But what about Lenci?"

"The police'll find her, if she's there," she responded. "There was a situation at an apartment building just a few blocks from the school."

"Is this reall—lly more important than finding Lenci?" His voice was beginning to shake.

"Try to pull yourself together, Wilson. We've got a crime scene at which we need your immediate presence."

"Understood," he replied.

He hung up and looked longingly in the direction that Lenci had gone. She was now only a tiny dot, hopping from one roof to the next and out of his life again.

* * *

Local police officers lined the stairwell and eyed the three Cooperative FBI agents suspiciously as they passed. The officers would not voice their opinions, however, because the Coop had expressed reasonable belief that the crime that had taken place in the apartment involved their person of interest.

"The manager doesn't even know who lives here. Says it's a 'pay and no questions asked' kind of place." Theresa pouted into her flake. "So, why are we bothering with this?"

"Because the results of CDP's analysis indicate that the bone structure of the body from the school was that of a Class 1 woman," Blair replied, "and *this* crime scene involves charred remains with what appears to be the bone structure of a Class 3 female, for which we all know our person of interest could easily be mistaken. Carmelita's Class 1 Gifted isn't far from here, so this female very well could be the ambusher from the school."

"Woman," Racky corrected under her breath.

"What was that?"

"A Class 3 *woman*," she said.

"The legal term is 'female,'" Blair responded curtly. "I won't apologize for that."

"You brought me back for *this*?" Karthik exclaimed. "I'm t—telling you, Lenci is *at the train station*. That's where we should be if we want t—to catch her, n—not looking at some corpse!"

"Wilson, CDP is handling the train station," Blair said. "They've got the numbers for a wide ranging search, and I need you at this scene to analyze it for traces of Lenci's typical patterns of behavior."

"Don't worry, K.," Racky told him. "If there's anything CDP is good at, it's foot chases and searches. If Lenci's at the train station, they'll get her."

"And if she's here, *we'll* get her," Blair said. "We're leaving no stone unturned."

Karthik did not respond, and his teammates let the matter drop for the time being.

"Apartment 9001, right?" Theresa motioned to the broken down apartment door.

"That's the one," Blair said. "Local police found the door closed and locked, so they forced their entry. They've already made a sweep for evidence, but I specifically requested that they leave everything just as it was."

"A reasonable request, but in vain, as always," Theresa said. "Look, they moved the body."

"They said it was like that when they arrived," Blair explained. "Police got a call about a noise disturbance and a heavy leak into the apartment below, but when the first responders arrived at 9001, there was only that charred body."

Karthik frowned pensively. "N—no furniture. Carpet is immaculate. N—no burn marks in sight."

"So, the body was burned somewhere else and brought in," Racky said. "That's some weird, kinky stuff."

"I'll see if I can get a viable DNA sample somewhere off this *thing*," Theresa sighed, moving forward with her sampling kit.

Racky smacked her shoulder. "Have some respect! That could be our Circus."

"It's n—not," Karthik said.

Theresa snorted. "But we haven't even—"

"It's *not* her!" he snapped.

"Watch your tone, Wilson!" Blair told him.

He continued more softly, "I just saw Lenci with my own eyes. She'd dyed her hair, but it was her alright. She broke my rental car window, and I chased her a good distance. So, I d—don't know who this is, but it's n—not her. Someone set this up."

"Someone like the Killer?" Theresa asked with morbid interest.

"Maybe," he replied, "or Lenci herself. She could be faking her own d—death to get us t—to stop l—looking for her."

After a brief silence, Racky said, "It's been a long few days, K., and we all want to find Lenci, too."

"It's just highly unlikely that she'd get into your cab," Theresa said, her voice dripping with mock-sympathy. "She was trained to avoid situations where she had to declare her destination."

"She sounded l—like she was in a hurry," he said. "She had new bruises on her n—neck. And she smelled like alcohol. Maybe she'd gotten into it with someone and was too d—desperate to follow protocol."

Racky shook her head. "Now, that really doesn't resemble the Lenci we know. Bourghin was opposed to her drinking since it could impair her judgment in life or death situations. From what I heard of the Killer's training regimen, he held a similar view. It must have been someone else who got into your car."

He sighed. "But why d—did she run?"

"Some criminals just run when they're being chased," Blair said.

Karthik's personal flake began to ring.

Looking at the caller ID, he said, "I'm sorry, if you can excuse me for a minute, I have t—to t—take this." He scooted toward the hallway and put the flake to his ear, whispering, "Hey, Maude! Yeah, I miss you too…"

Theresa stared after him with a haughty smirk. "Are they, like, an item now?"

Racky shrugged. "I think he's aiming for petty revenge on Lenci, which isn't at all fair to Lenci or that infuriating girl."

"Woman?" Theresa whispered mischievously.

"Get to work, ladies. Remember, debrief is immediately after landing in Corpus." Racky's flake chimed as Blair disconnected.

Someone pounded on the door, and a gruff voice called, "Five minutes Coopers! We're all set to go home at 0830, so don't keep us waiting."

"Got it!" Theresa responded. Then, clearly tickled by the fact that Racky was still bristling over Karthik's conversation, she chuckled. "I wonder if your disgust for Maude is rooted in offense for Lenci or for yourself. How loyal of a friend *are* you, Racky?"

Racky shook her head at Theresa and stooped to examine a small, strong-smelling stain in the carpet on the border of the hallway. Whoever had recently cleaned the apartment had missed a spot. There was a groove where the living room carpet met the hallway's hardwood floor. And in that groove, sticking up out of the smelly threads of the carpet, was a shiny speck. It appeared to be a media chip.

Using a pair of tweezers, Racky picked up the little chip and placed it in a baggie. She said nothing because she didn't want the officers outside to hear that she was going to take it without their permission. If Lenci had been there, that chip would almost assuredly be some link.

* * *

In a pile of hay in an eastbound cargo train, Valencia Chang was sobbing as if the world were crashing down around her. The train had left Carmelita South Station an hour before. Police had been communicating with each other and instructing bystanders to clear out as they searched the premises. The dispatcher had relayed the order to search all westbound cargo trains.

The Agent had fled from Karthik because she knew it was never a good idea to mix histories. Valencia was past. She had to be, for the sake of her survival and for Karthik's and for their family's.

But Karthik had encountered her in a very vulnerable moment. As she was transitioning from one life to another—as she was leaving one self behind and still learning to be someone new—there he was. He called her by a familiar name, and his voice dredged up all kinds of feelings that she had laid to rest the year before. She tried not to hear his voice, and she definitely did not allow him to touch her. But the damage had been done.

She remembered their bond, that she loved him deeply—not just in fact but in feeling and, perhaps, in some part of her being. But she was not Valencia, not anymore. She had yet to discover who she needed to be in this new life.

"Go back down," the Agent told Valencia. "I'll take it from here. Everything's going to be okay."

With a couple of last hiccuping sobs, Valencia did as she was told and sank down, down, down into the depths. The Agent wiped her eyes with her hand and looked at the tears on her fingertips like they were some kind of foreign substance. Then she wiped her hand on her gym shorts and settled down in the hay to try to keep warm.

CHAPTER 4

"Welcome back," Blair said, shaking hands with the members of her team as they entered the conference room. "Good effort, all. Have a seat."

They sat at the table in the center of the room. Theresa and Racky slouched immediately in their seats, but Karthik sat with his back as straight as a rod. He stared broodingly down at his briefcase, which lay on the table.

"Agent Wilson," Blair said. "I'm sorry to hear that the police search of Carmelita South Station turned up nothing, but you made the best spur-of-the-moment decision you could with the info you had."

His eyes were glassy as he replied, "I almost had her, and I l—let her slip through my fingers."

Blair shook her head. "You're sleep-deprived and emotionally worn. Why don't you debrief us on Cormorant, so you can head home?"

Something inside of him seemed to click into place, and he took a holopresentation device and a fingertip command attachment out of his briefcase. Stifling a yawn, he powered on the device. A 3-D image of the ruins of a building floated above the table.

He took a deep breath and began. "We responded to the report of explosions at the nature reserve in Cormorant to find that they were n—no accident. The image you see here is of the ruins of a facility that the WCE had secretly and illegally constructed in the heart of the reserve."

"No one noticed that big hulking piece of concrete?" Blair asked.

"With the d—district government shut down for the past couple of years, there's been n—no park staff to check on things," Karthik explained. "As for air surveillance, we now realize that there was WCE interference with our satellites over the area."

"But what is its function?" Racky asked. "The building, I mean."

"As far as we can tell, the WCE was using this facility to d—develop and test agents of biological warfare. One of their experiments must have gone wrong because the d—demolition of the building was performed by the WCE itself."

He touched his fingertip to his thumb twice. The image in the middle of the table dissolved and was replaced by a series of aerial snapshots.

"These are the images we pulled from a personal drone which the owner, a civilian, claimed had 'accidentally wandered' over the area around the t—time of the explosions. As you can see, it was a WCE bird that dropped the bombs."

Blair squinted at the grainy pictures. "I don't see anyone evacuating. Was the facility empty?"

Karthik ran a hand over his face as though it could wipe away what he had seen. "D—director Vincent invited me along with the team that searched through the d—debris. The facility was d—definitely n—not empty. We found the remains of facility staff as well as evidence of experiments that had been run on human subjects."

"And the kid?" Racky ventured to ask.

A somber silence descended on the room.

"There were a few children," Karthik swallowed. "Most of the remains were t—testable, and they have all been identified. Those tested were n—not related to Lenci."

His voice tapered off for a moment, and when he began to speak again, his words came slowly, forced and reluctant. "We found one cell sealed off in the juvenile section. There was n—nothing but ashes in that cell."

His voice cracked, so he stopped talking.

"Someone probably incinerated the subject before sealing off its quarters, seeing as how there were only ashes left," Theresa said in her matter of fact way.

"To make sure that test subject would never be identified," Racky said pensively.

"But we can't know for sure that the kid in that cell was the kid we're looking for," Blair said. "Ashes give us nothing. They just send us back to square one."

"We found the facility's population l—log in the rubble," Karthik said. "In the juvenile section, all of the children had commonly known n—names, but the sealed cell contained a subject referred to as 'Larva.'"

"Like *bug* offspring?" Blair asked.

"Salamander offspring, more likely," Theresa offered. "Very interesting given the tantalizing hints about the elusive 'Amphibians' in Bourghin's recorded message to Racky."

"It's like some kind of cruel joke," Racky grumbled.

"Anyways," Karthik said, "Director Vincent is convinced that Larva *was* the kid we've been looking for and that the kid is d—dead. So, as far as he's concerned, we should now streamline our efforts t—to find Lenci only."

"Is that so?" Blair looked down at the table to keep her anger from becoming evident to her team. "Well, thank you for your presentation, Wilson. Please, all, type up your reports for Carmelita after the DNA results come in for the body at the apartment building."

Racky looked at her sadly. "So, the search for the kid ends just like that?"

Blair stood. "We'll see. Dismissed!"

Her team members filed out one by one.

"Dinner?" Racky mouthed to Karthik. He nodded and said he'd message her.

After taking a minute to collect herself, Blair marched down the hall to Director Vincent's office. She tapped twice on the door, then opened it.

"You can't call off the search!" she burst out.

There were two men inside of the room, one on each side of the desk. Both looked toward her with an annoyed expression. The one behind the desk—a tall, lean man of ebony skin, chin-length twists, and a shimmering silver nose ring—gestured to the other one to give them some privacy. The dismissed man rose stiffly and brushed past Blair with an air of condescension.

"Take a seat, Lee-Smith," Vincent said.

He folded his hands in front of him such that his fingers interlocked and made the shape of a lean-to on his desk.

Blair sat in the vacant chair. "Wilson's report indicated that you didn't find any testable remains that could be linked to the child. How can you—"

"Supervisory Special Agent," Vincent interrupted. "That's your rank, the highest rank with *your team* in the field. But in this organization *as a whole*, I call the shots—even when your team is affected."

Blair's face tightened. "The code name Larva, if it is related to the Amphibians, could give us a direct line to the kid. We've got to at least look into this and follow the road as far as it goes."

Vincent drew a deep breath and let it out slowly before responding. "We've followed this road with the kid as far as we could. Meanwhile, the WCE has systematically demolished ten covert agencies and continues to prepare for biological warfare on a level that, by comparison, makes us look like toddlers in a sandbox. And now, we've got a heap of rubble, a pile of ashes, and a codename that points us right back to what we should've been looking at all along: the Amphibians."

"But—"

"I won't waste any more resources on this wild goose chase," Vincent said calmly. "We need your team's undivided attention on the search for Valencia Chang. Bourghin's recording identified her as a potential Amphibian, so she's the only hope we have of unlocking this whole damning mystery."

He paused, then continued. "You surprise me, Lee-Smith. What happened to your conviction that the *mother* was highly sought after by the WCE and, therefore, worth our every effort to find first?"

Blair tried not to look as exposed as she felt. "When you made that the priority, I believed Chang had enough of a mother's instinct that, if we found her, the child would be nearby. Over the past year, though, there's been no discernible pattern in Chang's flight. She's appeared in the same districts as three of the last six Cull events, but we could chalk that up as much to pattern as to chance. All things considered, Chang seems most to be running *away* from us and not toward her kid. She was young when Miller took her, so she's still got a teenager's mind. I think she's avoiding punishment rather than having a sense responsibility for her child—if that makes sense."

When she finished speaking, she looked down at the desk.

"You're an exceptional agent, Blair." Vincent's tone had softened, just a tad. "If we'd known your true connection to Beatriz Gomez and David Miller, we never would have allowed you to take the SSI assignment. That said, your durability and creative adaptability in obtaining the necessary intel convinced me that you'd be a good leader on the Chang case. Now, it hasn't escaped my notice that the unfortunately nicknamed Larva was your half-sibling."

Blair's heart skipped a beat. She raised her gaze to his.

He continued, "I arranged this term of desk duty for you, so you could process your emotions as you saw fit and prepare for the task of leading your team in the field. It's a big responsibility to lead a team, especially when that team has been given as much freedom as I'm giving yours. So, when your desk duty ends after the holiday, don't make me sorry to have you on the Chang case."

"Yes, sir," Blair said.

He nodded. "Dismissed."

* * *

In a dark corner of a helium billiards bar, Theresa was hosting an audio call on her disposable flake. A near-empty platter of potato skins and six completely empty shot glasses sat on the table alongside her portable web apparatus.

"No, no!" She laughed. "I really am Class 3, *pureblood*. I know most of the sopients at SSI were subclass, but *I* was one of the elite few."

She listened for a moment, then responded. "Well, it was really my pleasure to report Fire Salamander's pregnancy because I respect the tenets. It just drove me crazy that she'd seduced the Killer. How is he, by the way?"

After a couple of seconds, she shook her head sympathetically. "Wow, only just in rehab to learn to walk again, hey? She must have really done a number on him last year."

Her laughter faded as her interlocutor asked her a question.

She replied, "Of course no one suspected about the kid. They just ate up the story about the drone images, and we're going all in after Valencia Chang. So, you'll have the Coop off your back with respect to that, at least."

The call ended abruptly. Theresa checked the connection, and it looked fine. But the person with whom she had been conversing was not the kind one called without invitation. She would have to wait for her to call back.

A brightly colored ball zipped past Theresa, missing her head by a couple of centimeters. It stopped at the wall beside her and floated there, looking annoyingly jolly.

"Hey, keep your balls away from me, you yellow bellies!" she snapped at the group of guys playing at a table on the border of the Class 2 and Class 3 sections of the bar.

"You're welcome, brownie!" one of them jeered. He blew a cloud of glittering, blueberry-scented vapor at her and made a lewd gesture with his cue stick.

"Ugh! As *if!*" she replied with an eye roll. Then, as the guy and his friends hooted and whistled at her, she gathered her things and left in a huff.

* * *

Racky's cozy ranch-style home was filled with the aromas of gumbo filé and butter. She had changed out of her work clothes into gray sweatpants and a powder blue exercise shirt under which she wore a bikini top and a T-Shirt bra. The bikini top was for support, but the bra was mostly for storage.

She stood at the range, stirring a pot of gumbo. The aromatic steam was making her hair shrink up, but she didn't much care about that. There was something soothing about the stirring motion. And with the week she was having, soothing was welcome. She rolled her head to work out the kinks in her neck.

Her gray rescue tabby, Gustav, was curled up in his kitty bed in the living room. He was typically active in the early evening, but the smell of gumbo seemed to have a calming effect on him. This was particularly convenient because Racky was expecting company, and she preferred that Gustav not take running leaps off of the table or skid across the vinyl flooring.

At 1830, she heard footsteps on the porch. The visitor paused in front of the door. He was talking, and judging by his frustrated tone, it was not too happy of a conversation. He set something down near the pet door. Then the flap of the pet door folded up, and a grocery bag slid through the opening. As it thudded onto the floor, Gustav looked up. The pet door flopped shut again, and the cat began to shuffle back and forth energetically in his bed.

"Close enough, Gustav," Racky said. "That was *something* uninvited coming through the pet door. Good guard cat!"

She pulled a kitty treat out of her bra and tossed it to him. He caught it in his mouth and chomped on it enthusiastically.

When Racky opened the door, Karthik was standing on the porch, whispering into his flake. "Well, I d—didn't know you were going t—to surprise me with d—dinner. I'm working l—late."

Racky rolled her eyes and motioned him into the living room.

"Yeah, it's my special case," he said, stepping inside. "I kn—know, Maude. Rain check?"

At the sound of Maude's name, Gustav spat and hissed. Racky tossed him another kitty treat.

"Sounds great," Karthik said. "Yeah, you t—too. Okay, bye."

Gustav finished his treat and licked his chops. He glanced at Racky's colleague. Karthik had visited before, so there was no pressing need to investigate him. After he'd been there for a while, it was possible that he would be available for a petting session, and that was the only matter of great interest to Gustav.

"Sorry to ruin your plans with your lady friend," Racky said.

"A surprise isn't 'plans,' by d—definition," Karthik replied. And with a knowing glance, he added, "And n—no, you're really not."

She shrugged. "I just don't know what you see in that bourgeoise, ignorant, eugenist—"

He held up a hand. "Before you add any more adjectives, l—let me just stop you right there. Maude and I go way back."

"But Lenci and you go back even further, K.," she said. "And while I didn't associate with your families long enough to get a comprehensive history, I *do* know that Maude Jackson was Lenci's number one tormenter at Windsailing's Gifted. So, help me to understand why, of all the purebloods in the world, you chose to link up with one that bullied your best friend and hates the Subclass?"

"It's mostly her family that hates the Subclass," he sighed, taking off his coat and tossing it on the couch. "They have important political t—ties in the West, so they can be pretty extreme. But Maude is actually a really open-minded, kind, and caring person."

"Funny that I never managed to notice that," Racky said. "Well, the honest reason I bring it up is I'm concerned you're dating her to get back at Lenci for leaving, even if in a subconscious manner. Don't you think you owe it to *Maude* not to date while you still have feelings for Lenci?"

His face contorted into a glare fiercer than any she'd ever seen on his mild-mannered countenance. "Maude has n—nothing to d—do with my feelings for Lenci."

He'd said it in a way that made "nothing" sound like "everything."

Seeing that the discussion was going nowhere, Racky changed the subject. "What did you bring this time?"

"Red ale," Karthik replied, pulling a six-pack out of the bag by the door. "And brownies, for d—dessert."

She examined the brownies. They were double fudge chocolate chip, which she deemed more than acceptable. The drinks, however, left much to be desired.

"Ale?" she said. "Don't you drink hard liquor ever?"

His eyebrows rose. "L—like, what?"

"Tequila, man, tequila!" she exclaimed. "Or, at least, something that burns on the way down."

"T—tequila t—tastes l—like feet," he replied without a hint of humor.

One thing could be said of Karthik Ethan-James Wilson: he could transform a lively conversation into a dirge in one fell swoop. Anyway, he was definitely the straitlaced type that had never engaged in under-aged drinking, and he'd only been of age for about half a year. Racky decided that she could make do with red ale since he was still getting his bearings.

She jabbed his shoulder with her bony elbow. "Ey, Theresa got the results for the tissue test on our Class 3 body in Carmelita."

He stared straight ahead at the wall and didn't answer her.

Gustav emerged from his bed and headed for Karthik, undoubt-edly to initiate his first petting session of the evening. He had a way of finding the gloomiest people and drawing them out of their shells. At least, that was what he had done with Racky when she had gone to the shelter in search of a companion. The tabby rubbed his head and back against Karthik's shins.

Karthik started slightly and looked down at the cat. He hadn't grown up with furry critters—or so the story went—so he didn't always know how to interpret this kind of action. In any case, he seemed to figure that the cat was looking for some kind of acknowledgment. He patted Gustav's head absently. The cat took a couple of pats but even-tually shook out his fur and went back to his bed.

Racky tapped her friend's shoulder. "Karthik?"

He answered in a low monotone. "And it's n—not Lenci."

"It's a relief you were right about that," she said. "And we have another lead. I got a look at those dental records from the Class 1 body at the school, and they match that blond WCE broad who nabbed Lenci's baby a year ago! She still had an existing dental record from last decade, most probably before she joined the agency. Someone on their side missed a spot in their cleanup."

Karthik side-glanced her. "That's suspiciously lucky."

Racky beamed. "Yeah, but it strongly supports your claim that you saw Lenci in the area."

"So, she caught up with the woman who took her kid," Karthik said pensively.

"And messed her *up!*" Racky said proudly. "Multiple broken bones, uh, that weren't broken in the explosion."

In answer to his sickened expression, she said, "The WCE-issued cyanide molar was emptied before the explosion. Coroner cited the pill as the most likely cause of death."

"Oh, good. So, Lenci d—didn't *kill* the woman. She just t— tortured her to the point of suicide before t—torching her body." Karthik massaged his forehead.

Racky sighed. "You have to understand, Karthik: Lenci's just doing what she was trained to do."

"I d—don't care what she was trained to d—do!" he exclaimed. "Any friend of mine should know better than to d—do something l— like that."

"I'm sure she had her reasons," Racky said.

He shook his head decidedly. "N—nothing can justify t—torture. That's just evil—inhuman, even."

"Then, why are you even taking the trouble to help us find her?" Racky asked. "If she isn't even human enough to be your friend?"

He hesitated, then said, "Because all these things she d—does have consequences, and she's going t—to have to face them."

While she knew that he only spoke that way because he was hurting, Racky sat back and looked at him with such a profound disappointment that he squirmed in his seat.

After a moment, she stood. "I have to stir the gumbo."

"Mm! Gumbo!" Karthik stood as well. "I'll get the bowls. You kn—know, Maude makes a killer—"

Gustav hissed.

Racky banged her ladle on the gumbo pot. "You will *not* mention that prejudiced gorgon's name in this house!"

Then, remembering the cat, she tossed him a kitty treat.

"Are you *training* him to hiss at my girlfriend's name?" Karthik asked.

He didn't have to ask. He knew.

Racky tried not to look too pleased with herself, but it didn't work very well. "I'm training him to do a lot of things. He can take a whizz in the toilet and flush on his own. And he can dance bachata. Want to see?"

"The whizzing or the dancing?" Karthik said dourly.

"Oh, don't be a miserable wretch! I was endeavoring to change the subject."

"She's n—not a gorgon," he muttered, conveniently avoiding any discussion of prejudice.

"And you're not an immature nincompoop."

"Whatever, your up-highness."

"Up yours, as well." She slammed the pot of gumbo onto the table. "And dinner is served."

As they ate, Racky explained how she had found the chip in the carpet of the Carmelita apartment.

"It looks like a media chip," she said, holding the baggie up to the light. "Pretty fancy stuff for Carmelita—WCE-grade stuff."

Karthik munched thoughtfully. "And you think it's somehow linked to Lenci?"

"My gut says yes," she replied. She took another bite of gumbo and then hopped up to get a magnifying glass, some cleaner, and a couple of her fine-tipped probes. "Looks like the chip runs on organics, but I can probably tweak a couple of things to get it to project with a plain old electrical current as the prompt. If there is any information encoded on it, I will find it. Oo! I forgot the monkey bread!"

She ran to the kitchen to retrieve the monkey bread from the oven. Between "oo, hot"s, she carved out a couple of pieces and hurried back to the table. After taking a blissful bite, she blew the steam out of her mouth, wiped her hands on her pants, and took up her probes.

Karthik watched her distastefully, then cleared his throat. "Are you coming to the Changs' for the holiday n—next week?"

"Monica had extended an invitation to me," Racky said, staring intently at the chip through her magnifying glass. "Why do you ask?"

He cleared his throat again. "Well, Maude and I were considering a road trip—"

"Have you lost your ever-needy, numbskull mind?"

He took a bite of gumbo to avoid having to answer that question. Then he began tapping his fingers on the table from pinky to thumb and thumb to pinky. He sometimes did that when he was upset, although Maude had been trying to break him of the habit because it looked unsophisticated. Racky didn't care one way or another about sophistication, but she did feel a certain responsibility for Karthik as he was one of the people Lenci loved most.

She sighed, "I know that you are only being such a vindictive fool because you are injured on account of Lenci's skipping town, but if you are not the most gelatinous-brained, butt-dragging, selfish—"

"You're just full of flattering d—descriptions t—tonight, aren't you?" Karthik said sulkily.

"And I will remain so as long as you're keeping company with that gor—" She stopped herself. "Uh, gorgeous woman. I can admit she's beautiful, even if prejudiced. And no, I won't be spending *my* holiday listening to her highfalutin Neo-Eugenic garbage. Tell Monica I send my love."

Silence descended and remained.

Racky cleaned the sticky residue off of the chip. Then she began to probe it and move its tiny parts this way and that with a pair of tweezers. When Karthik was finished eating, he stood to look over her shoulder.

Gustav reemerged from his bed and rubbed his head against Karthik's legs. Karthik responded this time with emotionally available petting, and Gustav purred his contentment. At Racky's request, Karthik filled a small bowl with gumbo for the cat. Gustav devoured it greedily, and after he'd gotten his fill, he returned to his bed happy and rather sleepy.

As Racky probed further toward the chip's center, she discovered that she needed to use multiple tools to get the job done. Karthik held the magnifying glass for her and sometimes probed as well, although three hands were quite a lot to work on such a small chip.

It was 2316 when Racky gave a triumphant squawk. Karthik was so startled that he dropped the magnifying glass into Racky's half-eaten gumbo.

The chip sparked and projected a gaunt man's face, and a loud beat pulsed through the room. The beat was accompanied by a haunting melody of five simple notes that repeated over and over.

> *Hellbender, kill and end her*
> *Fire*
> *Salamander, full of slander*
> *Slip and slide*
> *Till she has died*

Then come
Home to me
And rest indeed

"It's Carmelita's former district head," Karthik said.

Racky nodded. "And it's no halfway kind of spine-chilling."

"What do you think it means?" he asked.

There was an uncomfortable pause in which they left unspoken the concerns that could arise from the fact that the chip had been in an apartment associated with Lenci *on the night of the district head's death.*

"I don't know," Racky replied at last. "But I've got to find out where this chip was made. Maybe that will lead us to more information about this 'Home' place. And if the message was for Lenci, maybe she'll be headed that way as well."

"Lee-Smith's going to want to see this," Karthik said.

"I'm sending her a recording of it as we speak," said Racky.

Her flake chimed almost immediately.

Blair: Find its source.

CHAPTER 5

The Agent awoke stiff and itchy in the train car. The hay had been a comfortable insulation against the cold two days before, but now it was simply irritating as it poked her from all angles—and it had caused her nightmare. In an attempt to avoid thinking about the detention cell, she began reminiscing about the warmth of intimacy with Karthik and about the innocent comfort of linking pinkies with him and about his laugh, which sounded so much like his mother's.

The Wilson boy had thrown a wrench in the works of the Agent's plan. As her new self was emerging, Valencia hovered beneath her consciousness, dredging up emotional memories. This was confusing because Valencia belonged in a different mental compartment, but her memories and feelings kept leaking into this new, yet to be defined space. The confusion reminded the Agent of the trigger-prompt experience she had had in Diablo, when select facts from Valencia's past had been made salient to her. That time around, it had also been difficult—though not impossible—to separate her emotions from the facts.

The Agent attempted to redirect her attention to a task more relevant to her current survival needs: retrieving the names and Songs of the Amphibians from the locked box of her mind. She would need these to gain the advantage over any Phibs who managed to catch up with her.

But her mind was overrun with rosy memories of Valencia's childhood and of unlikely safe spaces like the library at Windsailing's School for the Gifted. That had been the only place where Valencia's tormentors would not follow her. The pickings were slim as literature went, but she took an interest in the herpetological encyclopedia—a multivolume, comprehensive description of amphibians and reptiles—which she read cover to cover. That season of her life had been characterized by constant terror, but the library was one place where she had felt safe and at peace.

But now was no time for childish reminiscing. With no small amount of effort, the Agent successfully wrangled those emotional memories and began to stuff them back into their appropriate compartment. Then the memories seemed more like facts to her, and everything was in its proper place once again.

She stretched her aching limbs, but the blistering cold so accosted them that they retracted immediately. She exhaled and watched her breath whoosh out in a steamy stream. The train, which had started out traveling to the east, appeared to have traveled significantly northward. That was good, the Agent hoped, because it was possible that she could exit the train before it entered the Eastern States, where advanced technology would make her much easier to find.

Bracing herself against the cold, the Agent emerged from the hay and crawled to the edge of the train car. A fluffy white blanket covered the outside world. Snow had been a fairytale in the hot, dry streets of Diablo, where Valencia had spent her childhood. And the Agent, in all of her travels, had never come across it either. More of the curious precipitation was falling from the sky like great, white cotton balls.

The Agent, having been born in blood and fire and myrrh and water—among other environments—saw her next opportunity for rebirth in the cold, shimmering cushion on the ground outside. The train was not exactly moving at a crawl, but the Agent figured that a jump would not hurt too badly since the snow would break her fall. So, before she could convince herself to dive back into the warmth of the hay, she leapt from the train.

When she hit the hard ground, she realized that snow was not as great of a cushion as it appeared to be. She bounced to her feet and began shaking the fluffy substance out of her hair. The snow was like very cold sand, soft and crumbly. It rained down off of the Agent's head and onto her tank top, gym shorts, and stockings where it quickly melted. In the freezing wind, she regretted not having brushed off the snow while it was still in solid form.

Her extra help would need time to adjust to counter the vicious knife hands of the wind. Or—she feared to think—her extra help was already at work, and she only dreaded the outer cold because it reminded her of the cold within her. She entertained that unpleasant thought no further beyond the acceptance of the fact that she needed to keep the cold at bay to keep the past at bay.

In that expanse of snowy open country, the Agent was acutely aware of her need to obtain clothing and a warm place to stay. A town or village would be helpful, but she hoped to find the urban center of—whatever district this was. An urban center would have a larger population in which the arrival of a floater like herself would not create a stir among the locals. She waded about a hundred meters through the knee-deep snow to a whited-out signpost. When she kicked it, the snow fell off to reveal two different urban destinations.

CENTRAL NORTH PLAINS 830 KM WEST
CENTRAL LAKES 10 KM EAST

North Plains was a fairly advanced Western district, but the Agent knew that urban centers of Eastern districts, like Lakes, were far ahead of any district in the West. The advanced technology in Central Lakes would prove a great obstacle to her survival. Her anti-tech conditioning would likely impede her ability to carry out everyday tasks, but even if less advanced tech were available, there remained the danger of facial recognition devices capturing her image. And yet, the cold also was a danger in itself. After once more considering the distance to Central North Plains, the Agent decided that she would just have to take her chances in Lakes. She began moving eastward.

* * *

A definite advantage of traveling in the Free East was that travel rules were much more lax than those of districts in the Western States. The Agent had apparently ridden into the Eastern States undetected, and she had walked from the rural edge of Lakes to the urban center without encountering a checkpoint or a patrol.

It was midday and still bitterly cold when she reached Central

Lakes. As she moved further into the urban center, she gained more of a sense of wonder. At each street corner, she paused to admire the sparkling layers of snow collecting on the branches of the trees. The sidewalks had been shoveled recently, so they provided a more comfortable walk compared to the fields and backroads on the outskirts of the district.

There were many people trudging down the sidewalks, but none of them seemed terribly interested in the Agent. This nonthreatening indifference was most welcome after her recent encounters with the parties who were hunting her. High-rises lined the streets, and a large clock tower sat in the central plaza. Auto-cars hummed along at a moderate speed through the streets, stopping at floating traffic signals and continuing after a well-timed interval. The Agent noticed commercial drones and police drones alike flying overhead, but they were uncharacteristically silent.

Noise-canceling technology. The Agent smiled. She liked the Eastern States.

A strong gust of wind hit her, and she remembered the one reason she did not like the district of Lakes. If she could find a way to mitigate the effects of the cold, however, her appreciation would quickly return. Smoothing her hair away from her face, she peered through the snow flurries to locate the nearest clothing shop. There was a boutique only halfway down the block.

The Agent was so excited at the prospect of obtaining dry clothing that she didn't look where she was going and ran right into a passing business woman. The woman offered a rushed apology and continued on her way, waddling under the weight of a long, heavy wool coat. The Agent thought that the coat looked very warm. She decided that she would very much like a wool coat of her own.

The holographic salespeople at the boutique were both about one and a half meters tall and very thin. They were Class 1 women with strawberry blond hair and hazel eyes. Their makeup reflected the latest fad, heavy accents on the jaw and little to no emphasis on the eyes. The Agent took a couple of deep breaths as they approached, trying to manage the overwhelming panic that David had programmed into her to keep her from utilizing modern technology. She had at least seen salespeople like this before, when she had passed through the district of Forsythe.

The holographic salespeople greeted her with cool professionalism and asked if she needed anything.

"No, thank you," she replied, keeping her voice calm and even. "I'm just looking for now."

They followed a couple of paces behind her and made uninvited commentary about every item that she considered. Every thirty seconds, they reminded her that the self-heating, fortified cotton coats were on sale. Unable to take any more of their jabbering, she smoothly swiped her hands in front of her—right then left—and the holograms disappeared. Not too long after, a red wool coat with a thick lining caught her eye, and she decided to buy it.

The holographic salespeople returned to help her check out. No matter how she swiped and swiped, they seemed to believe that their presence was mandatory for any financial transaction. They did not recognize cash when they scanned it with their eyes.

"Is there a physical person here that I can talk to?" the Agent asked, beginning to feel lightheaded.

"Perhaps you are unfamiliar with the process of electrofund transfers," one holographic salesperson said. "We can walk you through the process. Please touch the red button if you would like a tutorial on electrofund transfers."

The Agent's throat was tightening. "No new process!"

She considered leaving the store without the coat, but the memory of the snow and the bitter wind kept her rooted where she was.

"I just want to talk to a person," she said pleadingly. "Don't you have any non-holographic salespeople?"

"We can certainly help you with this sale," the other holographic salesperson replied. "Maybe you will appreciate our Class 3 interface."

"Wait, why Class 3?"

Both of the salespeople struck a pose, and their pale skin suddenly turned mocha brown. Their limp, strawberry blond hair transformed into voluminous, black curls, but their hazel eyes remained unchanged.

"Is this more agreeable?" they asked together.

The Agent made a move for the door. The going was slow because she was out of breath, but she moved as quickly as she could. The salespeople had labeled her as Class 3, which meant that they must have captured an image of her face in order to run it through some kind of class analysis software. And if they had an image of her face, then anyone scanning the country's databases for it could find it.

As the Agent leaned on a shelf for support, she grunted, "If I could just manage to—"

"Did you say manager?" the salespeople said. "Would you like to speak to our human manager?"

That would work.

"Manager!" the Agent gasped. "Yes, a manager, please!"

And just like that, the holographic salespeople disappeared. A petite Class 4.14 teenager with similarly trendy jaw makeup came out of a door near the front of the shop. She sported waist-length micro-braids, a lavender dress, and spectacles with thick, lavender rims.

"The appellation is Maewyn," she said. "With what can I assist you?"

"Did they take a picture of me?" the Agent asked. "I need you to delete it."

"That is something with which I can assist you," Maewyn said in an unhurried manner. "I see that my assistants already prepared a profile for your account. You were attempting to make a purchase, correct?"

"Yes," the Agent said. "Please, I still want to buy the coat, but the photo needs to be deleted first. It's important."

Maewyn did not seem interested in the details of the Agent's back-story, which was a relief. She pinched the air in front of her and moved her index finger in a circle. The Agent saw nothing, but the manager nodded as if she were reading some important information in the lenses of her spectacles.

"A profile picture is mandatory for everyone paying with electro-fund transfer in this establishment," Maewyn said at last.

"But I don't *want* to use electrofund transfer," the Agent said. "I only have cash."

She pulled out a handful of money and fanned it, so the manager would know that she was serious.

Maewyn's eyes flicked over the money. "Cash transactions, for anything other than tips, are not customary in Lakes. If you want to pay with that tender, you must set up an account with us. It will be similar to a checking account but only for our store."

She paused, then said, "We can complete the account without a profile, if you wish. We will load the exact amount of money into the account for a single use."

"Fine, fine," the Agent said. "Delete the photo, please."

Maewyn flicked the air. "Your request is complete."

The Agent sighed with relief. The photo had been in the system for an uncomfortably long time, but there was a small chance that those who were hunting her had not thought to track facial recognition at Eastern boutiques. After all, they likely knew she had every incentive to stay in the Western States.

"Now, which item were you hoping to purchase?" asked Maewyn.

"I just want to buy this coat." The Agent said it like she was defending herself against a grave accusation.

"Genuine wool, not synthetic," Maewyn said, seeming intrigued, "a vintage option outside of our vegan-approved collection. I will be happy to assist you with this transaction."

And with that, the Agent forked over the cash. The manager touched the bridge of her spectacles, and a chime sounded by the door.

"Your transaction is complete," Maewyn said. "If you are on the web, leave us as kind of a review as makes you comfortable, and come visit us again when you return to Lakes."

"That's it? I—thank you," the Agent replied. "I will."

Donning the coat over her cold, wet clothing, she could already feel the difference. Of course, for all the trouble she had been through, she rather wished that she had stolen the coat. But the time was already lost. She would need to buy more clothes in the near future, but for the moment, she'd had her fill of Eastern retail. She nodded to Maewyn and moved to the exit.

The coat's protective capacity met the Agent's expectations. She could not feel the cold at all. This enabled her to focus on her next task of finding a place to stay—a task she hoped to accomplish before evening because camping outside overnight did not seem like a very pleasant option.

Just off of the main road, the Agent came across a Class 2-specific apartment complex. On the door, there was a poster of a waving lucky cat with a speech bubble that read:

Pure as gold.

The Agent could see how living in such a complex would be beneficial, especially given that there was an order out on her life. Living in class-specific housing would limit which Phibs could casually walk into the building in search of her. By the same principle, however, the Agent herself would have difficulty gaining entry to the Class 2 community. For reasons of a distant past life, she knew this to be true, but those memories were shrouded in a pain that could not be dulled by her pain management. She suddenly felt dirty and itchy. Resisting the urge to scratch her skin raw, the Agent readjusted her mental grip on reality by focusing on the facts of the situation at hand.

It was a fact that Class 2s notoriously aimed to be considered as close to wellborn as possible, which meant policing class relations down to the decimal point. So, a Class 2 community that welcomed all Class 2s was a rare find. Even so, the Agent knew better than to expect that that kind of open-mindedness would extend to the inclusion of the Subclass.

Yes, she was subclass, born in the furthest distant life to a Class 2.0 father and a Class 4.14 mother. After her encounter with the one to whom Valencia was tethered, her emerging self found this to be most salient. She still remembered that Bourghin had once registered Valencia as a Class 3 to give her some protection in a world that only recognized registered classes. However, this new self—likely affected by the contact with her childhood friend—was adamant that she acknowledge herself as the product of the love between members of separate classes. She found that love to be beautiful, though costly, and worth honoring.

Another block down, the Agent came across an apartment building with a sign outside that read:

Celebrate Heritage: Secure Housing for 4.14s or Subclass with One 4.14 Parent.

A woman with skin the color of vanilla pudding and wavy, sandy brown hair entered the building before the Agent and held the door open for her. The Agent nodded at her and waited at a respectful distance as the woman approached the reception desk.

"Good afternoon," the woman said to the cappuccino-colored man sitting at the desk. "I have a 4.14 grandma. Do you have any openings?"

The man finished typing one last sentence on his very sleek keyboard, then looked up at her. "I am the manager of this fine community, and I will grant you a place with us. If you please, do inform me of your appellation and flake."

"Josephine Freeman," she said, "and 555-4703."

"Exquisite, Ms. Freeman," the manager said. "Kindly connect your funds account in our app, and all of the information will be conveyed to your flake. In the app, you may select a four-digit access code in order to gain entry to your abode. Shall you make any queries?"

"No, thanks. I'll unload my belongings now."

It appeared to be an incredibly simple process. As Ms. Freeman headed for the door, the Agent stepped up to the desk confidently.

"Good afternoon," she said to the manager.

"I'm sure," he replied, pulling a plate of hummus and assorted vegetables out of one of his desk drawers.

Ignoring his munching and crunching—it was lunchtime after all—the Agent began to follow the path that she had observed in the previous conversation. "My mother is Class 4.14, and I was wondering—"

The manager stuffed a baby carrot in his mouth and lodged it in his cheek, so he could smirk at her with his mouth closed. She waited while he chewed and swallowed.

"We inhabit the Free East, but there are reasonable limits on freedom," he said disdainfully.

"But your sign says—"

"Our signage is of no import at all," he interrupted. He picked up a cherry tomato and inspected it for blemishes before biting it in half. "Only appearance is of import, and *you* appear to be Class 3. Imagine the manner in which the public would disparage this community if I granted access to a subber such as yourself."

The Agent scowled at his use of the word designated to malign members of the Subclass. "But what about me looks Class 3 as opposed to subclass with one 4.14 parent?"

"The most obvious characteristic would be the color of your skin," the manager said, swirling a carrot around in his hummus.

"Oh." The Agent looked over at a copper-colored woman with short, coiled hair leaving the building. "Kind of like hers?"

"Yes." The manager shifted uncomfortably. "But your hair has insufficient curl."

"Uh, huh," the Agent said, watching as three women of different skin colors—whose curls very much resembled her own—walked together across the lobby. "Like theirs?"

"A perm, a weave, and an accident of nature," the manager said, pointing at each of the women. "Your eyes are excessively slanted, and your nose is excessively flat."

"Like hers?" The Agent motioned to a woman with toasted pecan-colored skin, almond-shaped eyes, and a broader nose than her own.

"It must all of it be taken together, you subclass jezebel!" the manager bellowed. "This is the plain and simple fact: to have you in residence would convey the message that this community condones the tainting of blood. And that message, once conveyed, cannot be retracted! Therefore, you imperil the community with your attempts to claim membership. Now, *begone* before you are cast out!"

As the Agent's hands curled into fists, a heavy hand fell on her shoulder. She turned to find herself staring into the abdomen of a tall and rather sturdy Class 1 security guard, who made every effort to look intimidating.

The Agent imagined that she could make quick work of him in a fight, but after the situation at the boutique, she knew that she couldn't afford to draw any more attention to herself in this district.

"Fine," she said, heading back toward the door through which she had first entered.

"Kindly do not exit through *that* door," the manager said, crunching another hummus-covered tomato. "The one beside it is the one through which you ought to depart."

The Agent did not like his smug expression, but she figured that she would be able to handle an ambush or whatever was waiting for her outside the other door. The security guard, too, looked pleased to see her heading for that exit.

When the outside air accosted the Agent, she realized how hot it had been in the lobby. She'd never thought that the cold could bring her relief, but it did. A caramel-colored young man in an oversized coat was seated at a cart outside the door.

"And what's your story?" the Agent asked.

"Time and money are jealous bedfellows," the young man replied, looking as if the words embarrassed him greatly. "Having emerged from this doorway, you must give recompense—owing to the fact that you are not 4.14-descended and have therefore squandered the manager's time."

He motioned to a glass jar that sat on top of his cart. The jar was full of money.

"You don't say." The Agent whipped around and caught the door just before it closed. "Thanks for the info."

She strode back into the lobby, kicked the security guard in the shin when he grabbed at her, and overturned the manager's lunch plate. The hummus landed on his keyboard in an unappealing heap. And, despite his frantic attempts at corralling them, the carrots and tomatoes hopped and scurried like lemmings over the sides of the desk. Feeling gratified, the Agent turned and stomped on the guard's foot on her way to the door for 4.14-descended individuals.

Once outside, she circled back to the young man at the cart by the other door.

"Jealous bedfellows and all that," she told him as she took the jar from his cart and dumped its contents into her coat pocket. "You seem like a frustrated, underpaid worker. Here's a tip for the helpful tip."

She stuffed a couple of big bills into the young man's pocket. He protested neither to her taking the money nor to her tipping him.

"Your blood is tainted with Class 2." His voice lowered like he was speaking about a venereal disease.

"That's one way to describe it," she replied. "I can tell yours is, too, by your almond-shaped eyes and your flat nose."

"Truly?"

"No," she admitted. "You looked scared when you saw me, like you were afraid that what happened to me might one day happen to you. And you shave your hair close, presumably to hide the texture."

He looked sheepish. "It may do you great service to grace your speech with a lilt. Surely you understand the meaning behind my words?"

"Not all 4.14s speak that way," the Agent said, reflecting most notably upon her knowledge of Valencia's family. "But if I did it in hopes of acceptance, how much more of myself would I lose chasing an ever-changing standard?"

"That is one way to describe it, as you say," he shrugged. "Nevertheless, temperatures drop to inhospitable levels out there in that vast, hostile world."

"You have no idea," the Agent replied. Then, shoving her hands into her coat pockets, she walked away without looking back.

* * *

Karthik was returning to work from his lunch break when he got an audio call from Racky's personal number. On the inside of the tinted windshield, his auto-car displayed a picture of her cradling her cat.

"Answer," he said. Then, after the double chime to indicate that the call had connected, "Hi Racky. What's happening? I thought you had today off."

"Ey, K.! I do, but my tech never takes a precious moment's rest, and I finally captured something real handy! Blair's with us on a three-way. Say hi, Blair!"

"Hey, Wilson." She sounded excited in her cool and collected way. "When Wernicke called me, I knew you'd want in on this."

"In on what?" he asked.

"Wernicke's home-cooked facial recognition search successfully sidestepped the virus that's been preventing us from storing Lenci's image in our system," she replied. "We got a hit at an upscale boutique in Lakes, of all places. The recog picked it up before it disappeared. Chang is getting sloppy, which is good news for us."

Karthik frowned. "Recog's the exact reason she would have *avoided* the Eastern States. How clear is the image?"

"It's a ninety-eight percent match to that photo print you gave me, K.!" Racky squawked. "It's really Lenci!"

Blair's voice again. "We have to assume that she was actively working to cover her tracks and that she fled the area soon afterward. The image is from two hours ago, so we've got the recog scanning a radius equivalent to the distance she could have traveled in that time—including but not limited to the district of Lakes."

"Two hours on foot?" Karthik asked.

"By any sort of vehicle, even plane since she seems to be able to combat, if not prevent facial recognition. We figure the larger the radius, the better."

Karthik's mind was racing with thoughts about how and why Lenci could have ended up in the Eastern States, but he would have to ponder that later. "When do we leave?"

"I've got Wernicke on a special project with me, so you're co-leading with Cravenly on this one," Blair said. "You guys'll have a full tactical unit at your disposal. You're taking off from our airstrip in an hour."

"Understood."

The call disconnected. Warmed with a hope that he had long thought dead, Karthik set the auto-car's course for the airstrip, then sat back and smiled.

CHAPTER 6

THE AGENT TOOK A BREAK FROM HER APARTMENT SEARCH TO LOOK FOR a job so that she could remain aware of the happenings in the community. She wandered up and down six or seven streets before finding the ideal place. A restaurant named The Sweetest Rose was seeking help for per-diem shifts. In addition to the standard electrofund transfer, they paid in cash. There was a brightly lit flyer floating in the glass front door with all of the information in boldface type. A border of red roses marched around the edges of the flyer.

Upon closer inspection, the Agent found that the flyer was projected in front of the glass by a tiny, circular projector that hovered just beneath the second highest door hinge. She touched the projector curiously and jumped in surprise when it turned off and fell into her hand. The Agent closed her hand around the tiny projector, opened the door, and poked her head into the restaurant.

She was greeted by the inviting aroma of chocolate. The smell immediately calmed her nerves, and for one disorienting moment, she almost felt relaxed. It was a peculiar sensation, which she immediately rejected. She could not let her guard down, not at the start of a new life—maybe not ever.

A couple of meters from the door, there was a counter with a display case full of delicious-looking pastries, many of them drizzled with dark chocolate. There was no one in the dining room, but it was as cozy as an empty room could be. In the soft light of floating lamps that seemed to be held up neither by the ceiling nor by the floor, everything was enveloped in an aureate glow. The walls were hand-painted with large, deep red roses and emerald green leaves. Gold-gilded wooden chairs surrounded tables prepared with white napery, a porcelain tea set, shining silverware, and a floral centerpiece. At the far end of the room, there was a murmuring fountain decorated like a forest brook, on the surface of which floated fresh, red rose blossoms.

The coziness of the empty room made the Agent uneasy. She moved quickly to a door behind the counter, which she was sure must lead to the kitchen.

Little silver bells attached to the door heralded the Agent's arrival. The kitchen was pretty standard for a small restaurant: thirty-five square meters of space, a lowboy with a food preparation space, a counter for preparing pastries, sinks for dishes, and all of the standard kitchen appliances. There was a backdoor exit marked by a red sign and an unmarked door, which probably led to a storage space. Although there were a couple of windows that let in natural light, white fluorescents made the place seem sterile and almost harsh compared to the dining room. The Agent preferred that because it felt more professional.

An attractive man was kneading some dough on the pastry counter, but he did not seem to have noticed the Agent's entry. He had short, dark hair that waved at the ends, almond-shaped eyes, and golden-brown skin—making him some sort of Class 2, by the Agent's estimation. He had a lean, muscular build, like a player of association football. His shoulders nicely filled out his crisp, gray dress shirt, and on the front of his apron was pinned a name tag that read: **PETE**.

The Agent cleared her throat. "I'm wondering if you're still looking for help?"

"Not particularly," the man said, folding his dough into a ball. "I've made it on my own this long."

Frustrated about this rather dismissive treatment, the Agent flicked the tiny projector across the counter. It hit the man in his perfect pecs and glanced off onto his dough ball. The image of the flyer sprang to life, turning slowly in the air in front of his face.

"Hey, this is a Grade A establishment!" Pete's gaze shot up at her. "Do you know how many big chain restaurants exploit moments like this to oppress small bus—"

The Agent had instigated her first food sanitation lecture, but it was slow in coming. Pete had become quite at a loss for words. Self-maintenance had been shoddy at best in that train car, and the Agent's hair had admittedly become a rat's nest over the past couple of days.

She smoothed her hair. "Pete?"

A dazed, goofy smile slowly spread across his face.

"Holy wow!" he breathed.

The Agent shrugged off any guess at the kind of goofy thoughts that could be running around behind the man's goofy smile.

"Can I work here?" she asked.

A spark of recognition seemed to ignite in his eyes as she mentioned the work posting.

Coming to himself, he grinned with an unassuming winsomeness. He glanced at the holographic flyer and placed the projector on a nearby footstool.

"I, uh—" He cleared his throat. "The manager's not here right now, but I'll talk to him. I'm sure we—he'll find a spot for you. Just come by same time tomorrow in a long-sleeved, gray dress shirt and black slacks. Gordon'll start you right away."

"Thanks," she said, still a little whiplashed from the turn that the conversation had taken between the man's unfriendly overture and his guarantee that she'd be hired.

She had only been in this life for a few hours, but it was already a funny little life, riddled with all the quirks and mysteries of human interaction.

Pete hunched his shoulders and stuffed his hands into his pockets, betraying an unusual lack of confidence for a man so undeniably endowed with more than his fair share of natural beauty.

"You new in town?" he asked shyly.

"Just floating through," the Agent replied. "Kind of transient, I guess."

He might have looked a little sad, if there could be a reason for that at all.

"Speaking of which," she continued, "I don't suppose you know of any good places for a subclass female floater to lie low for a while?"

"Subclass," he echoed. "I don't know if I would have guessed that. You look just like some kind of Class 3."

"I get that a lot," she said. "It may surprise you to know that my father is Class 2 and my mother—"

"Oh, no, no!" Pete interrupted. "You *clearly* aren't from around here. In Lakes, it's illegal to ask someone about the specifics of their subclass designation."

"But you didn't *ask* me," the Agent said. "I was just telling you—"

"I must do my part to resist the perpetuation of the problems caused by our unjust classification system," Pete insisted. "And having grown up in a very Neo-Eugenically oriented Class 2 family, I know how bad that stuff can get. I don't *want* to know what you are. You are simply a human being to me."

The Agent stared at him in bewildered silence. She habitually banished unmanageable, pain-filled memories to the most inaccessible depths of her mind, but Pete's mention of family opened a direct gateway to the fact that—many lives back—Valencia had had regular exposure to a very Neo-Eugenically oriented Class 2 family as well. Despite her many lives since then, the residue of that family's anti-4.14 sentiment and not so thinly veiled eugenistic vitriol continued to corrode parts of her that were too deep to protect. So, she also knew how bad that stuff could get. The question remained, however, whether it would be a productive response to *never* consider anyone's heritages at all.

Pete nodded emphatically as though her silence confirmed the correctness of his behavior.

"Fine," the Agent said slowly, figuring it was not worth forcefully revealing her heritages to him when she only really wanted a place to live. "Just your average member of the Subclass, then."

"My dad is Class 2, too!" Pete offered, working with the little bit of knowledge that she had volunteered before he had educated her about district law. "I guess that's another thing we have in common."

Nothing else about the two of them had seemed similar to the Agent, but she smiled politely as he scribbled on a scrap of fabric that he'd torn off of a dry dish rag.

Pete handed the fabric to her when he was done writing on it. "Frin's Place doesn't consider class designation in the application process, and you can pay at whatever interval you like—so long as it's regular. Got cash?"

The Agent sized him up quickly, determining that—even though he was in impeccable shape—she could best him in a fight. Two minutes, tops, if it came to that.

"Cash's all I've got," she replied.

"Great. If the manager gives you any trouble, just tell him Pete Bae sent you. That's Pete, not Peter. I've been living in that building for a couple years now, so Frin'll take you on my recommendation. In fact, my shift ends pretty soon. You could wait here, enjoy some tea or something, and then I could accompany you?"

She folded the piece of fabric he'd given her. "Thanks a lot, Pete Bae. I think I can handle it from here."

As she turned to leave, he called out, "Wait! What's your appellation?"

She glanced at the Help Wanted flyer that still floated above the footstool. As she admired the cheery border of rose blossoms, it came to her.

"Rosa," she smiled sweetly. "See you tomorrow."

* * *

Racky sat on the floor of her living room with a bunch of flashcards in front of her. She held up a blue flashcard.

"Blue," she told Gustav.

The tabby flicked his tail. His eyes seemed to show understanding, but the true test would be whether he could remember any of the material they had covered in the past half hour.

Racky spread out the flashcards, one for each color of the rainbow. Then, folding her hands in her lap, she said, "Yellow."

Gustav thought for a moment, then confidently placed his paw on the blue card.

"We can keep up the practice," Racky told him.

Her flake began to vibrate. Blair was calling.

"Wernicke," Racky said.

Blair's voice came through in a loud whisper. "Uh, hi, Wer—uh, Racky. Can we talk?"

"Sure. What's up?"

The line went dead.

Baffled, Racky attempted to redial. But before she could initiate the call, there was a knock at her front door. She looked through the peephole to see Blair standing on the porch.

Opening the door, she said, "When you asked if we could talk, I got the idea you meant we would have an audio call."

"Yeah, sorry," Blair said, turning in a small circle as if admiring—or scrutinizing—Racky's décor. "It's kind of sensitive."

Gustav rubbed his back against Blair's shins, and she glanced down at him uneasily.

"You don't like cats?" Racky asked, shooing Gustav away.

"I've never had to find out," Blair replied.

"All these non-cat people coming to my house," Racky grumbled.

Gustav was reluctant to head back to his bed, perhaps sensing in Blair a lonely soul in need of some tender love and care.

"That one's beyond help for now," Racky whispered to him. "Go to your kitty bed."

He glanced wistfully at Blair but did as he was told. Then he curled up and went to sleep.

Taking a seat, Blair pulled out a small, circular device.

"Ey, what's your intention with that?" Racky exclaimed.

"I'm just going to sweep—"

"No, you will not," Racky said, snatching the device. "I have very sensitive equipment in this house. Everything is tuned plumb perfect. Crude bug killers like this throw everything out of whack! I have something of better quality that will kill bugs without frying my other gadgets. Watch."

She cleared her throat. "SecurityFriend."

A synthetic voice that sounded a lot like Racky responded, "Activated."

"Please initiate a sweep of the house, garage, and porch."

"Initiating bug sweep now."

Racky grinned at Blair, who smiled knowingly.

SecurityFriend beeped twice when the sweep was done. "Sweep complete. No bugs found. Would you like me to send out a routine pulse for pest control, just in case?"

"Please," Racky said.

After a few seconds, SecurityFriend beeped again. "Pest control pulse complete. Anything else?"

"Not now, thank you," Racky said.

"Deactivating."

"Impressive," said Blair.

"I'm over the moon about how well her beta period is coming along," Racky told her. "Only thing left is to get her to recognize the pet doors. Right now, she only monitors whole doorframes and windows. Anyway, you mind telling me why you're here?"

"I wanted to make sure we had some privacy to talk about that special project I mentioned earlier," Blair answered.

Racky crossed her arms. "Any chance I'm earning overtime for this?"

"It's not really something official," Blair said.

"I'm directing all my energy to tracking the source of that media chip," Racky sighed. "What more could there be, unofficial or not?"

Blair shifted uncomfortably. "Dr. Bourghin only just brought herself to clean out Agent Bourghin's study. It was a big to-do what with all of the priceless artifacts he had willed to family members. She had to sift through it all."

"And he left me a plethora of Bronze Age musical instruments?"

"No," Blair said. "After Dr. Bourghin distributed all of the artifacts, she was left with a collection of research and notes, things Agent Bourghin had been working on unofficially."

Racky's eyes grew wide. "You mean, all that stuff she turned in just after he passed—"

"That was his official documentation of Lenci's experience with the agency. It was the information he *wanted* SSI to have about her. This other stuff, though," Blair lowered her voice. "It's much—richer."

"So far, I'm comprehending all this," Racky said, "but why do I have to hear about it before everyone else?"

"Because, after Dr. Bourghin had sent Agent Bourghin's research by courier the other day, she found a canister that she'd stored in a closet. I happen to know the canister contains an antipersonnel agent that my—Beatriz Gomez attempted to test in Diablo last year."

Racky's forehead wrinkled. "Yeah, I took that canister to Dr. Bourghin directly on the night that SSI collapsed. If you want to study it, you should send it to the lab at HQ."

"I want you to sell it," Blair said, sitting up straight and putting her shoulders back. "Or, more accurately, I want you to put it up for sale, so we can get info."

"What sort of info?"

"I think Lenci's kid is still alive, and I want to know where he or she is."

Racky's brow furrowed. "I take it Vincent is not aware of this plan?"

Blair's gaze was unwavering. "So, can I count on you to put out an ad on the dark web? It needs to look legitimate."

Racky really took the time to think about it. Blair's plan was a fairly low-maintenance one. They only needed to post an ad and wait for someone with information to respond. They'd act when, and only when, they had a lead. In the meantime, they could focus all of their attention on finding Lenci.

"It will be *both* our behinds if we get caught," she said at last, shaking her head.

Blair nodded firmly.

Remembering the part of Samir's recording where he seemed to be hiding something in his office, Racky asked, "Ey, can I pick up the canister from Dr. Bourghin directly? If I can get a flight today, I'd beat a courier for speed. Plus, a personal touch usually soothes all involved when dealing with the family of the deceased."

"I assumed you would go," Blair said. "You've got a commercial flight. It leaves in two hours."

"Well, then, I will have to prepare Gustav to hold down the fort." Racky stood up, then paused to look at her flake.

"What is it?" Blair asked.

"I got another ping on Lenci," Racky said. "It's a ninety-nine *point five* percent match."

"Where?"

"Croon A Tune."

"That's just south of Lakes," Blair said, typing a message on her flake as she spoke. "Send me the coordinates, and message Wilson your findings. I'll contact the pilot."

Her flake buzzed, and she took the call on the porch.

Racky messaged Karthik about the switch-up. After all of the appropriate information had been exchanged, she asked him how he was holding up. He welcomed the change in plan because it meant that they were acting upon more up-to-date information.

> Karthik: It's weird, but I'm really looking forward
> to seeing her, almost like we're meeting to
> catch up over coffee or something.

> Sounds about right. I was saving up a hug for
> her this past year. Give it to her for me when
> you see her.

> Karthik: Mine first.

Blair came in from the porch.

"Okay, everything's set," she said. "It took some doing, though. The district of Croon A Tune insisted on involving Eastern law enforcement, but I made sure Wilson and Cravenly were understood to be necessary experts to have on-site with the team they dispatch."

Racky felt a sudden pang of sadness. "It feels just strange not to be there."

"For me, too," Blair said, "but I need you in Diablo to retrieve the canister. I'll finish my read-through of Bourghin's materials, so you all can get cracking on them in the next couple of days or so."

"What all *did* you find in that 'rich' research from Bourghin?" Racky asked.

Blair grinned. "Much of it is still very mysterious. You'll want to see for yourself. I'll distribute the original materials to the team, but I don't want any copies running around."

"You think the info's that much of a game changer?"

"It'll blow your mind," Blair said. "Now, I'll get out of your hair. You've got a flight to catch."

* * *

Frin—the manager of Frin's Place—was a paunchy, middle-aged, subclass guy with a broad nose, soft brown eyes, and pinkish brown skin. The Agent named Rosa tried not to stare at him, but she had never seen a subclass man who owned a whole apartment building.

True to Pete's word, her subclass designation was not considered in the application process because there was no application at all. Frin merely asked that Rosa state her first name and the interval at which she would like to pay: hourly, weekly, monthly, or yearly. He listed the rate for each interval and explained that since heat and electricity were sourced from the building's nuclear generator, they were included in her rent. After she gave him a week's worth of cash, he handed her a set of keys for Apartment 450, which he assured her would have classic appliances.

"Classic means ancient-but-mostly-functional," he explained with a wink. "Now, elevator's just down that—"

"Oh, no need," she smiled. "Can I get to the apartment by using good old-fashioned stairs, assuming they're, uh, mostly functional?"

Frin's jowls shook as he chuckled heartily.

"450 is on the west side of the building," he said, pointing in that direction. "So, you'll walk out the front door and turn left, then left again. That's the door to the stairs. Go up the stairs to the fourth floor, turn right out the staircase, and your room will be two doors down on the far side of the hall."

"Left, left, fourth floor, right, two doors down," Rosa repeated to let him know she had been listening.

"Far side of the hall," he reminded her. Then, with a kind smile, he said, "But that's the long way. Sure I can't convince you to ride the elevators? They even tell you your heart rate and blood pressure."

Lakes was just the type of well-endowed district that *would* install biometric scanners in their elevators to aid with security. The Agent knew to stay away from such technology that could be hacked by—or even directly wired to—government agencies.

"Thanks, no," Rosa replied. "I could use the exercise."

"Fine by me," Frin said with a shrug. "Welcome home, for now."

She nodded to him and exited out the front door.

The building was plain but well maintained. It was flanked on three sides by thick patches of trees. The stairs to the apartments were outside of the building, but they were covered and behind a locked gate. The steel steps were textured with X shapes and painted a gaudy yellow, probably to lessen the chance of slips and trips in the dimly lit stairwell. At the entrance to the fourth floor, there was another door that took the same key as the gate.

Not too far down the dark, musty hallway, Rosa arrived at Apartment 450. There was a box of chocolates sitting on her doormat. Feeling inwardly warmed, she smiled and picked up the box. She thought Frin very kind to have sent someone up to leave that housewarming gift for her. The delivery person must have gone up the elevator. After noting that the original packaging was undisturbed, Rosa popped a couple of candies into her mouth, turned her key in the lock, and threw open the door.

As the unfortunate mix of mint, raspberry cream, sea salt, and caramel exploded in her mouth, she noted with delight the homeyness of the small apartment. The common area was already furnished with a loveseat, an armchair, a coffee table, and a dining set. She ventured in and placed the still-open box of chocolates on the dining room table.

There was a well-equipped kitchen that very nearly sat in the living room. In the bedroom, there was a firm, twin-sized bed and a climate control panel, for temperature and humidity. The panel was an older model, one that Rosa had seen before and was comfortable using. She was grateful that Frin's building still offered apartments with classic appliances. Not many places could be doing *that* in the Eastern States.

The bathroom, which could only be accessed through the

bedroom, was by far her favorite part of the new living space. Aside from the mismatched fixtures in three different silver tones, the creaky commode, and the shower head that leaked, there was a heat lamp installed in the ceiling. That heat lamp alone would be worth the entire week's rent on a cold Lakes morning.

Rosa returned to the living room and sat in the armchair, feeling grateful. She'd gotten a job and a place to live before sundown. Since Pete Bae lived in the same building, she may even have gained a friendly neighbor. This was a fortunate turn of events, and yet, she was not quite sure that she was ready for another neighborly friendship. Crispin suddenly reappeared in her memory as a chilling reminder of the consequences of opening her heart and life imprudently.

But this was a different situation, the Agent named Rosa reminded herself. Crispin had moved in *after* Posy. Pete, however, had been living in Lakes for years before she arrived. Plus, Pete was kind of dorky. Phibs were generally versed in enticement and by necessity *not* dorky.

Rosa concluded that she really needed to stop being so paranoid and maybe to become a little dorkier herself. It would make a good cover. She retrieved the box of chocolates from the table and selected one that was shaped like a haystack.

As she was closing the box, a piece of paper fell out of the lid. It was a note written in elaborate, looping script:

BuY A WeB ApparatuS
StaY ConnecteD
StaY AlivE

The Agent's heart skipped a beat. She hurried to the corded landline in the kitchen and called down to the front desk.

Frin answered. He sounded tired. "Yes?"

"It's Rosa, in 450," she said hurriedly. "Could you check your security footage to see if anyone came up the stairs in the past hour or so bearing a box of chocolates?"

"You're the only person who's used that staircase all day," Frin said. "Everyone else is availing themselves of our very modern and lavish elevators."

Rosa laughed. "They *do* sound tempting when you put it that way. Any footage from the elevators?"

"No one's been riding. Most people won't even be off work for an hour or so."

"Of course," Rosa said. "Well, thanks, Frin."

"What's all this about chocolates?"

"It's nothing, probably," she replied. "Goodbye."

She hung up feeling quite puzzled.

Someone had gone to great lengths to get her that message. Someone who had been watching her, maybe even since before she had arrived in Lakes. Someone with enough tech savvy to override Frin's security visuals. But who?

Clearly someone who did not know that the Agent had been conditioned against new technology like web apparatuses.

She turned over the note, and on the back were the words:

TimE TO AdapT

Okay, so maybe it was someone who knew about her conditioning. But, again, who?

The only person she knew who was gifted enough to pull a stunt like this was Rackelle Wernicke. But what possible reason could Racky have for playing a game like this? They had been friends in the Agent's life as Valencia Chang and pre-teammates a few lives before that. However, while it was heartwarming to think of a kleptomaniac, dance-teaching, coding genius pre-teammate pulling for her, the Agent figured Racky would have left some kind of hint—if it were really her.

If it weren't Racky, the message-sender would be an unknown player, a wildcard, and only time would tell whether they were pulling for the Agent.

Say it again. She refused to give in to the panic rising within her.

Say it again. Say it again.

CHAPTER 7

IT WAS SUNNY AND BRISK IN CROON A TUNE WHEN KARTHIK AND Theresa descended onto the tarmac. Across the Bygone River, the district's already distinctive skyline was augmented by impressive drone advertisement displays. The river, which ran southeast to northwest through the district, shimmered like a golden ribbon in the late after- noon light. On the riverbank nearest to the airstrip, there was a large hologram of a beamed pair of eighth notes—undoubtedly an homage to the district's well-known music production industry. Next to that was an area filled with bright, flashing lights. That was the pleasure center, which contained the district's sex-oriented businesses.

A black sedan was waiting at the edge of the airstrip. The driver got out and opened a door for Karthik and Theresa. He was an austere figure in a black suit and black sunglasses. He didn't speak for the entire ride, dropped the Coop agents off in the financial center, and drove away in a hurry.

The financial center was still busy, but it was likely to empty out in an hour or so. Maximinus Brown, the head of the Eastern FBI's SWAT team, met Karthik and Theresa by the Central Bank. He was tall, muscular, and very direct.

"SWAT?" Karthik said after Brown had introduced himself. "We thought Croon A Tune Police would be here to assist us."

"That was before your person of interest blew up the district morgue," Brown replied. "There were no casualties, but you know how

CAT-PD gets over explosions. Anyhow, this is now our case, and *you're* assisting *us*."

Karthik and Theresa exchanged a glance. Neither of them knew how CAT-PD could get about explosions, but the Eastern SWAT team's presence was certainly an escalated response. Karthik messaged the update to Blair who told him to defer to Brown's leadership and that she'd be in contact with the Eastern FBI.

Brown, it seemed, had already been briefed on the Coop agents before their arrival.

"I get you're the supposed 'expert' on the target," he said to Karthik. Then to Theresa, "I'm not sure why *you're* here."

"Just another pretty face," Theresa said, batting her eyelashes. "And I'm forensics and biochem."

Brown huffed. "If we found a body, we could have had it bagged up for you. This no place for a female."

"You do know that all special agents at the Coop are field trained, don't you?" she said.

"Field training isn't the same as what SWAT does," he shrugged. "See, I just don't want you to get yourself into some kind of trouble. None of us are going to be able to—"

"You should watch your own back," Theresa interrupted. "I can take care of myself."

"I hope for all our sakes that you can," he said.

Karthik shifted uncomfortably. "So, you said you were going t—to orient us?"

Brown nodded. "This way."

He led them around the side of the building. "About an hour ago, our surveillance first caught sight of Chang carrying what appeared to be a bodybag out of the district morgue. The building exploded twenty seconds later. Then Chang set up shop in this abandoned renovation project."

It appeared that they were going to have a chance to catch Lenci in the middle of her death-faking process. Karthik was not entirely gleeful about the idea, but he hoped that they'd be able to apprehend his friend this time and bring her home.

"Where's your surveillance team now?" he asked, glancing around.

Brown smirked. "They're in an unmarked van at the end of the block, riverside. Been monitoring the building using AI-assisted 3-D imaging since she arrived. She's still in there, and she's alone."

He brought one hand to his earpiece and held up the other as if to request silence, even though he had been the one speaking.

A second later, he nodded. "We'll be in position in sixty seconds."

Theresa tapped his shoulder. "Shouldn't we get comms, too?"

"No."

"Did they say which floor she's on?" Karthik said, looking up at the building and estimating that it must be about three or four stories tall.

"She's on the second floor," Brown said. "Jones'll join us at the back. Got two other teams going in through the sides."

"No one's going in through the front?" Theresa asked.

Brown shook his head. "Rich, our sniper, is posted on the roof of a building across the street. He's got a clear view of the front and sides, so he'll keep an eye on things."

They walked toward the river and passed the surveillance van at the end of the block. When they rounded the corner of the building, there was a man in SWAT gear standing by the back entrance.

He held out a hand to Brown. "Brown, good to see you again."

"Jones," Brown replied, stuffing his hands into his pockets.

Jones gave Karthik and Theresa a once-over. "And you are?"

"Attractive and incredibly capable," Theresa replied with a flirtatious smile.

"I don't mind it," Jones said with a grin.

Not sure how to follow that, Karthik held out his hand. "Wilson."

"Ah, the expert," Jones said, shaking his hand. "You know anything about this Chang witch that'll help us nail her?"

Karthik stiffened. "She's a friend. I'm hoping we won't need to resort to violence to get her to come with us."

Jones raised an eyebrow. "She blew up a government building this afternoon. They don't usually call us in unless they have reason to expect a violent conflict. "

"A man can hope," Theresa said, looking at Karthik scornfully.

Jones' gaze snapped toward her. "Yes, a man *can*."

"Banter's over," Brown said. "All units moving in."

They entered through the back door and trudged down a dark hallway to get to the building's atrium. While the outside of the building had looked quite polished, the inside was bare and some places were almost completely gutted. Scaffolding lined the walls, and a couple of walkways were suspended from the high ceilings. The place smelled like mildew.

"Oh, you've got to be kidding me," Brown said.

"What?" Karthik and Theresa asked in unison.

Brown waved at them dismissively.

"Surveillance can't find her," Jones whispered, sliding his finger around the outside of his earpiece to turn up the volume. "Nothing wrong with our camera system, but it sounds like she's found a way to cloak herself."

"So, she just disappeared?" Karthik said.

"If you're going by the images on the monitors, yes," Jones shrugged. "But people don't just disappear into thin air. She's got to be in here somewhere."

"And trying a mind game on us, no doubt," Theresa said, sounding as if she almost relished the idea.

"A dangerous game," Karthik said.

"That may be the truest statement you've made all day," Brown told him. "I don't like my time being wasted."

* * *

"How was your flight, Rackelle?" Esperanza Bourghin asked.

"It's always a smooth trip on those supersonics," Racky replied with a smile. Then her face became sober again. "I missed you a whole lot."

"I'm glad you came," the older woman said, pouring her a cup of tea. She set a plate of cookies on the table between them and motioned for Racky to help herself.

Racky picked one that was covered in powdered sugar and bit into it. "How are you holding up?"

"Oh," Esperanza sighed. "Life is beginning to normalize. I miss Samir still, of course, but with the research papers to grade and that big conference in March, I'm plenty busy."

Racky had always admired Esperanza's work. Esperanza was a tropical disease specialist whose research carried her to the remotest parts of the world. About once quarterly, she presented her findings at the most prestigious conferences. She also taught full-time at Diablo's District College.

"Where's the next conference?" Racky asked.

"Windsailing," Esperanza replied. She paused, then said, "I'm planning to stop by the Changs' house. Do you think there's anything Mrs. Chang would like?"

"She's always been partial to teas and infusions," Racky said, reflecting on the many beverages she had tried at the Changs' place in Diablo.

"I've got plenty from my travels. I'm sure I can assemble a sampler she'll enjoy." After a moment of contented silence, Esperanza looked at the time display on her wall. "I am conscious of the time, Rackelle. You told me your plane leaves in an hour and a half?"

Racky nodded. "Just a turn around trip for me today, I'm afraid. When I come out to Diablo next, though, I hope to stay for at least a weekend."

Esperanza smiled sadly. "I would love to have you, my dear. The house does feel awfully empty at times."

"In that case, maybe I'll bring Lenci with me, once we get her home safe."

"All the better," the older woman said. "Samir loved that girl so much."

"We all did—do," Racky corrected herself. "It's what keeps the team going on the hard days."

Esperanza cast her a sympathetic glance.

"When Agent Lee-Smith told me you were coming today," she said, "I wondered if there might be something that you needed urgently, more than just the canister."

"You just about pegged it," Racky replied. "The only trouble is I don't know exactly what I need. Maybe, can I just get a glimpse inside of Sam's study?"

"Of course." Esperanza rose and led the way down the hall. "Take what you need and put it in your bag before coming out to say good-bye. The less I know—"

"The better," Racky agreed.

They stopped outside of Samir's study. Esperanza unlocked the door and let it swing open.

"I hope that whatever you find in there is helpful in your search," she said.

"Me too," Racky told her.

"I'll be in the living room, my dear, if you need me."

"Thanks so much."

The door to the study closed softly behind Esperanza. As Racky looked at the empty shelves on the wall and the dusty, furniture-less floor, her heart leapt into her throat. Samir had spent hours upon hours in this space, strategizing about Lenci's recovery and rehabilitation. Even though the study was now mostly emptied out, just the knowledge of all the time Samir had spent in there made the space somehow seem fuller.

"Why'd you have to go, Sam?" Racky whispered.

Months before, Blair had given her a patchy and confused account of what had occurred on the evening that Sopient Solutions, Inc. was destroyed. But there was still so much that they didn't understand about Samir's true reasons for showing up at HQ that night and how he had ended up with a bullet in his gut.

The canister was sitting in the corner behind the door. Racky immediately placed it in the carrier that she had brought with her. In the corner, she saw a small, metal stand, which must have been overlooked—perhaps due to its size—when everything else was moved out of the room. It was a stand for a hologram recorder.

Racky rummaged through her purse for the holoprojector that contained Bourghin's recording. She placed it on the stand, turned it on, and smiled as her mentor's image popped up.

Hey, Racky. If you're seeing this…

"Hey, Sam," she replied, speeding up the recording.

She paused it right before the end and went behind the life-sized hologram to catch a glimpse of what Samir had been trying to reach. He was sitting at his desk, facing the wall to the right of the door upon entry. It was an accent wall, made of a sleek white material in contrast to the other walls, which were constructed more traditionally and painted blue-gray.

As Racky followed Samir's gaze, she saw the faint remnants of a handprint on the glossy surface of the white wall. It could have been left over from anything, even a mover leaning on it for a break. But Racky suspected it was a wall safe, the really good quality kind that required a handprint verification—the kind which she had regularly burglarized before she joined SSI. She didn't tend to toot her own horn about it, but she was kind of a specialist.

She put her hand over the smudged handprint, and the wall beeped at her, flashing a red light.

"Alright," she said, cracking her knuckles. "Talk to me, lovely."

After making a quick estimate of the safe's dimensions, Racky tapped in a square on what she guessed to be the four corners of the door. A dialogue box and a holographic keyboard popped up in blue lights, prompting her to enter her command. She entered a small line of code, which indicated that she was a servicer from the safe company. From there, it was a piece of cake accessing the administrative account and changing the handprint verification to accept her own hand.

As the door of the safe swung outward, a strong, bitter aroma filled the room. The safe contained a peach-colored journal with a bloody handprint on the cover and an outdated piece of recording equipment that Racky identified as a cassette tape recorder. The azimuth angle of the tape head had been adjusted, probably intentionally, to conceal a message on it. When she fixed it, she discovered that there was indeed a message on the tape. It was a message from Lenci, but she sounded unsettled and angry. And she was talking to herself.

Not sure what to make of that, Racky put the tape recorder in her bag and took up the journal. There was a pink piece of paper taped to the front cover with a message scribbled in Samir's writing: **There's more of them**. When she opened the journal, she discovered that its pages were the source of the bitter aroma that filled the room. They had been soaked in some kind of oil and dried into crinkly, bitter-smelling leaflets.

"Pungent enough to beat a skunk at its own game," she mumbled, flipping through the pages.

The name 'Bathsheba' caught her eye at once, although she couldn't think of a logical reason that the name should be connected to Lenci. The sloppy writing in the book was a poem that repeated over and over. Since it was with the recording of Lenci's voice, Samir must have seen a connection between the Bathsheba poem and Lenci. And since he hadn't mentioned them in his recorded message to Racky, he seemed also to have wanted to keep these things off the official record. She put both items into her bag and closed the safe. She needed to get back to Corpus.

* * *

It had been half an hour, and none of the SWAT parties had reported so much as a brief sighting of Lenci. They had searched the building from top to bottom, but she was nowhere to be found. The two parties that had originally entered through the side doors were posted on the second and third floors.

Brown, Jones, Karthik, and Theresa were snaking through the hall-ways of the first floor. They peeked into empty rooms and unfinished closets, behind debris, and even in hollowed out walls. Eventually, they returned to the atrium.

"Maybe she really duped us," Jones said, looking up at the dark shadows in the suspended catwalks and scaffolding. "Maybe she's gone."

"No, she's here somewhere," Karthik said. "She hasn't tried to make fools of us, yet."

Brown snorted.

"She does tend to make things dramatic," Theresa said, as if *she* were the expert on Lenci.

Karthik side-glanced her irritably.

"Well, I don't like it," Jones said. "The longer we go without a sighting, the bigger the chance we're going to be the mice in her game of cat and mouse."

"I hate to admit it, but you're right," Brown said.

The entire building rumbled.

"That was an explosion!" Brown exclaimed, bringing his hand to his ear. "Rich, what's the source?"

"It's—she got—don't have it under—"

"You're breaking up," the SWAT leader said, adjusting his earpiece.

He looked back at Jones who shook his head.

"Repeat, Rich," Brown said.

"Van—ploded—side parties—dows—by their necks—" Rich sounded more angry than afraid. "Don't ha—shot—watch your—"

"Rich?"

No response.

"The van exploded," Theresa said, her face drawn tight. "That means our live connection to HQ was severed?"

Brown nodded. "And sounds like the other parties met trouble."

"And there's something interfering with cell and satellite connectivity," Karthik said, looking at his useless flake.

"Back up radios are down, too," Jones added. "She's got us completely cut off."

Brown set his jaw. "Alright, folks. The sole objective now is to get out of here alive. We're on our own inside, but our best bet is to get to the front of the building where Rich might be able to provide us some cover as we exit."

"But what about Lenc—Ms. Chang?" Karthik asked.

"If she crosses us, I'll extinguish her daylights myself," Brown replied, leading the group along a wall to get to the other side of the atrium.

Karthik began thinking of ways to branch off from the group, so he could find his friend before she crossed paths with Brown.

"But she's probably on the run after taking out the first two parties and the van," Jones said. "I mean, no one with half a brain would stick around to take on a whole SWAT team."

"Unless she had a reason," Theresa said.

"Like what?"

"Like she *wanted* all of us to die and planned to personally oversee the process," she said nonchalantly.

Jones shrugged but looked somewhat convinced.

"She would never do that," Karthik said.

"And you know her so well," Theresa replied.

There was a *CLANG* and a sort of screeching groan. One of the suspended catwalks was shifting out of place, and it certainly had not disconnected itself from the wall. Someone was up there.

All of a sudden, Jones pushed Brown forward. The SWAT leader hit the floor with a *SMACK*.

He turned angrily and looked up at Jones. "What in the name—"

Jones' eyes crossed as he brought a hand to his neck where a small, silver dart protruded. He collapsed into a prone position.

Karthik and Theresa drew their guns, keeping their eyes trained on the shadowy area of the second floor scaffolding where the shot had originated. Brown checked Jones' pulse, then sighed and got to his feet. On the opposite side of the atrium, the groaning of the teetering catwalk served as a reminder that the gunman with the darts was not the only danger.

All of a sudden, Brown yelled, "Fall back! Fall back!" He was hit shortly thereafter but managed to take a shot before crumbling to the floor.

Karthik reached toward him to try to pull him up and support some of his weight, but Theresa grabbed his arm.

"He's finished, Wilson!"

The bodies of Brown and Jones as well as their uniforms were dry and shriveled. A puddle of some kind of liquid had accumulated around them.

Theresa squinted up into the darkness. "Brown was a decent shot, though. He got her dominant arm, which probably bought us a couple seconds."

"It's *been* a couple seconds," Karthik said.

"Exactly!" Theresa exclaimed, shoving him into a supply closet with four walls and no ceiling.

She hurried in after him, slammed the door, and maneuvered him as far from the door as was possible with the crowd of empty boxes that shared the space. A couple of *THACK*s followed as two darts hit the outside of the door. From two points the size of pin pricks, the wooden door began to shrivel in a tree-like pattern that quickly spread to the doorframe.

"Those were injector darts," Theresa said, looking very scared.

"Yeah, I'll say!" Karthik responded.

Ignoring his sarcasm, she explained, "They were filled with dehydrators. It's nanobot technology, used for treating water retention. I've never seen one that fast-acting—or lethal."

"Me n—neither," Karthik said. He put his gun back into its holster and turned his attention to the door. "D—do you think it's safe to use the handle? It's metal."

"Even though the bots only affect organic substances, they might be able to pass through inorganic ones," Theresa said. "And we don't know how long the bots stay active. We'd better wait here for someone to lift us out."

Karthik kicked the pile of boxes beside him. "Not again! We were so close."

"Not that close," Theresa said. "And now, we're trapped and have no way of knowing which way—"

"She's going out the back," he said, noticing that the walls of the closet seemed unaffected by the shrinkage that had made the door unusable. "It's the only path that makes sense. The front and sides could have high pedestrian traffic, but the back is a secluded alley that borders the river. Now that Lenci's t—taken out the van, she's got multiple means of escape back there."

The walkway above them—which was hanging by a ripped strap that looked to be weakening by the second—rumbled and groaned. Recognizing that his window of opportunity was rapidly closing, Karthik began to climb up the boxes.

"What are you doing?" Theresa asked.

"Getting out while I have the chance," he replied, eyes focused on the catwalk which was tipping downward. "She's n—not going to get away this t—time."

"That catwalk is set to fall any second."

"I'm going t—to get her," he said determinedly.

"But what about me?" Theresa tried to crawl up the first couple of boxes, but she slipped, and they fell on top of her.

As the entire pile of boxes slid out from under him, Karthik slung his arm over the wall of the closet and hung on as if his life depended on it. There was a loud, metallic screech as the catwalk came completely dislodged.

"This is going t—to be the safest place in the whole building," he told Theresa. "I can come get you l—later."

"Oh, come on!" she whined. But he was already pulling himself up over the wall.

Just as his fingers unhooked from the top ledge, the catwalk crashed down onto the closet. The walls and door held solid, but pieces of insulation flurried about the cramped space. Karthik's footsteps echoed away from the closet and down the hall.

Theresa sneezed and looked up at the grating that enclosed her like a cage. Then she pulled out her flake and pressed the redial button.

"He's out," she whispered, "and he's going around back."

CHAPTER 8

KARTHIK HAD BEEN RUNNING AT TOP SPEED TOWARD THE BACK EXIT, BUT he halted suddenly at a stairwell. There was a small blotch on the bottom stair, which he stooped to examine in the dim light. It was blood, probably from Lenci's injured arm. So, she had descended the stairs to get to the back exit, just as he had predicted.

Congratulating himself, Karthik jumped up a little too quickly and became dizzy. He gripped the banister for support but immediately retracted his hand. His palm was covered with blood. Wiping it on the inside hem of his shirt, he bent to get a look at the angle of the bloody handprint on the banister.

Lenci had gripped it going upward. So, she *hadn't* exited the building yet!

Karthik stood slowly and tiptoed up the stairs. As he neared the top, he could hear soft murmuring in a room just off of the stairwell. He paused outside to listen.

"Can't knock him out because I need them to heal," Lenci was whispering softly. "She'll hurt me if I kill him."

Then she began to scream as if someone were ripping her limb from limb. Unable to bear the sound of her anguish, Karthik drew his weapon and entered the room.

After establishing that they were alone, he asked her, "*Who* will hurt you?"

His friend sat in the middle of the floor with her back to him. At his voice, she stopped screaming and looked over her shoulder but did not look him in the eye. She was gripping her upper arm, and a peach-colored foam frothed between her fingers.

There was a charred corpse about Lenci's size lying on the far side of the room. It was the final bit of evidence Karthik needed to prove that she had taken to planting bodies in order to fake her own death. An empty water bottle lay beside the body—no doubt to serve as some sort of misleading evidence. It was a twisted game, but he imagined that Lenci played it only because she was unwell. No one knew the extent of the horrors that she had experienced while in the custody of David Miller.

Letting out a deep breath, Lenci released her arm, and Karthik saw in her cupped hand a blood-covered bullet. His gaze shifted from her right arm to her left and back again. The left one was smeared with blood and the peach foam, but neither arm showed signs of a bullet wound.

"Where were you hit?" he asked, stepping closer.

She raised her gaze to his, and he subconsciously took a step backward. Her regard was cold, not just in the way of lacking warmth but in the way of extinguishing it. After all that she had been through, Karthik understood that some of the light and laughter would have dimmed from her eyes, but he was shocked by the toll that the past year alone had taken on his friend.

"Lenci?"

In a split second, he found himself winded on the floor with his gun dismantled beside him, and Lenci was running down the stairs. He pursued her, reassembling his weapon as he ran.

As he descended the stairs, he remembered Lenci's escape from Carmelita. She had taken the train eastward, knowing that she would end up in the Eastern States where advanced technology would put her at a disadvantage. He had been predicting Lenci's actions based off of how she had always acted, but something had changed for her. He didn't know all of what, but she was purposely taking risks that she would never have dared to take before. She was making illogical choices.

No, there certainly was a logic to them, just a logic of opposites.

So, if it was clearly the most logical thing to flee out the back where she'd have fewer witnesses and multiple means of escape, maybe Lenci would flee out the front. In fact, Karthik was sure that she would. And because the SWAT van had exploded over ten minutes before, it was probable that Eastern FBI backup would be on the scene. He sprinted for the front of the building, hoping to get to Lenci before they did.

When he arrived in the foyer, he saw Lenci lowering herself outside one of the windows. She must have found another set of stairs somewhere because she was clinging to the molding above the front door. Karthik noted how at ease she seemed relying upon her upper body strength. That was certainly a change. In all the time that Karthik had known Lenci, even after she had resurfaced, she had relied mainly upon her leg strength.

Lenci swung to the ground, and her gaze met Karthik's. She seemed surprised but also delighted that he had figured out she'd be escaping by the least likely route. The coldness of her eyes made her smile seem contemptuous, like she was convinced that he could not keep up with her. Incensed, he reached for the door handle. Lenci looked a little sad, but her smile didn't disappear as she shook out her curls and turned to walk away.

The street in front of the building was surprisingly empty, no flashing lights, drones, or squad cars. But that didn't mean that FBI backup wasn't in the vicinity.

Karthik began to follow Lenci but stopped as he questioned why she had exited the building from the second floor. There would be no reason for that, unless there were some danger associated with the front door. He released the handle.

Ordinarily, this would be the time that he gave up, the time that he'd report that they'd had another close call. But he had meant what he'd told Theresa. He had come to Croon A Tune to apprehend Lenci, and that was just what he intended to do.

Lenci was crossing the street at a leisurely rate, almost like she hoped that he would follow her. He would, as soon as he could figure out a decent way out of the place.

There was wiring around the lobby's window frames with a node and a timer at each window. While Karthik's flake was useless for communication, its explosives analysis software still worked. After a quick scan, Karthik found that only the door was set to blow up but that breaking a window could trigger it. While the plastic explosives would provide a large blast, they had been molded to direct the blast upward and in the opposite direction of the one in which Lenci had walked.

Lenci had reached the other side of the street and was walking westward, in parallel with the windows on the side of the foyer furthest from the door.

Karthik charged at the window on the westernmost side of the lobby, tucked his head, and dove through it. Midair, he heard the front door blow. The outer edge of the blast slammed him into the ground. He rolled and tucked again until all of the debris had settled.

Almost immediately, he was on his feet and running in the direction that he'd seen Lenci go. He whipped out his badge as he ran, ready to explain his presence to any members of Eastern law enforcement. But there was no sign of a law enforcement presence besides some yellow tape that had been put up about a block from the building. Beyond the tape, there was a small number of people trickling out of the skyscrapers and onto the street. The overtimers of the Croon A Tune financial district were finally heading home.

When Karthik got to the next intersection, he flashed his badge at a short, bald guy who was standing on the corner.

"Cooperative FBI," Karthik said. "D—did you see a—a Class 3 female with blood on her arm?"

Lenci would have berated him if she'd heard it since she was proudly Subclass 6.14, but he'd described her as Class 3 because exploiting stereotypes of pureblood phenotypes could save a whole lot of time.

"A real looker—brown skin, long curly hair, gym clothes?" the guy asked.

"That's her."

"She went into that bank over there."

"Thanks," Karthik said, heading toward the building.

"But you know," the guy called after him, "she was starting to remove her clothes. I bet you anything she was preparing to take a dip."

Karthik turned around. "This bank exits onto the river?"

The guy nodded.

"I know where she's going," Karthik said. "Thanks, again."

How he knew that Lenci was returning to see her work's completion was not a matter of logic. In fact, the knowledge might have been born merely of his own wounding. His childhood friend had shot dehydration darts at him, tried to drop a catwalk on him, rigged the exit with explosives, and looked him right in the eye as he was on the verge of blowing himself to bits. He wanted her to feel remorse or at least to feel the need to know what had become of him. So, he returned to the abandoned building and approached from the riverside.

In the fading light, he saw that there was indeed a woman sitting on a slab of concrete beside the Bygone River, but it wasn't Lenci. The woman was tall, olive-skinned, and quite voluptuous—chest and hips at about 105 centimeters and a waist of seventy centimeters. She wore a luxurious white robe, the kind that one might expect to find in a hotel spa. Her chestnut brown hair was dripping water, and she was drying it with a luxurious white towel. Perhaps it was her shampoo or her sparkly lipgloss that smelled faintly of artificial cherry.

In addition to its artistic fame, Croon A Tune was known for its booming sex industry. Karthik assumed that this woman was either not affiliated with any of the district-funded establishments or that she had a gunk addiction that prevented her from maintaining a permanent residence. Those were the only reasons that he could imagine she would bathe down at the river in a district as affluent as Croon A Tune. It was a sad but fairly common situation.

"Excuse me, ma'am," he said, coming around in front of her so as not to catch her off guard. "Have you seen a Class 3 female with l— long, curly hair around here? She was in the water at some point, so she would have been wet."

The woman smirked in a way that made Karthik blush a deep shade of purple.

"No, sugar," she said in a deep, sultry voice. "Want a quickie?"

Karthik could see the back door of the abandoned building from where he stood. There was something with blinking lights near its hinges.

"A quick what?" he asked absently.

The woman's perfectly shaped eyebrows rose. "Beg pardon?"

"You kindly offered me something. I just d—didn't catch—"

"Sex," the woman said bluntly.

"Oh," he said. "N—no, thanks. I'm a federal agent, uh, and I'm on d—duty."

"As you like," the woman shrugged.

Karthik jogged up to the back exit of the abandoned building. Up close, there was no mistaking it: an explosive device was attached to the door. What may have once been the small seeds of bitterness in Karthik's heart broke ground and began to sprout when he walked to each of the side doors and found that every exit had indeed been rigged to explode.

Was there that great of a difference between Lenci rigging only one of the exits and her rigging all of them? Probably not. But there was something inescapably chilling about her thoroughness.

Karthik had previously understood Lenci's antics to be cries for help or, at most, threats because she was afraid. But rigging every exit of a building to explode while he was still inside—that wasn't just a threat. That was an attempted murder.

The thought made him sick, literally. He doubled over at the eastern exit and vomited.

"Hey, Wilson," a male voice said. "Wilson?"

Karthik wiped his mouth and turned to see a man with the name "Rich" sewn onto his Eastern FBI uniform.

"You look like hell, kid," Rich said.

"I feel like hell," Karthik responded. Then, horrified, he said, "Cravenly's stuck in a supply closet!"

"She's safe," Rich reassured him. "When the comms went dead, I called for backup from the drugstore on the corner, but backup ended up being more like cleanup."

Karthik cast him a weary glance. He felt like vomiting again, but there was nothing left inside him to surrender.

"The team's all bodies in bags now," Rich told him. "You, me, and the female Cooper—we're all that's left. HQ managed to keep CAT-PD off our backs long enough for our crew to collect the bodies and sweep the space. Your person of interest flew the coop—"

The sniper suddenly looked embarrassed. "Uh, she escaped. Anyway, CAT-PD is itching to do their own investigation. The Coop wouldn't okay it until I brought you in. Come on back with me to HQ. We'll take yours and the female Cooper's reports and have you on your way."

Karthik nodded, accepting the sniper's help to stand upright, then followed him to the waiting car down by the river. The woman who had been bathing there was gone.

* * *

True to Rich's word, Karthik and Theresa gave their reports to the Eastern FBI in Croon A Tune and then they were released to board their jet back to Corpus. Just after takeoff, Karthik's flake chimed. A picture of Racky and Gustav popped up along with an invitation to a 3-D chat.

Glad to see a friendly face that hadn't experienced the horrors that he had that day, Karthik linked his 3-D projection attachment to his flake and answered the call.

A life-sized, 3-D image of Racky popped up in the aisle next to him.

"Hey, Racky," he said. He noticed that the connection was glitching slightly. "Are you in transit?"

It looked like she was in a car, but she appeared to be alone.

"Yeah, but I can't say from where."

"Okay." He rubbed his forehead with his fingers.

"I heard things got rough," she said. "You okay?"

"I'm fine, in case you were wondering!" Theresa called from her side of the plane. "And Lenci's a turd!"

Karthik glared at her.

"Just ignore her," Racky said. "She should have been born with duct tape over her mouth. What happened with Lenci? I saw in the summary that there was a violent conflict, but the Eastern FBI was tight on details."

"Well," he said, "I'll elaborate in the debriefing, but I can give you a short overview now."

The floodgates opened, and his long, sad story poured forth.

At the end of it, Racky said, "None of that sounds like something that Lenci would do."

"I don't know what she wouldn't do anymore," Karthik sighed.

Racky's image wavered, but her voice was resolute. "She has always been mule-stubborn and independent, but not to the point of murdering people who want to help her."

"But people can change, can't they?" Theresa butted in. "She always thought she was on a higher level than us. Maybe she's finally become convinced that we *normal* people slow her down. So, she wants us out of the way."

"Oh, listen to yourself, Theresa," Racky said.

"It's possible," Theresa said with a shrug.

Karthik frowned. "Do you think that she keeps tabs on our personal lives?"

"Well, she wouldn't need that to want me out of the way," Theresa said with a hint of pride. "But, Wilson, is there anything happening in *your* life that she might have a murderous reaction to?"

Racky laughed. "I think she's too caught up in whatever she's doing—avoiding us or searching for her Kiddo—to be all up in our business."

Karthik cast her a miserable glance. "I gave Maude a key to my apartment yesterday. We're going to move in together."

"Lenci would not try to kill you over that, despite the fact that no one would blame her," Racky said. "There has got to be some other explanation."

"I'm happy for you and Maude," Theresa said, snapping open a bottle of soda. She tilted the bottle toward him. "Would have been great to see Lenci's reaction to that news. If I'd known it was so easy to get under her skin, I would have made more of an effort in the right direction."

Racky rolled her eyes and hung up.

After thinking about it, Karthik figured that Racky was right. Lenci hadn't cared about his personal life since the day that she had joined SSI. For his role in that, he had since felt the need to punish himself, but Lenci never had. It would have been less hurtful if she *had* been trying to punish him because it would have meant that she still cared about him. But she didn't. She only wanted to get away from him, to completely separate their life into unshared existences—which admittedly made it seem strange for her to go to the trouble of luring him to Croon A Tune to kill him.

The deathly cold look in Lenci's eyes in that upstairs room and the sad look that she had given him before he almost blew himself up at the front door—they were looks that recognized him, perhaps, but there was no understanding in them. And that wasn't the only thing that was different. The more Karthik thought about it, the more he realized *everything* about his friend had been different: the way Lenci held her face and her body, the way that she walked, and her heavy reliance upon upper body strength. These things had seemed abnormal before, but now they were suspicious.

Although Karthik did not yet know how it could be possible that someone who looked like Lenci could *not* be her, he did know his friend. And the woman who had nearly blown him up that day was not Lenci. Who she was, well, that would take some investigation, and he had a fairly good idea about where to start.

He thought about the patch of smeared blood on the inside of his shirt. Finding out whose blood it was could give him the next piece in the puzzle. He scraped a decent amount of the dried flakes into an evidence container and put it into his pocket.

CHAPTER 9

"SAY IT AGAIN!"

The Agent struggled against the laser net that restricted her legs, and it began to glow red hot. With a final push, she kicked her legs as far apart as they would go, and the net gave. Searing pain shot through her legs as her flesh was cut to the bone. Her shrieks echoed throughout the yard.

It was the shrieking that catapulted the Agent back from the depths. Her eyes popped open, and her shriek diminished to a sigh. She peeled the blankets back. The cold morning air knocked the nightmare right out of her. She was in an apartment in Lakes, not at Home, and this was the beginning of her first full day in the district.

Dangling her legs over the side of the bed, she rubbed her eyes and fluffed out her voluminous bedhead. She ran her fingers gingerly over the reticulated scars on her legs. Only the year before, the scars had been a network of shallow, cream-colored valleys in her copper skin. But now, the scars were fading. In another year or so, they would probably disappear entirely.

Although she endeavored for survival's sake to act as unphiblike as possible in public, the Agent privately clung to discipline to maintain her focus—discipline and the image of her son's tiny red body on the day of his birth. She began her morning exercise routine with sit-ups. For each of her thousand sit-ups, she thought of her son and was motivated to survive so that they could both live one day.

Her gym clothes and stockings were dry, having sat under the heat lamp in the bathroom all night. Their warmth on her skin was a welcome comfort. She slipped into her heavy wool coat and trotted out the door for her morning run.

It took one fall for the Agent to realize that she needed to watch the sidewalk for hidden patches of ice. For a while after that, she ran with her gaze toward the ground. The brisk morning air burned in her lungs, but it was exhilarating. She liked this new place and this new life.

As she ran, the Agent searched for an apparatus store in order to follow the directions from the message in her mysterious house-warming gift. While she was unsure of how staying connected to a web apparatus would help her to stay alive, she figured that—on the condition that she could actually learn how to use the machine—it could help her to find information about her son.

In theory, one could use a web apparatus to initiate a link to the dark web, where the WCE conducted much of its business. So, the Agent simply needed to learn *how* to use the apparatus at an expert level, then infiltrate WCE messaging platforms. She had certainly faced and overcome more difficult obstacles.

She passed a few web apparatus stores, but she entered the one that accepted cash payments. It was a poorly lit, dingy little shop. There were no decorations, only shelves and shelves of apparatuses and a counter at which to purchase them. Some of the apparatuses were bigger than others; some looked sleeker, but they all looked like a plastic rod with a tiny hole in the middle, a power button at one end, and a power plug at the other. Eventually, the Agent selected the most expensive one with all the attachments and access capabilities.

The salesperson, who most thankfully was not a hologram, was so happy when the Agent offered to pay him in full and in cash that he gave her a free satchel with the store logo on it. She departed with the apparatus in her new satchel.

There was just enough time to run to a small store to buy work clothes. At the store's entrance—much to the Agent's relief—there was a good old-fashioned, physical screen on which she could customize her shopping experience. She declined virtual help, chose to create a guest account with no profile picture, and requested the presence of a manager in order to pay in cash. After purchasing a couple of gray dress shirts, two pairs of black slacks, and a pink, frilly dress that seemed so unphiblike that she had to have it, she changed into a shirt and pants in a dressing room. Then she shoved the rest of the clothes into her satchel and hurried off to her first day of work.

* * *

Gordon Fritz—the owner of The Sweetest Rose and brain-parent of the restaurant's delightful dining room décor—was a chiseled Class 1 man with a square jaw, a piercing stare, and a supreme talent for interior design. His hair, which had been buzzed into a thin film around the sides of his head, was so blond that it was almost white. Although his employees wore dress shirts under their aprons, Gordon wore a tight, white T-shirt that unapologetically showcased his physique. He stood with an impeccably straight back, and his arms were constantly at his sides. When he pointed, he pointed with his chin, which irked the Agent to a degree that she could not find words to express.

After Gordon had given her a tour of the restaurant, they sat across from each other at a table near the door.

"Remind me of your name, again, kid?" he said. "And where're you from?"

She noticed that Gordon had not used the regional term "appellation." It seemed that he also had moved to Lakes from another district.

"Rosa," she replied. "And I spent most of my life in Diablo, but I've been around."

He grunted, whether from approval or disapproval she could not tell. "Hot and dry out there."

He didn't ask her for a surname, and she didn't insist on disclosing one.

"You'll be in charge of the display case and presentation in here," Gordon said gruffly, chin-pointing to the glass case. "And serving."

"Any chance you could use help in the kitchen?" the Agent named Rosa asked, attempting to lessen the chances of being caught in the crossfire of customers' photographing activities in the lovely dining room.

Gordon smiled condescendingly. "I need *males* in the workroom who can knead my dough in a timely manner. More bang for my buck, if you know what I mean."

"Oh." Knowing nothing of kneading dough, Rosa was not sure that she did.

"Pete'll show you what to do," Gordon said, pulling out his phone to check the time.

It was a satellite phone that appeared mainly to function as an audio conversational device and a clock, unlike the omnifunctional flakes that so many people had begun using. Such a phone might have been common in the Free East, but the Agent had only seen phones like that in the hands of soldiers. It seemed out of place on the owner of a small restaurant.

"You military?" she asked casually.

His eyes narrowed. "Does it matter?"

She shrugged. "My cousin was Army, and he had a phone just like that. Just an office guy, but they made him carry one anyway. It just reminded me. I just miss him a lot is all."

Her feminine hedging paid off. Gordon's face softened.

"Medical discharge after a couple knee replacements," he said. "They gave me the low-tech ones, so no bionic super-soldiering for me."

He laughed humorlessly.

"I'm sorry," Rosa said.

"It was high time I got a life outside the service," he replied. "Anyway, I got this phone from a recycler. It reminds me of faster-paced times, you know?"

The Agent hooked her pinky fingers. She understood the value of a good replica. When shifting from life to life, it was important to have reminders of the most significant aspects of one's experience.

"Hey, there's the newbie!" Pete said, leaning into the room. "Good thing you're done with your tour. There's a crowd out there ready for lunch-dinner."

"Welcome aboard, Rosa," Gordon said, shaking her hand firmly.

"Thank you," she said with a sweet smile.

"You're going to love working here," Pete said.

"We're throwing you in the deep end, Rosa, starting you on a Friday lunch-dinner," Gordon told her. "We get twice the amount of diners in two thirds of a normal day because of our alternative hours. Good luck. At least your suffering won't be drawn out."

Those were not the most encouraging words to hear before a first shift, but the Agent had not survived as long as she had on encouraging words.

To Pete, Gordon said, "I'm going market-ways to pick up some more flour, sugar, potatoes, and the like. Orient the kid. Make sure she knows about the menu and the procedures and the regulars and all that, then get back to the kitchen. But look in on her on occasion, alright?"

"On it, Gordon." Pete motioned for Rosa to join him behind the counter.

Gordon nodded to each of them, then exited out the front door.

"This is for you," Pete said, handing Rosa a waist apron with a notepad and a bunch of straws that were individually wrapped in wax paper.

He proceeded to rattle off instructions faster than Rosa had previously thought humanly possible. "We offer three-course meals—mostly French cuisine—tea services, and individual baked goods. The brioche buns and almond croissants are always a hit. Our diners appreciate the human touch since most other restaurants use those government subsidized food service bots. So, talk to them, ask them how they are, and all that. You'll write down the orders on your notepad and read them to me in the kitchen. It's all a part of the experience. Most diners have charge accounts, and they'll scan themselves out at the register here when they've finished. But if there are any physical tender customers, you can cash them out. When you're almost out of anything, just yell that you're almost eighty-six, and I'll bring you more. Totally off-topic, but our straws are made of sugar and a mix of vitamins and minerals. They're tasty, nutritious, and good for the environment!"

He gesticulated enthusiastically and accidentally knocked over a small container of edible toothpicks. Rosa tried to catch the stream of toothpicks as it trickled over the counter, but she missed some.

"Sorry," Pete said, scrambling to stuff the picks back into their holder. He looked toward the door. "Oh, man, we need to open. You okay getting the rest of these? I have to unlock the door."

"Sure," Rosa said, mentally reviewing the information Pete had given her.

He had told her about the menu and the procedures, but he hadn't told her about the regulars.

"Good afternoon, everyone! Welcome!" Pete said, throwing open the door. "This is our new server, Rosa. She'll be helping you today."

A small crowd entered such that the room was filled to capacity, and there was an hour-long waitlist.

With everyone seated, Pete joined Rosa behind the counter once more. "I've got to get back to the kitchen. Take all of the orders by table, then just come to the doorway and read them to me. Make sure to project your voice, so I can hear you over the kitchen fans. Good luck!"

"But what about—"

"You'll do great." He smiled at her before disappearing into the kitchen.

"The regulars," Rosa sighed. She'd have to figure it out.

The first few hours of her shift were fairly easy. She followed Pete's instructions and took all of the diners' orders. The only challenges she encountered were a few requests for substitutions and this one guy who insisted on receiving a straw every couple of minutes. He wasn't using them to drink. He was eating them like an hors d'oeuvre.

When Rosa wasn't serving anyone, she sat behind the counter and helped takeout customers. She had to ask for replenishments of brioche buns and almond croissants multiple times because they were very quick to sell out. Whenever she called "eighty-six," Pete appeared a few moments later with a fresh tray of pastries. The operation was seamless.

A few hours later, Rosa was placing a new tea set on a recently vacated table when something touched her rear end. The Agent grabbed backward and seized the hand of the man who had been eating the sugar straws as hors d'oeuvres.

"*Don't* touch me there," she said, bending his fingers so far back that he squealed.

"Hey, hey!" Strawman said. "I'm sorry; I was just getting a straw from your apron."

His eyes were wild with pain, but they were honest. He'd had a very leisurely tea service and apparently desired yet another straw for dessert.

"Ask next time," she said, releasing him roughly.

He muttered some insult about where she had learned customer service, but her attention shot toward a group of seven hooligans who had come in off of the street. They were scooping armfuls of baked goods out of the display case and shoving them into large paper bags. Each of the hooligans jostled to get in front of the others, and they seemed to be barring one another's way. When the ones in front occasionally dropped pastries, the ones behind hurriedly claimed them.

The Agent could not have thieves robbing the restaurant on her first day—not when she could stop them. She ran into their midst and approached the biggest thief to make an example of him. She grabbed his bag of pastries and tried to shove it back into the case, but he was not so excited about relinquishing it. He grabbed after the bag, but she closed his hand in the door of the case and drove her palm up into his nose.

His companions did not seem concerned by the confrontation. In fact, they seemed to think of it as somewhat of a favor as they continued to shovel pastries into their bags and the pockets of their coats.

"That server's going crazy!" Strawman yelled. "Someone call Gordon!"

The diners all began to talk at once. Some of them ran outside and watched the scene unfold through the windows.

The Agent moved through the thieves effortlessly, dislocating a shoulder or hip—whichever was nearest and most convenient—on each of them. She did not notice until her fifth takedown that the dining room had become very quiet.

Pete leaned through the kitchen door and cheerfully called, "It's about 1600, Rosa, which means it's almost—"

Upon seeing the pile of people with dislocated joints behind the counter, the cheery expression on his face gave way to horror.

"Oh, Rosa!" he exclaimed. "Not the *regulars!*"

"Regular whats? Regular thieves?" She stomped her current thief into the floor to keep him from moving and looked up to find that everyone in the room was staring at her fearfully.

A couple of law enforcement drones with red and yellow flashing lights were hovering outside of the front door.

"Sorry, everyone," Pete told the few brave customers who remained in the dining room. "It's her first day, so she's a little jumpy."

He looked nervously at Rosa, who returned his stare with some bewilderment. Gordon, who had been restocking the pantry with the food he'd purchased at the market, came out of the kitchen. Seeing the pile of men moaning on the floor, his face became ashen. Then his managerial persona activated and, after motioning for Pete to help Rosa clean up, he went outside to communicate with the terrified diners and the law enforcement drones.

"*These* are your regulars?" Rosa asked. "Haven't they ever heard of standing in line and paying for their food?"

"I can't imagine what it must have been like in Diablo, Rosa, but in most Eastern districts, people don't have to stand in line for simple purchases," Pete said, patting the face of one of the downed men. "Our regulars have subcutaneous payment chips, and they're charged each time they reach into the display case. The cost increases the longer they linger inside there. So, they're pretty motivated to move quickly and to collect as many pastries as they can in one attempt."

"Oh. I didn't know." Before that day, Rosa had never—in any of her lives—encountered the mayhem of lineless life or the privileges afforded those who could take advantage of the newest technology.

"You couldn't have known," Pete said. "I forgot to tell you, and I didn't realize how important it would be."

Rosa pulled the guy nearest to her to his feet.

"This is going to hurt a little," she told him. He cried out when she maneuvered his shoulder back into its socket, but he looked more comfortable afterward.

Pete handed him a bag of fresh croissants and brioche buns.

"Free of charge," he said with an apologetic smile. "Come back and see us soon."

"Yeah, right!" the man said. He pulled out a bun and bit into it ferociously. His face slowly changed as he chewed. It became relaxed and more peaceful. He took another bite.

"You guys are lucky these things are so damn delicious," he said, glaring at Rosa. "See you tomorrow!"

Rosa had not expected that interaction to be so easy. She and Pete gave the rest of the injured regulars similar treatment. The regulars all left with smiles, even as Rosa reminded them to take a hot shower and ice their joints when they got home.

Gordon remained in front of the restaurant, talking with his diners until they felt comfortable to return to their tables. He comped their meals and went to the kitchen to personally prepare a free dessert for them. Each diner had the choice of chocolate soufflé or strawberry crêpes. Pete stayed with Rosa at the display case and showed her how to open the door to restock while standing aside for any additional regulars, who were usually in a hurry.

By half an hour to closing, every diner had left satisfied. Gordon exited the kitchen.

"I've got to get home now," he said, observing Rosa with an indecipherable stare. "We're on track to close up at the normal time. Pete, the lowboy needs restocking. And, uh, after Rosa does the dishes, you can walk home together, can't you?"

"We can," Pete said as he closed the window shades on the far side of the dining room, "but something tells me Rosa could handle herself walking home alone in the dark, if she needed to."

She dropped her gaze self-consciously.

"I was suggesting that for your benefit, Pete," Gordon replied. "With her around, you'll never get mugged again."

"Mugged?" Rosa repeated, as if she could not imagine how an act of such violence could ever occur.

Pete rolled his eyes. "You'll never let me live that down, will you, Gordon?" Then, turning to Rosa, he said, "In my defense, it only happened once: before we got door-to-door service from the bank. Some guy figured out the timing and route of my bank run, clubbed me over the head, and made off with three-days' worth of cash."

"And Pete didn't even land one punch!" Gordon laughed.

Pete shrugged. "I'm a pacifist."

"But look at you, and look at her!" Gordon gestured to Rosa. "She's *tiny*, but she wouldn't have taken it. Just look what she did to the regulars!"

"About that," Rosa said apologetically. "I didn't know—"

"Think of it no more," Gordon said. "I was deployed for the stabilization of the Chinese Cooperate in Peru on my second tour. Was jumpy as hell when I came home."

He began, once again, to study her with an unnerving fascination.

Pete cleared his throat. "You said you were in a military family, Rosa?"

"Just my cousin," Rosa replied. "But, I lived in Diablo from a young age, and I've heard people compare *that* to living in a war zone."

"No wonder you're so cool in a fight," he said. "I almost pissed my pants just watching you."

"Takes practice," Rosa chuckled. "Fighting, I mean, not pissing. Although, for men—"

"Now, now," Pete said, "no need to disparage a whole gender."

"Yes, lots of practice," Gordon said, finally shifting his gaze toward the door. "Well, good night, you two."

"Ahem, wait," Pete said, coming out from behind the counter with his arms spread wide.

"Oh, not with the hug stuff, now," Gordon said. "Come on, man."

"There were some tense moments today, Gordon," Pete replied, grinning invitingly. "Let's hug it out."

Gordon looked like he thought his manhood was in jeopardy, but he reluctantly lent himself to Pete's arms. Rosa watched in amusement as Pete embraced their boss with all of the tenderness of a mother hen sheltering her offspring. He very sincerely seemed to believe that his hug could absorb or dispel any negative effects of Gordon's workday. The effect on Gordon was even more amusing and slightly endearing. His tense upper body relaxed, and he seemed more at peace.

"How do you feel?" Pete asked, releasing him.

Gordon nudged Pete's shoulder with his fist. "I don't know what kind of witchery that is, but it always works like a charm."

"You're welcome," Pete said cheerfully.

Rosa stifled a giggle.

"Do you want one too, Rosa?" he asked.

"No," the Agent said. Then, remembering her manners, she added, "Thank you, though."

"Standing offer," he told her. "Positive touch is good for the soul."

Gordon looked at his phone to check the time, then grabbed his satchel.

"Well," he said. "Good first day, Rosa. See you kids tomorrow."

"Good first day?" Rosa said after he left. "In what world?"

"In the world where I nearly burned down the kitchen on my first day and destroyed a quarter of the property," Pete said sheepishly. "Gordon's got an eye for diamonds in the rough."

There were only two customers before closing, neither of which was a diner and one of which was a drone. Both transactions went smoothly. The door was locked by 1800, and Rosa and Pete moved into the kitchen to start on the dishes.

Pete grinned goofily as he soaped up his sponge. "It's actually pretty exciting because what Gordon says is true: I'll have an armed bodyguard to escort me home tonight!"

She gave him a quizzical look, prompting him to add, "I mean, a bodyguard with arms—that she's not afraid to use?"

He was dorky but sweet in his own way.

Rosa found that she enjoyed doing the dishes with Pete. He made interaction easy because he didn't pry into the details of her past. In fact, he did most of the talking about sports, fighting unjust systems, cats, the oppressiveness of the meat production industry, donuts, and whatever other topics traipsed across his mind.

At 1902, they put the last dish in the drying rack and headed for Frin's Place. It turned out that Pete lived on the third floor in the apartment just beneath Rosa's. He offered to walk Rosa to her door, but she declined his offer and he did not insist. He wished her a good evening in the stairwell.

Finding her apartment bitterly cold, the Agent turned up the heat. While the place was warming up, she showered and sat under the heat lamp in the bathroom to muse about her first day at work.

Although she was as far as ever from finding any information on her Kiddo, she had done a stellar job of maintaining her cover in Lakes—well, an adequate job, anyway. It was actually more of a patch-up job. Gordon had been surprisingly gracious about her incident with the regulars. He seemed to have developed a liking to her because of the military family connection, which was to the Agent's advantage. But she couldn't get his piercing stare out of her mind.

It was probably nothing—hopefully.

Then, thinking of how much money she must have cost the restaurant in comped lunch-dinners and apology baked goods, she chuckled, "With arms I'm not afraid to use."

* * *

Early in the evening, Karthik's auto-car pulled into the parking lot of the personal storage area down the street from his apartment.

He and Theresa had given their debrief presentation on the Croon A Tune assignment that afternoon. They each shared from their own experience, but Karthik left out the part about the blood sample he had collected. He also left out the part about how he thought Lenci might not have been herself at all. During a moment of silence for the fallen members of the Eastern SWAT team, Theresa lit a candle that set off the fire alarms. The sprinklers went off, prompting a quick close to the meeting and an evacuation of the entire floor.

Before leaving for the day, Karthik stopped by the basement lab to drop off the blood sample for manual testing against Lenci's blood. The tech was preoccupied with inspecting the lab for any water damage that may have leaked from above, so she accepted the sample rather unceremoniously and told him she'd get to it in half an hour. Feeling empty and exhausted, Karthik had driven directly to the storage area.

He wandered down the rows of units until he reached his own. His heart rate increased, and his hands shook so hard that he had difficulty unlocking the unit. He eventually succeeded, and the door rolled back to reveal a baby grand piano and a bench. There were other items in the unit as well: a loveseat, some dining room furniture, and artwork. However, it was the piano that Karthik sought.

Feeling very small all of a sudden, he sat down on the bench and slid his fingers onto the piano keys. He exhaled deeply, and C-sharp minor flowed from his fingers. The mournful, brooding tones of *Moonlight Sonata* swirled around him. The acoustics in the storage unit left much to be desired, but Karthik found some comfort in that. He felt awful, so why shouldn't the song sound awful as well?

Moonlight Sonata was his and Lenci's song. They had grown up listening to it before bed at their sleepovers, and whenever they'd had a big fight, Karthik played the song because Lenci couldn't help dancing to it. It was how they reconciled. But more recently, Karthik had found himself visiting the storage unit to play the song, even though Lenci wasn't there to dance.

His fingers slipped, and he hit two keys at once. The discordant result cut at him more deeply when it was dampened by the cushioned furniture around him. He tried to reposition his hands and pick up where he left off, but his fingers stumbled over the keys and into each other. *Moonlight Sonata* devolved into a train wreck.

With a frustrated grunt, Karthik brought his fist down on the keyboard. The sound that came from the baby grand resembled a reprimand, which made him apologetic. He ran his hand over the surface of the keys and sighed.

He looked at his flake. It had been over an hour since he'd dropped off the blood sample at the lab.

Suddenly, the flake vibrated in his hand. It wasn't the lab tech, though. It was Blair.

He answered. "Wilson."

"Did you think I wouldn't know?" She sounded angry.

"Kn—know what?"

"You had blood tested today."

"That's true," Karthik said. "I d—didn't intend for it to stay a secret, though. I just know that I haven't been on t—top of my game recently. But I had this hunch, so I figured I'd just follow it and l—let you know if I found anything."

"Well, the lab tech had to tell me because she wanted access to our limited sample of Lenci's blood. Those mirror shards are all we have, so we don't test injudiciously."

"I would have t—told you—"

"It's not Lenci," Blair told him.

The words hit Karthik like a ton of bricks. Happy bricks, though, if he thought about it hard enough.

Maybe he didn't want to think about it that hard.

"Well, the person I got it from sure l—looks a l—lot like her," he said. "Who is it?"

"He's an agent from a covert agency called Warbuck. He went

missing around the same time that Lenci did. As I recall, Lenci was seconded from SSI to Warbuck for a mission with him.”

“And that's when the WCE t—took her?”

“And him, too, it would seem,” Blair said. “Warbuck collapsed about a year ago, so he's not acting on *their* orders. In fact, we were able to match his DNA using intel from WCE records. His public record had been scrubbed.”

“Huh.” Karthik rested his chin on his hand, then started when his elbow struck a sour chord on the piano. He closed the fallboard.

“I'm going to alert Vincent about this,” Blair said. “I, uh, just wanted you to know before I announced it to the rest of the team.”

“Well, that's thoughtful, Lee-Smith,” Karthik replied. “I'm glad to know it's n—not Lenci. Kind of weird that it's a guy, but—”

Blair emitted a tight-throated sound that was more like a hoarse cough than the laugh it was meant to be. “Oh, no, Wilson. You must think I'm coddling you. It's not that at *all*. There's a reason I wanted to talk to you one-on-one about this.”

“Okay, shoot.”

“The former Warbuck agent whom you caught pretending to be Lenci is a Class 3 male named Arjun Thomas.”

Karthik's blood ran cold. His mind was flooded with images from the year before when his cousin Arjun had accosted him and Lenci at the wedding reception of another relative. Arjun showed himself to be an expert in hand-to-hand combat, and he also displayed a rather uncomfortable level of familiarity with Lenci. Karthik had tried to ask Lenci about it at the time, but she had been very tight-lipped. And now, Lenci was on the run, and Arjun was pretending to be her.

“I looked up the little we have on him,” Blair was saying, “and I know he's your cousin.”

Karthik thought of the coldness of Lenci—or, Arjun's gaze in the upper room in Croon A Tune. Arjun had never been nice to Karthik, but there was something about his gaze that seemed cruel, even by Arjun's standards.

“Wilson?”

He came to himself. “Pardon?”

“I just said I know this must be difficult for you.”

“N—not much more than it has been,” he said honestly. “In l—losing Lenci, I l—lost a part of myself. Arjun and I are blood, but we were n—never half as close.”

Blair was silent, perhaps because she was unsure of how to respond to such an emotionally vulnerable statement.

At last she said, "Look, I'm sorry to ask this, but having a record of your answer will set a lot of minds at ease: Did you request the blood test because you suspected the imposter was your cousin?"

Karthik gave a rueful chuckle. "I'm not that imaginative or pessimistic. You know, Arjun had a way of disappearing and showing up again. Our family thought that he had a drug problem, and after his recent year-long absence, my aunt and uncle actually assumed he was dead."

"It's better that they continue thinking that," Blair said. "The Arjun they know and love basically *is* dead—in a manner of speaking."

Karthik gulped, wondering if she also thought that way about Lenci. He couldn't yet adopt that line of thought.

"There's something else you should know." Blair's voice wavered slightly. "His blood was full of nanobots, just like Lenci's."

Karthik's heart sank. "Sounds like they've been involved in similar activities. Is there anything linking Arjun to the Cull directly?"

"I don't know yet," Blair said. "But let's not lose sight of our goal from the agency's perspective: bringing in Lenci. Vincent may have some ideas about how to deal with Thomas' copycatting. I'll get Wernicke and Cravenly in the loop. You sure you're okay?"

"Just ready to get to the bottom of all of this, for sure," he replied.

"Hang in there." The line went dead.

Karthik opened the piano's fallboard and plinked out the chords of *Moonlight Sonata* as separate notes. He wove the left and right hands in and out of each other until it sounded like a completely different song. When it ended in another train wreck, he took his head in his hands and wept.

* * *

That night, Rosa found hardly any rest in sleep because she dreamt once again of Valencia Thomas. That was who she had been, briefly, before she'd become the Agent. That was past, but the past had a way of erasing well-constructed barriers and forcing its way into the present—especially when her guard was down. And *that* made sleeping real work.

Valencia Thomas could hear David Miller's approach, even before he spoke to the guard. Everyone at Home referred to David as the Killer. Valencia gathered that it must be a term of respect, but she still thought of him simply as David, one of her trainers from back at SSI. This was the fifth time in five days that he'd come to see her in the detention cell block. He seemed to be checking for some kind of progress.

"How do you make a monster?" David said, repeating the question that the guard had asked him in the hall. "Easy. Just take away a person's human dignity. Then, at the right moment, offer him or her agency—one thing to have control over. It's all downhill from there."

Valencia morosely glanced over at the two chuckling men. They stared at her through the bars like she was a caged animal. To them, she was a pathetic spectacle, dirty, bruised, and bedraggled. That was what was visible to them. Not so easily visible were her mind's loosened grip on the truth about her mission and the aches in her pelvic region as well as in her demoralized spirit.

"It's not so bad, Fire Salamander," David told her. "Stop feeling sorry for yourself, and you'll see the way out."

He paused and a look of pity settled on his countenance.

"If there's anything I know from the past couple years training you," he said, "it's that you're quite capable. The only reason they're doing this to you is because you're allowing it."

There was a shadow moving in the corner on the far side of Valencia's cell. It was an enormous cockroach with a segmented body that was reddish brown and bright yellow. Its long, thin legs clicked on the cold, hard floor as it walked alongside the wall.

"I proved I was fit," Valencia said miserably. "They're doing this to me because they want to. And they will keep at it until there's nothing left to humiliate, dehumanize, or violate."

"Then, choose something else, Fire!" David exclaimed.

After gazing at her for a moment, he said, "Well, well, you're a fire salamander who's lost her fire. How about that?"

The roach seemed to tire of pacing the one side of the cell. It headed toward Valencia. She scooted as far from it as her chains would allow. When the bug continued its advance, she stepped over it and moved to the other end of the cell.

"Just crush it already," David said amusedly.

Valencia looked at the roach. Her stomach turned at the thought of killing it. The only living being she had killed in recent memory was one she had killed on accident: the woman in the arena. No one had known it was an accident, but it was. In fact, Valencia had no idea how it had happened. As she bowed to her opponent in the arena, she felt a surge of strength unlike any she'd experienced before. The next thing she remembered, she was outside in the sun with her opponent's dead body. She felt sick just thinking about it.

"Blind are the eyes of one who feels no pain," David whispered.

Fat lot of good that saying was. Valencia still felt pain.

He continued, "Focused is the mind of one who has an established purpose."

It occurred to her that David was, in some fashion, showing her the way out.

Then, as if to assuage any last concerns she might have, he said, "What is necessary must never be lamented."

There was a clang. Valencia started as the guard threw open the door to the neighboring cell. He began spraying something that made the air taste bitter.

"The cell next to yours has been empty for a few weeks," David told her as he headed for the door. "I took the liberty of ordering it cleaned out. So, you might have a few extra visitors. Call for the guard when it's time, and let me know when you've chosen your path."

Valencia listened for the message between the words, and even though she did not understand it explicitly, she knew that the necessary thoughts and actions would come to her at the right time.

That time was coming.

CHAPTER 10

THE FOLLOWING DAY, THERESA SLIPPED OUT OF THE MEETING WHERE Racky was giving her long-awaited presentation on the creepy video of the chanting face. Racky had shared how she'd set up a global scan to locate the source of the media chip using some high-tech doohickey that could detect the gas emitted during the cultivation of the microorganisms. A great concentration of the gas in one area could indicate the presence of a farm or a production site, which would be a good place to start asking questions.

As the group began to discuss the finer points about how such a chip could even survive inside of a human body, Theresa saw her chance and ran out of the room holding her stomach.

"I'm on a cleanse!" she whispered loudly over her shoulder.

Karthik groaned. "Way t—too personal, Cravenly."

She simpered at him before closing the door. Immediately, the ridiculous smile disappeared from her face. Her new disposable flake, which had been silently ringing during the meeting, began to ring again.

"I'm sorry," she said when she answered. "I can't just get away whenever I want. Our team works very closely."

The voice of the woman on the other end was quiet but harsh. "Get us copies of at least half of Bourghin's materials by tomorrow."

"Tomorrow? But—"

"We need to know what your team knows in order to stay ahead of them. Don't fail us, or the Assistant Vice will want *your* head next."

"I'll do it now," Theresa gulped. "Just give me five minutes and have your team stand by. If they're worth their salt, they'll be able to catch a scan in transit, am I right?"

The chime in her ear indicated that she was now in a one-way conversation.

Blair was planning to distribute the boxes of Bourghin's secret records that afternoon, but they were still in a locker in the evidence storage area on the basement floor. Theresa used her own thumbprint to gain access to the area and open the locker. Inside, there were two large boxes that were packed solid with notebooks and binders.

Theresa heaved one box onto her hip and headed for the door. Each item in the box had a barcode, but she scanned only one journal at the exit in order to give the appearance that she'd only taken that one book rather than the whole box. Then she went up to the imaging room, which was just a couple of doors down from the conference room.

Her dimwitted teammates were probably still talking about how the organisms that fueled the chip could exist inside the host without triggering an immune response. That conversation was riveting to them, but Theresa had mastered those concepts before the end of primary school. She could afford to skip out on the discussion.

She keyed in her print code and fed the notebooks into the imaging machine one by one. The machine assessed the materials, then scanned them at a rate of about seven seconds each.

When Theresa was partway through the box, Racky leaned into the room and exclaimed, "Why are you in here?"

Theresa masked her fear with nonchalance. "You guys seemed like you were in the thick of it with your science discussion when I left, but that's all primary school stuff for me. So, on my way back from the restroom, I decided to get a head start on our homework."

Racky stared apprehensively at the machine. "I could use some reassurance that you are *not* copying those classified materials."

"Of course not," Theresa said. "I'm scanning them because I can't stand the idea of lugging this huge box around when I could just read the materials at home on a screen."

Racky shut off the machine and shoved all of the materials back into the box. "Even when there's only an *intermediate* hacker looking for mischief, scanning is as troublesome as copying. And there could be more advanced folks looking for this info."

"Oh, lighten up, Racky," Theresa replied. "You're the only person around here that would be obsessed enough with Bourghin to steal the light particles of his journals."

"I'm putting these back in the locker," Racky said. "And if I ever catch you doing something so lunkheaded again, I'll report your sorry behind."

"Tattle, tattle," Theresa said. "Well, if you feel that way about it, why don't you just give me your notes, and I'll sign my timesheets to say I did my reading?"

Racky sucked her teeth, then left to go to the evidence room. Theresa let out a deep breath. She'd scanned a quarter of the total materials, but it would be a bear to have to sort through them again after Racky had jumbled them. Theresa hoped that the portion she had scanned would at least placate the WCE until she could send the remaining information.

* * *

"So, the chip is a l—living organism?" Karthik said slowly.

"No," Racky said. "Well, yes. I mean, I don't know. It's a colony, I guess. Basically, the chip runs off of the waste of the electrically charged little critters. And the fact that it's self-powered suggests it can be used as a transmitter or a beacon of some kind."

Blair had gone home a couple of hours before. She had told Karthik and Racky that they could take Bourghin's journals to their own residences, but they had decided to use Racky's lab as a secure workspace instead. There would be no chance of loss or theft if the materials never left HQ. Theresa had said she wouldn't read anything until after the holiday, so she had gone home at the same time as Blair.

Racky was flipping through Bourghin's notes on Lenci's mental state post-resurfacing.

"But how d—do they stay alive?" Karthik asked. In the two hours they'd spent there, he hadn't even gotten through one notebook.

"Glucose in the host's blood," Racky said, "or, in the case of the Carmelita chip, the alcohol it fell into—like I said in my presentation. Will you read tonight at all?"

He sighed. "I'm sorry. I just can't seem t—to focus. What are you l—learning?"

She looked at him concernedly but chose not to pry regarding his uncharacteristic lack of focus. It probably had to do with the announcement that Blair had made about the Lenci imposter who was actually Karthik's cousin. No one could blame him for needing some time to get his act together.

"Crazy stuff," she replied. "In the recording, Bourghin said that the Amphibians were subjected to mind control, which never struck me as too far out of the ordinary since SSI was well acquainted with hypnotic ops. Lenci herself was trained to respond to certain fluctuations in Bourghin's tone of voice. In these here notes, though, he says the WCE may have relied upon Songs—with a capital S—for a similar effect."

Karthik sat up straight. "A Song l—like the Song on the chip you found in Carmelita! There were t—*two* names of amphibians in that."

"True," Racky said. "Without a doubt, though, that would tie Carmelita's district head to WCE covert ops."

"I bet it's more common than we'd think," Karthik said with a shrug. "Most politicians have some kind of association with the WCE, and the WCE's always blurred the lines between social responsibility and covert activity. Anyway, how do you think Lenci got a chip with a recording of District Head Mitchell singing a Song?"

"Well, I thought maybe the Song on the chip could be *her* Song," Racky said. "According to Bourghin's notes, all of the agents of Lenci's cohort at the WCE were named after an amphibian, marked with its image, and controlled by a corresponding Song."

"But of the Amphibians mentioned on the Carmelita chip, would Lenci be Hellbender or Fire Salamander?" Karthik wondered.

"Neither sounds all that agreeable," Racky sighed, flipping a couple of pages back and forth. "Somewhere here, I read that Gomez called herself Poison Arrow when she resurfaced from her own tour with David Miller a couple of decades ago. She even had a tattoo of a frog on her neck. And Bourghin notes here that Lenci considered herself to be similar to Gomez, like an updated version or some such."

"But Lenci d—didn't have a t—tattoo," Karthik said.

"She might have, underneath those frumpy stockings she always wore," Racky said.

He shook his head. "N—no, d—don't you remember when we were in Forsythe? She had no stockings and no t—tattoo."

"Maybe it was elsewhere on her person," Racky said, clicking her pen. With a playful grin, she added, "Unless you've seen every other nook and cranny where it might have been hiding?"

His face flushed a deep shade purple. Then, looking at his flake, he gasped. "Is that really the t—time?"

"Yeah. So?"

"T—tonight was my rescheduled 'surprise' d—dinner d—date with Maude. We're supposed to d—discuss flights to Windsailing since the Croon A Tune assignment ate up our t—time cushion for the road trip. With Arjun and the chip and the n—new case materials, I completely forgot! What am I going t—to t—tell her?"

"'Let's break up?'" Racky offered.

He threw her a look. "I'm just going t—to step out to make this call."

When the door shut behind him, she sighed. Sometimes she wanted to take Karthik's flake and shove it up one of his nostrils.

She looked at the transcript of the Song from the Carmelita chip. Just at a glance, it looked like an order to Hellbender to kill and end a female Fire Salamander. And if it were, then perhaps it was not too far of a leap to hypothesize that Lenci was the Fire Salamander. After all, Karthik believed that he had seen Lenci near Apartment 9001. Perhaps Hellbender had used the charred Class 3 corpse to try to cover up an unsuccessful attempt to execute Lenci according to the Song's command.

The Coop had recently encountered someone faking Lenci's death in Croon A Tune. Maybe Arjun Thomas, previously of Warbuck, was Hellbender. That he looked like Lenci was a point of mystification, but perhaps shapeshifting was one of the Amphibians' many unknown abilities. But why would the WCE order one member of the Amphibian cohort to kill and replace another?

Racky sighed again and turned back to the box of Bourghin's research. This puzzle would definitely necessitate some overtime.

CHAPTER 11

ON THE HOLIDAY, RACKY WAS CHECKING ON HER BIOFUEL GAS detection process in her lab when Theresa and Blair left for the afternoon. They had all completed their obligatory half-day of holiday overtime, but while Theresa and Blair were going to celebrate over drinks, Racky planned to celebrate by making progress on Lenci's case. Both boxes of Bourghin's research materials sat on the ground a few feet from her worktable.

"You sure you don't want to come?" Theresa asked. "Blair knows this place down on the Avenue that is just the *cutest*."

Blair nodded as she put on her coat. "You'd be welcome, Racky."

"No, thanks," Racky replied. "I appreciate the offer, but I'm better off right where I am."

"Happy holidays, then," Theresa said dismissively. "Have fun with Saint Bourghin."

Racky glared at her.

"Happy holidays, Racky," Blair said as they walked out the door.

"Back at you, ladies," Racky said. "Enjoy yourselves."

When they were gone, the room felt very empty, but it was an emptiness that was begging to be filled with achievement. And Racky was hungry for the breakthrough.

Her equipment had been detecting emissions in the Northwestern State. So, she fine-tuned her algorithms and narrowed down the search to a couple of districts. She then put Bourghin's recording on loop and picked another journal from the boxes of case materials.

Hey, Racky! If you're seeing this, I've finally met my maker, and—more likely than not—Lenci is in the wind…

A while later, Racky's web apparatus began to beep and chime. The emissions sensor had found something.

"Got you!" She muted Bourghin's recording and leaned toward her apparatus to get a better look.

The coordinates were in the southwest corner of the Farm And Forest district. Judging from the size of the gas cloud, it was possible that someone in that area had a large farm of those microorganisms, or they were storing the critters in order to produce a lot of chips at that site. And those possibilities did not have to be mutually exclusive.

She looked at the grainy image of Samir. Even though the recording was muted, she knew that he was talking about the missing SSI agents. She had watched the recording so many times that she could probably recite it by heart, but she got new insight every time she watched it.

"What were you trying to tell me, Sam?" she asked, increasing the volume.

Anyway, one of my sources was—for a price—able to get me limited, supervised access to a homing chip. Every Phib handler has one implanted in their finger with slightly different coordinates, all within the boundaries of the compound where the Phibs were trained.

"A finger chip with coordinates, you say." She looked back at the screen of her web apparatus. "Did they say anything about unsettling music videos?"

No one was able to tell me why this is a useful thing to have. The chips aren't only trackers; they're some kind of reminder. You know how the WCE is always inside of everyone's head. Anyways, I've written the coordinates in my green notebook, but I…

"Green notebook!" Racky hollered.

For the past year, she'd heard him say that again and again, but now she knew what to do with that information. She scrambled to the boxes of materials and rifled through them until she found the only notebook with a green cover. It was thick and stuffed with extra sheets of paper that made it even thicker. A large rubber band was stretched around the sides of it to keep the loose sheets from falling out. Racky got to work skimming each page carefully.

At last, she found it: a series of numbers scrawled in the margin of a page and enclosed in a square with an arrow pointing to a description of the chip in detail. None of it mentioned music or having a projection of someone's face. And yet, the coordinates in Bourghin's book—marking a location within the Phib training compound—were only a few hundred meters away from the coordinates of the site where the Carmelita chip had likely been produced.

Be careful, Racky, but you've got to find her. You've just got to find her.

"I think I got my breakthrough at last, Sam," she said with a smile.

* * *

Karthik stood on the porch of a large, gray house in the district of Windsailing. It was the first time he'd been there since his mother's celebration of life, and he was returning for a different kind of celebration. He rang the doorbell, stepped back, and made an effort to look as happy as he wanted to be. Maude Jackson stood next to him with her hair in ringlets about her shoulders. She linked his arm and squeezed it softly.

The door opened to reveal Monica Chang. Her graying, curly hair was pulled back into a bun, and she wore a cable knit sweater beneath a holiday cheer apron that highlighted the red undertones in her milk chocolate-colored skin. She looked burdened by an inescapable fatigue, but her face brightened considerably at the sight of the young man standing on her doorstep.

"Karthik!" She embraced him at once.

A rush of warm air that smelled of ham hocks, browning garlic, and copious amounts of black pepper washed around them. The aroma awakened feelings that Karthik hadn't acknowledged in the months since he'd last seen the Changs. He had missed them terribly, and coming back to them was like reattaching a piece of his broken heart.

After squeezing him for what seemed like forever, in the best possible way, Monica drew back and smiled at his companion.

"And you must be Maude," she said warmly.

Maude stretched her thin, plum-colored lips into a line. "Pleased to finally meet you. E.J. says you're like a mom to him."

Monica looked puzzled for a moment before recognizing that Maude was referring to Karthik by his two middle initials.

"Yes," Monica said, motioning them into the house. She took their coats in the entryway. "His mother and I were very close. He really is like another son to me."

"You have another?" Maude asked, her voice limp with practiced politeness.

"My youngest," Monica said. "Lorenzo! Come say hello. Lorenzo!"

"Two minutes, Mom!" he called from upstairs.

Karthik marveled at how Lorenzo's voice had deepened since their conversation via flake only the month before. Some crashing around in the bathroom indicated that the teen was conducting a last-minute cleanup.

Monica sighed. "He might be a while. This way, please."

As they made their way to the living room, Maude paused to look at the family pictures displayed in a slideshow on the walls of the hallway. Monica came and stood beside her.

"That's my girl, Valencia. She won't be joining us today." Her voice trembled a little. Then she pointed to another picture. "And that's Kingston, my husband. He's stepped out for some last-minute groceries, but he'll be back shortly."

Maude's face hardened in a way that Karthik recognized and yet did not fully understand.

"What is your maiden name, if you please?" she asked Monica.

Monica raised her eyebrows. "Thomas—same as Ethan's mother's maiden name, actually." She smiled at the memory of Preeti Wilson. "She passed away from cancer about nine months ago."

"After a good fight," Karthik added, as if to reassure himself.

"Yes," Maude said with a tight jaw.

"Poor James became a bit of a workaholic in his grief," Monica said. "We never see him anymore, really."

Karthik nodded. "It's just dad's way. I d—did catch him when I called today, though. He's in Salamanca on a business d—deal."

"I'm glad you spoke with him. He hasn't been answering Kingston's calls."

Just then, Lorenzo bounded down the stairs.

"Karthik, man!" He strutted up to his older friend, trying to play it cool.

"Get over here, Renzo!" Karthik swiped him into a hug.

Lorenzo—who had undergone a growth spurt since Karthik had last seen him—used his favorite jiu-jitsu move on him, and they ended up in a laughing, wriggling heap on the floor.

"Boys," Monica said, smiling fondly.

"Males," Maude corrected her.

Monica cleared her throat. "Lorenzo, come and meet our guest. This is Karthik's friend Maude."

Lorenzo rolled out of the grappling match and bounced to his feet.

"Hi," he said, extending his hand to Maude. "Nice to meet you."

Maude stared past him, seeming not to hear him at all. Then she blinked a couple of times and looked at Monica.

"Ms. Thomas, do you have a powder room where I might freshen up? It was an uncomfortable flight from Corpus."

"My married name is Chang," Monica said as she motioned down the hall toward the bathroom.

Karthik looked uneasily between the two women. With their shoulders back and their chins raised, they appeared to be preparing for battle. Poor Lorenzo looked like he wished he was small enough to hide under a piece of furniture. Karthik rather wished that he was small enough to join him.

"I don't recognize miscegenetic partnerships." Maude wrinkled her nose as an exclamation point. "And really, I'm being generous to consider you a 4.14. In the West, you'd be a member of the Subclass."

"You can keep your generosity because I never stopped being Class 4.14, regardless of Western antics," Monica said with no small amount of pride.

The battle was in full swing. Karthik kept looking for an opportunity to intervene. However, since he was so nervous the words stuck to his tongue, and he wasn't able to articulate anything more than a few stuttering syllables that never became words.

Maude sniffed. "Just so you know, I'm of the liberal few who recognize that the 4.14 community needs numbers to maintain the little bit of power we've gained. It's a shame how our numbers have dwindled."

"There was a time when our community accepted anyone of 4.14 descent who was willing to share in our sorrows, joys, and efforts for progress," Monica told her. "So, the 4.14 community lacks numbers these days mainly because we, as a group, bought the lie that so-called purity of blood would lead to power."

"The Subclass excised itself," Maude retorted. "That's what brazenly associating outside of the class does—for you and your progeny." She glared so fiercely at Lorenzo that he shrank back from her.

"That's enough!" Monica thundered. "*Who* do you think you are?"

Almost out of reflex, Karthik clasped her arm. She struggled to compose herself for his sake.

"In any case," she said in a strained voice. "Ethan calls me 'Auntie Monica.' Feel free to do the same."

Maude rose abruptly. "Pardon me, Ms. Thomas."

Once she had disappeared down the hall, Monica took Karthik by the arm and dragged him into the kitchen.

"How could you bring that woman into my house?" she asked in an injured tone. "She is incredibly disagreeable, not to mention prejudiced! Lenci would have punched her in the face by now, and I'm frankly starting to think about it myself. Oh, your poor mother must be rolling over in her—"

Her voice cracked, and she stopped talking. She turned away from Karthik and looked out the window by the sink. Knowing that she was doing her best to keep her tears from him, he hugged her from behind.

"I'm sorry, Auntie Monica," he said. "Maude's usually so n—nice. I d—don't know what got into her."

"Let me tell you something, boy," Monica said, still facing the window. "If she's only nice to *you*, she won't be for long. People who are only nice to the person they like in the moment they like them are *not* nice people. And that kind of vicious eugenistic prejudice takes a lifetime to unlearn, even when a person is willing. Don't think yourself exempt from it just because she's being 'nice' right now."

Karthik took Monica by the shoulders and turned her gently toward himself. "When Lenci l—left us again and my mom passed away and I moved to Corpus, Maude was there t—to pick up the pieces. She's given me a chance to actually l—live my life again."

Monica looked up at him, the hurt still evident in her eyes. "Just don't let her drive a wedge between you and your family—no matter how hard she tries, okay?"

"N—never, ever," he promised. "N—now, will you *please* give her another chance?"

She looked apprehensive.

"For me?" He flashed her a winsome grin.

She took a deep breath and wiped her eyes. "*Only* for you, Karthik."

He kissed her on the cheek. "Thank you, Auntie Monica." He kissed her again. "Thank you! Thank you!"

"Yeah, yeah," she said, brushing him off and moving to stir a pot of greens on the stove. "But if she mentions miscegenation again in *my* house, I will shove this wooden spoon down her throat."

"Oo." He shuddered. "And *that's* where Lenci gets that from."

"Like mother, like daughter," Monica said coolly. "Now, go have a conversation with your friend and make sure we're all on the same page."

And so he did.

CHAPTER 12

The noise in the neighboring cell continued—*spraying, sweeping, mopping, and more spraying. The bitter smell of the pesticide became stronger.*

There was a hole in the back corner between Valencia's cell and the empty one. Light shone through it, looking warm and inviting, but Valencia only admired it from afar because the brown and yellow roach was still pacing over there.

Suddenly, two long, hairlike antennae poked through the hole. A large cockroach followed. To Valencia's horror, the bug took flight. She ducked, and the roach landed on the wall behind her. Then the rest of them came—dozens of roaches of various sizes—barreling through the hole between the cells and flitting around her.

Valencia squeezed herself into a ball in the furthest corner and hoped that the roaches would find their way out through the bars of the cell. Some of them did, but most of them headed for her corner to escape the poisonous spray. They enveloped her in a swarm of legs, wings, and antennae, and their cold, segmented bodies ran over her like ice water.

In that moment Valencia—desecrated, humiliated, enchained, and terrified— finally chose her path. She knew what she would need to become to survive. This was the one bit of agency that she was to be given, and she would embrace it wholly. She sank down, down, down to somewhere very dark. It was dark like the arena, where she had first found the strength to do what was necessary.

The Agent stood up and brushed the panicked roaches off of her. She no longer felt her aches and pains. Her purpose was to locate that first roach, the brown and yellow one. There were other dual-colored roaches in the cell with her, but she remembered that first one's markings. It did not take her long to find it scuttling along in the damp filth at the back wall. She crushed it with her bare foot.

"Oh, guard!" she called, her voice husky with victory. "Come here. The Killer told me to call you when it was time."

The guard tossed his tools on the ground. Around Home, the Killer's command was nearly as powerful as that of a member of the WCE board. The Agent smiled at the thought as she dislocated her thumbs and slipped her hands from their manacles. Just as the guard approached, she popped her thumbs back into their sockets.

He looked at her through the bars of the cell. The space between the bars—the Agent happened to notice—was just wide enough to accommodate one of her arms.

"What's it time for?" the guard asked.

"Lean in close, and I'll tell you," the Agent said, acting as if she were still enchained and struggling to move toward him. "No one should hear."

He obeyed with such urgency that the Agent almost felt bad for what she was about to do.

"What's going on?" the guard demanded.

"I'm going to kill a roach!" the Agent hissed. In one smooth motion, she thrust her hands through the bars and caught the guard by his neck. His head banged against the metal bars, but instead of reaching up to fight for his life, he reached downward.

The Agent heard his radio chirp.

"Fire—loose!" he choked.

She snapped his neck and watched him slide to the floor.

"Admirable last move," she said, plucking the keys from his belt. "And I appreciate your confidence in my ability to free myself."

With that, she turned the key in the lock and stepped over his body. She looked back, but she did not see the swarming roaches or the body of the man whom she had just killed. She saw nothing.

Rosa's eyes popped open. It was the holiday, but for her it was just another morning of feeling like she had been awake all night. What point was there in having a new life if the old ones could intrude whenever they pleased?

She peeled back her sweat-drenched sheets and immediately dropped onto the floor to do push-ups. With every push-up, she tried to push away the past, but her arms gave out before her mind was rid of the horrific images from her nightmare. She collapsed and rolled onto her back for some sit-ups. She tried to think of nothing as she sat up, but after a thousand sit-ups, she accepted that she couldn't exercise away the nightmare.

Defeated, she struggled onto her feet and headed for the bathroom. She turned on the heat lamp and looked in the mirror.

"Your life is not the only one at stake here," the Agent said. "I have to remember, for my son."

* * *

The Sweetest Rose was open for a special dinner that evening. Rosa figured it was just as well. After the nightmare she'd had, she didn't feel much like celebrating, anyway, and working meant getting paid. After the regulars incident, Gordon had her working back of house most of the time. He'd discovered that she had a knack for operating the grill and stove, which thankfully kept her away from the disorder of the dining room and the regulars.

When Rosa arrived at the restaurant, Pete and Gordon were hanging strings of decorative lights on the far side of the dining room. Tea lights floated along with the rose blossoms on the fountain brook, and garlands woven of bay laurel, roses, and more lights lined the floors. The tea sets had been removed from the tables—replaced by crystal champagne flutes—and the floral center pieces had been upgraded to include sweet-smelling branches and some with plump, red teaberries.

"You've outdone yourselves," Rosa called to the guys. "It's positively enchanting!"

"Thanks, Rosa!" Pete said, handing another string of lights to Gordon.

"Hi," Gordon said over his shoulder. "French onion soup is on the stove. Can you check it and then whip up some chocolate mousse? Pete'll be back in a sec to start salad prep. Pest control's coming for a quick touch-up. Shouldn't take more than twenty minutes to start and finish, plenty of time before everyone arrives. Got extra pastries for the party favors and champagne in the wine cooler."

"He's got a lot on his mind," Pete explained. He and Rosa shared a knowing smile before they each turned to their respective tasks.

The kitchen smelled like caramelized onions and beef broth. It was the kind of aroma that made Rosa feel full and happy without even eating anything. She peeked into the pot on the stove, gave it a stir, then gathered the ingredients for the chocolate mousse. Gordon had left the necessary utensils out on the counter, so Rosa got to work separating the egg whites from the yolks. As she did so, Pete entered.

"We're done in there," he announced. "I'm so glad we went with the classic white lights instead of the platinum ones. Platinum was bright but just too sterile."

"It looks wonderful, Pete," Rosa said. "Where's Gordon?"

Pete opened the doors of the lowboy and crouched to take stock of his vegetables. "He's out meeting his scallop vendor. The guy only comes to town once a month with all manner of fresh seafood, but he was delayed with the recent snows. Last year, I told Gordon I know this really great animal-friendly alternative for bacon-wrapped scallops, using king oyster mushrooms, but he wasn't buying it—not for the holiday, anyway."

"What would you use for bacon?" she asked skeptically.

"Shiitakes," Pete said with a proud grin. "If you flavor them just right, you can barely taste the difference."

After picking out a number of fresh vegetables, he stood and began to prepare them for the salad arrangements.

"Mushroom on mushroom?" Rosa's nose wrinkled. "That's just *wrong!*"

"Why?"

"It lacks diversity," she said.

"You just have to develop a sensitivity to the nuances of flavor and texture," Pete said, shaking a cucumber at her. "And it *is* diverse within the mushroom realm and actually very delicious. It also saves the lives of animals from both land and sea."

He looked at her with such sappy puppy dog eyes that she burst into laughter.

"A worthy cause, to be sure," she said, "but I'll have to take your word for it about the deliciousness."

Suddenly, there was a thump and a low grating sound. Rosa's gaze shot toward the door to the dining room.

"It's the exterminator," Pete said somberly.

"Are there really pest problems here in the dead of winter?" Rosa asked.

Pete sighed. "The poor things come inside to wait out the cold weather. They don't mean any harm. But Gordon got a complaint from a couple of the regulars. And just yesterday, too."

"Well, what did they see?"

"A roach."

Before she could stop it, a whirlwind of anxiety overtook her. She beat the hands of the past off of her mind and reached for anything in the present that might ground her. She was making chocolate mousse for a holiday party in Lakes, roughly two thousand kilometers from Home. She focused on the whirring of the beaters and the frothing of the egg whites. The aromas of French onion soup and semisweet chocolate mingled to produce a unique anchor to the present.

At last, the mousse was finished. Rosa crossed the kitchen to put the dessert in the refrigerator, so it could set. She grabbed a broom and a rag to tidy her workstation.

Suddenly, she spotted a brown blotch moving along the floor by the wall. It was a sizable cockroach, about eight or nine centimeters in length. She told herself that it made sense for a roach to make an appearance since the exterminator was just in the other room. But as Rosa watched the spindly legs work their way along the floor, she had a sinking feeling like she was about to go away. She swept the roach into the corner furthest from the fridge, which looked to be the best place to keep such an intruder. Then she began searching for the opening by which the bug had entered.

Pete watched her creeping along the wall that bordered the dining room.

With some amusement, he asked, "What are you doing, Rosa?"

"I'm going to plug up their entry, so they'll be trapped in the dining room and die," she replied.

"Oh, let them be," he said. "If they manage to survive the treatment in there and find a safe haven here, what does it matter?"

"They're gross and ugly, and they carry disease," Rosa said.

"But they're really highly intelligent and sensitive creatures," said Pete.

Rosa brandished her broom. "Better hope they're intelligent enough to stay away from this kitchen, or they'll be sensing this broom crushing the life out of their nasty little bodies."

Pete was horrified into silence. He went back to arranging the salads. There were many things about which Rosa could keep an open mind, but she drew the line at the virtues of cockroaches.

Right about then, she saw two long, hairlike antennae peeking out of a small hole in the corner opposite of the one which she had designated for the containment of intruders. When the roach emerged, she prepared to sweep it into the corner where the first roach was still milling about, but the new roach took flight and one, two, three, four, five, six, seven more erupted into the kitchen. The bugs scattered, some flying and some crawling, as fast as they could go. Rosa felt herself slipping down, down, down into the depths.

Legs, antennae, and wings seemed to be everywhere—and those horrid segmented bodies. The legs went *TICK* *TICK* *TICK* on the floor, and the wings clacked against the walls and the refrigerator. There was no containing them in their frenzy, and the sight of them overrunning everything would have instilled fear and helplessness in anyone.

Filled with rage, the Agent pursued the first roach that had taken flight, which she simply named Number 2. It flew past her and would have brushed her face if she had not dodged. With her broom, she swatted at the bug but only knocked over pots and cooking utensils that had been hanging from the walls.

When they clattered to the floor, Pete turned around. His mouth dropped open.

"Rosa, please stop!" he exclaimed. But Rosa couldn't hear him right then.

The Agent chased Number 2 around the kitchen twice, then followed it back toward the ill-designated containment corner. Many of the roaches had assembled there, so she jumped into their midst, hacking, stomping, and smacking.

It wasn't until Pete snatched the broom from her that Rosa came to herself and froze, swatting arm still raised.

"I'll take them outside myself," Pete told her, "but, *please*, no killing in the kitchen."

Rosa lowered her arm. "Take them outside? They'll just come back in."

"No, they'll listen to me," he said. "They *know* me."

"This I've got to see."

After casting her one last exasperated glance, Pete banged the broom handle on the wall a couple of times. He repeated the action all around the kitchen until the roaches, perhaps responding to the vibrations, congregated in the middle of the floor.

"Come on, folks," Pete said to the bugs, sweeping them toward the door. "Rosa says it's time to go outside."

"Rosa said it was time to die," she corrected.

"They won't go, if you talk to them like that," he said curtly.

The roaches did seem to have calmed considerably. In response to Pete's nudges with the broom, they sauntered toward the open back door. And when they got to it, he swept them over the weather strip one by one.

"Okay," he said as he swept them, "that's Emma and Gary and

Alistair and Barbie, Felix, Darren, Harriette, and Iphigenia. Where's Carlisle?"

Rosa's stomach flipped as she looked under her right foot. Number 2 was the one roach that the Agent had managed to target and eliminate. She hadn't known that he'd been named by someone who would miss him.

"Carlisle!" Pete called, peering under the refrigerator. "It's safe to come out now. I'll escort you to the door myself."

"Uh, Pete?" Rosa said uncomfortably. "Would you be able to identify Carlisle from 2-D remains?"

"Oh, Carlisle!" Pete breathed, staring sadly at the gelatinous, green-brown smudge.

"I'm sorry," Rosa said, a tad perplexed. "I didn't know they were your friends."

He sighed. "What you don't seem to understand, Rosa, is that *all* animals are our friends. We can live in harmony with them, even if they look scary or carry diseases. Acknowledging the fact that we are all a part of the same cosmic network of living beings can be the basis of our respect for all life."

Her expression said, *If you say so.*

Pete moved past her to collect Carlisle's remains. He did so with an air of reverence that seemed slightly excessive for the situation at hand. But that was Rosa's opinion.

When the deed was done, Pete approached Rosa and stared down into her face with a gaze full of pity.

"Oh, don't look at me like that, Pete," she said. "I'm no monster. You and I just have different values."

"No, it's not values," he said, regarding her more incisively than she would have liked. "Something happened to you—something bad, right?"

Weary from warding off the images from the awful dreams she'd been having, Rosa found herself blurting out, "I was seventeen."

Interestingly, the pity in Pete's face gave way to sorrow. And that was quite a relief because Rosa understood pity to be a spectator sport. It trapped everyone involved into the inhuman roles of the spectator and the spectated. Sorrow, on the other hand, brimmed with relational possibility.

Pete spread his arms. "Want a hug?"

It was curious that he thought a hug could be the answer to

anything. Maybe he thought of it less as an answer and more as a salve. Or, maybe it was just his way of changing the subject.

The Agent would not have approved of a hug, but she wasn't there right then. Rosa shuffled a couple of centimeters forward and let Pete wrap his arms around her. She fit neatly inside of his frame and immediately felt warm all over. The past apparently couldn't reach her in there.

A car pulled up in the driveway behind the kitchen.

"Gordon is back," the Agent named Rosa said, pulling back self-consciously. Her mind felt foggy, but she happened to notice that—even though she was pushing Pete away—she enjoyed the warmth of his body at her palms.

"Where?" Pete asked.

"I heard his car in the back," she said. "I—we should—"

"Yeah." He somewhat reluctantly returned to his workstation.

Only seconds later, Gordon's booted feet crunched up the icy back steps. He barreled through the door grasping a cooler with three boxes stacked on it.

Rosa took the boxes off the top of the cooler while Pete grabbed a mop.

"Freshest scallops in the district!" Gordon beamed, tracking dirt-filled slush into the kitchen. "I had to take on a couple of shrewd businessmen for them, but it was worth it. They're really beauties!"

Pete went to work with the mop.

"I'm glad you were so fortunate," Rosa said, placing the boxes on the floor beside the fridge. "Pete was ready to whip up his king oyster mushroom scallops with shiitake bacon."

"Never in my kitchen!" Gordon declared. "Or, not on a holiday, at least."

"Ha. Ha." Pete purposely swirled the mop over his boss' boots. "You guys contribute to the problematic systems of the world."

Gordon's eyes lit up. "Speaking of a problem, you've got a solution for me, Pete. I decided on my way up here that it would be a nice touch to include a hardboiled egg in the appetizer course along with the soup and the salad. We've got enough for tonight, but we'll need more eggs, day after tomorrow, for prep. Can you get me a dozen by then?"

"Of course," Pete said. "Everyone produced today, and they likely will tomorrow as well."

"Every who?" Rosa asked.

"Pete tends chickens, and I sometimes buy eggs from him," Gordon explained. "I don't know how he does it, but his fresh eggs'll beat any supermarket. He's an authentic urban farmer."

"Well, any fresh eggs will beat the supermarket," Pete said, his face reddening. "And I wouldn't call myself a farmer. I just try to do my part to create humane conditions for animals that contribute to human flourishing."

"I see," Rosa said.

"I'll be out front," Gordon said. "Rosa, grate the gruyere, then look in the pantry for the recipe labeled 'Scallops Provençal.' It's for the third course, so take a look at the recipe and whip up a pilaf to complement it. And Pete, cut the beets for the salad in those little rose shapes everyone loves so much and get the bread in the oven for the French onion. We're open in an hour."

He'd been speaking a mile a minute, and the door closed after him before either of his employees could respond.

Pete regarded Rosa almost as shyly as when they had first met. "Would you like to come with me to get eggs after the shift? It's only a couple of blocks from Frin's Place."

Rosa considered accepting his invitation, perhaps more for his sake than any curiosity about urban chickens, but she thought better of it. Even though their work had continued since their embrace, Rosa was experiencing the odd sensation that the embrace had not concluded. That seemed like a potential problem, so she figured it would be best to go back to her apartment to address the issue.

"Maybe another time," she said with a smile. "I think I might be tired after this shift, but would you walk me home?"

The disappointment in Pete's face paired somewhat appropriately with a flicker of hopefulness.

"I would be honored to," he replied.

* * *

The holiday dinner was a huge success. Gordon was a real ham, acting both as the server and the master of ceremonies. He had invited a few local poets and musicians to perform while people dined, which Pete told Rosa was not a common happening in Lakes. Most artists moved southward to Croon A Tune to jumpstart their careers, and those who had not yet had the opportunity stayed in Lakes, working two or three jobs to fund their art. Gordon had a soft spot for these hardworking people and wanted to give them every opportunity to showcase their gifts. And apparently, he had an eye for talent because Rosa and Pete could feel the vibrations of the diners' applause from the kitchen.

After the diners had departed and the performers had been paid, Gordon cleaned the dining room and came back into the kitchen where Pete and Rosa were finishing up the dishes.

"The artists enjoyed the meal so much they wanted to share their tips with you," he said, pulling out an enormous wad of cash and handing them each a half.

Rosa stared at the money. It was enough for two weeks' rent.

"We have a very wealthy clientele," Gordon told her. "They're willing to pay top dollar for food cooked by humans and to appreciate art created by humans."

"It's really a niche industry," Pete added. "Most things are automated in Lakes."

"I noticed," Rosa said, thinking about her struggles with shopping during her first days in the district.

After a short silence, Gordon clapped his hands together. "Well, kids, the kitchen looks great. There's only the mopping to do, and since it's the holiday, I'll finish up for you. You head on out."

Rosa and Pete thanked him, wished him a happy holiday, and put on their coats.

As they were exiting out the back, he called after them, "Be safe. And Rosa, make sure to protect Pete. Use lethal force, if necessary!"

Gordon's laugh was lighthearted, and Rosa tried to remind herself that he'd had no way of knowing that she would not find the joke humorous.

CHAPTER 13

THE DAY AFTER THE HOLIDAY, BLAIR WAS BRIEFING KARTHIK AND Theresa on what to expect with her return to field duty when Racky burst into the conference room. Her hair was uncombed, and her clothes were disheveled. That, combined with the watery brightness of her eyes, suggested that she had not slept recently.

"I got it!" she said, slamming her portion of Bourghin's journals onto the table. "I know where Home is!"

"What are you talking about?" Theresa asked irritably.

"I got it. I got it," Racky mumbled as she rummaged through her large purse. She dumped the contents of the bag onto the table. Receipts, pens, and used tissues flew everywhere. On top of the pile was the holoprojector that contained Bourghin's recording. It was still projecting, though paused. Ignoring her teammates' reproachful glances, Racky straightened the holoprojector and played the recording.

The chips aren't only trackers; they're some kind of reminder. You know how the WCE is always inside of everyone's head. Anyways, I've written the coordinates in my green notebook, but I don't—

Racky stopped the recording and held up the green notebook. "The Carmelita chip was produced only a few hundred meters from the coordinates that Bourghin recorded from the homing chip of an Amphibian handler! I checked out satellite images of the area, and it's for sure a manufacturing compound. I found paper trails proving that the compound is still WCE-affiliated, mostly for manufacturing and light administrative functions. It's the 'Home' we're looking for from the Song, I'd bet my subclass buns of steel. It's the old Phib training ground, and it's right up in the grand and green district of Farm And Forest!"

Her teammates were stunned into silence. They all looked at her, then at each other.

"You d—did it," Karthik said in amazement.

"Surprised?" Racky asked, smoothing her hair only to have it spring straight up again.

"N—no," he replied sheepishly. "I mean, I just never imag—wow."

"This is going to answer so many questions for us, Racky," Blair said. "If we can get into that compound, we might finally get some substantial information about the Amphibians' main function. That intel could just be the boost our team needs."

Racky smiled. "All these good feelings make those sleepless hours and having to work with your pain-in-the-behind behinds worth it."

Suddenly, the lack of sleep seemed to catch up with her. She yawned and brought a hand to her head.

"Good work, Wernicke," Blair said. "I'm going to call it a day here, so I can get the director up to speed. Expect finalized itineraries sometime in the next twenty-four hours. We'll leave for Farm And Forest at the end of the week, most likely. Dismissed."

Theresa hurried out, looking at her flake, while Karthik congratulated Racky on her breakthrough.

"And thanks for getting us unstuck!" He clapped her on the shoulder and departed with a broad grin on his face.

As Racky was gathering all of her junk back into her purse, Blair approached her.

"I think we should couple this trip to the WCE compound with— our other task," Blair whispered. "Do you think we can make the arrangements in time?"

"I think we could have a decent shot, if we get the ball rolling tonight," Racky replied.

"I trust your expertise," Blair said. "Now, please, go home and get some sleep."

"On it," Racky said, yawning again. "But maybe I'll drive through Chubba's for a snack first."

She tried to exit and bumped into the doorframe.

"Maybe not," Blair said concernedly. "Next paycheck, you really need to upgrade to an auto-car. Come on, I'll take you home."

* * *

The Sweetest Rose was closed the day after the holiday. Rosa came back from her morning run to find a tiny basket with two eggs in it sitting outside her door. Pete had left them with a note to wash them before preparing them.

Rosa thought it very kind that he had shared the eggs with her. And when she had fried them up, she discovered that Pete and Gordon were right about fresh eggs being better than store-bought ones. The yolks were creamy, substantial, and almost butter-like in their richness.

After breakfast, Rosa continued her exercise routine. No matter how she tried, she couldn't stop thinking about the embrace that she and Pete had shared the night before. Maybe it was the physical movement of his hands—that he had grasped her so gently—or maybe it was his humble heart that made it seem as if he had been giving something to her. And what he'd given was a mystery to Rosa, but it appeared to have been something that she wanted, maybe even something she needed. That kind of need was vaguely familiar to Rosa because Valencia had experienced some version of it with a family in Diablo. Sadly, it did not take much imagination to see how easily that need could be exploited.

Growling away the vulnerability, the Agent dropped to the floor and did a hundred push-ups. She had enacted an unassuming flirtation for an unassuming man. That was what she had been doing. Pete felt compassion for individuals—whether animal or human whom he understood to be disadvantaged. The uncontainable fragments of the Agent's troubled past were beckoning to him, for he wanted nothing more than to embody the compassionate, pacifist ideal to which he aspired. In her brokenness, Rosa had found a soft entry point, the gateway to Pete's desires and self-image. It was ingenious, really, but so terribly phiblike. What did he have that she wanted anyway?

"Don't entice the dorky cook, Rosa," she said. "We've got more baggage than Pete Bae can handle."

Her understanding of people's fragility had solidified during her experience as Valencia Chang in Diablo. The Agent's life was unpredictable and dangerous, and even though she usually took pretty good care of herself, it was the vulnerable people around her—family and friends that tended to suffer because of her way of life. Sweet, dorky Pete would have to remain at arm's length.

The Agent rolled onto her back and thought of her son for a thousand sit-ups. Then she figured it was time to resume her attempts to pick up her Kiddo's trail. Her web apparatus was sitting on the dining room table, unused since the day she'd bought it.

Just prior to the holiday, she had taken a trip to the local library and borrowed some books on how to use a web apparatus to access the dark web. She had to learn methods other than the conventional ones, which had become increasingly traceable in the past couple of decades. The kiosk, nicknamed "E-Lib," had spit out projection capsules in addition to the hardcopy books, reminding her in a friendly synthetic voice that she'd have to learn by capsule eventually.

If we can learn any of this stuff at all. The Agent looked doubtfully at the pile of books and capsules next to her web apparatus.

The capsules were each about the size of a horse pill and bright red with the crest of Central Lakes Library stamped in yellow on the broad sides. The Agent took one in her hands to examine it. It looked benign enough. She accidentally discovered how it opened when she pinched the crested sides. There was a quiet click, and a holographic copy of *Never Leave A Trace: Phantasmic Chat Functions and Tracking on the Dark Web* appeared on the table in front of her.

The Agent had a distant memory of using similar technology, perhaps as a teenager. Yes, Windsailing's Gifted Library had provided shared use of big, clunky holoprojectors onto which an ebook file could be downloaded. Besides the sleeker design of the capsule from Central Lakes, the book it projected onto the table seemed to function fairly similarly.

She pulled the edges of the page to make the print larger. If she tapped the top corner of a page, it would stick to her finger so that she could turn the page. The interface was basically the same as the one that Valencia had used as a teenager. Of course, Valencia had been diverting herself with random facts about frogs and salamanders in the herpetological encyclopedia, but the Agent was going to learn useful information that would enable her to find her son.

When she flipped past the book's introduction, a familiar, musty smell enveloped her. Apparently, the book had been infused with a fragrance to give it the classic "book smell." *That* was new. The Agent's stomach turned, and she decided that that was enough new technology for one day. She switched to the hardcopy of the book. And when she had finished that one, she moved to the next and then the next. Learning to access the dark web most securely involved some synthetic languages as well as 3-D programming, which required a certain artistic flair, but she grasped the concepts fairly quickly.

By mid-afternoon, she felt a surge of confidence because of all that she had learned. She reached down and touched the plug of the web apparatus. When nothing happened, she plugged it into the wall. Still nothing. She pressed the power button. That's when she noticed her arms going weak.

"Say it again," she whispered.

A green holographic screen popped up and hovered in front of her, prompting her to create a username and password. It seemed to be tracking her eye movement because it followed her no matter which way she turned. A keyboard also popped up in the same green light on the table.

The Agent shook out her limbs and reached for the keyboard. As soon as she touched it, a shock went through her. She blacked out and woke up on the floor next to the table. Learning theories could not overcome her conditioning against *using* new tech. Frustrated, the Agent picked herself up and went out for a run. That, at least, was something that she could do without fainting.

* * *

Late at night, Racky sat in her living room, typing furiously at her web apparatus. Theresa was filing her nails next to her. And Karthik had bowed out of the unofficial overtime with the excuse that he was still recovering from his trip to Windsailing. His team knew he was probably sitting at home, distressed about the case yet unwilling to participate in the preparation for this unapproved operation.

Blair verbally affirmed his commitment to integrity. She also affirmed Theresa's and Racky's commitment to doing what was right. Racky wasn't completely convinced that tacking another mission onto the trip to Farm And Forest behind Director Vincent's back was actually right, but she guessed that she understood that the operation was well-intentioned.

"Okay, how's this?" she asked, flicking the holographic screen so that it twirled over to her supervisor.

The ad read:

Got Cull cani$ter. Exchange info Re: Larva.
  Contact xx

"What's the significance of the dollar sign and the 'xx?'" Blair asked.

"The dollar sign is to indicate that the buyer will provide money for the middleman's fee," Racky said. "And anyone knowledgeable enough to make this exchange would accept without question that Lenci would be seeking info on Larva. The exes are my placeholder for some kind of alias we need to create to suggest Lenci is the seller while side-stepping any automatic algorithms searching for her known aliases."

"And we're the middleman, I'm guessing, to explain why Lenci won't be at the exchange. But what do you propose we do with the money?"

"Use it, leave it there, I don't care!" Racky sputtered. "It would look phony if we didn't collect."

"Okay, okay," Blair said. "What about the alias?"

Theresa smirked. "We could use the name '*Bathsheba*.'"

Racky's eyes shot toward her. "Why?"

"Well," Theresa said, "I thought it rather poetic, what with her previous relationship to David Miller the Killer. Anyone who knew of their, ahem, affair would think of her on seeing that name and the Cull mentioned together."

Racky thought about the journal she had found in Bourghin's office, which mentioned the name 'Bathsheba'. SecurityFriend had not reported any breaches at the house over the past week, so it was impossible that Theresa had seen the journal. But it could not be a coincidence that she just so happened to connect *that* name to Lenci when Samir had done the same.

"I don't know," Blair said. "That assumes an awful lot. We might miss the mark."

"Or, we could use a name that's more to the point," Theresa said, "the name of an Amphibian."

"If you know her WCE agency symbol, do share," Blair said.

"She's Fire Salamander," Theresa replied. "That's fairly obvious, don't you think?"

"How do you figure?" Racky asked.

Theresa blinked rapidly as she answered. "Well, if Lenci was a WCE target in Carmelita, which we assumed because of the charred Class 3 body, then we can also assume that the Song on the chip we found at the site—which very clearly makes Fire Salamander the target—is talking about her. So, use the name and just change it a smidge."

"I'm not sure that completely follows either," Blair said. "Maybe we should—"

"Actually, yeah," Racky interrupted, staring suspiciously at Theresa. "I had the same thought a while ago. Thanks for bringing that up, Theresa."

"Happy to help." Theresa went back to filing her nails.

Racky couldn't quite put her finger on it, but there was something very strange about Theresa's sudden spurts of knowledge—especially since she constantly bragged about not having gotten around to reading Bourghin's materials. But that was a matter for later investigation.

"This should be close enough," Racky said, typing in the alias 'BlazingMander'.

She posted the ad and then sat back with an expectant look on her face.

Blair cleared her throat. "Okay, so what do we do now?"

"We wait for someone to respond to the ad."

The apparatus chirped.

"What's that?" Blair asked.

Racky leaned forward to get a better look. "I think we're getting a response."

"That was fast." Blair sat down next to her.

A chat box had opened, and someone was typing a message.

B.F.: You're supposed to be lying low.

"Who do you think B.F. could be?" Blair asked.

Racky shrugged. "Someone who knows Lenci and who knows tech. The only reason we are able to view an alias is because B.F. is displaying it on purpose. They doubtless have the knowledge and ability to send an anonymous message because they can initiate a private, untraceable chat with me. Best to record this now as it will disappear when the conversation ends."

Blair tried to use her flake to record the conversation, but her display only showed Racky looking at an empty screen.

"Uh, Racky? The flake can't recognize the images."

Racky grinned broadly. "An untraceable phantasm—that inspires awe, even by my standards. We're dealing with a techie *par excellence* here. Guess we'll just have to do it the old-fashioned way. Theresa, write it down."

Theresa glowered at her, but with one look from Blair, she got up to get a notebook. Meanwhile, Racky typed a response in the chat box.

> BlazingMander: Desperate times, desperate measures. Got a buyer?

> B.F.: I'll ask around. What's your price?

> BlazingMander: Info on Larva and 6MM.

> B.F. is still typing...

"Why aren't they responding?" Blair asked after a minute or so. "Do you think you said something wrong?"

"Maybe they're just thinking about whether or not they can deliver on something like this," Racky said, typing another message.

> BlazingMander: I want the coordinates of Larva's current location.

> B.F.: I want the Songs.

"The *Songs*," Racky mumbled.

"You have that weird Song from the Carmelita chip," Theresa reminded her. "Maybe you can bargain with that."

"This could get out of hand fast, Racky," Blair said. "Wrap it up."

> BlazingMander: I only have one right now, but I'll toss it in with the canister for the $ and info on Larva.

> B.F.: Interesting. I'll be in touch.

> B.F. has disconnected

"What just happened?" Blair asked.

"I think we've got a lead," Racky replied.

Theresa shrugged. "Or you just outed us *before* we got the lead."

Racky simply shook her head.

"We should delay the trip to Farm And Forest until B.F. gets back to us," Blair said pensively. "Keep an eye on your messages, Racky. I'll buy time with Vincent."

"So, what? We're just supposed to be packed and ready to go *if* B.F. ever gets back to us?" Theresa asked.

"Within twenty-four hours of their response," Blair said, heading for the door. "And *you* aren't coming with us."

Theresa didn't look very sad about that. "Why not?"

"You got your share of action in Croon A Tune," Blair told her. "I thought you might appreciate working admin on this one, and we can afford it since I'm returning to the field. I wish I could give Wilson a break, but he's our resident expert on Lenci."

"Poor him," Theresa said, "and poor all of you, if the buyer isn't actually interested. You might be waiting a long time for her—or whoever they are—to get in touch."

"If they weren't interested, they would have just disconnected without any mention of being in touch," Racky said.

There was a lot about the situation that seemed precarious, and yet, after her recent breakthroughs, Racky was hopeful.

CHAPTER 14

Rosa enjoyed working with Pete and Gordon. They were concerned with simple things like pastries, customer satisfaction, and having enough ingredients for the week. So was Rosa, too, during the days, as a sort of respite. And in the evenings, the Agent would sit under her heat lamp, pondering how she might seek information about her Kiddo without attracting the Phibs who were out for her head.

A couple of weeks after the Agent's initial arrival in Lakes, she very nearly blew her cover again. It was Friday lunch-dinner. Gordon was cooking in the kitchen, and Pete and Rosa were working the dining room as efficiently as they could. It seemed that the line at the counter was never ending. As soon as five satisfied customers exited, fifteen hungry ones entered. The regulars were emptying the display case at twice the normal rate, and although Rosa had given the eighty-six warning on almond croissants twice, fresh pastries were nowhere to be seen.

"Now we really are eighty-six on almond croissants," Pete said after handing the last one to an elated customer.

Rosa looked over her shoulder at the door to the kitchen. Gordon had probably stepped out for a break. The middle of Friday lunch-dinner was not the best time for that, but he was the boss.

"I'll get them, Pete!" Rosa said. "Don't worry!"

And with that, she ran into the back.

"No! No, running!" Gordon's plea registered just as she collided with him.

The tray of almond croissants that he was carrying flew from his grip. With a grand leap, the Agent caught the tray and displayed it proudly to show that not one croissant had been displaced.

Gordon's face went white. "You—"

"I'm *sorry*, boss," she laughed. "But I hope you'll accept this offering of unharmed croissants to appease your wrath."

"But you—your—your *hands!*" he stammered.

The croissants on the tray were steaming, and bits of melted butter sizzled around them. The tray was fresh out of the oven, but the Agent's pain management had kept her from feeling the searing heat. She was in danger of being exposed.

"Ow!" Rosa shrieked theatrically and threw the tray straight into the air.

It came right down into Gordon's mitted hands.

"Good thing you have such good reflexes," she said. "I should soak my hands. I think I'm in shock."

He gave her a scrutinizing look, but before he could ask any questions, Pete called eighty-six again.

"Get some ice and use the sink to soak, then go to the emergency room down the street," Gordon commanded.

Rosa headed for the sink. "But who'll walk Pete back after work?"

"I'll drive him, if you're that worried about it," he said.

"Would you?" Rosa grinned. "He's a very good pacifist."

"Yeah, hell of an excuse for not fighting back when you're getting mugged." And with that, Gordon slammed the door to the dining room.

Rosa filled one of the sinks with ice water and shoved her hands into it. She hated the cold, but despite her best efforts, she could not *not* feel it. Cold was always present, lurking beneath the surface of every warm and comfortable moment of serenity—waiting to drag her to the depths, the depths where she was trying to convince herself that she did not belong. The ice bath made her hands cold and stiff, and that reminded her of dark water and kelp, which reminded her of being separated from Kiddo.

"You're forgetting," the Agent said, "and this is something you must not forget."

She looked toward the door to the dining room. There was much to keep Gordon busy in there, and Rosa was supposed to be off for the weekend, anyway. Her boss would not have to know that she had abandoned her unnecessary ice bath. He would not have to know that she would heal without it. In fact, that was one thing that he *must* not know. No one could know, not even the staff at the emergency room down the street. The Agent's last visit to an emergency room had given away her position to WCE operatives and had led to the kidnapping of her son.

However, as the Agent thought about it, her position was already compromised—potentially in a way that she could turn to her advantage. The mysterious correspondent who had left the note in her housewarming gift seemed familiar with her history as well as with the newest technology. The person had not yet attempted to harm her, so the Agent figured that they might be an ally. If she could manage to overcome her conditioning enough to use the simple chat functions on her web apparatus, she would be able to petition the correspondent's help in obtaining a lead on the location of her son. It was worth a shot. She removed her hands from the ice water and dried them, then departed for her apartment.

* * *

It was 2130, and the Agent was staring at the web apparatus on her dining room table. She had assimilated all of the appropriate material, maybe more than was necessary for what she intended to do. And yet, she could not apply any of what she had learned. When she powered on the apparatus, she became short of breath, and when she touched the holographic keyboard, she would black out and wake up on the floor.

The Agent abhorred this residue of her time with the Killer. While she had once managed to circumvent the conditioning against guns by allowing Valencia to come to the surface, she knew that there was a difference between going back to something one already knew—even if in a different mental compartment—and trying to learn something entirely new.

Adaptation was the Agent's goal, but so far, she could not achieve it. She could learn any human being at an unparalleled rate, but she still could not learn to operate one of the most commonly used technologies of her day. And if she could not learn to use it, she might never see her son again. That thought sent all of her pent-up frustration surging into an uncontainable rage.

With a furious scream, the Agent hurled the apparatus across the room. It bounced off of a cushion on the loveseat and landed unharmed on the floor. The release felt good, so the Agent overturned her table as well. Everything that had been on it—the books, their associated capsules, and an empty plate—hurtled to the floor. Then she screamed at the mess, too.

The Agent was summoned out of her rage by a knock at the door. She looked at the mess on the floor, disgusted by how much it reminded her of the Killer's rage fits. At least no one had gotten hurt—this time.

"You okay in there, Rosa?" came the voice of Pete Bae.

The Agent named Rosa had known that a visit like this could be possible, and she was prepared. She accidentally stepped on one of the book capsules, causing a ghostly version of *Just Try It: Accessing the Dark Web for Beginners* to flicker to life, and tripped over a couple of physical books on her way to the bathroom.

"I feared she'd go home instead of to the emergency room," Gordon was saying, "and now, she's screaming in agony and dropping everything with those crispy hands."

"Just a minute!" Rosa called as she fumbled around in her medicine cabinet.

She grabbed some burn cream, squeezed a thick layer of it onto her palms, wrapped both hands in gauze, and hurried to open the door.

"Hi guys!" she said, keeping her hands behind her back. "How're you?"

"Fine," Pete said in his usual happy-go-lucky way. "We finally finished cleaning up at the restaurant, and Gordon said you wanted him to take me home. I *think* he just wanted an excuse to check in on you."

Rosa cast an embarrassed glance at Gordon. He was staring incredulously at the mess in the living room.

"Uh, sorry about the mess," she said. "I was just trying to catch a spider. Sucker was as big as a mouse!"

Gordon didn't take his eyes off of the mess. "A spider, huh? Maybe you've got a nest in your cabinets. Wolf spiders do that sometimes. I'll find the nest, and you won't be having any more problems."

He pushed past her.

"Oh!" She resisted the urge to grab him back.

Remembering her incident with the regulars at The Sweetest Rose, she knew that she would have to make an extra effort not to out herself as specially trained and belligerent. Gordon was a military man who would be able to recognize a combat trained person. He fortunately hadn't been present for most of the regulars incident, and Pete's inexperienced explanation of the event sounded more like a gang fight than a skilled engagement of well-assessed targets.

Pete was still standing in the hallway, looking tentative.

Rosa cleared her throat. "Come in?"

He took his time considering her invitation. He didn't look like he particularly wanted to come in, probably because he knew that this was her safe space and Gordon had just intruded upon it. However, it would be the most polite thing to come in after she had extended the invitation, and it would be more appropriate for her to entertain them both rather than Gordon alone.

She glanced uncomfortably at Gordon who was emptying all of her pots and pans onto the kitchen floor. She had nothing to hide in there, but his rummaging felt invasive anyway.

"Sure," Pete said. Then, reaching into the darkness beside the doorway, he picked up a basket of eggs. "I brought you these. The hens send you their warmest greetings."

"Do send my greetings back to them," Rosa smiled. "I really enjoyed the last batch you brought. You were right that fresh eggs are better than store-bought. They're so rich and delicious!"

"Maybe I'll keep that part to myself," Pete said with a wink. He held the basket out to her, but she kept her hands behind her back. So, he stepped into the apartment and placed the eggs just to the left of the door.

After giving the living room a once-over, he nodded in approval. "Frin always does a great job with the furnishing. Do you feel at home yet?"

"Getting there," Rosa said with a wry smile. "Want to see my favorite part of the whole place?"

"Alright!" He followed her to the bathroom where she flicked on the heat lamp.

"This thing is better than everything else in the apartment added together," she gushed, pointing to the lamp with both hands. "The cold weather has been kicking my desert-raised behind, but this little lamp has been the brightest spot at the end of my cold, dark days."

"High praise, indeed," Pete said. Then, with a concerned expression, he motioned to her hands and said, "Those don't look right."

"Oh, they're fine," Rosa said. "I applied burn cream before I did the wrapping. The stuff's practically magic."

"It's for mild burns only, though," he replied. "From what Gordon told me, your burns are far too severe for that kind of treatment."

"And who made you an expert?" She backed away as he advanced toward her.

He looked embarrassed. "I was a premed in college. Spent a couple semesters in a burn unit for clinical research. Now, please, let me see?"

After a moment's calculation, Rosa determined that it would likely be more trouble to *not* let Pete take a look—and all the more suspicious when she turned up completely healed at work on Monday.

Sighing, she held out her gauze-wrapped, goopy hands. Pete seemed relieved that she was allowing him to take a look, but there was something else about his expression that looked weary.

He unwrapped the gauze somewhat laboriously, appearing to hold at bay the pain of some traumatic memory—perhaps something from the burn unit. He had insisted on examining her burns despite knowing full well that it would catapult him back in time. Rosa found that sweet and selfless but quite unnecessary.

"Hey," she smiled.

He met her gaze and some of the angst of his protective blocking dissipated.

"You alright?" she asked.

"Yeah," he said. The past was gone.

He looked back down at her hand. "This is actually pretty remarkable. You do have minor burns. But from the way Gordon described it, I thought your palms would be melted to the bone."

Rosa laughed. "Oh, he's sweet! But I really only held the tray for a fraction of a second. Gordon actually caught it when I realized I was burning myself."

They moved back into the common room.

"Gordon's always been a bit of a fibber," Pete chuckled, "or, at least an exaggerator."

"He *is* a master of hyperbole," Rosa agreed. "I barely even touched that tray."

"It had to have been ten whole seconds, at least!" Gordon hollered from the kitchen. "I could *smell* her flesh burning. It was—"

"Yeah, yeah, and my getting clubbed over the head *once* makes me a mugging target for life," Pete said. He touched Rosa's palm ever so gently. "How's that feel?"

"It doesn't hurt," she said, retracting her hand. "That burn cream works like a charm."

"At this rate, you'll be back to work on Monday as planned," Pete said. "Heck, you could come in tomorrow just to hang out with us, if you wanted."

"That isn't possible!" Gordon rushed out of the kitchen with dust bunnies falling from his shoulders. "I was there at the scene!"

"So was I, Gordon. Look." She extended her hands, so he could see for himself.

"Unbelievable," he said, staring at the fading marks of the tray corners in her palms—now merely raised, pink skin with no blisters. "It's like a miracle."

"Well, I'm glad," Pete said. "It could've been a lot worse, sounds like."

Rosa nodded. "I feel very grateful. Would you guys like some tea or something?"

"Might be nice to warm up before heading home," Gordon said.

He picked one last dust bunny off of his shoulder and sat down in her armchair. As he did so, the Agent thought she might have seen something on the inside of his upper arm.

Maybe it was nothing.

"I like tea," Pete was saying, "especially the whole-leaf kind. I use hand-woven, reusable bags that are distributed by a company that pays its workers a living wage."

"I'll put some water on, then." Rosa hopped over the downed table on her way to the kitchen.

"Whose old-style books?" Pete motioned to the large heap by the table. He moved to get a closer look.

"Central Lakes Library," Rosa said from the kitchen. "The E-Lib insisted on giving me capsules, too, but I've always loved an old-fashioned, physical book."

Pete chuckled. "I don't know many subclass females who read books on synthetic languages and the dark web."

"But this female's not your average subber, is she?" Gordon laughed, leaning around the side of the chair to get a glimpse of the books.

"'Subber' is an ugly word," said Rosa. "I prefer the term 'naturally unclassified.' And 'woman,' if you don't mind."

"I'm sorry," Pete replied in an astonished but sincere tone. "I meant no offense."

"Ditto," Gordon said, scratching his head.

"None taken, fellas," she replied. She knelt to retrieve a sachet of jasmine green tea from one of the lower cabinets.

There was a low scraping sound as Pete turned her table upright. She stood to find him stacking the books on top of it. He gave them a caring pat.

Suddenly, he laughed out loud. "I just noticed that, if you take the words of the titles of each of these books in sequence, it makes the sentence 'Just Leave Me Alone'. Is that some kind of subliminal message you're trying to send us?"

Rosa glanced at the books. From the way that he had stacked them, she could see that the first, second, third, and fourth words of the respective book titles did indeed add up to 'Just Leave Me Alone'. It would have been a clever mode of communication, if she had had reason and intention to use it.

"You give me too much credit, Pete Bae," she said. "It would take an incredibly sharp mind to come up with a code like that. And remember, the books were in a messy pile before you guys got here. Perhaps *you* are the one with the subliminal message?"

"No chance of that." His already wide grin broadened. "So, you might actually want me around?"

She mirrored his grin, but before she could answer, Gordon rapped on the side of his chair.

"Hey, enough with that!" He reclined in the seat and put his hands behind his head. "I don't want to be a third wheel, here."

"I hope you like jasmine," Rosa said, placing the teapot on a tray and bringing it into the living room.

As she set the tray on the coffee table, she looked up at Gordon, who had begun to doze off with his hands still behind his head. She had only ever seen him with his upper arms at his sides. He often seemed to go out of his way to keep them there, like he was standing at attention. She had never given much thought to his posture beyond imagining that some aspects of military service must stay with a person for their entire life. But now that she was faced with the true reason for Gordon's secrecy, she wished that she'd never met him at all.

Tattooed on the inside of his upper arm was a green, tailed creature, maybe a salamander of some sort—salamander, as in Amphibian. While the Agent was impressed by the ostensible normalcy of one of her own cohort, the very thought of what Gordon might be able to do to her was sobering. He was at least half a meter taller than her and quite a few pounds more muscular. He'd be more agile than Crispin had been, and his judgment was not impaired at the moment.

The Agent figured it would be most advantageous to eliminate him while he was sleeping. It would be as easy as snapping his neck and making it look like he'd fallen out of the chair at the wrong angle.

"Sleek web apparatus!" Pete said. He plugged in the device and set it on the dining room table. "Mind if I take a look?"

The Agent named Rosa moved to join him. There was little sense in trying to eliminate Gordon with a witness in the room.

"Knock yourself out," she said. "In fact, I'd like to look over your shoulder. Growing up in Diablo, we didn't have all these fancy gadgets. I just bought it hoping to learn as I go."

"Oh, well, in that case"—he pulled out a chair for her—"have a seat. I can walk you through setup."

She sat awkwardly in front of the holographic screen.

"You don't have to be so tense," he said, putting a hand on her shoulder. "The device won't bite you. It's just a tool for you to use."

The warmth from Pete's hand radiated down to Rosa's, and in that moment, she had a wonderful idea.

The conditioning against tech didn't have anything to do with Rosa. It was solely the Agent's problem. Rosa would repeat the process to which the Agent had subjected Valencia—only more kindly, she hoped. She would not keep secrets from the Agent or violently stuff her into some cramped nether space of the mind, but she would be quite content for the Agent to keep to herself all of the weaknesses that the WCE had programmed into her.

There was no place for a tech-disadvantaged human weapon in Rosa's new life in Lakes, and now was the time to adapt. She only had to remember one thing: there was a little child whom she needed to deliver from the WCE. The rest of her life she could cultivate to her liking.

The Agent could recognize an efficient path to survival when she saw one. She sank down, down, down until Rosa found that the conditioning against technology was only a fact, not experience. Well, not her own experience, anyway.

She refocused on the warmth of Pete's hand on her shoulder. She felt most herself with him since he had been the first to know her by her current name. That was as safe of a place as she could create for herself in this life. In a leap of faith, she touched the screen of the web apparatus.

She remained upright in her chair, conscious and alert. So, with a smile, she set up her username and password and proceeded to initiate a secure link to the dark web.

"Holy wow!" Pete whistled. "Seems like you don't even *need* me here. This stuff goes way over my head. I'm going to have tea."

Rosa grabbed his hand and held it on her shoulder while she used her other hand to type new strings of code that would bolster her anonymity.

"Don't move. I'm almost done," she said.

"Okay." He sounded bewildered but not unhappy.

Some time later, she leaned back in her chair and exclaimed, "Ha! Incredible."

"No kidding," Pete said. "You're like a pro, but you borrowed those books only a few days ago, right?"

"Yeah, but I really studied *every* word of them." Rosa stood. "How about that tea?"

"It's about time," Gordon said groggily. "You said we were going to have tea half an hour ago."

"Well, we *would* have if you hadn't fallen asleep on us like an old man," Rosa teased.

He snorted.

She touched the outside of the teapot, admiring the material that made it cool to the touch while steam still trickled from its spout.

Looking at Pete with gratitude, she said, "Gordon, Pete just helped me with some techie stuff while we were waiting out your nap."

Pete looked confused. "I—I didn't do all that much. I mean, I just—"

"He was a real lifesaver," she insisted, as she poured the tea. "I don't know what I would have done without him."

"Good job, Pete," Gordon said, staring at Rosa with a strange look on his face. "Keep making yourself useful and maybe she'll stick around. I'd hate for her to slip from our grip."

She raised her teacup, and her boss and coworker both cheered her good health. Their conversation turned to trivialities such as the weather and the need to order more edible straws, but for the rest of the evening, Rosa could think of nothing other than Gordon's tattoo.

At 0045, Pete yawned loudly.

"Well, Gordon, I'd hate for us to overstay our welcome," he said. "Can I walk you to your car?"

Gordon waved him off. "I'm not a pansy, I mean, a *pacifist*. I'll be alright."

"I'll walk you down, anyway." Pete handed Gordon his coat. "Thanks for having us, Rosa."

She smiled. "Thanks for coming to check on me, guys. It means a lot."

"Thanks for being okay," Gordon said. "Listen, since you've made this miraculous recovery, I'd like you to come in tomorrow night, say around 2000?"

She followed them to the door. "But I thought I'd be off this weekend."

"Uh, yes," he said with a warmer smile than she'd ever seen him smile before. "But I just remembered that we're having butter delivered tomorrow night. And I'll need help getting it all into the freezer in a timely manner. Should only take about half an hour or forty-five minutes, tops. Just helps to have it done before the start of the day. No good trying to portion out butter in the middle of a rush; Pete can tell you."

"It's true," Pete said. "I would join you, but I have to take one of my hens to the vet for her yearly checkup right after closing tomorrow. The appointment's at the edge of the district, so I don't think I can get back by 2000."

Rosa masked her suspicion with a smile. "Oh, alright, Gordon. I think I can spare 'half an hour or forty-five minutes, tops,' especially if I'm being paid for it."

"My kind of employee," Gordon said. "Well, bye!"

Pete began to follow him into the hall but turned back.

"Hey, Rosa," he said hesitantly. "I've been watching you, uh, from my window—I mean, I was wondering if you'd like to—I mean, you seem pretty fit and stuff and, well—"

She didn't know how to help him out of his floundering. Was he asking her to dinner or referring her to his gym?

"What I mean is, I've noticed that you go running every morning—"

Seeing her chance, she offered, "Maybe you can join me this Monday before work? I usually do ten kilometers."

"Yeah, sounds great." He grinned sheepishly. "Good night, Rosa!"

"Good night, Pete," she said.

He didn't make a move for the door.

"I'm getting old out here!" Gordon called to him from the hallway.

Pete snapped out of his reverie and walked out, saying, "Newsflash, Gordon! Rosa said you're *already* old."

"Better old than a pansy."

Rosa chuckled as she closed the door. She looked down at her palms, which were almost back to normal. That was good because she had some work to do. She sat down at the web apparatus.

An incredible thing had happened that evening. Rosa had side-stepped the Killer's anti-tech conditioning simply through compartmentalization paired with positive touch. Yes, she dared to think it: she had liked Pete's warm, gentle touch, and with his unassuming support, she had overwritten her conditioning—hopefully.

Rosa touched the screen, and when she saw that she would remain conscious, she created an algorithm to search the dark web for Gordon Fritz. Other than a mention of his years of military service, there was precious little information about him. There was even less available in public searches.

Gordon's previous military experience should have raised some red flags from the day Rosa had met him. She should have left the district and never looked back. But she couldn't do that now. He had dropped the hint about their coming conversation when he invited her to the restaurant the following night. She couldn't bring herself to leave without going to that conversation. It would be dangerous, yes, but the Agent could not leave unaddressed the possibility that Gordon had been the Phib to transport her son to the WCE.

Rosa sighed, frustrated that even her unphiblike living had not thrown the other Amphibians off her scent. In fact, it had brought her right into the path of another Phib. She heard the faint sound of Pete's happy-go-lucky whistling in the stairwell. He was returning from walking Gordon to his car. For a moment, Rosa felt comforted and warm. Then the door to the third floor closed, and she heard Pete no more.

Her web apparatus chimed and a small, holographic icon of an envelope popped up. It hovered in front of her face, flitting around as her gaze wandered about the room.

She touched the icon with her finger, which initiated an animation of a piece of stationery slipping out of the envelope. The piece of paper twirled around in the air and floated, as if carried on a breeze, until it landed at her feet.

It was a note of only three words, scribed in the same elaborate, looping letters as the note from her housewarming gift.

Watch His Maid

Rosa jumped onto the keyboard and quickly developed a program that could track the source of the message. The search yielded no results.

While she was combing the program for errors, a series of anonymous messages popped up in a plain white box.

> That won't work on me.
>
> Stay connected.
>
> Stay alive.

The white box disappeared. Rackelle Wernicke never would have been so mysterious. It was clear that the mysterious correspondent had eyes on many different players in the game called Survival. And without any knowledge of this person's motives, there was no way to know whether they could be trusted. That was disconcerting enough, but of further concern was the correspondent's confirmation of the Agent's fears about Gordon.

Rosa had been born in sparkling snowfalls, croissants, and holiday parties, and it had been easy to direct her path when all was going well. As she began to feel targeted and powerless, she felt her grip on reality loosening. She held on with all of her mental strength, and instead of sinking down, down, down, she felt compelled to run. So, she burst from her apartment and ran out into the night.

As she tore down the block, she whispered over and over, "Say it again. Say it again."

* * *

Karthik was in his living room, staring at a picture of him and Lenci in a digital frame that sat on the coffee table. The year before, they had spent the holiday at Fairwaves Beach in Diablo. It had been a bizarre day, but the moment captured in that photo was the goodness that kept him going in this difficult time.

The photo was slightly blurry because he and Lenci were falling. Lorenzo had asked them to squat down in the sand, but he had taken forever with the old, point and shoot digital camera. One or the other of them had lost their balance, and both Karthik and Lenci fell sideways just as Lorenzo snapped the picture.

Despite the blurriness, the photo was one of Karthik's favorites. He loved the amusement, the bliss, and the surprise in their faces. And he loved it that he and Lenci, for once in their adult lives, were reaching toward each other. For just a precious moment, they were frantic to be near one another, frantic for the stability of the other's presence and support. Yes, it was a very precious moment.

"Missing her again?" Maude asked, turning the picture facedown on the table.

He didn't respond as she sat on the couch beside him.

"She only ever brought down your status with her loud-mouthed critiques of the classification system," she said. "The WCE puts that kind of female on a list, you know."

Karthik took the picture from the table and gazed at it broodingly.

"She held you back then, but you don't have to let her hold you back now." Maude took the picture from him and placed it back on the table. "She kept you on society's margins with her, but *I* can bring you into the center where you belong."

He began tapping his fingers on his knees, from thumb to pinky and pinky to thumb, but Maude took his hands in hers and intertwined their fingers. She kissed him with a hunger that fed him deeply.

Every day, Karthik felt as if his heart were being ripped out again and again. And this—whatever it was with Maude—filled the hole. Suddenly overcome with a passion that scared him as much as it excited him, he pulled her body closer to his.

She drew back and said, "Set a date with me, E.J."

He sighed. "Why do you keep pushing this on me?"

"We're living together, and I met your 'like a second family,'" she said, pursing her lips. "I'm ready to be your wife."

"I just need some time," he told her.

Maude regarded him disappointedly for a moment, then smiled and stroked his hair.

"I don't know what you need time for, E.J.," she said sweetly. "More of the Eastern States are becoming unaffiliated, so they can adopt that law about subbers taking on the class of their spouse. I could make you 4.14 by association."

He chuckled humorlessly. "Because you wouldn't want to be married to a member of the Subclass."

"I wouldn't have to be, if we got married in the Free East," she said, pecking him on the cheek. "Besides, you present like a 4.14 well enough. We'd at least keep the appearance of 'keeping the average.'"

He flinched away from her, saying, "Your maternal grandmother is Class 1, so your mom *and* you would be subclass if anyone official knew."

Maude huffed. "*Someone* official knew, but that all got erased when my parents proved their commitment to the Neo-Eugenic ideals as adapted by the 4.14 community."

"Proved with their money?" he asked bitterly.

"With their well-known scientific discoveries and involvement in politics, of course, although I'm sure their wealth didn't hurt," she said. "Anyway, if you marry me, our children and all of our associations will be 4.14s, and your father's indiscretion will be forgotten."

"That ind—discretion is my family!" Karthik retorted.

"What family?" Maude shot back at him. "Your mother is dead, and your Class 3 'family' doesn't even acknowledge you. I'm just saying that if you marry me, you could have a place to belong with people who look like you—as is proper and right."

Karthik wanted to tell her that his Class 3 family—especially his mother—was none of her business, but he swallowed his anger and decided to come at the issue from a different angle.

"D—doesn't it feel wrong t—to cut off a whole side of your family?" he asked. "You have Class 1 and subclass cousins whose existence you completely ignore."

Maude looked like she had never thought of it that way before, but her moment of revelation was short-lived.

"Here's the point, E.J.," she said. "My parents proved they were *assets* to the Class 4.14 community, not societal contaminants like other watered down blood. Usefulness is the main currency of the community, and status is what's most useful. You *do* understand that it's an issue of status more than genetics, right?"

"Status," he echoed, the word souring on his tongue. "And what contribution do I bring that makes me *useful?*"

"Well, you do work for a prominent law enforcement agency," she said. Then, with an impish smile, she added, "And you're incredibly fine."

She kissed him lightly on the lips and patted his shoulder. He outwardly smiled, but he felt like his insides had been scraped out.

CHAPTER 15

"Say that again," the Agent growled, stretching her legs so that the laser net became hot again.

"Say it again," the Agent whispered through the burning pain in her legs.

"Hey!" Someone grabbed her wrist.

The Agent pulled her assailant off-balance and kicked at his abdomen. Displaying excellent reflexes, he caught her foot and held onto it.

"Holy wow, Rosa!" she heard Pete Bae's voice say as she unleashed another combination of strikes. "It's just me: Pacifist Pete! Hey, I've only got two hands to hold you off with!"

Embarrassed beyond belief, Rosa stopped swinging at her coworker. "Oh, Pete! I'm sorry. I don't know what got into me."

"You look like you've seen a ghost." His face was full of concern.

He had almost assuredly noticed that she was wearing the same clothes as she had been when he last saw her. It had been night when he'd left her apartment, but now the sun was climbing well above the horizon.

"Out for your run?" he asked.

She nodded, suddenly feeling weak in the knees. Her body was shuddering but not from cold, not even from fear anymore. She began to collapse, and he caught her forearm to steady her.

"I'm okay," she said. "Just finishing up. Need to stretch is all."

Pete put her arm around his waist and began walking her back to the apartment complex. "You're drenched. When'd you start?"

He was very warm.

"Hm?"

"Your run. When'd you start running?"

"Uh, maybe 0100."

Judging from the position of the sun, Rosa figured she'd been circling Frin's Place in a haywire flight response for at least seven hours. She hadn't stopped for water. She hadn't stopped for anything, until Pete had interrupted and nearly gotten his liver bruised. Although she was too exhausted to look her coworker in the face, she could tell from his deep, controlled breathing that he was holding back many admonishments.

Good. She wasn't a child and therefore did not need a lecture on healthy exercise habits.

"Let's get you home," Pete said, opening the door to the western stairwell.

Even with Pete's support, Rosa felt like millstones were attached to her ankles, and each laborious step was more painful than the last. This was not the life that the Agent had envisioned when she leapt from the train in the snow. She had expected that she would be able to live a life free of broken bones and bloody conversations as she strategized about how to find her son. But she was going to have a conversation with Gordon that evening that, if she survived it, would mean losing this small semblance of a life that she had managed to cultivate. She wished she'd been more intentional about enjoying this little life.

When they got to her apartment, Rosa ignored Pete's suggestion that she have some orange juice. She went to the kitchen sink and drank water straight from the faucet. Soon, her dizziness dissipated, and she was able to keep her balance.

"I should probably shower," she told Pete. "Thank you for helping me out."

"Happy to help," he said, moving for the door. "See you later."

Before she knew what she was doing, Rosa caught him by the hand.

"Don't go," she said. "I'll only be a couple minutes."

She pushed him into the armchair where he sat in dazed contentment. Then she showered, pulled on a pair of stockings, and slipped into her pink, frilly dress. She glanced in the bathroom mirror to ensure that she looked innocent and unphiblike enough, then curtseyed.

When she returned to the common area, the armchair was empty. Pete was in the kitchen, beating some eggs. A wonderful aroma filled the room.

"Egg drop soup," he announced.

She looked into the pot on the stove. "This is great. It's almost like the kind I grew up eating."

He smiled goofily. "It's so weird that you eat things like this."

"No weirder than you eating it," she replied, grabbing some scallions out of the fridge and handing them to him. "Your dad *was* Class 2, was he not?"

"Well, yeah." He went to the sink to wash the scallions. "But so was my mom."

Ignoring his assumption that the woman of the house would be the main cook, Rosa stayed the course with respect to Pete's exploration of interclass relations. So often one had to pick and choose which line of thought to pursue in a conversation of this kind.

"People can learn to cook dishes of other people groups," she said, turning to search through the cupboard for sesame oil. "It's called cultural exchange."

"Oh." He grabbed a knife from the dish drainer and looked around for a cutting board. "Is that like appropriation?"

"Not exactly," she said. "Invitation, respect, and love arc usually involved. Cabinet next to the stove."

"Thanks." He began chopping the scallions in pensive silence.

As the broth came to a full boil, Rosa poured the eggs into it and watched the convection currents froth the eggs into the shape of a flower with innumerable, feathery petals. When she tasted the soup, she remembered a childhood in Diablo and a family whom she had hurt terribly.

It needed white pepper.

The Agent crossed the kitchen to the seasoning cabinet, trying to pry the past's cold, clammy fingers off of her mind. She was not in Diablo anymore. She was far away from the Changs and the Wilsons, where she could no longer bring them into harm's way. She needed to think of her son and of surviving that evening's conversation with Gordon. A stunt like Rosa's flight response the previous evening would not be effective. She would have to fight.

When she turned to go back to the stove, she found herself face-to-face with Pete. He might have been looking for some salt. He seemed lost, anyway. But when he saw her troubled expression, a friendly grin spread across his face.

"You alright?" he asked.

The past was gone. It had to be.

As she stuffed it back where it belonged, Rosa returned his smile. "What do you mean?"

"I don't know," he said. "You just looked sad."

A bit of truth would be enough to satisfy his curiosity.

"My son was taken by some bad people," she said. "I think about him a lot."

Pete looked perplexed. He was processing all of this new information: that she had a son, that she had tragically lost him, and that her child was probably the reason that she was a floater at all.

"They're telling me he's dead, but I don't believe them," Rosa said, shrugging back her tears.

"I'm sorry," Pete said. "I hope you find him."

"I intend to," she replied.

With a little hop, she pulled herself onto an unused portion of the counter and took a long look into Pete's earnest face. There was something about his good-humored, glass-half-full, believe-the-best attitude that beckoned to her. In him, she did not see the loss that she saw in the mirror, the loss that had smothered every other area of her life. Pacifist Pete—who had gotten mugged and spent his free time caring for urban chickens and tried to make everyone's day better with a hug—was so utterly untainted by the treachery and betrayal that had become the only relational occurrences she expected with any certainty.

Driven by a desperate longing, she threw her arms around his neck and pressed her lips onto his. Pete, though caught off guard, promptly began to kiss her back. His warm hands caressed her so gently that she felt pain—or maybe it was sorrow. She could not remember the last time she had been touched so tenderly. Maybe she had never at all been touched quite like that.

Up to that point, physical contact had been the main tool of those who sought to dominate her as well as the means by which she negotiated her own survival. However, while she couldn't quite define what was happening with Pete, it didn't feel like domination or negotiation. It felt like something warmer. Between passionate kisses and hot, desperate breaths, she ran her hands up underneath his shirt. His warmth radiated onto her, melting away the past to expose her great, incomprehensible need.

Rosa tried to ignore the intensifying uneasiness she felt as Pete's hands slid up her stockinged legs. She figured he probably wouldn't notice her scars because his attention was—otherwise engaged. Slowly and with great relish, she began rolling up his shirt on his body.

"Oh!" Pete caught her hands and pulled back abruptly.

Chest heaving, he tugged his shirt down over the waist of his pants and ran his hands through his hair. Thoughts raced across his face at a million times a second. It seemed that he had liked where this was heading, and yet—and yet.

Rosa straightened the neckline of her dress, trying to make a graceful transition away from what had clearly been a massive misjudgment on her part.

"I'm sorry," she said sheepishly. "Too soon?"

"Sorry," Pete panted. "I just wasn't thinking—"

She didn't need him to elaborate. She had pushed him to give something that he had not been ready to give. Despite his open demeanor, Pete—like any other person—had restricted spaces to which she could not assume he would grant her access.

"No, I shouldn't have assumed." Rosa smiled and hopped off of the counter. "I apologize, really."

"No, don't," he replied. "I liked it. I like *you*. I'm just—"

"Not ready," she finished, fluffing out her frilly dress. "I get it."

The Agent thought it fortunate that all of the excitement had ceased before Pete had a chance to remove her stockings. After all, her scars were a fairly unique identifier, and Pete seemed just like the honest kind of person to unwittingly blow her cover her to any inquiring party.

He looked out the window and grinned. "It's snowing again, Rosa! Maybe as a Diablan, you wouldn't know this, but *fresh* snow is the best snow. And I've still got a couple hours before work, so let's go play!"

An olive branch. After they had donned their coats, Rosa extended her arm, and Pete hooked it immediately with his own. They walked down the yellow, steel staircase to the lawn behind the building where they stayed a good while, trampling every fluffy patch of undisturbed snow into a mess of powder. As they did so, the past was far from Rosa, and the present was pleasant enough to stave off the future for just a little longer.

* * *

"Yeah, I took care of the agency jet, and commercial flights are obviously out of the question," Theresa said as she adjusted the climate control buttons in her luxury auto-car. "So, their only choice is to drive. You have them right where you want them. Have you finalized with Wernicke yet?"

"I will soon," said the woman on the other end of the call. "Can you verify that she has the canister?"

"I'm about to." Theresa peered out into the darkness beyond her headlights. "I'm pulling up at her house now, and I think she is, too. Lee-Smith told me to get the canister from Wernicke and load it into the rental car. "

"And you received the virus?"

"Everything's in place, B.F.," Theresa reassured her. "I'll monitor the car from the moment it leaves the Coop, and I can even retrieve the canister once the deed is done. I'll bring it to you myself."

"Our operatives will retrieve the canister," B.F. said. "Just do your part."

Theresa gave an exaggerated sigh. "It's sad that you don't trust me with something this simple, but I'll prove my loyalty. You'll see."

"Don't fail us." The line went dead.

Theresa was still getting used to the WCE's not-so-veiled threats, especially those of the Amphibian with whom she most often interfaced. But that was the price of working with the elites of the world. And if she was going to prove that she had what it took to be a WCE operative, she needed to complete this assignment with the utmost precision.

She saw Racky running up the porch steps. Racky waved to her before entering the house, leaving the front door ajar. Theresa gathered her belongings and trudged up the porch steps.

"Knock, knock!" she said, stepping inside the house.

She heard the top drawer of Racky's desk slamming shut in her office down the hall. When Theresa peeked into the room, she saw Racky hiding the drawer's key in the flowerpot behind her desk.

Pretending not to notice, Theresa entered and sat nonchalantly across the desk from her teammate. "So, I never asked you about how that trip to Diablo went, and we never got an official debrief presentation."

"It was okay," Racky said as she rifled through the mess of papers and files on her desk. "Esperanza was sad and lonely, so wish I could have stayed longer. But what can you do?"

Theresa yawned. "Indeed, what? So, did you find anything interesting while you were there or just the canister?"

Racky's gaze briefly flickered toward the top drawer of her desk before she resumed her search. When she found Gustav's color flashcards under a book, she breathed a sigh of relief.

"Only the canister," she said.

"Well, alright, then." Theresa made a mental note to visit Racky's house again at some point in the near future.

Racky's flake chimed. "It's B.F.! At last!"

"Congratulations," Theresa said. "And might I say, it's quite impressive that you're able to chat on the dark web from your flake."

"Perks of being a tech genius," Racky said, typing as she talked. "Oh, they're trying to haggle now. Give me a minute."

Theresa smirked, but Racky didn't notice. B.F. really had her agitated.

After a very tense minute of typing, Racky finally let out a deep breath. "Okay, we're all set for three days from now, 1600, at Home. Can you message Blair and K. and let them know that everything's a 'go' for tomorrow?"

Theresa nodded, taking out her flake. "Making the swap at 1600 that day will be more than enough time when leaving from here. You could probably meet in the morning, if you wanted."

"Yeah, but I'm hoping this will give us time to snoop around before we make the exchange. We need to have some kind of intel to bring back, too, you know."

Racky continued talking about how much she hoped the team would get information about the origin and function of the Amphibians, but Theresa tuned her out. She had heard all of that before. Instead, she was thinking about the spare house key that Racky always left underneath the lawn gnome sitting on her doorstep.

CHAPTER 16

The Agent arrived at The Sweetest Rose at 1945, having changed out of her frilly dress and into her work clothes. Gordon's car was not parked outside, and the door was locked. So, the Agent broke the pantry window in order to gain access to the kitchen. She was familiar enough with the space, but she wanted to make sure that her treacherous boss had not changed the layout in order to gain an advantage.

The prep area was dark and silent but for the hum of the refrigerators. Everything was clean and ready for another day of work. Only a couple of pairs of tongs, some wax paper, and a rubber spatula were out of place. The Agent cringed at the idea of death by spatula, but she had undoubtedly seen worse in her days with the Killer.

She sat on a footstool to wait for her boss and wondered what she would say when he arrived. She figured that Gordon, if that was really his name, might actually be willing to reason with her since they had worked together for the past few weeks. If not, the Agent wondered how she might obtain information about his agency symbol in order to utilize his Song to defuse him.

Of course, Gordon likely would not appreciate being compromised in that way. And since there was a chance that he could fly into a murderous rage upon hearing his Song, the Agent decided that she should prioritize the solicitation of any information about her son. Information about Gordon's mark would have to remain of secondary importance.

A key turned in the back door lock.

"Hello, Gordon," the Agent said, standing.

"Whoa!" He dropped the stack of boxes he was carrying. "You're early!"

He fumbled with his keys and the boxes. Each time he picked up one box, he dropped another. With this flustered response, he was trying to disarm the Agent, but she wouldn't be fooled by his theatrically clumsy entry.

"I figured I'd see what I was working with," she said, motioning to the utensils on the counter.

"Oh, yeah," he said dismissively. "By all means, choose your weapon. Whatever you feel most comfortable with."

The Agent gave him a scrutinizing glance. This was not at all how she expected this confrontation to unfold. Gordon was much too casual and open about the whole thing. Still, she imagined that every Phib had his or her own distinct flavor.

She slid the spatula off of the counter. As she thought about the possibilities, she much preferred for that tool to be in own her hands.

"Excellent choice," Gordon said, placing the largest of his boxes on the counter. "We'll just have to see how it'll stand up against the butter."

"Butter," the Agent repeated with a coy smile. "Are we still going on about that? I think we both know the real reason we're here tonight."

"Come on," he responded, ripping the tape off of the package. "You've got to let me do this at my own pace. I've really thought this out."

"Have it your way," she said. She twiddled her spatula and watched bemusedly as he pulled out some champagne glasses and a basket of chocolate-covered strawberries.

He set his devices of trickery on the counter and delved back into the box for more. "You're a very special fem—er, woman, you know that, Rosa?"

"So, I've been told." At last, they were getting down to business.

He opened the bottle of champagne and poured half a glass for each of them.

"Are you quite sure we should start this way?" the Agent asked, thinking of how she had nearly lost her life in Carmelita because of her impaired reflexes. "People in our line of work must have our wits about us. We are, after all, held to the highest standards of precision."

He chuckled, raising his glass to her. "Well, as your boss, I can't force you to drink my champagne. But I hope you won't begrudge me indulging in a little liquid courage myself."

As he knocked the drink back, the mark on his inner arm became visible. Seizing her chance, the Agent poked the tattoo with her spatula, causing Gordon to choke on his drink.

"You're going to wash that before you use it, right?" he asked.

"I actually prefer to work with my hands." She grabbed his right arm, twisted it behind his head, and kicked his knees.

With a sickening crunch, he fell to the floor. When he squawked in protest, she shoved the rubber end of the spatula into his mouth.

"Now, hopefully, we can do this the easy way," she said, "I'm just looking for some information."

Although she had left his other arm completely free, he did not make a move for her. His arm trembled, like he was actually resisting his defensive reflexes. Additionally, he did not seem very well able to manage pain. His eyes were watering, and he gagged pitifully on the spatula, which had been a tad too large to fit in his mouth. The Agent had made it fit.

Maybe his pain management just needed a while to activate because he'd been undercover so long. Well, hurting him brought the Agent no pleasure. The sooner she was done with this part, the sooner she could be on her way.

"*Where'd* they *take* my *son?*" she demanded.

He gagged on the spatula again, so she removed it. However, remembering the manner in which Hinny had cut short her last interrogation, the Agent caught hold of Gordon's jaw and forced his mouth to stay open.

"Can't take any chances," she said, using the handle of the spatula to move his tongue out of the way. He grunted and began to writhe, but she tightened her grip on his jaw and said, "I'm just looking for the tooth. Don't make me remove your whole lower row."

When she turned his mouth toward the light, she was puzzled to find that none of his molars had a WCE insignia on them. The Killer had specifically requested that *she* not be equipped with a cyanide tooth in order to lower her suicide risk during their tour. It was possible that Gordon's handler had done the same for him. Maybe none of the Phibs had the tooth. With pain management, there should be little need for one. She released him, and he crumbled onto his side.

"Rosa, what are you doing?" Gordon asked with wide eyes and a pale face. His lower lip was even trembling slightly.

It seemed that Gordon did not know what he was. Whether he had rearranged his memory for survival's sake or someone else had done it to him, the Agent did not know. He would need a gentle ramp up to rediscover the truth.

"What animal is this?" she asked, poking his mark with the spatula.

Confusion overran his face, and his breaths were rapid. "It's a gecko—from my tour in the Sovereign Nation of Hawai'i."

"A gecko," she said, "not some kind of *amphibian?*"

He shook his head. "What's that got to do with anything?"

"It's clear that you were trained to be dependent on conventional weapons," she said, moving over to the smaller boxes that Gordon had brought with him. "So, let's take a look at your *mail* and see what you had planned for me tonight."

She ripped open the first box and was shocked to find another box inside it. The inner box was labeled: **Butter**.

"Cute," she said, opening the butter-labeled box and dumping out its contents.

Six industrial-sized blocks of butter spilled out onto the floor.

Horrified, Rosa tore into the other boxes. Both contained butter. That, in conjunction with the fact that Gordon had not yet found a way to attack her, convinced Rosa that her boss was not a Phib. He didn't even have any pain management. Poor Gordon had actually intended to spend that evening drinking champagne and packaging butter for the freezer.

"What are you into, kid?" he sputtered. "You in trouble or something?"

"I'm so sorry," Rosa whispered, kneeling by him. "You've been so good to me, Gordon."

And with that, she banged his head on the floor and knocked him out. With some duct tape she'd found under the sink, she fastened his hands behind his back and his feet to each other. She used a piece of tape to cover his mouth and wrapped it around his head a couple of times.

Then she took his phone and messaged Pete to announce that there was water damage in the dining room and that the restaurant would be closed the next day for repairs. Hopefully, that would give her a decent head start. Pete would come into the restaurant in two days and find Gordon, and Gordon would be okay. With the advanced medical care in Lakes, he would be as good as new within a few weeks. Maybe he'd even get bionic knee replacements this time around.

The Agent leaned him against the shelves in the pantry, then closed and locked the door. She hurried out of the restaurant and tossed his phone into the dumpster behind the building.

* * *

It was accursed sentiment that brought the Agent named Rosa to Pete Bae's door when every bit of her training dictated that she should be in the wind. She had only known Pete for a short while, but he had made an impression by helping her to become aware of feelings besides pain. The last person who had done that—well, he was of no consequence in this life. But leaving him had been like tearing out a piece of her own heart.

A bit of Rosa would remain in Lakes, even after the Agent had departed. She linked her pinkies for a moment, then took off her satchel containing the web apparatus and its fancy attachments and placed it on the doormat. She planned to take her chances returning to an untraceable, low-tech life in the Western States. In the West, she would be able to get information on her son the old-fashioned way. So, it made sense to unload the machine, and she wanted to give it to the person who had enabled her to use it.

The space beneath Pete's door was dark. It appeared that he was still across the district, attending to his chicken's health. That came as a bit of a relief.

"Goodbye," Rosa whispered, "and thank you."

Suddenly, the space beneath the door illuminated, and before the Agent could take evasive action, the door swung open.

"Pete Bae!" Rosa gasped. "I didn't know you were here!"

"Evidently not, or you probably would have knocked," he grinned.

She drank in the sight of him, goofy, unaware, and wonderful. "I just came to—to—"

"Well, you don't need an excuse to come see me, especially after this morning," he said, motioning for her to enter. "But, if you don't mind, you're letting out all the heat."

"Oh." She really needed to get on the road, but Pete's warm, innocent presence was a welcome salve after her conversation with Gordon.

She stepped inside wearily.

"You alright?" He was quite emotionally aware.

That was not so welcome.

"I'm fine," she said.

She studied him as she sat down on his couch. His T-shirt was damp, and he looked fatigued.

"You look kind of frustrated yourself," she said. "Everything okay?"

"Yeah," he said, sitting down next to her.

On the cushion between them, there was an open package with a bunch of tissue paper hanging out of it. Pete looked at it with a hint of annoyance. Rosa eyed the package as well, resenting that it reminded her of her faulty suspicions about Gordon's mail—and about Gordon himself.

Pete continued, "I just got back from taking my hen to the vet a few minutes ago. I jogged back to this neighborhood instead of hailing a car. Want some tea?"

Before she could answer, he stood up, taking the package with him. He placed it on the windowsill on his way to the kitchen.

"Ginger good for you, Rosa?" he asked with his head in the cabinet.

"That'll warm me up, for sure!" she said. "It's good for circulation."

"And digestion," he added, filling the kettle from the faucet.

She smiled at him, but her eyes wandered back to the package on the windowsill. There was something about it that troubled her beyond the fact that she had misjudged Gordon. She had been warned to watch "his" mail. Of course, her mysterious correspondent might have known that she was employed by Gordon, but how could she have watched *Gordon's* mail other than that which came through the restaurant?

No, no, it was simpler than that. It had been right in front of her, or downstairs from her, the whole time. She reminded herself that, although Pete had been living in that building before she had, he had also been the one to recommend the place to her.

"So, Rosa, I was thinking that tomorrow, we could—" Pete paused to look at his flake. "Oh, I should get this."

The Agent named Rosa nodded, and when he retreated to the far corner of his kitchen to answer the call, she crept over to take a peek inside of the package on the windowsill.

"Gordon?" Pete said, sounding alarmed. "Slow down. Are you okay?"

As she peeled back the wrapping paper, dread sank into her bones. Nestled in the paper was the body of a dead fire salamander, gutted and limp. It was a message that she could decipher, but it was not meant for her.

"Rosa did *what*?"

Gordon's military training had enabled him to free himself sooner than she had intended, and now he was blowing her cover. She threw open the window. Three stories would have to be not too far to fall. The front door was too close to the kitchen and to Pete. He was telling Gordon that he hadn't seen her, and she knew why.

"Rosa, stop!"

She didn't look back at him before leaping. As she plummeted toward the ground, she thought of the web apparatus that she had left in the satchel on his doormat. She remembered it and released the memory.

That evening's drop in temperature had caused the ground to ice over. Her feet broke through the icy snow and hit the cold, hard ground—yet another reminder that snow definitely was not as soft of a landing as it appeared to be. The impact reverberated up her legs and into her pelvis, almost certainly causing decent-sized fractures.

The Agent looked up at the man who had been sent to kill her.

"Rosa!" he yelled again.

He was surprised and hurt, but he was not confused. He knew what she was, just as she knew what he was. They were the elite of the elite, set in an unnatural and unkind opposition for the sake of pride and power.

The Agent had so many questions for Pete, foremost how he always managed to be so cheerful and, of course, if he knew anything regarding the whereabouts of her son. But now was not the time to conduct an interrogation. She was his target, so she had to take evasive action until she could regain the advantage.

She tore her gaze away from his and willed her legs to move. Running through the knee-deep snow made her legs feel like lead. Behind her, there was a loud, rolling crunch, indicating that Pete also had jumped from his third floor window. He had been more prudent about his landing, probably because he did not have the same ability to heal as she did. In rapid, crunching footsteps, he began closing the distance between them.

His crunching stopped about ten meters behind the Agent, but she continued onward without looking back. Shortly thereafter, two gunshots shook the night air.

The Agent didn't bother to dodge as a couple of bullet holes appeared in the snow in front of her. She brushed aside her surprise that Pete, despite having undergone the same basic training as any Amphibian, was able to operate a firearm. In any case, he'd left his apartment in a hurry. Chances were that he hadn't had time to grab extra ammunition. The Agent hoped that she could outlast however many bullets he had left.

That hope was short-lived. Another shot rang out, and she felt the impact in her right shoulder. Recognizing her need for cover, she made for the wooded area behind Frin's Place. Pete's swift footfalls resumed, which was sort of good news because he had to focus on running rather than shooting.

When the Agent reached the edge of the wooded area, Pete's short, intense breaths could be heard no more than three meters behind her. He was within two meters, no, one meter of her when she heard him strain. She jumped, fully extending her body, and grabbed the nearest tree. She swung around it, aiming for Pete's face with her heels.

He batted her away with his forearms, and the force sent the gun flying from his hands. It landed in the snow with a weak crackle. That bought the Agent the half-second she needed to hightail it into the shadows.

Pete didn't waste time trying to retrieve his gun. As a Phib, he *was* the weapon. He chased the Agent in and out of the trees, which she sometimes used to pivot and change direction. But he didn't appear to be thrown off by her swiveling. Somehow, he could anticipate her little tricks. He kept up with her every move, and too soon, he was again within an arm's length of her. There was a loud crunch as he crouched in preparation to lunge at her.

She kicked back at him, but he caught her leg and brought her to the ground. When he moved in to pin her on her back, she kneed him in the chin and then kicked him in the shoulder. He reeled backward and grabbed onto the base of a slim tree branch for balance. Once steadied, he effortlessly snapped the branch off of the tree.

"You should never have come here, *Rosa*," he said, his voice deeper and richer than it had been before, "if that's even your name."

He swung at her, and she dodged right into his weapon. He was so fast that she could not very well predict the trajectory of his strikes.

Everything about the way that he moved seemed perfectly normal in one sense, but he changed direction incredibly quickly. As a consequence, he could react to her reactions to his strikes before they had even been fully executed.

She grabbed his branch, and it broke such that she had the bigger piece. But Pete had the sharper end. Before he could stab her, she rammed him into a nearby tree. Their wooden weapons fell to the ground.

Pete shoved the Agent off of him and unleashed a combination of high kicks. She ducked to take out his supporting leg, but he spun out of the way and stomped on her ankle mid-sweep. A sound ensued, somewhere between a pop and a crack. The joint was broken, for sure.

It was beyond a shadow of a doubt that Pete had made a space for himself among the WCE's best by virtue of his extraordinary reflexes and agility. The Agent had learned him, but she simply was not fast enough to gain an advantage over him. She would need a different strategy in order to survive this fight.

Pete retrieved the long end of the broken branch, and the Agent pulled herself to her feet. She felt no pain, but her left ankle could take no weight.

As he approached her, she told him, "You don't have to do this."

"Yes, I do," he said, striking the tip of the branch to transform it into a long, rugged knife. "I'll never be able to live in peace otherwise."

She dodged two of his strikes effectively, but she had to buy some time if she wanted to get any distance between them. On his third strike, having observed that he left his face unguarded whenever he stabbed at her, she conceded a wound in her left shoulder so that she could headbutt him.

As he stumbled backward, she leapt into the nearest tree. It was a small but sturdy evergreen with plenty of branches, and most importantly, it was taller than Pete was. The Agent's one-legged leap got her to the second branch from the ground. She pulled herself up into the shadowy cover, and she didn't stop there; she climbed. About three meters up, she found that she could easily reach the branches of a couple of neighboring trees. She crawled across to another tree, trying to make as little noise as possible.

Pete had retrieved his firearm and was crunching around the base of her tree. The gun was a six-shooter. Two bullets were in the snow and one was in the Agent's shoulder, which meant that there could only be three bullets left in gun's cylinder.

"I should've known it would be you," Pete laughed bitterly. "Your irresistible charm, the way you were just 'floating through,' your combat skills—I just didn't want to believe it."

He paused right below her, but he wasn't looking up. He was listening, possibly for her breathing. She held her breath.

"You must've been in tech," he continued, crunching a few steps forward. "Is that how you found me? Hacking into traffic cameras? The only elevator I've taken in this district is Frin's, which he swears is immune to hackers."

Found him? The Agent inched back the way she had come, hoping that Pete would assume that she wasn't stupid enough to run in such small circles. She saw a branch just above her that would enable her to swing to the tree on the other side of the one she'd first climbed. She stretched her stiff, cold fingers to reach for it. The branch beneath her creaked, and a gunshot quickly followed. There was a bullet hole in the tree trunk about six centimeters from her head.

Immediately, she swung backward out of the path of the next bullet. Hanging by her knees, she found herself staring down the barrel of Pete's gun. She threw her hands sloppily around his and forced the gun to the right of her head just as it discharged. That was the last bullet. Although her head was reeling from the proximity of the noise, the Agent knocked the gun from Pete's grip. It landed a couple of meters away.

Pete lunged at the Agent. She flipped off of the branch and caught his head between her knees to bring him to the ground.

This was where the Agent finally gained the advantage. While Pete was fast and agile, his understanding of grappling and submission holds was rudimentary. With their bodies pressed together, the Agent was able to feel his intention and predict his next moves— switch-ups included—with ease. She used his basic survival instincts to maneuver him limb by limb into a crucifix hold, then rolled him into a choke.

"Why couldn't you just let me live in peace?" he asked, struggling to loosen her hold. "I wasn't hindering WCE activities. I just wanted to be left alone."

"That's a little hard to believe with you hunting me!" the Agent replied. She tightened her chokehold.

"*Hunting* you?" He coughed. "You mean defending myself?"

This would be an interesting story to hear, if there were any truth to it.

She released him and stared incredulously as he fought for his breath. "You *were* assigned to kill me, were you not?"

He rolled over to face her. "*You're* Fire Salamander?"

There was no good answer to that.

CHAPTER 17

"I can't believe I'm doing this," Pete said, helping the Agent up.

He left her balancing on her good foot, so he could retrieve his gun. He tucked the weapon into his pants and covered it with his shirt.

Then he returned to her said, "Well, let's go."

"How do I know this fight is really over?" she asked, eyeing him warily.

"You don't," he replied, "but you won't make it very far running from me on that floppy ankle. Now, come on."

There was no arguing with that. She leaned on Pete for support, and they slowly made their way out of the trees and up to Frin's Place.

As they were passing the front entrance, Frin leaned out the door with a concerned look on his face. "You kids okay?"

Rosa glanced at Pete's bruised neck and disheveled appearance. She was glad that her shoulder with the gunshot wound was hidden in his side.

"Yes," she said, searching for an explanation that would account for all of their injuries. "We were playing hide-and-seek tag in the woods, and I fell out of a tree—onto Pete. Good thing he broke my fall, too. It could have been a lot worse for me."

"Hide-and-seek tag, hey? In the woods. At night." Frin looked at each of them once more, then smiled broadly. "Well, I'm glad you kids are okay. I heard gunshots out there and thought, for sure, Pete'd been mugged again."

"Does the whole district know about that?" Rosa asked, looking mischievously at Pete.

He sighed. "It's hard being a pacifist."

"Poor, *helpless* soul," she said. Then to Frin, "Don't worry. I'll get him home."

"Handle him with kid gloves, hey, Rosa?" he laughed.

"Absolutely." Her voice rose to a squeak as she accidentally stepped on her bad ankle and pitched forward.

Without missing a beat, Pete stepped forward to support her.

"You kids aren't trying to go up the stairs like that, are you?" Frin asked. "I know Rosa hasn't been too fond of our *very modern and lavish elevators*, but it seems to me that if you were going to try them out any time, tonight—"

"That's a great idea," Pete said, steering Rosa into the lobby. "Let's take the elevator."

"But—" she began.

"Really, Rosa," Pete said loudly enough for Frin to hear, "taking the elevators just this once won't hurt. I know you *love* exercise, but with that sprain, you've got to be kind to your body."

Frin sat down at his desk. "He's right, Rosa. Give 'em a try. They don't bite!"

"Thanks, Frin!" Pete said, ushering Rosa down the hall. "Good night!"

"Good night, kids." Frin chuckled and turned on his radio.

When the Agent was sure that Frin wouldn't hear over his smooth jazz, she elbowed Pete in the ribs.

"Hey!" he exclaimed, pulling up his shirt to examine the purple and green blotch that she had struck.

"Are you crazy?" she whispered. "I don't know about you, but there are people *hunting* me."

"I promise you won't get caught from this," he told her. "You'll be glad you saw it."

She sighed and reluctantly hobbled the rest of the way to the elevators with him. There was one waiting for them with its doors open. It looked benign enough.

"I'll find a way to kill your speedy behind if you compromise me with something as stupid as this," she grumbled.

"Noted," he replied. "Now, please step in."

The doors closed behind them. Then the walls lit up with green light, and a red scan ray enveloped them.

"Scan in progress," a synthetic voice droned.

"Damn it, Pete!" The Agent slammed him into the wall.

He caught her forearm as she attempted to jam it into his already bruised throat.

"Listen," he said.

The red lights of the scanner passed over them three times.

Finally, the elevator beeped. "Scan complete. Live cargo for delivery to Floor 3."

The colorful lights faded to white, and the Agent could feel the elevator moving upward.

"Live cargo?" she repeated. He nodded.

The elevator doors opened on the third floor with a friendly chirp, and Pete helped the Agent named Rosa down the hall to his apartment. Seeing that there were two cups of tea sitting on the kitchen table, she excitedly hopped forward on one foot.

"I bet it's just the right temperature!" she said.

"No!" Pete dove in front of her and grabbed the cups.

In answer to her puzzled look, he explained, "I, uh, prepared these when I thought you'd been sent to reprogram me."

She didn't mean to laugh, but she couldn't help it. "I'm sorry, it's just you thought—I thought—and you had—"

There wasn't much breath leftover between pulses of laughter for her to convey anything of much significance. In any case, the absurdity of the situation pretty much spoke for itself. Pete seemed like he wanted to smile or laugh, but he wouldn't allow it.

He motioned for her to sit on the couch, then went to the kitchen to dump the tea in the sink. "I'll put the kettle on again and get new cups."

She shrugged, pulling off her boots, and elevated her broken ankle. It was swollen and bruised, but she had seen worse. This was definitely not how she had envisioned her evening, but it was quite a welcome surprise—at least, after the bit where she and Pete had tried to kill each other.

Pete returned from the kitchen and sat down beside her.

She looked at him expectantly. "So, why did the elevator scanners equate us to a crate of lobsters going to a restaurant?"

He shook his head. "Let's talk about you. I brought you here on good faith that you actually are Fire Salamander."

"Fine." She undid her pants and began to roll down the waist of her tights.

"Hey, hey, hey!" Pete exclaimed. "What are you doing with those?"

She rolled her eyes. "I promise not to strangle you with my tights. You wanted to see my mark, did you not?"

He nodded.

"Okay, then." She slipped out of her pants and tights and set them on the floor.

"I don't understand," he said, staring at her scarred legs. "Where's your mark?"

"It *used* to be right here." She pointed to an area on her left hip that was covered only with cream-colored, scarred skin.

With wide eyes, Pete said, "You're the one the Killer renamed. There were rumors, but no one knew who—"

"I moved beyond that name." She folded her good leg under her. "Now, let's see. Judging from your shielding this morning, I'm going to take a wild guess and say that your mark is right there."

She touched the right side of his chest.

He smiled wryly and removed his shirt. Sure enough, on his right pectoral, there was a tattoo of an Eastern Newt. It was green with a yellow underside and red spots on its back.

"*He* called me 'Yellow Belly,'" Pete said. "And yes, *he* meant it to double as a slur."

He was not the Killer, since the Killer had made himself available only for the initiation of the other Amphibians. *He*, then, could be none other than Pete's handler—apparently a rather maliciously eugenistic handler. One could expect nothing different from the WCE.

The Agent placed her hand over the mark and marveled at how whole Pete looked without it. Yet, with it, he didn't seem any less of an admirable man. He spoke of his handler in the past tense, indicating that he was free. That explained why, despite the fact that he had opened the package containing the fire salamander, he had been able to decide not to kill her. Somehow, he had managed to make his Song ineffective and to live apart from the WCE.

"How did you do it?" He cleverly asked the question before she could ask it of him.

Folding her hands in her lap, the Agent took a deep breath. "I had help: a family, a Kiddo, and a former trainer who wouldn't give up on me. I owe my freedom to them."

It seemed the most respectful way to reflect upon her experience in Diablo.

After a moment, she asked, "You?"

He began to rub his thighs with his hands. "I sang my Song into the mirror and ordered myself to be free?"

"Liar," she laughed.

He shot her a cheeky grin. "Can't get anything past you."

A sorrow for which there could be no comfort crept into his face. She touched his shoulder to bring him out of its shadow.

"It was an accident," he admitted. "But when it happened—"

"You took your chances in the big wide world," she smiled.

Pete nodded. "I thought I was completely off their radar, so I stopped taking the DNA masker last year and found a facial reconstruction guy to get my face back. No one at the WCE really followed up with me until the mail order to kill you. Even that seemed halfhearted on their part. They didn't even send me a picture of you."

He seemed fascinated by her hands, and as though he were working out a puzzle, he began intertwining her fingers with his own.

"Is your name really Rosa?" he asked.

"It can be, for now," she replied.

"Nice to meet you, Rosa," he said, leaning toward her tentatively.

She met his lips with care. The two of them were exposed, his tattoo and her scars, yet it seemed that they were more secure than they could ever have been in all of their lives as Phibs. They moved toward each other, pursuing the warmth of that security from the cold shadows of their innermost selves.

All this time, the Agent had thought she was the only one to break free from the WCE. It had been a profoundly lonely existence, necessarily so. But now, even though many of the details of her complicated life as a Phib remained the same, Rosa found hope in the idea that there was someone else facing the same obstacles and finding a way to survive.

Suddenly, Pete groaned in pain. His lips slid away from hers, and he collapsed backward onto the couch.

"Oh, my," Rosa whispered as she watched him convulse.

She supposed it was most efficient that, beyond their basic anti-gun conditioning, all Phibs should be programmed to have different weaknesses. After all, Crispin clearly hadn't been conditioned against technology like she had. Given that Pete used a flake and didn't seem troubled by her web apparatus, he likely hadn't received anti-tech conditioning either. Indeed, it appeared that he had been conditioned against something more fundamental than technology.

Everything had been fine while he was more guarded. Their earlier encounter in her kitchen was proof. But in the vulnerable intimacy of their camaraderie, he was catapulted back into his troubled past. He was exhibiting the typical rapid eye movement and limb paralysis that came with the territory. Nothing out of the ordinary.

"Shake it off," she told him. "You can do it. Get back in the fight."

Pete cried out, but his voice sounded strained as if he were being choked. The muscles around his neck were tight, and he clutched at his throat helplessly. Psychosomatic scars appeared all over his torso. They looked like burn marks, purposeful ones, probably from his handler.

Rosa grieved for Pete. She knew, only in part, what he was experiencing. But she chose to believe that, in time and possibly with positive exposure, he would heal—just as she was healing.

She massaged the tension out of his rigid, claw-like hands.

"Come back to me, Pete," she said. "He can't hurt you anymore. You're here, not there."

He opened his eyes with no small effort and croaked, "Rosa?"

"Yes," she said, squeezing his hand.

He brought her hand to his chest and curled into a self-protective posture. Even though he had successfully beaten back the past, his body was still trembling. Rosa, utterly spent herself, patted Pete on the head and then lay back against the couch cushions.

CHAPTER 18

AT 0515, BLAIR, RACKY, AND KARTHIK EXITED AN ELEVATOR IN THE parking garage at HQ. They were there to meet Theresa, who was prepping their auto-car from Peaceful Rentals. When they arrived at the vehicle, she was rummaging around in the front seat.

"What are you up to?" Racky asked.

Theresa started, hitting her head on the ceiling of the car. "Just looking at the receipts. Peaceful said they'd give us a discount for providing the coordinates to our destination up front. I went ahead and registered everything at their office, so you guys should be good to go."

"N—no programming n—necessary?" Karthik asked, admiring the oblong-shaped sedan's omnidirectional wheels and its lack of an electrical port.

"All done," Theresa said. "In fact, they said there's no reason to touch the console at all. "

"Great!" He tossed his bag into the trunk. "Remind me t—to go with Peaceful for my n—next rental."

Racky placed her luggage beside Karthik's, but she held onto the bag that contained all of her gadgets.

"Auto-cars give me the creeps," she said. "I don't see why we can't just drive to Farm and Forest in a human-operated car."

"Get with the times, Wernicke," Blair said good-naturedly. "Auto-cars are the way of the present day."

"That, and the Coop is paying for this rental through one of our front companies, which is in tech," Theresa said. "Everyone knows that tech people are supposed to use the most current tech. It would look suspicious if we rented a non-auto-car in a district where they are readily available."

"And as auto-cars go, this has got to be the sleekest ride ever!" Karthik said. "What d—does it run on, anyway?"

Theresa grinned. "It's got a hydrogen powered internal combustion engine, so you'll get highway-appropriate speed *and* consistent performance in freezing temperatures. You're all set for a smooth ride!"

"Alright!" Karthik nodded approvingly.

He and Blair got into the front seat of the auto-car while Racky sat in the back with her bag of gadgets.

"Well, have a good trip, all," Theresa said, leaning on Blair's door. "You're programmed to stop at refueling stations three times on your outbound trip and, of course, you'll stop for the night at the halfway point and also at the nearest urban center to the compound. I've already got a reservation for you at the hotels. Be safe out there, and don't hesitate to call if you need anything."

"Thanks, Theresa," Blair said. "See you when we get back."

Without another word, Theresa stood back and smiled. As the car pulled out of the garage, Blair could still see her standing in the dim light, staring after them with an odd air of melancholy.

* * *

There was only one purpose in the Agent's mind: to find the chief medical director. And she did so with ruthless efficiency. Her path across the compound was straight, though unhurried. She killed only those who intentionally obstructed her path, and after she had killed them, they were gone. She could not remember their faces or even how their tense bodies had relaxed as their life slipped away. She remembered only her goal.

Soon, she arrived at the medical facility. By that time, the alarm had sounded, and a small crowd of administrative staff was forming. The containment team— three men in uniform—stood at the front of the crowd. They seemed reluctant to engage the Agent directly.

The chief medical director came to his third floor office window and looked out at the Agent. "Why all the fuss, Fire?"

"I'm giving notice: I'll no longer cooperate with the additional 'enticement training,'" the Agent declared.

"You're not any different from the others, just because the Killer favors you," the medical director said contemptuously.

The Agent charged forward and leapt onto the side of the building. Onlookers chattered and shouted as she climbed. When the medical director slammed the window shut, the Agent glanced down at the men in uniform. They were assembling a very large gun. She quickened her pace up the side of the building.

When she reached the window where the medical director had been, the men in uniform fired the big gun at her. A laser net shot out of it. She tried to dodge by slipping down a couple of meters, but the net utilized an intelligent technology that recognized her face and followed her.

She fell the rest of the way to the ground, and the net expanded to envelope her. When it contracted, she managed to fold the net against itself so that it couldn't fully close. The resultant mild burns on the Agent's hands were worth it because her upper body remained free. The net clamped down on her lower half. Bruised and muddy, she rolled onto her side to get a better view of the building's exit where the medical director and the Killer were emerging.

The Agent tried to move her legs apart, but the lasers in the net became very hot and began to burn her. She brought her legs together, and the net cooled down.

"I think you're scared, Fire," the medical director said, kneeling beside the Agent, "which is good because fear breeds respect."

The Agent wriggled her legs and opened and closed her burnt hands. She had not come that far to be denied. She had been crushed, and she had killed and climbed and fallen—and there was mud oozing down the back of her shirt. She hated mud.

"Say that again," the Agent growled, stretching her legs so that the lasers became hot again.

The medical director stood back with some mix of condescension and admiration in his face. "Fear breeds respect."

"Say it again!" the Agent said, digging her feet into the net as she forced her legs into a forward split.

She shrieked in pain as the lasers overloaded and blew, cutting deep gashes in her legs. Some of the onlookers began to scream, too, probably more at the idea of the injury than anything else. There wasn't any geyser of blood or uncauterized flesh; there wasn't really much to see at all. The Agent's bones were exposed in some places, but she supposed that was to be expected.

Blind are the eyes of one who feels no pain.

The cool mud sucked at the Agent as she pulled herself to her feet. The medical director froze in terror as she approached in jerking movements.

Focused is the mind of one who has an established purpose.

Seizing the medical director and forcing him into a headlock, the Agent commanded, "Say it again!"

The Killer stood only a couple of meters away, but he didn't intervene.

"Fear," the medical director choked. "Fear—breeds—"

**SNAP* The Agent let the medical director's lifeless body fall to the ground, and as she did, the Killer looked incredibly proud.*

What is necessary must never be lamented.

The Agent's mind was cloudy with the past when she awoke. She was in an unfamiliar room on an unfamiliar bed. The bed was impeccably made, and she was lying on top of the undisturbed covers.

She had the feeling that she had been in a violent conflict the night before, but many of the details eluded her—except for those pertaining to her injuries. She could feel that the bullet had been removed from her right shoulder, and all of her stab wounds were bound with gauze. Her ice-pack-covered ankle was elevated on a couple of couch cushions.

The shower was running. Many times before, she had waited on the bed for a man to get out of the shower. Often, she had done so in fear. Her handler, the Killer, had a very hot temper and a very short fuse.

Bothered by the cold that gripped her ankle, the Agent removed the ice packs and slid off of the bed. When her feet met the floor, she felt solid. After taking a couple of test steps, she confirmed that she could walk fairly well. Her ankle was still a little weak, but it had mostly mended. Just in case, she figured that she should probably wait a day or two before jumping from any unreasonable heights.

As she made her way to the kitchen, she noted that two cushions were missing from the couch and a thin throw blanket lay crumpled on the remaining cushion. Someone had spent the night out there. She put the ice packs in the freezer and returned to the bedroom.

The water in the bathroom had stopped running. All of a sudden, the door swung open, and a billow of steam emerged.

The Agent shrank back, filled with dread. But the man coming out of the bathroom was not the Killer. He was Pete Bae, her neighbor and cohort-mate, looking clean and happy. Fighting to gain control of her rapid breathing, the Agent told herself that this reaction was unnecessary. She was not in Chile. She was not on tour with the Killer at all.

Pete's smile disappeared when he noticed her murmuring to herself in the doorway.

"You okay, Rosa?" He cautiously stepped toward her.

"Give me a second," she gasped, gesturing for him to come no closer.

He gave her the space that she needed to come back to the present. When he could tell that she had fully returned, he grinned.

"I see you're already up and around," he said, motioning to her ankle.

Intending to skip the part where he asked how such a quick recovery could be possible, Rosa nodded. "So, I guess I should go now. I mean, you were here first."

Phibs were trained to operate in isolation. They never collaborated, which meant that they could have no sense of loyalty, even to members of the same cohort. While the Agent had gained her freedom, her basic instincts about survival hadn't changed. Pete's likely hadn't either. So, they had to part ways. That was the only way to make sense of the situation.

Pete looked bewildered. "I don't want you to go."

Rosa sighed. "But staying together could make us more vulnerable. What if the WCE finds a way to turn us against each other?"

"You still don't trust me." He seemed genuinely wounded.

"It's not that," she said. "It's just—how can two people like *us* stay near each other?"

"One day at a time," he said, walking with a spring in his step into the living room. "And today's an *interesting* day to be near each other because I've got news from the deepest dark web!"

Rosa followed with the couch cushions and plopped them in their places before sitting down beside him. The apparatus she had left on his doormat was now sitting on the coffee table, fully configured.

Pete slung one arm around her shoulders and used his other hand to navigate the apparatus. Rosa noticed this smooth move, but given all that had transpired in the past twenty-four hours, she felt comfortable with that level of familiarity. In fact, she liked Pete's arm around her shoulders.

Admiring how well the apparatus was functioning, Rosa chuckled, "And you said all this went over your head."

"Well, a guy's got to keep his cover intact somehow."

"The vegetarian, animal-loving, pacifist thing would have been enough," she said. "'Respect for all life?'"

"I am certainly a vegetarian, and I *do* strive to respect all life," Pete said.

"But Carlisle the Cockroach?"

"Okay, Carlisle was overkill," he admitted. "But I had you fooled, didn't I?"

Rosa nudged him with her shoulder.

"Now, take a look at this!" He turned the screen toward her. "These screenshots were sent directly to your apparatus via the dark web, late last night."

The images were of chat boxes. Someone named B.F. had been chatting with someone named BlazingMander.

B.F.: My buyer will pay 2MM.

BlazingMander: I said 6MM.

B.F.: You'd want to deliver yourself along with it at that price.

BlazingMander: What would your buyer want with me?

B.F.: In my experience a live specimen is always better than a dead one.

BlazingMander: The intermediaries will have to do. I'm trying to lie low as best I can.

B.F.: Bring them along, then. The more the merrier. I'll meet your price if you make an appearance.

BlazingMander: I'll check my calendar.

B.F.: Excellent. What venue do you suggest?

BlazingMander: Meet at Home. Come alone.

"BlazingMander is posing as *me*!" Rosa exclaimed. Then, more quietly, she added, "And I'm guessing if *I'm* the live specimen, then the dead one must be my son. But a specimen for what?"

Pete's expression indicated that he'd put together many of the pieces of the puzzle regarding who had her son and why they wanted him.

"Before I got out of the WCE, I heard rumors of research on genetic disease resistance in humans—the search for a gene that, when turned on, can cause uncompromisable immunity to every disease," he said. "If your son has half the healing rate that you do, I can see how both of you would be of interest to their project. Do you know B.F.?"

She shook her head. But the unspoken thought lingered between them: if B.F. and BlazingMander both knew about Home, they were intimately connected to the Amphibians.

A message icon popped up and floated around Pete and Rosa. The holographic envelope wavered between the two of them because the apparatus didn't know which pair of retinas to follow.

"I'm really going to have to turn off that function," Rosa grumbled.

She touched the envelope, and a note in flowery script floated out of it.

So, The Game Is On. Quick Chat? —B.F.

A private chat window popped up.

B.F.: You are cordially invited to the rendezvous.

"Try to be careful what you say in the chat," Pete said. "B.F. seems happy to share their private conversations with interested parties."

"I'll do my best," Rosa replied, her fingers hovering over the keyboard as she thought about what to say.

Rosa del Desierto: Why would I be interested?

"You named the apparatus Rosa del Desierto?" She looked amusedly at Pete, who dropped his gaze. "Look Pete, about my heritages, I should really clear something up—"

He held up a hand. "Carlisle may have been a smokescreen, but I really was raised in a Neo-Eugenically oriented Class 2 household. So, please understand my staunch commitment to anti-Neo-Eugenic practice. I only see you as human, so I don't need to know your heritages."

"Need" was such a strong word, but Rosa didn't see the benefit of Pete mistakenly believing that she had Class 3 heritage—which she assumed he did since he'd bestowed on her a Hispanic surname. Her brow wrinkled in exasperation, but before she could say anything, the apparatus chimed.

> B.F.: Out of curiosity.

> Rosa del Desierto: Not curious enough for an ambush.

> B.F.: How about for info on your son?

Rosa's heart skipped a beat at the mention of the child. But she remembered how B.F.—just in that previous conversation with BlazingMander—as well as Hinny had mentioned her son's death. Well, B.F. had referred to Kiddo as a dead specimen. But that was close enough.

> Rosa del Desierto: You mean, my dead son?

> B.F.: Affirmative. I've got info you want, and you've got something I want. Come Home, and we'll work something out.

"I don't like the sound of this," Pete said.
Rosa ignored him.

> Rosa del Desierto: What do I have?

> B.F.: It's what's inside of you that matters most. Be Home in two days' time at 1600.

> B.F. has disconnected

"Okay, so let me get this straight," Pete said, staring at the screen. "B.F. has been arranging some kind of exchange with someone who is pretending to be you. But they also want *you* to be at that meeting?"

"Apparently, yes," Rosa responded. "I can't quite figure what B.F.'s motivation is. They've been dropping me notes about how to survive here in Lakes, and they even tried to warn me that you'd been activated to kill me."

"Then, I bet they're also the one that tampered with the elevator sensor after you got here," Pete said slowly. "That does lend credence to the idea that they're trying to help you in some way."

"We'll see," Rosa replied. Then standing, she said, "I guess I'm going Home, then."

"When do we leave?" Pete asked.

"I think I should go alone," Rosa said. "It's really my problem to handle."

"But I've been waiting for an opportunity like this!" Pete said. "Of all the oppressive systems in need of dismantling, the WCE would be the most worthy. I would consider having a hand in its downfall the crowning achievement of my miserable life. You wouldn't deny me that chance, would you?"

"Well, I don't know about causing its downfall. I just want to rescue my son," Rosa said.

"The way I see it, one might lead to the other," Pete said. "Or, at least, rescuing your son will cripple the WCE's search for uncompromisable immunity. And it would make you happy, so it seems like a win-win."

Her happiness was not the main issue. It seemed unlikely that B.F. would show up at Home alone, and since there was an order out on the Agent's life, there was a high likelihood that at least some Phibs would show up to ambush BlazingMander. If they found Rosa there, they would not hesitate to kill her. And if Pete went with her, he would be in danger, too.

"Furthermore, I have yet to disclose to you my most coveted power," Pete said, as if he were reading a persuasive essay. "I have magnetoreception!"

Rosa's eyebrows rose. "So, you mean to tell me that you use the Earth's magnetic field to make you a human GPS *and* you have super reflexes? What did the WCE do to you to make that happen?"

Pete chuckled. "I came by both honestly, but the reflexes were mostly a bonus. With respect to the magnetoreception—it's common knowledge that human brains interact with the Earth's magnetic field. I guess I'm just more sensitive to the interactions and know how to use them to my advantage. It's kind of like the advantage of your accelerated learning rate."

In answer to her astonished expression, he said, "I figured that from your lightning fast mastery of synthetic languages and programming. You didn't acquire that ability from the WCE, did you?"

"No," the Agent named Rosa replied.

Noticing her guarded tone, Pete did not pry.

"Anyway," he said, "the hint about magnetoreception was in my mark. You know how the WCE loves a good symbol. Eastern Newts aren't particularly known for their speed or reflexes. But they *are* known for their homing behavior, even over distances. I'm less traceable than a GPS, and I could get you Home by the most direct route!"

The Agent had never thought of the Amphibians' marks as having anything to do with their abilities. But Beatriz Gomez *had* hinted that there was some meaning to her Poison Arrow symbol as it related to her experience and perceived purpose. Crispin—Hellbender—had been incredibly large, much like his namesake. And goodness only knew who else was out there. The idea was fascinating, though terrifying, given the broad array of mechanisms by which amphibious organisms managed to survive.

More than ever, the Agent wished that she could access her mental roster of Phib names in order to get an idea of what abilities her opponents could have. But all that came to her mind was the library at Windsailing's Gifted. Childish reminiscing aside, she knew that she would need all of the help she could get. Two Phibs would certainly prove much stronger than one Phib on her own—no matter what advantages she might have.

"So, I'll ask again," Pete said. "When do we leave?"

"Five minutes," Rosa grinned.

She showered and when she returned, Pete was on his flake in the kitchen. She stood across the counter from him. The call rang a couple of times, and a machine picked up—just a voice reciting the target number, then a tone.

Pete drew a deep breath. "Gordon, it's Pete. I hope your recovery is going well."

Rosa looked down ashamedly. Pete leaned over, put his hand under her chin, and raised it. When she met his gaze, he smiled.

"Listen," he continued. "I know this isn't the best time what with the restaurant being closed and all, but I've run into some personal trouble and I have to disappear, at least for now. The hens and their eggs are yours to keep. I hope you understand and, uh, thanks for everything. Bye."

When he ended the call, he exhaled. From the weary look on his face, Rosa could tell that he had done that before—more than once.

"It doesn't get easier, does it?" she said.

He shook his head. "But just like with the gun conditioning, I'll adapt."

"Yes, I believe you will." After a moment, she asked, "How *did* you learn to use a gun, anyway?"

"I've been out of the life for a while," Pete replied, seeming a little sad. "But you know, I really only bought it to use on Phibs."

Rosa nodded with understanding. "The only people you can't afford to give a fighting chance."

"Exactly," Pete said. "Even then, it would be incredibly difficult to take a life."

CHAPTER 19

When Rosa and Pete entered the antique section of a car lot in Western Lakes, Rosa immediately gravitated toward a gasoline-powered jeep with a manual transmission. Despite Pete's concern over the car not being fully automated, she insisted upon buying it.

"I trust myself more than I trust an auto-car," she said. "Besides, jeeps remind me of a dear friend of mine."

Perhaps knowing the value of a good replica, Pete didn't press the matter.

"As long as you don't mind driving the whole way Home," he said. "I've always ridden in auto-cars."

She paid for the jeep in cash, and off they went. They traveled with blankets and food enough for one meal per day—plus first aid supplies because Pete had insisted, and shampoo and conditioner because Rosa had insisted. The web apparatus also made the trip, secure in its satchel and nestled under the blankets.

To the average person, Rosa and Pete would look like the typical young couple on a cross-country road trip—well, except for their difference in class, especially in the Western States where they were headed. So, they were to be two strangers thrown together by fate, which seemed a fairly accurate description.

Rosa had never driven in snow and slush before. When Pete asked her if the car was supposed to stall so regularly, she said yes, and he had to take her word for it because he'd never ridden in a car with a human driver. With time, however, their ride became smoother, and the jeep was practically gliding as they reached the quiet roads leading out of the district.

About a kilometer out from the Meridian, the border between the Eastern and Western States, Pete indicated that Rosa should pull off of the road and drive through the woods. There were westbound checkpoints along every road that crossed the border. Leaving the road meant that they only had to watch for patrols, which seemed preferable to passing through a checkpoint where they would almost certainly be harassed as an interclass party.

Surrounded by trees, the jeep was well hidden. The ground rose and dipped beneath the vehicle as it bumped along.

"So, those scars on your legs," Pete said, ending what had been a long bout of comfortable silence. "Did you get them from the arena?"

The Agent named Rosa responded, "After. It was a disciplinary action gone wrong, I guess you could say. What do you know about the arena?"

"Nothing much," Pete said. "The only reason I knew about it at all was because they had me on the medical team developing the nanobot inhalants for the unfit ones."

"And you heard that one of the unfit ones survived the procedure," she said.

"Rumors, more like. You know how the WCE hates to admit a failure," he replied. "Just imagine the scrambling it took to cover up that you'd also survived the execution in the arena."

She gave a wry laugh. "Clever that, between me and my opponent, you figured I'm the unfit one. What tipped you off?"

"Your healing rate was proof enough for me," Pete said with a shrug. "If you survived the nanobots and they're still in your body, maybe they're not doing nothing in there."

Rosa cast him a curious glance. "Like they randomly decided to heal me instead of kill me?"

"The bots are programmed to respond to certain hormones and neurotransmitters," he said. "That's how they find their targets within the body and interact with them. Maybe your body adapted to interact chemically with the bots and reprogrammed them to help you instead of harm you—like by healing your injuries and maybe even preventing disease."

"I'd be lying if I said I'd never wondered about it," Rosa said. "It's probably the reason the Killer refused to allow testing on me or the fit one's body. I guess I just thought that, in the world of the WCE, there could be a lot of reasons for my—extra help."

"I guess," Pete said, "but the idea of a genetic reason for your ability to reprogram the bots is very compelling. I mean, I didn't hear any other rumors of unfit subjects surviving the procedure."

"No," Rosa said, feeling chilly all of a sudden. She turned up the heat.

Pete turned his vents toward her. "If the WCE discovers a gene for uncompromisable immunity or a way to epigenetically cause what happened in your body, they could do a lot of damage."

"Having an uninfectable agent *would* serve their bioterror goals," Rosa agreed.

"Or a whole cohort of uninfectable agents," Pete added.

"But you know," Rosa said, frowning. "If B.F. wants to help me, they can't be with the WCE. The Assistant Vice is out for my head. Everyone connected to the Phibs should know that by now."

"I just don't get why the Assistant Vice is trying to kill you," Pete said. "I mean, why dispose of something so potentially useful?"

After a pause, he must have realized how that statement sounded. "I don't mean any offense by that."

"None taken," Rosa replied. "Anyway, to answer your question, the Assistant Vice has had it out for me ever since she found out that my Song wouldn't work—although I'm sure it didn't help that she also discovered the Killer's fixation with me that same night."

Pete shifted uncomfortably. He, too, had been initiated by the Killer. They had that in common, and yet Pete had been passed along to another handler while *she* was the one whom the Killer had kept.

Feeling sorry that she had brought it up, she cleared her throat and continued, "But that's why I'm sure our son is still alive. The Assistant Vice wants to terminate me because she *still has* a live specimen with my genes to experiment on. She's just lying about him being dead to keep other interested parties off her back. I'm sure of it."

"Your son," Pete said. "The Killer's son?"

He was perturbed, but she could not discern whether he was bothered more by the Killer's abuse of her or by their miscegenation in general. She had a few words for him if it were the latter.

"B.F. has information on my son," she said, "and I have to rescue my son."

"I'll help however I can," he said.

When the jeep emerged from the cover of the trees onto a snowy plain, Pete suggested that Rosa drive back to the main road. In the right side-mirror, she could see the lights of a border checkpoint glimmering a kilometer and a half to their northeast. They'd crossed into the Western States without being detected. She breathed a sigh of relief.

Pete sighed as well, looking out the window.

"I can feel it out there, you know," he said. "Wherever I am in the world, I can feel that vile place trying to pull me back."

Rosa knew something about that, except whatever was pulling at her was internal rather than external.

Pete laughed ruefully. "After I got free, I never thought I'd ever go with that impulse. What do you think it'll be like—going Home, I mean?"

Rosa thought about the Agent's experience with a trigger-prompt in Diablo. "Maybe like getting stabbed in the brain with a poisoned shaft?"

"But only if we encounter something familiar, right? It's been a few years. I mean, how similar could the place be?"

"I don't know," she said, "and I'm not really looking forward to finding out. If there's any way to avoid the arena and the medical facility—"

"And the initiation quarters," Pete said, folding his arms across his chest.

Rosa cast him a sympathetic glance. "Yes, *especially* the initiation quarters."

"Glad we have an understanding," he replied stiffly.

He continued to look out the window, but Rosa noticed that his chest was shuddering. She knew it was not tears he was resisting but intrusive memories. The very mention of their old training camp had brought troubling images to his mind. She was sorry to have disturbed him.

* * *

The auto-car from Peaceful Rentals hummed along the cliffside portion of the Pacific Highway, northbound for Farm And Forest. Racky had dozed off in the back seat, but she was awakened by the frantic chattering of Blair and Karthik.

"I'm t—telling you it's been hacked!" Karthik was saying. "The car should have t—turned inland back there, but it missed the t—turn and it's n—not going back."

"Maybe it's taking us on a detour," Blair replied. "Maybe there's traffic on the normal route."

Racky sat up. "What's the matter?"

"The car's t—taking us the wrong—" Karthik stared in horror at the dashboard.

Blair followed his gaze, then groaned. "The 'check engine' light is on."

"Huh." Racky cocked her head and listened. "Engine sounds fine, though."

"Yeah, but we should run a d—diagnostic anyway," Karthik said. "Just to make sure the car isn't about to explode on us or something."

"Makes sense," Blair replied.

"Diagnostics is the blue button on the console," Racky said.

Karthik pressed the button, and all of the lights on the console lit up. A loud whirring ensued.

"I don't think that should sound like that," Blair said. "Racky, can you take a look at the console?"

As Racky unhooked her seatbelt, the car suddenly lurched to the right. The vehicle collided with the wall of the cliff and bounced off it, skittering wildly on its omnidirectional wheels across the four-lane road.

"Now, I *know* it ought not to be doing that," Racky said. "The machine must have some kind of virus. I can get to the bottom of this."

She took her portable web apparatus out of her bag.

"Has anyone else noticed that we're accelerating?" Blair asked.

"I hope we'll t—turn if we get too close t—to the edge," Karthik gulped.

"I hope I'll get into this machine and kill the virus, so we never have to worry about that," Racky said, unfolding her holographic keyboard.

She typed with urgency to gain access to the service account on the car. The diagnostic report listed ten failures in various engine parts and counting.

"Hurry, Racky!" Blair urged.

The car was moving erratically and far too quickly. There was a huge *BANG* as they crashed into another car and glanced off in a different direction.

Racky decided to use 3-D programming to better visualize and interact with the problem at hand. She typed in a command for the car to report all of the codes that it considered relevant to the trip, and her apparatus projected a large, intricate web of codes in red light.

There were invasive codes intertwined with the original ones, but they were so closely linked that Racky was afraid she might not be able to remove the harmful ones without nicking the good ones. She fished around in her bag of gadgets and pulled out a fine-tipped tool that she could use to manipulate the web.

"Now we're talking!" she exclaimed, using the tool to drag connections this way and that.

The car beeped, and the red web flashed on and off repeatedly.

"What's happening?" Karthik asked.

"Still trying to discern what blend of synthetic languages these morally diseased mad hackers used," Racky muttered. "The car just took my command to engage the emergency brake as a request to empty the main fuel tank."

"Well, that could make us stop, right?" said Blair.

"As l—long as we d—don't blow up first," Karthik said.

"If we were going to blow up, we would have done it already," Racky told them. "Our fuel was dumped a few hundred meters back. The car's got emergency power from a flow battery, which isn't nearly as combustible. Now, hush, you two. I need to concentrate."

WHAM They hit the guardrail. Everyone jolted forward, then all was still.

"Phew!" Karthik said. "L—let's get out of here."

"No!" Racky cried. But it was too late.

When he engaged the door handle, an alarm went off.

A synthetic voice droned, "Vehicle still in childproof mode. You must not exit the vehicle until you reach your destination."

"Well, can you t—turn it off?" Karthik asked, jiggling the handle again.

A metal sheet closed over the windows and windshield.

"Hyper-security mode activated. You must remain in the vehicle until you reach your destination."

"Would you stop touching things?" Racky snapped. "I have bigger fish to fry!"

"Bigger than our being l—locked in an out-of-control auto-car?"

Racky pointed at a snarl of codes in the web. "These extra codes are telling the car to run us over the side of this cliff. We'll start ramming the guardrail in ten seconds. So, if you don't mind—"

"I'll shut up."

"Thank you."

Ten seconds passed like an eternity as Racky hurriedly cut connections and reestablished them elsewhere. Finally, the car began to reverse.

"That was close!" Blair said.

"Wait a minute," Racky said, still messing with the web. "Someone knew I would be able to disarm that level, and there is a gnarly one underneath. We are not yet in the clear."

"N—not yet in the clear?" Karthik echoed. "What does *that* mean?"

Before she could respond, the car zoomed forward and rammed the guardrail. Everyone braced themselves as the car began backing up.

"There must be a d—different way of d—doing this," Karthik groaned as they slammed into the metal railing again.

"Can you program the car to do something else?" Blair asked. "Maybe, instead of trying to counteract whatever virus has been put into the machine, can you teach it to do something completely different?"

Racky smiled. "Now, *that's* a good idea, Ms. SSA."

After another fifteen seconds, when the guardrail was nearly ready to give, Racky threw down her tools with a victorious squawk. "Got it! Hold on, lovelies!"

The car accelerated toward the guardrail and, with a terrific crash, broke through it.

As the car plunged over the cliff, Karthik yelled, "I thought you fixed it!"

"Worst last words ever," Racky said calmly. "Just press that red button on the console, then the green one. They're service functions, but I switched up their meanings, so it should work."

"Red says 'eject engine,'" he said concernedly. "You sure?"

"Yes! Red, then green!"

With the metal sheets over the windows, there was no way to tell how close they were to impact. Karthik executed the command.

The car jolted upward, and as Racky continued to weave in new webs of code, its movements stabilized. Eventually, the car lowered safely onto what could only be the rising and falling surface of the ocean.

"How d—did you kn—know that was going t—to work?" Karthik asked.

"A little bit of history goes a long way," Racky beamed. "These auto-cars with the hydrogen internal combustion engines were originally designed to be flying cars. But with all of the political madness with the Divisive Round, no one got the legislation passed for road cars to travel in the sky—sharing airways with drones and planes and such. Flying cars were relegated to land use only and that was that. So, anyways, I just tapped into the old systems and redirected the flow of the car's fluids and waste to the thrusters to stabilize our landing. Ejecting the engine made us lighter, so we didn't need much thrust. And, being feather light, we won't sink. But we definitely cannot use the car to get to Farm And Forest."

"I'm just glad t—to be alive," Karthik said.

"Me too," said Blair. "Incredible work, Wernicke. You saved our lives."

"No thanks to Theresa," Racky said. "I bet she's the one that planted the virus that confused the car. Didn't you see her messing around by the console before we left?"

"It's t—terrible to say, but I wouldn't be surprised," Karthik muttered.

"Those webs showed a rare degree of programming sophistica-tion," Racky said. "It's a certainty that Theresa was acting on someone else's behalf. I'd bet money it was someone at the WCE."

"She and I will have a long talk when we get back," Blair said, her face stern and disappointed.

Racky looked at her solemnly. "If she's even still there."

"Maybe I had this coming to me," Karthik sighed. "I t—took Maude ring shopping."

"You did *what?*" Racky exclaimed.

"She had been pressuring me t—to set a d—date, so I figured the ring was the n—next logical step." He said it almost like it was a confession. "She chose a t—two-carat round cut solitaire in platinum."

"Well, the gor—woman has good taste," Racky said. "Can't deny that."

"Oh, I d—deserved this," Karthik groaned piteously.

"I hate to interrupt your guilt fest," Blair said, "but you've got to table this discussion until after we complete our missions. Now, let's call a tow truck."

"And a cab that can to take us to another rental car place," Racky said, "a place where we can get a car that *hasn't* been tampered with."

"Peaceful Car Rentals." Karthik shook his head. "If only the experience had lived up t—to the n—name."

CHAPTER 20

THE ROAD WAS LONG AND THE SKIES WERE GRAY IN THE DISTRICT OF Farm And Forest. Everything about the place—the oppressive atmosphere, the pothole-covered roads, and the constant drizzle—was hellish. The one positive aspect of being there was that the manual transmission jeep was not so out of place since older cars were still quite common in those parts.

"We should find a place to camp soon," Rosa said when the sun was setting. "Can't be caught out here after sundown."

Pete turned toward her. "They allow civilian patrols here?"

"Last I heard," she replied. "And there may be some kinds of curfews, too."

"Well, there aren't too many houses around, and the coastal woodlands are only about five hundred kilometers away," he said. "We could arrive tonight, if we just chance it."

Rosa shook her head. "I heard locals watch the roads for strange cars. We could have a nasty confrontation. I know it's a drag to stop here, but we'll have plenty of time to get Home if we just resume driving tomorrow morning."

"Okay, but where would we camp?" he asked. "These fields could be someone's property."

A man stepped into the road about a hundred meters in front of them. He was waving for help.

"Don't stop," Pete said. "It looks like a trap."

As Rosa slowed down to maneuver around the man, she glanced at his truck. It was propped up by the side of the road with its front right tire removed. The tire looked new and undamaged. And there were a couple of motorcycles leaned against the front of the vehicle.

Definitely a trap. She began to accelerate past him, but there came a *THUMP* *BUMP*.

"Damn!" she exclaimed. "Tire shredders!"

The shredders had only affected the tires on the left side, but from the tilting and wavering of the jeep, it was clear that the vehicle was in no shape for a chase. A motorcycle would easily overtake them. Rosa pumped the breaks and put on the flashers.

The man who had been standing in the road made a gesture and another man came out from behind the truck. They both carried semi-automatic pistols.

"Do you see any others?" Rosa asked.

"No, just the two of them," Pete said, looking out through the back windows.

As the men were approaching, one on each side of the car, Rosa unlocked the doors. Before she could open hers, though, the man on her side raised his gun.

"No need to get out," he said with a scowl. "Roll down the windows. We just want to talk."

"Well, can you set the guns aside to talk?" Rosa asked, pressing the button to open the windows only halfway.

Scowler scoffed and did not lower his weapon.

Pete cleared his throat. "Is there something you gentlemen need?"

"We need directions to the nearest gas station," the man outside of Pete's window chuckled.

Rosa decided that the man looked like a 'Walter'. Walter motioned for Scowler to go around to the back of the jeep.

"We're not from around here," Pete said.

There was a slashing sound as Scowler cut the jeep's soft top. Rosa reached for her door handle, but Pete touched her arm. He shook his head ever so slightly.

Scowler's voice rang out from the behind them. "Just some snacks, medical supplies, and shampoo back here."

"Interesting," Walter said. "What are you two doing all the way out here with hardly any supplies?"

"Just passing through," Pete said.

"You two together?"

"We're traveling together."

"But are you *together?*" Walter demanded, nodding in Rosa's direction.

"Whose business is that?" Rosa shot back.

Pete's gaze flickered toward her in alarm.

"Ours," Walter replied, "since we have the guns."

"Got something!" Scowler shouted. "They were hiding a real nice web apparatus. Bet we could get a few thousand for everything."

"Well, then, let's take what's ours and be off," Walter said with a grin.

Rosa's eyes narrowed. "Come again?"

"Rosa." Pete's voice said to drop it.

She knew that escalation wasn't ideal, but it wouldn't be the end of the world since she and Pete were specially trained and these common thieves surely were not. Besides, she had overcome her conditioning against technology on that apparatus, and she figured she might need it later to communicate with B.F.

"Think before resisting," Walter said with a raspy laugh. "If you call the police on us, they'll arrest *you* miscegenists instead."

Rosa bristled at the idea.

"Better shut your eugenist mouth and move along empty-handed," she said. "My patience is wearing thin, and I'd hate for this to get messy."

Pete looked at her pleadingly.

Walter aimed his gun at her. "Only mess around here's going to be your brain matter on the dashboard, you uppity female."

Scowler was loading their supplies into the truck. His gun sat in the highway shoulder.

"I gave him fair warning, right?" Rosa asked Pete.

"A world minus a miscegenist is a better world," Walter said.

She replied, "The same could be said of eugenists."

Pete's face hardened in a way that told her that he understood there was only one way out of this now.

As Walter's finger twitched over the trigger, Pete forced the gun upward. The shot went into the sky, and a struggle ensued.

The Agent slammed her door into Scowler, who had come running at the sound of the shot. And having stunned him, she leapt out of the car and wrestled him to the ground. He was stronger than he looked and a better grappler than the average joe, but his abilities diminished after the Agent broke his elbows.

Just as she was wrapping him up with her legs, another gunshot rang out near the jeep. Scowler frantically wriggled in her grasp, but she squeezed tighter, breaking a couple of his ribs.

"What *are* you, you bone-crunching animal from hell?" he wheezed.

Better an animal only than a slave and weapon. She had come a long way since her days with the Killer.

"Subclass 6.14, I think," she replied. "Anyway, you really stopped the wrong car today."

And with that, the Agent ended Scowler's misery. She was slower getting to her feet than she would have liked. There was gravel embedded in her back, and blood was dripping down her arms. They must have rolled over the tire shredder at some point. Scowler had shred marks on his knuckles.

The Agent could hear Pete breathing deeply, but she couldn't see him until she went around to the passenger's side of the jeep. He had removed Walter's sweater and used it to cover the dead man's face.

"We wrestled over the gun," he said with eyes and fists screwed shut. "And when he tried to fire at close range, I just tipped the gun up as far as it would go. Guy blew his own head off."

Inexplicably drawn in by Pete's agony, the Agent reached out and touched the back of one of his fists. His hand unfolded to accept hers, but his eyes remained shut.

"It was as easy as breathing," he continued, his voice shuddering. "There was no moral quandary, no dialectic of right and wrong in my mind. It was him or me, and I chose myself without hesitation."

This crisis of conscience was simply incomprehensible to the Agent. She had been taught that what was necessary must never be lamented. The months she spent carrying Kiddo had instilled in her the novel idea that someone else's survival could be as important as her own, but the Agent had never second-guessed the use of deadly force in the case of self-defense. Pete, however, had been out of the life for a few years. That was probably why he was so tortured about it.

At length, he opened his eyes and stared once more at the body of the man whom he had killed.

"Why are we like this?" he whispered bitterly.

"Because we were broken," the Agent replied.

"Don't you hate it?" he asked.

She gave a rueful grin. "It just is."

He sighed. "But hopefully not forever."

Rosa loved his optimism.

They shifted into cleanup mode. They buried the bodies about two kilometers from the road and—after retrieving their supplies from the thieves' truck—Rosa put on the jeep's spare tire. Pete observed her as she worked and stepped in as an extra pair of hands when she indicated a need for assistance. They communicated through eye contact and hand motions, no words.

After their work was done, they had to find somewhere to stay for the night and repair the car. Rosa drove the car off the road and toward the nearest town, which was just a tiny band of glimmering lights about ten kilometers to their west. There were no patrols out in the fields, which was fortunate. When they found a decent hiding place for the car, they took their supplies and headed into the town on foot.

Rosa had figured that Pete was using the silence between them to collect himself, but she noticed that he also seemed to have trouble meeting her gaze.

Finally, she asked, "You okay?"

Pete hesitated before saying, "Can I ask you something?"

"Sure."

"When those guys started harassing us about class stuff, why didn't you just keep quiet?"

Rosa's blood nearly boiled, but when she saw that Pete didn't intend the question to be an accusation, she took a deep breath.

"As a member of the Subclass, I have spent too much of my life bending to people like that," she said. "Things never improve when you just stay quiet and let ignorant people do whatever they want to you."

"But we might have been able to get by without a bloodbath," Pete protested.

"Maybe," Rosa shrugged. "But do you honestly think, with the way they were going on about the two of us, that they would have let us go without any violence?"

Pete's brow wrinkled as he truly thought about it, then he replied, "No. I think they would have gone beyond taking our supplies. They probably would have tried to harm us."

"And there's your answer," Rosa said. "It didn't end well for them, but those were the consequences they chose. You *do* know that Survival is the name of the game, don't you? What's necessary must never be lamented."

"Yes," Pete said tentatively. "But I don't think you were only thinking about our survival. It almost seemed like you *wanted* to have a violent standoff."

"Spoken like a true pureblood." Rosa's voice had a bitter edge. "You don't know what it's like to walk in this world with everyone asserting their power over you, even those who claim to be oppressed."

"Hey, I'm not exactly Class 1," he retorted, "and I'm a Phib, too."

"Which is why you *should* understand that I baited no one today. Those men ended up dead because of their own violent intentions! I only did what was necessary."

Even as the words came out of her mouth, Rosa knew that they weren't entirely accurate. The rage that seethed within her was a dead giveaway. In past lives, rage had been the source of her strength whenever she'd been frightened. It had given her the courage to do what was necessary.

"But *what* is necessary?" Pete asked exasperatedly. "You made yourself judge, jury, and executioner today without ever considering that there might be another way."

His words rang true. She had indeed learned that what was necessary must never be lamented, but somewhere along the way, her rage had begun to drive her decisions about *what* was necessary. And she had come to believe that it was necessary to make victimizers pay, at all costs.

"I'm sorry, Pete," Rosa said. "I guess my anger over past experiences affected my judgment. I didn't feel angry, but I really wanted to make them stop."

He smiled sadly. "But you *did* egg them on toward the end."

"I was standing up for us!" she said.

"And I'm glad you did that, sort of," he responded. "It's just—well, I hope that next time we're in that kind of situation, you'll maybe try to think of a response where fewer lives might be lost."

Pete's value of life, even of the most unworthy life, was admirable. Rosa didn't know how practical it would be for a couple of Phibs to be governed by such a value, but she did very much hope it could be possible—for Pete's sake.

"I'll make an effort in that direction, if it would make you feel better," she said, at last.

"It really would," he grinned.

A pickup truck was approaching them from behind. It slowed down and pulled toward the side of the road.

A Class 3 man of russet-colored skin hopped out on the passenger's side. He waved at Pete and Rosa.

"Evening, folks," he said. "Everything alright?"

Rosa gave him her most brilliant smile. "Our jeep hit a rough patch, quite literally, back there: a pothole the size of Carmelita. Both left tires took damage, but the back one's unable to be patched and we don't have a replacement."

"Tough break, kids," the guy said, running a hand through his curly, salt-and-pepper hair. "Got a spare, at least?"

"Yeah," Pete said. "It's on the car, about a half a kilometer from here. But we're headed toward the coast, and we'll need actual tires to get there."

"We've got a couple standard tires that might work for you," the man told him. "Our place is only about a five-minute drive from here. I can walk with you to fetch your car, since we're right up against female curfew. If the lady doesn't mind hopping into our truck, she can ride to our house. And we can host you for the night, if you'd like."

"That's very kind," Rosa answered. "May I ask who 'we' is?"

The man's laugh was bright and friendly. "'We' is me and the missus, of course. I'm sure you'll have a lovely chat on the way back to the house."

"Thank you," Rosa said.

She shot Pete a furtive glance before approaching the charcoal gray pickup truck in which the wife of their new acquaintance was already waving at her. The woman had dark eyes and pink lips set in a pale, thin face that was framed by straight, black hair.

"Good evening!" the woman beamed. "Hop on in!"

Rosa tried to contain her surprise, but it was rather unusual to meet a Class 3 man with a Class 2 missus in a district like Farm And Forest. It seemed that she and Pete had stumbled into a shelter from anti-miscegenist sentiments, at least for the evening.

There was a buzzing sound overhead, and the red and green lights of a drone shone through the darkness.

"We should get going," the woman in the driver's seat said. "There are eyes everywhere, and I'd hate for there to be unrest tonight."

Rosa nodded and climbed into the passenger's seat.

"Marie," the woman said, putting her hand over her heart and nodding.

"Nice to meet you," Rosa said, mirroring her gesture. "I'm Rosa. Thanks for stopping to help us."

"It's dangerous out here," Marie said.

"I wouldn't have guessed it," Rosa replied, adopting a clueless mien. "It's so quiet out here in the country."

Marie smiled kindly. "I guess you're not from around here?"

"Oh, no," Rosa said. "Pete and I've been living in Lakes."

"A very modern district in the Free East," Marie said, taking on a probing tone. "You know, things are different here in the Western States."

"I've heard some stories," Rosa said. "But it can't be all *that* bad, can it?"

Marie gave a wry chuckle. "It's probably worse than you've heard."

"What do you mean?"

"Well, for starters, it's illegal for people from different classes to have"—she cleared her throat—"relations."

Rosa's eyes widened as if she couldn't believe such a thing. "But how could anyone possibly enforce that?"

"Incarceration is rare, but they do find ways," Marie said. "And when some eugenists take the law into their own hands, law enforcement tends to back *them* rather than the victims of their crimes. So, young couples like you two just need to be careful out here."

"Oh!" Rosa exclaimed. "Pete and I aren't—well—"

"I'm sorry," Marie said. "I didn't mean to imply—"

"No, no, it's not, um—"

Marie mercifully changed the subject. "So, what are you two doing out this way, anyway?"

"We're—" There was no simple way to put it, and Rosa knew she would never be able to sell the story of two platonic friends on a road trip from Lakes to Farm And Forest.

She started again. "We're running from family. They've been very unkind to us."

Marie's expression took on a soft grimness that Rosa had only seen a couple times before. Hers was the expression of a person who had absolutely no reason to be so emotionally invested in a stranger and yet decided to care nonetheless.

"Please don't mention to anyone that you've seen us in these parts," Rosa pleaded. "Pete and I are just looking for a place to lie low for a while."

"Jason and I won't tell a soul," Marie smiled. "You know, that's part of the reason we moved out here to the country. There's just more space around here. It's a little like the Wild West, but we can handle ourselves."

Rosa returned her smile. "I sure am glad you picked us up."

"Me too," Marie said. "And we'll be happy to have you stay the night. Are you planning to stay with someone out west?"

"We've been corresponding with a friend from—from school who plans to meet us near the coast."

"Good," Marie said. "And you know you'll always have a place with us, if you happen to pass through again."

"You're too good to be true," Rosa said gratefully.

Marie laughed a charming, chirping kind of laugh. "I just remember what it was like the day Jason and I announced our marriage. It was just us against the world. We had no family but each other."

Rosa regarded her with authentic admiration. "You're made of stronger stuff than I am."

"I'd wager you're stronger than you give yourself credit for." Marie took her hand off the gearshift to squeeze Rosa's, only briefly. "In any case, you've gotten this far. That's got to be worth something."

"I suppose so." Rosa smiled inwardly at the thought, although she wasn't entirely sure why.

CHAPTER 21

Pete and Jason arrived at the house about half an hour after Marie and Rosa had. The women had been chatting in the living room, but when the men walked in, Marie rose to get some more coffee and cookies from the kitchen. Pete and Rosa begged her not to serve them, making an excuse of their fatigue.

"Of course! Where are our manners?" Marie exclaimed. "The guest room is down the hall, second door on the right. I'll bring you some sheets."

"Good night, you two!" Jason called. "Pete, I'll help you with the car in the morning."

Rosa and Pete expressed their thanks before heading down the hall. Pete peeled off to use the bathroom while Rosa entered the guest room. It had yellow walls and a full-sized bed with an orange bedspread. There were trinkets on the boudoir-style dressing table as well as what appeared to be the high school senior photo of a young woman with cinnamon-colored skin, dark eyes, and long, wavy black hair. Her smile was bright, but her eyes spoke of prolonged pain. The photo was faded, but there were no newer pictures of her on display in the house.

"Here we are!" Marie sang. She entered the room carrying a pile of crisp, orange and white striped sheets and laid them on top of the bed. When she saw Rosa admiring the photo, she sighed. "That's Darlene, our daughter."

"She looks like she's got strength of spirit," Rosa said, "enough to overcome a lifetime of pain."

Tears came to Marie's eyes. "She was so excited to leave high school behind. We just didn't understand that she wanted to leave us behind, too."

Not knowing what else to say, Rosa grasped her hand.

"It's okay," Marie said. "It really is. She struggled through life as a subclass child. Her peers were so cruel to her."

She took a deep breath before continuing, "She moved to the Free East, and for a while she kept in touch. But not long ago, she married a wealthy Class 3 man and took on his class designation. That's when she cut all ties with us. I hope and pray every day that she's okay."

Rosa smiled, drawing upon feelings that mysteriously bubbled up from the depths. "I'm sure she is. And even if she can't express it, she loves you very much. Maybe she even *wishes* she could come home, but she's worried that she's hurt you too badly."

"I would have her back in a heartbeat," Marie said, wiping her eyes, "in a *heartbeat*."

Before she knew what she was doing, Rosa found herself hugging her hostess. There were regrets she had about her past lives, despite having made the best decisions she could. In this moment, she found a brief respite from the burden of regret.

Pete cleared his throat, and the women turned to see him standing in the doorway. He entered the room, wearing fresh clothes and smelling like soap.

"I'll give you two some alone time," Marie said.

She moved to the door, then looked back at Pete and Rosa. Her eyes shone as if the sight of them warmed her heart.

"How long have you two been together?" she asked shyly. "If you don't mind my asking."

"Well—" They both started, then stopped in order to avoid giving different answers.

Rosa smiled at Pete, granting him permission to answer for them. He got the hint and adopted a bashful expression.

"Well, if we're counting from the first date," he said, sliding his hand around her waist, "about six months. But if we're talking about the day I absolutely knew she was 'the one,' I guess about two years."

Well-played. He had accounted for their hesitation by suggesting that there was more than one answer to the question.

"I knew three months ago," Rosa added, much to their hostess' amusement.

"Well, I'm glad you made it through the early stages until now," Marie chortled.

After giving them a final once-over, she wished them a good night.

"Good night, Marie," they replied in unison as the door clicked shut behind her.

Alone at last, Rosa and Pete shared an amused glance. They sat on the bed and filled each other in about their respective rides with their hosts.

"I said I'd sprained my wrist pushing the jeep off the road and couldn't shift, so Jason drove," Pete said. "We talked sports, mostly. Jason watches a lot of association football."

"Your car sounds like the fun car," Rosa said. "We talked about interclass relationships."

His eyebrows rose. "Diving in the deep end, hey?"

"I guess," Rosa said. "Marie was just giving us advice on how to handle ourselves here in the West. She thought we were together, as you could see."

"Yeah."

She couldn't get a read on the thoughts behind Pete's pensive expression.

"I told her we weren't together," she continued hurriedly. "But she kind of assumed I was keeping it under wraps because of, well, things like what happened earlier on the road."

"Yeah," he said again. "Besides, she's some kind of Class 2 and she married a 3, so she's probably hyperaware of those kinds of things."

"Probably," Rosa agreed. "But at least her husband wasn't subclass like me. You know how Class 2 families can look down on people who are naturally unclassified, especially those with one Class 2 parent. Group betrayal, impure blood, and all that?"

Pete frowned at the space between them on the mattress. Perhaps he was thinking about his experience growing up in what he'd termed a "very Neo-Eugenically oriented Class 2 family."

Blood purity was an idea born of Class 1 polemics and adopted by the other pureblooded classes. The concept, though based in pseudo-science, had the power to divide families, communities, and even whole countries. A pureblood would be prudent to consider this before associating with a member of the Subclass, perhaps especially when shared heritage was a part of the equation.

At last, Pete looked up at Rosa and grinned. "Well, what advice did Marie have for us?"

She shrugged. "She just wanted us to be careful in these parts because people tend to take the law into their own hands. It's dangerous just for us to be *seen* together—even if we are just friends."

"Oh, right." Pete scratched his head. "It's kind of weird how people just assume we're *not*, uh, just friends."

"Yeah, we'll just have to be prepared for when people get the wrong idea." Rosa stood. "Well, I can barely keep my eyes open. You can have the bed. I'll sleep on the floor tonight."

"I wouldn't dream of it!" Pete said. "I'm sleeping on the floor."

"But you slept on the couch at your own house while I slept in *your* bed. I intend to return the favor."

"You're insane if you think I'd go for that," he said, snatching the sheets. He made the bed much quicker than Rosa could have done it in any of her past lives, and in no more than fifteen seconds, he was motioning for her to climb into it.

"Fine, I'll sleep in the bed, but you take the comforter." And with that, she tossed it onto the floor. "I'm going to shower and all that."

When she came back from the bathroom, Pete was wrapped in a sheet and snoring on the floor. The comforter was back on the bed. Rosa tossed the blanket over Pete, knowing that it would likely get very cold on the floor that night. Then she turned out the light and listened to Pete's snoring.

* * *

With the Killer watching close by, the Agent reached for the medical director. Her breath rasped in her throat as she seized him.

"Say it again."

The Agent awoke with a start and shivered in the darkness. The cold made her long for the heat lamp back in Lakes. And that reminded her of how much she longed for her son. And that reminded her of how much some part of her longed for the safety of family and friendship, a place to belong. In the darkness, her thoughts began to whirl around her in great, confusing spirals.

She knew that she was most efficient on her own, but this soft, weak side born of her time in Diablo drew her toward people. Valencia had become convinced that she *needed* her family, that she *needed* her friends—her wonderful friends who were probably out there in the world somewhere, barking up the wrong tree.

What was she doing here, in this house, in this room, on this road with this man—this Phib? Deep down, she knew that there was no good way for their story to end. Her experience with the Changs and the Wilsons had taught her that destruction followed in her wake. For her friends and family, that had meant bodily harm and psychological trauma. But what could it mean for Pete? Likely something much worse, if the WCE ever caught up with him. She had not considered that throughly enough when she had allowed him to join her, but his reaction to their encounter with the road thieves had shown her that he, too, was fragile in a certain way.

And yet, Rosa had grown attached to Pete. She did not need him in the same way that Lenci had needed her family, but she felt comfortable with him because her past could not terrorize him—not much more than his own could, anyway. Pete knew what it was to be brutalized into a monster. And because of that, he understood her in a way that no one else could.

"I'm sorry!" Pete yelled.

He cried out again, this time unintelligibly, then thrashed about in the comforter, whimpering and sobbing.

"Pete!" Rosa whispered. "Wake up!"

The comforter became still. Pete's limbs were sticking out from under it, trembling tensely like he wanted to move them but couldn't. He was moaning loudly. Concerned that he would awaken their hosts, Rosa sighed and slid out of the bed.

"Pete," she whispered again, taking his hand so that she could massage the paralysis out of it.

Suddenly, he grabbed her around the neck. The Agent took him to the floor, but as they wrestled, she noticed that his eyes were rolled back in his head. He was still asleep.

"Wake *up*, Pete!" she hissed. "Damn it, man!"

He had her pinned on her side, but she managed to create enough space between them to loosen his grip and throw off his balance. Then she straddled him and jammed her knees into his elbows. This was where her exceptional leg strength came in handy. He was pinned with both shoulders to the floor.

Giving his face a few soft slaps, she entreated him to come back. After about a half a minute, Pete opened his eyes.

Noting their peculiar position, he smiled goofily. "Hey, third time tonight! I could get used *this* dream."

Rosa scoffed, then sat beside him on the floor. "Would that be the one where you try to kill me in your sleep?"

His smile gave way to pure horror. "You're kidding."

She shrugged. "Well, you were trying to kill someone else, probably, but I guess I got in the way."

Pete brought his hands to his head. "Oh, no. I'm so sorry."

"It's okay," Rosa said. "My past tends to attack while I'm asleep, too."

"I'd never hurt you," he replied.

"Don't make promises you can't keep," Rosa said wryly.

He grinned. "That's one I feel fairly committed to."

Then he threw the comforter around both of their shoulders and said, "I know the only reason you came down here was because you wanted to share the blanket, so how about we both stay warm for the night?"

"I'll take you up on that," Rosa said, shivering as she lay back-to-back with him. "It was freezing up there on the bed. Just better hope no one walks in on us."

Pete yawned. "They think we're together, anyway."

"About that," Rosa said, "I underestimated how much of a target we'd be in this area. I mean, I knew it would be bad, but it was worse than I'd imagined. Do you think we should—"

"If today is any indication, I think we'll be just fine."

After a moment, Rosa said more to herself than to him, "We *do* work pretty well together."

"In more than one way," Pete mumbled, his voice becoming loose and relaxed.

She rolled over and grasped his arm, jolting him awake once more. "You think so?"

"Well, yeah," he said, patting her hand drowsily. "I mean, we get each other, and we've had the luck to cross paths after outgrowing the WCE—so to speak."

Luck, maybe. Valencia's handler had called it "Providence," and thinking on that made Rosa feel all the more grateful—like maybe there was some directionality in all of this chaos, some purpose.

"Not to mention, we look really good together," Pete said, "like stunningly good."

"Hard to argue with that," she chuckled, "but people will target us for it."

He turned over and grinned at her. "And just like we did today, we'll be able to handle ourselves."

"The bullying of those common road thieves is nothing compared to the full wrath of the WCE," Rosa reminded him.

"Well, it's a good thing the agency doesn't own us anymore. So, there's nothing to worry about." He moved in to kiss her, but she pushed him gently in the face.

"I'm serious, Pete," she said. "The WCE deals treacherously in these kinds of situations. They didn't know I was subclass, but my son—"

"Is going to be safe in your arms in the near future, if all goes well," Pete finished. "And if there's anything that being a Phib has taught me, it's to *not* be afraid of treachery."

"Good point," Rosa smiled.

They chatted awhile longer and must have talked themselves to sleep because they were still wrapped up together in the comforter at twilight when the Agent awoke to the sound of gunshots. A light turned on in the hallway, and two sets of footsteps thumped toward the front door.

"The shots came from the front yard," the Agent said, jumping up to pull on her shoes. "Just warning shots, I think, though. Get up, Pete!"

Pete rolled over and pulled down the edges of the comforter to keep the cold air from getting under it.

"Right behind you," he said groggily.

"Oh, no you don't!" She ripped the blanket off of him.

"Holy wow!" He leapt to his feet and turned away from her. "You can't do that to a guy when he's sleeping!"

She tossed his pants at him. "Phibs aren't shy about those things."

"Well, I don't always feel like a Phib when I'm around you," he said, pulling on his pants.

"Interesting." The Agent put her ear to the door.

"It's just, when I'm around you—"

She shushed him and whispered, "Listen!"

Their hosts were in a heated discussion with someone at the front door.

"There's got to be some mistake," Jason was saying. "They're just a couple of kids."

"We know they're here, Singh!" a gruff voice accused. "Tim Robinson here has drone footage of them walking out of his field. *Your* truck picked them up."

"We helped them out, sure," Jason answered coolly, "but they were eager to be on their way."

A new voice, presumably that of Robinson, chimed in. "Then, you won't mind if we take a look around, hey?"

"Actually, we do," Marie said. "You can't just come waking us up out of our sleep whenever you get a crazy notion."

"Get your female under control, Singh," the gruff voice said.

"Get yourself under control, Hampstead," Jason replied. "If the missus says you aren't welcome here, then you aren't welcome. Go on home."

"You miscegenists are all the same!" Someone else shouted.

At least three men entered the house, and it sounded like things were getting physical. Rosa put her hand on the doorknob, but Pete tugged on her sleeve and shook his head.

"Garage," he mouthed. "Fix the car."

He was right. They couldn't blow their cover that way. Marie had said that she and Jason were used to dealing with situations like this. From her reference to the Wild West, Rosa figured it was likely that there were multiple firearms in the house, if the need should arise.

"This is an outrage!" Marie was yelling. "How dare you?"

She and Jason were being restrained. Intruders with booted feet clunked through the living room, overturning furniture as they went.

Rosa and Pete looked at each other and, without a word, sprang into motion. They folded the sheets and the comforter and put them in the closet. Just as the intruders arrived at the guest room door, the two Phibs hurled themselves down into the shrubbery outside the window.

The lights came on in the guest room. Marie's protestations could be heard over the tumult of the angry men kicking the bed and slamming the sliding closet doors into the walls.

Rosa's ears pricked up when she heard Marie saying, "Don't touch that. We haven't seen our daughter since her graduation. It's the most recent photo we have of her."

"That *is* a shame," Robinson said. "Why don't you just tell me where those miscegenists went, then?"

"I don't *know*," Marie replied. "They were very secretive, as you can imagine."

She gave a shrill, anguished scream, and the sound of glass

breaking followed. Filled with a protective rage, Rosa lurched toward the window, but Pete grabbed her back. Jason and another man entered the guest room.

"As you can see, there's no one here," Jason said. "Now that you've humiliated us, why don't you just leave us the dignity to clean up without you folks hovering around?"

Pete released Rosa and motioned to their right. Now was their chance to get to the garage. She took one last look at the guest room window, then nodded. They tiptoed around the side of the house and found the garage door already open.

Rosa pointed toward the far wall where there were a couple of decent looking tires. While Pete dragged them over to the jeep, Rosa grabbed a lug wrench. Jason had jacked up the car the night before, so they were able to set about their work quickly and quietly. In a couple of minutes, they had the tires on the car and were ready to depart.

Returning the lug wrench to its place with a stack of cash for compensation, Rosa sighed. "I'd really like to say goodbye to Marie."

"Not with all those guys in there," Pete said. "Maybe we can just leave them a note with the money."

"But Jason sent them away. It'll only take a moment." Rosa ran out the door and right into a portly man. From the way that he breathed, she identified him as Robinson.

He pressed a gun into her side and whispered, "Don't scream, brownie. Now, tell me where your yellow-skinned beau is, and we'll finish this off the right way."

"You eugenists are all the same," she muttered.

"And who cares about the opinion of a Class 3 female?"

"I'm subclass!" She forced the gun up out of his grip and stomped on his foot. When he was off-balance, she threw him onto the ground. Pressing her foot into his back, she broke his gun arm at the shoulder and elbow, then one of his knees for good measure.

As the Agent watched the cruel man squirm and scream, she thought it wouldn't be so very much trouble to stomp on his chest to crush his heart. Of course, such an action would bring Pete much grief, but it would keep the eugenist from terrorizing anyone ever again. And wouldn't the world be better with one fewer eugenist?

Before she could make a decision one way or another, Marie and Jason came running with guns in hand. While Jason kept his weapon aimed at Robinson, who still lay groaning on the ground, Marie holstered hers and mobbed Rosa with a hug.

"I'm sorry it had to happen this way," she said. "But it's been a pleasure having you kids with us."

Rosa squeezed her tightly. "It was our pleasure. Thank you for your kindness."

"No, thank *you*." Marie pulled back and wiped her tear-filled eyes. "For a few hours, there was life in my Darlene's room. Such a gift."

Rosa suddenly found herself near tears, as well. She crossed her arms and looked at Robinson.

"Don't worry about him," Marie said. "These kinds of things happen every so often. Nothing much will come of it. All this took place on our property. We simply stood our ground. And it'll be our word against his, *if* it ever makes it to court. Isn't that right, Mr. Robinson?"

He spat in her direction, earning himself a kick in the hip from Jason.

"Good luck meeting your friend," Marie said. "Be safe out there. And our invitation for a place to stay is open, always."

Rosa covered her heart and nodded. "Thank you, Marie."

Pete had pushed the jeep out of the garage into the yard. He came over to exchange firm handshakes with their hosts.

"Thanks for everything," he said. "You really stuck your necks out for us."

"Just treating folks the way we would want to be treated." Jason clapped him on the back. "Come back any time."

"*Any* time!" Marie echoed, squeezing Pete's hand.

"We'd love that," Rosa said as she climbed into the driver's seat.

Pete got in on the passenger's side.

"Would you look at that, Marie?" Jason said. "Last female I knew that could drive a stick-shift—well, I *married* her!"

"They are quite a bit like we were in our younger years, aren't they, Jason?" Marie said.

Jason put his arm around her. "If you say so, hon."

She chortled quietly and waved once more at Pete and Rosa as the jeep pulled away.

Rosa glanced back at them in the rearview mirror repeatedly until she turned onto the main road. The sun was up by then, bathing the world in pale golden light. Everything was quiet, and it was only the sputtering of the jeep's engine that intruded upon the glorious stillness of winter morning on the country road. Pete fell asleep after a couple of minutes, and Rosa was content to listen to his snoring.

CHAPTER 22

IT WAS 1430 WHEN THE COOP TEAM ARRIVED IN A HUMAN-OPERATED rental car at the WCE compound known as 'Home'. They had made good time up the highway, off-roaded through the woodlands for about twenty kilometers, and parked right outside the barbed wire fence of the compound. The fence enclosed about four square kilometers of land on which sat a few clusters of buildings, a helipad, and a training yard. While the compound supposedly ran on a skeleton crew, no members of the staff could be seen milling about the area.

"Let's get some good intel," Blair said. "Carry this, Wilson."

She handed the carrier containing the canister to Karthik.

Racky took out her flake and a pair of wire cutters, then pulled on her backpack. After using the electricity sensor on her flake to confirm that the fence was not electric, she clipped a decent-sized hole for their entry.

"Maybe we shouldn't enter here," Blair said, motioning to a security camera that was posted in a nearby tree.

The camera was pointed at the yard in front of them, just inside of the fence. There were three other cameras in sight, and while they were all clearly designed to oscillate, they seemed frozen.

"Huh," Racky said, fishing around in her bag of gadgets.

"What are you looking for?" Karthik asked.

"These." She pulled out a pair of spectacles and blew on their lenses before donning them. The lenses made her eyes appear twice their normal size. "They help me to see reverse phantasms—you know, the kind that are invisible to the naked eye but can be seen through lenses with a certain angle of refraction."

Blair grinned. "A creation motivated by our first communication with B.F., no doubt."

"B.F. helps me to be a better version of myself," Racky said, pushing the spectacles up on her nose. "And it's already paying off. Somebody—my money's on B.F.—disabled the cameras by using hanging webs to rewrite the cameras' command codes from the outside. The webs are invisible to the naked eye, so you'd have to be looking specifically for phantasms to find them!"

"Seems excessive," Karthik said. "Why not just use a regular looped feed?"

"Looped feeds are easy to trace, even if they take a roundabout path," Racky replied. "These webs are self-contained, artificially intelligent tools that can adapt to counteract opposition to the hacker's nefarious goals while managing to stay undetectable and untraceable, at least to the average security system."

"Well, that's to our advantage today," Blair said. "Let's get in there. We've got two hours before the exchange."

"Do we know where specifically to meet B.F.?" Karthik asked.

"No," Racky said. "Guess we'll just have to wander around until we bump into each other and jump out of our skin with fright."

She popped the trunk of the rental car and pulled out her gigantic shotgun, Bambina Extraordinaire.

"Wernicke, you can't bring that," Blair said. "You have an agency-issued weapon for a reason."

"But the range is so much better with Bambina Extraordinaire," Racky grumbled, putting the gun back into the trunk.

"If by 'better' you mean 'more expansive,' I agree," Blair said. "Those look important." She motioned toward a couple of buildings. One looked like a typical rectangular office building or hospital, and the one next to it was a large, white dome.

"The hospital looks interesting," Racky said. "I bet it could have records."

"Let's move," said Blair.

* * *

The building's entrance opened on a lobby and reception area. It was dark, and the light switches didn't work. A thin layer of dust covered everything, and there was a single trail of footprints that led from the entrance to the nearest hallway.

"They're fresh," Karthik said. "T—tiny feet, probably a female."

Racky rolled her eyes. "So, my long flipper-flappers would make you think I was a male?"

"I'm just saying that, statistically speaking, the feet of females t—tend to be sm—"

"Fascinating, Wilson," Blair interrupted from the reception desk. She held up a large binder. "I found the directory that will tell us where the visitor *went*. Now, I don't know about you, but I feel like that is a *much* more useful piece of information than their sex."

"You got a map on that directory?" Racky asked.

"No, just the names of the rooms next to the numbers. Let's take it with us and follow the footprints."

The lobby fed into two different hallways, one to the right and one to the left. They followed the footprints down the lefthand hall. The room names in the directory were alphanumerically assigned and primarily medically themed with the exception of common spaces like the cafeteria and the restrooms.

The footprints in the dust led to a room marked R721. The door was slightly ajar, its keypad lock flashing with green and yellow lights.

"R721," Racky read. "What does the directory say about it?"

"It's not in the directory," Blair replied.

Instead of entering through the cracked door, Racky stopped to examine the sides of the doorway.

"What are you d—doing?" Karthik asked. "The d—door's already open."

He tried to walk through it, but she grabbed him back.

"It's rigged," she said, motioning to the thin wire that was stretched taut between the door and the wall.

"Oh, thanks," he said, experiencing a strong sense of déjà vu. He still hadn't quite gotten over the last time he'd nearly walked through an explosive doorway.

Blair sighed impatiently. "Can you disarm it, Racky?"

Racky was already removing the cover of the lock. "Our visitor might have bummed off this circuitry. Give me a minute."

She pulled out a handheld device and hooked it up to the keypad.

"What's that?" Karthik asked.

"It's a translator that will help me to have a decent conversation with this keypad."

He grinned mischievously. "Wild, Racky. D—do you often converse with l—locks?"

"They make a lot more sense than illogical, vindictive people," she said. "Hush, now."

"But seriously, what l—language d—do they speak?"

"Shut your mouth, crumb-butt."

"Shape up, you two," Blair said. "We don't know what's waiting for us in there. Understood?"

"Understood," they replied in unison.

Then Racky whispered, "Spawn of Pandora."

Karthik's eyebrows rose. "What?"

"That's the language the lock speaks."

"Good grief," Blair groaned. "Just do your job, Wernicke."

"I'm almost in," Racky said. "I just need to—"

She typed in a command, and the keypad beeped in response.

Racky huffed. "You sneaky bugger. You're not going to get me on that one."

In answer to her teammates' inquisitive glances, she explained, "Titty trap."

"I think the appropriate t—term is 'booby trap,'" Karthik said.

"Takes one to know one," she mumbled.

"Don't start, Racky," Blair said. "What is *with* you guys? You've been at each other's throats for the past couple of days."

"Personal issues," Karthik replied with an eye roll.

"Gorgon issues," Racky muttered. "Can't believe you bought that wretched woman a ring."

He opened his mouth to retort, but the keypad beeped again.

"Got it," Racky said proudly. She clipped the tripwire with her cutters and pushed open the door. It swung inward silently, and Karthik was relieved at the lack of an explosion.

"Personal feelings aside," Blair ordered them. "I need you at your best."

She led the way. Karthik was right behind her, and Racky took up the rear.

Room R721 was painted plain white. There were screens on every wall, and there was a holoprojector in the ceiling that pointed right to the middle of the floor.

"What *is* it?" Blair asked.

"It looks like it could be their records department," Karthik said.

Motioning to the rows of empty shelves, Racky added, "And it looks like they went paperless some time ago." She turned toward the screen nearest to the door. "I bet this is the access point."

"Do you really think that they could *still* be storing records about the Phibs here?" Karthik asked, staring at the dust covered floor. "It looks like no one's been here in a long time."

"What better way to keep secrets than offline, sequestered away on a chip manufacturing compound with 'light administrative functions?'" Racky plugged in her cloning device. "Anyway, whoever came right before us just tried to explode this stuff along with us. So, it's worth checking out."

"Get me everything on there," Blair commanded.

Racky ignored her because the device she was holding had already done just that. "Let's follow the virtual breadcrumbs to find the source of the homicidal, tiny-footed visitor's viewing pleasure."

The holoprojector in the ceiling flickered to life and surrounded the Coop agents with moving 3-D images of young men and women in separate containment cells along one side of a long hallway. A deep voice narrated.

Replacing the weak things of the world. The Amphibians are the WCE's elite cohort of agents—the world's best and brightest pureblood agents, trained as efficient politicians, doctors, lawyers, tech developers, and of course, human weapons. Through the use of the newest DNA-masking technology, these agents will replace their subclass counterparts and remain completely untraceable by way of their unregistered status. After all, who regulates or even watches the Subclass? There is no better cover for agents who must be able to appear and disappear at the drop of a hat.

The scene around the Coop agents changed. They were in a room in a medical facility with a doctor, lab assistants, and a patient.

This is Number Nineteen from the list of agents selected for review: a female, Class 3.5 pureblood.

"It's Lenci!" Karthik exclaimed.

Blair and Racky shushed him.

Nineteen's situation is unique in that her counterpart is also a Class 3 pureblood. The two were tested rigorously to see which would replace the other for the privileged responsibility of eliminating the first Amphibian and taking over the country's greatest supplier of subclass covert agents.

Number Nineteen was assigned to the group that nature deemed unfit. Note that the doctor administered the same dosage of the euthanasic nanobots as was given to the other unfit subjects.

The doctor put a mask with tubing on Lenci, who did not seem to know that she was being euthanized. She was smiling and chatting animatedly with the lab assistants.

But the results were confounding, to say the least.

After a few seconds, Lenci began to writhe. She was clearly in pain, and when she kicked her legs free of the restraints, multiple assistants had to hold her down.

"I can't watch this," Karthik said, turning away.

Racky jabbed his shoulder with her elbow. "No, look! Look!"

Lenci's movements became less frantic until, at last, she lay still. The doctor felt for a pulse, then made a gesture to the assistants. As soon as they took off her mask, Lenci sprang into action. From her slower and more measured movements, it was clear that this recording had been made before her intensive one-on-one training with the Killer. Even so, Lenci made a mess of the room and the staff.

"Amazing!" Racky said as Lenci bit off the doctor's ear. "Watch her go!"

"She's tough; I'll give her that," Blair said. "And now we know where the nanobots in her blood came from."

Thinking of his cousin Arjun, Karthik said, "I wonder what the chances are that *two* people could survive that procedure."

"Anyone's guess," Racky shrugged.

The hologram's narration continued.

The chief medical director insisted that a more thorough method be used to put down the sturdy SSI agent. However, an appeal came from the most surprising of sources: David Miller the Killer, longtime friend of and contractor for the WCE.

"Wait just a precious minute!" Racky squawked. "The Killer saved her life?"

Blair's jaw tightened, but she did not take her eyes off of the scene unfolding before them.

The Killer suggested a more theatrical and entertaining showdown. Having friends in the highest places of WCE leadership, he went over the chief medical director's head. At the Killer's request, the Assistant Vice gave the order for the event to take place, although she herself was not in attendance. The unfit agent and her fit counterpart faced off a week later in the arena where the dead pile was kept, for easier disposal of the body afterward.

"Oh, that makes more sense," Racky said. "Well, more sense than him trying to save her life."

"Yes, he just wanted a more *entertaining* death," Blair said, shaking her head. "I can't believe that man is my birthfather."

The hologram flickered as the autoplay function moved to the next recording in the system. The recording looked like it had been made on a personal device. The cameraperson was walking into the white dome that the Coop agents had seen on their way into the compound. There was a lot of chatter around the camera.

"The arena is in the dome!" Racky said. "Let's go there after this!"

Blair looked at her flake. "We're good on time."

"This'll be pleasant," Karthik said, glancing at the pile of bodies by the arena's entrance in the hologram.

"Don't worry about them," Racky said. "They're probably not there anymore."

"Or, if they are, they don't look like that," Blair added.

"It's n—not the bodies," Karthik said. "I d—don't think I can watch Lenci kill herself."

The two contestants—one with a red band on her arm and the other with a black band, both with Lenci's face—stood in front of each other. Their faces were devoid of emotion as they bowed and took their starting positions.

"I have a hunch you won't have to," Racky said, cocking her head.

The starting bell rang, and the contestant with the black band jumped straight into the air. The picture went dark. Rustling and panicked shouting indicated that the recording was still playing.

"She went for the l—lights," Karthik remarked. "Out of all the things she's capable of, she just went for the l—lights."

Racky scratched her head. "Maybe that one wasn't our Lenci."

"Or maybe it was, and she felt outmatched," Blair said.

The crowd of people that had been so excited to enter the arena began jostling against each other to get out of it. Shadows flickered around the Coop agents as the people in the recording tripped toward the exit. The records room was filled with blinding light for a few seconds before the lenses on the recording device adjusted to the lighting outside the building.

All of the panicked people congregated in the yard outside of the dome. They slammed the door and locked it. Then the spectators huddled together, asking questions and exchanging information.

How long do we wait?

Who's going to make sure she's dead?

I heard the fit one's nearly rabid.

I heard she got a dishonorable discharge from Winehill for disemboweling a guy.

"That's d—disgusting," Karthik said.

I heard she got discharged for eating *her kill.*

"*That's* disgusting," said Racky.

A guttural yell came from the arena. A tall man in a white coat hurried forward and cracked the door just enough to shove something through it. Then he jumped back as the door swung open.

One of the contestants dragged her dead opponent out into the sunlight. The living one had blood on her hands, and her opponent's neck was broken. Neither of them wore their armband, and both of their arms were ripped and bloody.

The identifier chips we implanted have been torn out!

The tall man frowned at the panting, blood-covered contestant. He grabbed her by the face and examined her.

I want a blood test.

The Killer stepped into the frame.

No tests. He put the living contestant behind him. *She beat her opponent, so she's proven herself fit. I'll train her myself.*

Blair huffed. "Turn it off, Racky. You can watch the rest on your own time."

"But why—"

"I said, 'turn it off.'"

"Okay, okay," Racky said, powering down the projector.

Her SSA was already heading to the door with Karthik in tow.

"Let's see if we can stop by the arena and get a sample," Blair said.

"You think they really l—left those bodies undisturbed?" Karthik asked.

"I bet they buried them in the dome eventually," she replied. "But I'm not opposed to supervising you two while you exhume them."

"You've got t—to be kidding me," Karthik sighed.

They rounded the corner to get to the lobby and headed for the door by which they had entered. When Blair tried the door, she couldn't get it to open.

"Locked from the outside," Karthik noted grimly.

"Here's hoping there's another way out," Racky said. She motioned to the tiny footprints that trailed around the lobby and down the other hallway. The tiny-footed visitor had gone through there while they were in the records room.

"Yeah." Blair drew her gun. Karthik and Racky followed suit.

They started down the hallway slowly and silently. It was dark, and the air smelled strongly of artificial cherry flavoring, like someone had waxed the floors with cherry lipgloss.

As they were passing the restrooms, a shadow shot down from the ceiling. Blair tried to yell a warning, but the shadow, which was a person, kicked her in the face with a tiny, booted foot. The tiny-footed ambusher was incredibly agile, flitting in and out of the dark spaces of the hallway. Before Racky and Karthik could figure out where to aim, their guns were dismantled on the floor.

Silhouetted against the light from the exit sign at the end of the hall, their ambusher struck a pose. Although her face was obscured in darkness, the intense curvature of her figure stood out. Hers was an unnaturally dramatic hourglass, which Karthik recognized immediately.

"Sorry, folks," she said in a sultry voice, "this wing is off-limits."

"Who are you?" Blair asked.

"The only one with any sense here," she said, sighing deeply. "Now, sleep."

Blair and Racky immediately collapsed. The cherry fragrance grew stronger. Karthik clung to the wall, feeling lightheaded.

"Interesting." The ambusher approached him as his knees buckled.

She was indeed the woman he had seen at the river in Croon A Tune. Only now, she wore a short-sleeved, red jumpsuit rather than a bathrobe. Her cold eyes looked disappointed to see him.

Helping him the rest of the way to the floor, she said, "We meet again, *Agent* Wilson."

He tried to respond, but his tongue was stuck to the roof of his mouth.

"Don't worry; I'll make sure your friend is safe." She shook her wavy, chestnut brown hair out of her face. "Incidentally, I *do* believe you managed to uncover more about me than I was ready to reveal. That will be remedied shortly."

She blew into his face. Her breath was hot and smelled like artificial cherry flavoring. She gave his face a final pat and used a zip tie to bind his hands. Karthik's body relaxed, and his eyes closed. He heard the woman bind Racky. Then she dragged Blair out of the nearest exit.

* * *

At 1540, Rosa and Pete were zooming down a lonely road in the jeep. Scraggly rows of ferns lined the sides of the road, and beyond them was a seemingly infinite expanse of trees.

"You've been awful quiet," Pete said. "What are you thinking about?"

Rosa had been thinking about the night before when Pete had attempted to kill her in his sleep. She trusted him, and yet—and yet.

"Honestly, I'm getting cold feet about having brought you along," she admitted.

He looked out the window as he responded, "Because my choosing not to kill you in Lakes and then fighting beside you against murderous eugenists isn't proof enough that you can trust me?"

"Well, with the WCE, it isn't always about our *choosing*," Rosa said.

Pete side-glanced her. "We're both free, aren't we? You know my handler is dead, so my Song doesn't work anymore. And I choose to trust you even though your handler's still alive."

"And your trust is well-founded," she smiled. "The Killer *is* still out there somewhere, but I beat the snot out of him the last time he used my Song."

"That inspires confidence as well as a healthy dose of terror," Pete replied. "One would not want to live life snotless."

"Ha. Ha." She scrunched up her face at him.

"Seriously, though," he said. "I came along because I want to help you."

"And you want to do your part to dismantle the oppressive systems of the world," she reminded him.

He grinned. "And the WCE is the hegemon worth targeting, for sure. But I want you to know that I'm not here only because our interests are aligned in that respect."

She didn't bother reminding him that hegemony was of secondary concern to her while her son was still a lab rat and developing weapon.

Pete continued, "I really care about you, and I won't ever do anything to hurt you."

"Oh, Pete, I believe you," Rosa told him. "And I care about you, too."

She smiled, but she couldn't help thinking about how many times she had unintentionally hurt people whom she very much cherished. The past threatened to cloud her vision, so she stuffed it back where it belonged—somewhere deep, somewhere dark.

"We're getting close," Pete said. "Better turn off the road here."

The jeep jolted and hopped over the uneven terrain. It had rained earlier, and the car seemed ready to get stuck in a mud pit or on a rogue tree root at any moment.

"You sure about that leaving the road thing?" Rosa asked after a couple minutes of extra rough maneuvering.

He shrugged. "Unless you want to go right up to the front gate and ring the doorbell."

"Point taken," she chuckled.

Only minutes later, the edge of the compound was within view. Rosa experienced no psychological fireworks or poisoned shafts upon seeing it. It just looked like a barbed wire fence running through the trees.

Although no meeting place had been specified between Blazing-Mander and B.F., Pete and Rosa figured that the involved parties had probably arrived and could easily be tracked. They climbed out of the jeep by the fence at the far west corner of the compound.

In one place, the fence had been clipped and soldered back together. The security cameras, which looked like they should have been able to oscillate, never moved. They were all pointed away from the repaired hole in the fence.

"Someone made decent arrangements for this rendezvous to be as private as possible," Rosa remarked.

"Yeah," Pete said, looking toward a treeless area about six meters away. "And looks like there was a struggle to make that happen."

Rosa followed him to investigate. The area was simply a shallow, barren, tree-fringed basin. There were a bunch of footprints and body prints in the mud. Two of the sets of footprints were undoubtedly from standard-issue WCE security uniform boots. It was impossible to tell exactly how many people had been fighting. At least four, maybe more.

It appeared that the security guards had not prevailed. At the base of a tree on the far side of the basin, there lay a security badge. Rosa pocketed it, in case it should prove useful later. Under it was a deep red, striated, fleshy object with what looked like tubes sticking out of it.

"Is that what I think it is?" Rosa asked.

"Without a doubt," Pete replied, poking it with a stick. "Human heart."

"So, we're dealing with a Phib," Rosa said, "a Phib pretending to be me."

"Or a Phib trying to trap you," Pete said.

"Or both," they said simultaneously. The thought was sobering.

There were tire tracks that led away from the site.

"We can follow those on foot," Rosa said.

"Good plan." Pete checked to make sure his gun was loaded, then tucked it into the back of his pants.

"You're really going to bring that?" Rosa asked.

He shrugged. "It's useful against a Phib—at a distance, anyway."

She couldn't argue with that. She just hoped there wouldn't be anyone else at Home who could handle a gun better than Pete could.

They followed the vehicle tracks and ended up at the southernmost tip of the compound. Inside of the fence, there were multiple sets of footprints in the mud. A small group of people had walked eastward, toward the arena.

Rosa's heart sank.

"You okay?" Pete asked.

"I'll have to be," she replied, "for my son."

He cast her a sympathetic smile. "It can't be too similar to what you remember. After your, uh, event, they buried the bodies."

"I was still Home for that," Rosa said, trying to return his smile. The past was just facts, after all. "But I haven't been inside of it since they made it into a gym. I think it'll always be the arena to me."

"That's understandable," Pete replied. Then, after a moment's silence, "What I can do to help?"

Rosa widened her smile. "Watch my back?"

"Always," he said.

His gaze wandered to the fence. It had been clipped and soldered there, as well.

"We might as well climb it," she said. "The barbed wire is only at the top, and it doesn't look so bad."

Pete took off his sweatshirt and wrapped it around his hands. "Don't you want something more for your hands?"

"I brought a blanket from the car," she said, pulling it out of her satchel. "I would do it barehanded, but then I wouldn't heal in time. And I might need my hands for whatever is waiting for us in there."

"And *whoever*." Pete turned and began to climb the fence.

Rosa didn't tell him that the only person she was afraid of encountering at Home was herself.

CHAPTER 23

When Blair regained consciousness, she found herself tied to a chair at one end of a long, dark room with a domed ceiling. The wooden floor was dusty and marked like the floor of a school gymnasium.

In the middle of the room, there were two females whispering underneath a single hanging lightbulb. One of them was tall with tan skin. Her jet-black hair must have been incredibly long because it was twisted up into a bun that was half the size of her head. The other female was taller still, brunette, olive-skinned, and curvaceous.

"She's awake," the brunette said. "Now, I'm backing down, but just make sure not to disturb my note."

Blair looked down to see that there was a note pinned to her jacket, just above her left clavicle. She couldn't make out the words in the dim light, but she could tell that the script was fancy and had a lot of flourishes.

"I'm well able to operate with top-notch precision," the one with the bun was saying. "I've been in the life at least as long as you."

"Of course," the brunette replied. "I wish you luck."

"I don't need luck, but thanks for, hm, sharing your opportunity."

"Always happy to share a good opportunity with a fellow Phib," the brunette said in a somewhat sour tone. "Besides, I'm outmatched."

"Yes," the one with the bun said, looking her up and down. "Cheers, then."

"Best." The brunette exited out the front door.

So, they were both Amphibians, but they were not exactly working together.

Once the brunette had left, the Amphibian with the bun approached Blair and said, "You're not Fire Salamander."

"My seller will be furious about this," Blair threatened. "Where are my partners?"

The Amphibian smirked. "I care nothing for the canister, but I saw in the ad that there were two parties: B.F. and Fire Salamander. Only now, B.F. has left the premises, and Fire Salamander is nowhere to be seen. It has turned out that no one who is *supposed* to be here is actually here. Curious, isn't it?"

"Why did B.F. turn me over to you?" Blair asked.

"She calculated the cost of facing me one-on-one and decided it would be better to concede," the Amphibian said with a shrug.

"So, what do you want with me if you really want Fire Salamander and you know that I'm not her?"

The Amphibian's eyes began to gleam. "You know that Fire is female, indicating that you and she have been acquainted in *some* way. I intend to return this rather elusive operative to the agency as soon as possible, so I'd be interested to discover what else you might know."

"I never really made contact with Fire Salamander," Blair said. "There was some chatter—"

"There is no chatter about Phibs," said the Amphibian. "I want information that will help me to track her, like her former aliases, names of trusted connections, *places* that are important to her, and the like."

Blair set her jaw.

"Clamming up, are we?" The Amphibian socked her in the face. "Anything come to mind now?"

Unable to wipe the blood trickling out of her mouth, Blair spat it onto the floor beside her chair and remained silent.

"Tough one, hey?" the Amphibian said, pulling a knife from her leg holster. "I'll break you in two minutes."

She stuck the point of the knife into Blair's right shoulder and twisted it.

As the Coop agent cried out in pain, the Amphibian whispered in her ear, "This pain can go away as slowly or as quickly as you want. Tell me what you know, and I will end it."

Blair looked her in the eye. "I know all of the districts of the Western States: Forsythe, Diablo, Carmelita, Cormorant..."

The Amphibian's upper lip curled back. "Poor choice."

She drew back her knife to stab Blair again but was interrupted by a commotion at the door.

"H.F.!" A slight man with beige skin and a platinum beard stumbled toward her. "I found the couple B.F. left tied up in the medical facility. I hid the male outside, but I had to leave the female because I couldn't carry them both at once. I got a charley horse trying to maneuver in that mud out there, and it's just plain disagreeable to walk."

H.F. sighed and sheathed her knife. "I'll get her, Knuckles. Why don't you knock this one around a little? B.F. took care of security, and the second harvest of the day just came in. So, all facility staff are over at the manufacturing area. No one will hear her scream."

Blair scowled at her.

"Got it, boss," Knuckles said, rolling up his sleeves.

"Despite his unassuming demeanor and his cramps, Knuckles lives up to his name," H.F. told Blair. Then, turning to Knuckles, she said, "She'd better be ready to talk when I get back."

And with that, she strode to the door and exited without a backward glance.

"She always gets what she wants," Knuckles sighed, pulling a pair of brass knuckles out of his pocket. "And she can be downright bloodthirsty at times, so why don't we just get this over with now? Won't you tell me what she wants to know?"

Blair looked at him solemnly. "Okay, fine."

"Really?"

"No."

"Oh." His face hardened as his hands tightened into fists. "Well, in that case—I'm sorry, little lady—this is going to hurt."

* * *

The layout of Home had changed since Pete and Rosa had last been there, at least on the side of the compound where they entered. There were a couple of familiar buildings, like the medical facility and the domed arena. But the dormitory and the detention area were gone. In their place stood a couple of large, factory-like buildings with clouds of something pouring out of their roof vents.

A group of people in lab coats had gone into one of the buildings and come out with containers that—Pete told Rosa—looked equipped to carry some kind of nonpathogenic microorganisms. The people in the lab coats took the containers to the second factory building.

The arena stood against the eastern fence of the compound, and there were multiple sets of footprints leading right to its front door. Pete and Rosa only had to get to the building undetected, which they figured would be a simple task since the compound now ran on a skeleton crew and a Phib had taken out their security. But just in case, they dropped to the ground and stayed close to the fence.

The mud was fresh from the earlier rain, and it got everywhere. Rosa hated mud. She tried to ignore the feeling of it seeping through the front of her shirt and sneaking down the waist of her pants. B.F. had information about her son, and B.F. was in the arena. Therefore, she was going to the arena. Behind her, Pete's breathing was measured and calm.

"I think someone's following us," he whispered.

"Is that your magnetoreception talking?" Rosa asked. "Like, can you sense the magnetic fields of other humans, too?"

"My handler died before we finished that training," he replied. "I just have a creepy feeling about all this."

"Maybe it's the human heart we found wandering around outside its owner's chest cavity," Rosa said. "That was plenty creepy."

Pete only grunted in response.

Avoiding the high-traffic area near the front entrance, they went around to the arena's rear, the side facing the fence. When they stood, a sharp wind immediately began drying the thin layer of mud that coated the front of their bodies. Dried mud was better than wet, Rosa supposed.

There was a small, hinged window in the wall of the arena, about an arm's length above Pete's head.

"It looks unlocked," Pete said, looking up at the window. "I'll boost you in."

"Great." Rosa was already taking a running start. She bounced off of Pete's hands and grabbed the bottom of the window frame. Hanging on with all her might, she walked up the wall to get her head, shoulders, and arms through the window.

The window led to a large supply room. In the dim light, Rosa could just make out the outlines of a few rows of shelves with different kinds of equipment on them.

She wriggled her top half through the window, flipped, and landed on her feet with a *THUD*. The noise echoed, and a cloud of dust rose up around her feet. Rosa began searching the shelves for something to toss through the window so that Pete could climb into the room, too.

A snorting noise startled the Agent. It was coming from the area of the room kitty-corner to the window, behind a couple of rows of shelves. She moved to investigate.

When she rounded the last shelf, she jumped back in surprise. Tied up in a chair against the far wall was Blair Lee-Smith of the Cooperative FBI. She was unconscious and in a very bad way. Her face was beaten and swollen, and her hair was caked with blood. She was breathing with much effort—short snorts in and long, laborious wheezes out.

The Agent sighed. She should have known that the Cooperative FBI, would attempt something as foolish as posing as an Amphibian— and under a name as obvious as 'BlazingMander'. And since the communication had taken place on the dark web, it was not too great of an assumption that Rackelle Wernicke had been involved with this scheme in some capacity.

In addition to the facial injuries, Blair had a knife wound in her right shoulder, three broken ribs, and her left clavicle was sticking out of her skin. There was a piece of paper pinned to her jacket, on which was written in looping script:

Had To Head. Catch You Later.

B.F. had bowed out, which could only mean that a greater threat was looming. The Agent's eyes darted around the room. Suddenly, every shadow, every cobweb, every dirt smudge on the floor became suspect.

"Rosa?" Pete called.

"I'm okay," she replied, "but there's no rope or anything in this room."

"Since it's a gym, maybe there's some kind of rope in the special equipment room."

"I'll look. Just stay put."

The Agent crept to the door and peered into the arena, which was completely empty. It was lit by a single lightbulb that was suspended by a cord from a rafter in the center of the room, and it looked nothing like the dirt-floored arena in which she had fought to survive. The glossy floor was made of screw-fixed plywood and painted with markings that one might expect to find on the floor of a school gym.

Even so, the sterility of the glossy, serene gym could not overpower the Agent's memory of uncleanness due to what she had accomplished in it for the sake of survival. She had executed many purposeful kills since then, but that first kill was the one that most haunted her because she had not yet recognized the force by which she was driven to act.

There was a loud *THUMP* over by the wall where Rosa had left Pete. She ran toward the closet to boost herself back through the window and help him.

"Don't come out!" Pete yelled. "It's B.F.!"

There were sounds of a struggle and some clanking, then a gunshot from Pete's gun. A body hit the wall.

"Pete?" Rosa whispered as loudly as she dared.

No response.

Someone was walking away, dragging a body through the mud. Rosa ran for the front door to pursue them, but there were voices on the other side of the door. A woman and a man were deliberating about which one of them had the access card.

As they were establishing that it was in one of the man's pockets, the Agent ran on tiptoe, bounced off the nearest wall, and leapt for the rafter with the lightbulb. Her jump was too short, but she caught the cord and swung up onto the rafter. The cord came untied, and after the Agent stopped fighting for her balance, she realized that the lightbulb was in her hand. She extinguished it just as a slight man with a beard and a tall woman with an enormous, jet-black bun entered. They were each dragging a blindfolded body. From the limpness of the bodies, it seemed that the captives were unconscious.

When they came closer, the Agent's heart sank. The woman with the bun dragged a man with red-brown skin and tightly coiled, black hair while her companion dragged a creamy-skinned woman with curly, golden hair. These were friends whom the Agent had known in Diablo, although they were now associated with the Cooperative FBI, which was based in Corpus.

The bearded man labored, rocking from side to side as he walked, like he was sore from a bar fight. He would be no threat at all. The bun-wearing woman, however, practically glided across the room. Her hips and shoulders swayed in harmony with each other, exuding the confidence of one from whom most had been taken and who, therefore, had little left to lose. Without a doubt, she was an Amphibian.

"What happened to the light?" Beard asked.

"This is an old building, so anything could have," Bun replied. "Just leave the door open for now. With the staff still tied up at manufacturing, we'll have a fair amount of privacy.

They dragged the bodies to the center of the room, right below the Agent, and set them down roughly.

"Maybe we've done all we could do," Beard said. "Maybe we're done here, H.F."

H.F. The Agent wracked her brain to remember which Amphibian had the initials H.F. since her life would soon depend on that knowledge. But she was unable to remember.

"No," H.F. said. "These Coopers were posing as Fire Salamander. They *know* something."

"Well, if they do, their leader hid it pretty well. She didn't give me anything to work with."

"The male looks more fragile. I'll start with him." She pulled a knife from her boot and flipped it open.

The Agent stretched her neck to get a glimpse of what H.F. was doing. Suddenly, there was a loud cry from the man who was tied up on the floor. Blood trickled down the side of his face.

"Do you really have to do your 'death of a thousand cuts' routine?" Beard asked.

"It's more fun this way," H.F. replied.

It was to H.F.'s advantage that she had trained with blades while the Agent had not. But the Agent knew there to be a fine line between an advantage and a crutch, and an opponent with a crutch was the best kind of opponent to face. She figured that if she could kick the crutch, her chances of survival would increase greatly.

"Where is Fire Salamander?" H.F. demanded.

The man whom she was torturing did not respond fast enough, or she just felt like cutting him again. This time, she sliced his inner thigh. He yelped but did not answer her question.

Having seen enough, the Agent dropped from the rafter onto Beard. She knocked him flat on the floor and snapped his neck before he knew what had hit him. H.F. tackled the Agent immediately, which was to the Agent's advantage. Her strong suit had always been one-to-one combat in close quarters, body to body. At her first opportunity, she banged H.F.'s wrist on the ground and forced her to drop the knife.

They rolled over and over, and H.F. ended up on top. She pinned the Agent's arms at the wrists and leaned in until they were nose to nose.

"You *are* fiery." She bit the Agent on the cheek as a sign of her dominance. "And you look the part well enough, but there've been some imposters today. I'll need to see that mark to confirm you're *truly* Fire Salamander. How about a striptease?"

"How about I break every bone in your body?" the Agent replied, headbutting her.

In the half second that H.F. was off-balance, the Agent hooked her assailant's ankle and flipped her. The Agent landed a messy jab that knocked H.F. flat on her back. H.F. answered with a solid kick in the gut that floored the Agent.

The Agent was quick to regain her footing. She leapt to snap H.F.'s neck and end the whole thing, but her opponent kicked her out of the air. Claw-like blades sprang from the tips of her boots, one of which caught the Agent in the upper arm.

Rolling into her landing, the Agent wiped the blood from her arm and bounced to her feet. She motioned for H.F. to make her move, which she gladly did. H.F. thrust her knife at the Agent, who in turn grabbed her forearm and broke her ulna. The knife slipped from her grip.

"That all you got, *Fire?*" H.F. jeered.

The Agent hated that name. It dragged her down, down, down into the dark, cold places that she did not like to remember.

H.F. used her other hand to pull out a butterfly knife and whirled it around menacingly. "In the big leagues, you're going to have to do better than a broken forearm."

And that was the key. Somewhere in the intersection of thoughts about broken bones and the thrill of knives that emerged from unexpected places, the Agent began to access the information she needed, but that information also emerged from a rather unexpected place: the library of Windsailing's Gifted.

From the herpetological encyclopedia, Valencia had learned that a horror frog could break its own bones to produce knife-like claws. She figured that, if ever there were to be a knife-wielding Phib, the horror frog would be an appropriate namesake—and it had the initials "H.F." Valencia, despite her childish and emotional constitution, could also play the Survival game.

When H.F. took another slice at her, the Agent targeted her wounded arm again, breaking the ulna in a second place. She twisted her opponent's arm slowly and in such a way that the broken bone protruded from the skin. Despite H.F.'s squirming and futile attempts to strike her, the Agent pulled the piece of bone out of H.F.'s arm and waved it at her tauntingly.

"I know who you are, Horror Frog," she said. "And you're not the only one who can pull knives out of unexpected places."

Horror Frog growled and rushed at her. The Agent dodged and slashed her opponent's cheek with the sharper end of the bone. Wiping her face, H.F. looked at the blood on her hand and then at the male Coop agent whose face she had slashed earlier.

"Payback." She smirked at the Agent and stepped toward the man. "Do I sense a *personal* connection?"

She drew her leg back to kick him with her bladed boot. The Agent dove onto his body and took the blow in her thigh. It was a deep puncture wound that would probably take almost a week to fully heal at her accelerated rate. She stared up at her opponent defiantly.

"Interesting." Horror Frog looked between the two of them in fascination.

"Lenci?" the Coop agent croaked, struggling to sit up. "What are you doing here?"

Although Karthik remained blindfolded, it seemed that he knew his friend by touch. The Agent placed her finger over his lips and said nothing. Her eyes moved to Horror Frog's bladed boot, which was swinging down toward them at a diagonal, set to make a nasty gash in both of their sides.

The Agent rolled sideways and kicked Karthik in the hip, sending him sliding about five meters on his behind. The tip of Horror Frog's blade slit about seven centimeters across the Agent's back, but that was better than a nasty gash in her side. When the Agent wrestled the bladed boot off of her foot, Horror Frog was quick to strike with the other. But the Agent caught her leg and broke it at the knee.

"That's quite enough of that," she said.

Lest the Agent believe that their scuffle had concluded, Horror Frog plucked tiny blades like hairpins from her bun. It became evident that they were smart blades when she threw them. The blades spread in the air, following the outline of the Agent's body, and pinned her to the wall by the seams of her clothing.

Behind Horror Frog, the two Coop agents—still blindfolded—were crawling like inchworms toward the door. Hoping to buy them some time, the Agent let out a loud laugh.

"Killing me at a distance, so you don't get any literal blood on your hands, I see," she scoffed. "You're no Phib! Dependence on external weapons has made you *weak*."

Training in isolation had led the Agent to believe that she was the best there was, and Horror Frog was no different in that respect—which is why her pride became the Agent's soft entry point. Fire flashed in Horror Frog's eyes as she hobbled over to the Agent. She drew out a spear point machete and went in for the kill, but the Agent broke free at the last second.

The side seams of the Agent's shirt popped such that, below the neck hole, the garment hung in two separate flaps. The strike that had been intended for her heart caught her in the fleshy part of her left forearm. Without missing a beat, she ducked and swept Horror Frog's legs. Her opponent attempted to regain her footing, but her broken leg failed her.

The Agent dove onto her and began to do what she did best.

Horror Frog was too good of a grappler to fall into basic traps that could endanger her life, but the Agent had a different plan. It was simply a matter of exploiting the broken leg and twisting her opponent into a position from which she would have to tap out to get free. They ended up in such a convoluted knot that the Agent could hardly tell where her own body ended and Horror Frog's began.

"You can't kill me from this position," Horror Frog said. "You've just brought us to a stalemate."

"A stalemate only if I wanted to kill you," the Agent replied.

She had a clear view of a tattoo behind her opponent's ear. It was a meaty frog with hairy fringes along its sides and claws protruding from its feet—a Horror Frog. It was the last confirmation of which Song the Agent needed to sing.

> *Horror Frog, come use your knives*
> *Leave behind your old, past lives*

"No! No!" Horror Frog shrieked, arching her back and writhing.

Blind are the eyes of one who feels no pain. Focused is the mind of one who has an established purpose.

"Yes." The Agent tightened her grip. "I'm sorry."

> *Give up the fight*
> *I own your might*

Horror Frog's shrieks devolved into sobs, anguished and despairing, which struck a chord in Rosa's heart.

What is necessary must never be lamented. Still, tears came to Rosa's eyes as she felt the strength drain from her opponent's limbs.

"Go away, Rosa," the Agent growled.

The next two lines were supposed to be the command. Whatever she wished for Horror Frog to do, she would do. And yet, the Agent had to wonder what was really necessary in this situation. Never in any of her lives had she been capable of doing to another human being what had been done to her. Broken bodies could heal, but a broken spirit—well, that remained to be seen.

There had to be another way.

Rosa briefly considered releasing Horror Frog so that they could indeed fight to the death. After all, she had made her weak, not just in body but in spirit. In a moment, she could end Horror Frog's miserable existence. But who was she to make that decision?

No, she could not be judge, jury, and executioner. Not this time. Rosa released Horror Frog whose body immediately sprawled out on the floor.

Everything was still except for Rosa's ragged breathing. She thought she might remember sitting on the dirt beneath that wooden floor, covered in blood, and panting. Perhaps she had wondered about what purpose that air whooshing in and out of her lungs could possibly serve. Even now, she was not entirely sure, but the fact that there remained air in her opponent's lungs seemed to be a great victory.

Shoving down any self-congratulatory thoughts over how she had chosen a better path, the Agent went to the supply closet to retrieve Blair. The Coop agent was fully conscious but unable to open her eyes or speak.

The Agent grabbed a pair of wire cutters from one of the shelves and hauled Blair, still tied to the chair, to the front door. Outside, there were footprints coming from the eastern side of the building and two small grooves that looked like the marks made by someone's heels as they were dragged across the compound toward the western fence. There were two other wider, messier grooves that looked like a couple of people had belly-crawled around the other side of the building.

The coast was clear, so the Agent carried Blair up to the eastern edge of the compound. After cutting a sizable hole in the fence, she pulled Blair through it and set her on an even place where the chair wouldn't sink too much in the mud.

When she returned to the entrance of the arena, Horror Frog was waiting for her. She had a knife in each of her hands, and she looked confused—maybe even angry. Rosa raised her hands in a gesture of non-escalation.

"What should I do?" Horror Frog demanded.

"Whatever you want," Rosa said. "You're free now."

Horror Frog looked at her knives. Her brow furrowed as if the idea of freedom did not register. In fact, she seemed afraid of it.

"All I ever wanted was to survive," she said.

"That's all any of us ever wanted," Rosa replied. "I hope, after you've accomplished that, you'll find a way to live."

Horror Frog cast her an inquisitive glance. "Have you?"

Rosa smiled wryly. "Working on it."

"Cheers, then," Horror Frog said, moving past her.

"Wait!" Rosa called. "Can I ask you something?"

Horror Frog turned back with an expectant expression.

"Do you know where the Assistant Vice is keeping my son?"

"Sorry," Horror Frog said, "I didn't even know the WCE took in children."

"Oh." Rosa's heart sank.

"I just came here because I'd been putting out feelers for anything related to Fire Salamander, and 'BlazingMander' wasn't too far off," Horror Frog told her. "A Phib named B.F. orchestrated this whole thing, you know. So, she's the one you should ask about your son."

"You spoke with B.F.?"

"Briefly, before you arrived. She left when she realized I planned to take you. Last I saw her, she was dragging some guy into the woods."

That confirmed it: B.F. was a Phib, too, and she had taken Pete. Rosa hoped she wouldn't hurt him.

"Well, thanks, Horror Frog," she said.

"Call me Freedom," the woman replied, seeming to find comfort in naming herself after the very thing she feared.

"Thank you, Freedom," Rosa said, putting a hand over her heart. "It's nice to meet you."

A crooked smile that could almost be described as happy graced Freedom's face. And without another word, she hobbled away. She seemed to have forgotten all about Beard, but perhaps that was what the joy of newfound freedom could do to a person.

The Agent brushed away all traces of warm fuzzy feelings and set about locating the two Coop agents who still needed to be reunited with their superior. She found them on the northern exterior of the building, still wearing their blindfolds and covered in mud. They were huddled by the wall and working furiously to remove their bonds.

When she grabbed them by the back of their jacket collars, they both stiffened.

"Lenci?" the man whispered.

"Hush, K.," the woman told him.

"I know it's you, Lenci," he insisted. "Why won't you answer me?"

The Agent did not respond as she dragged them around the building to the hole that she had made in the fence. She pulled them through and carefully laid them beside each other.

Blair was shivering in her chair, but she otherwise seemed no worse than before. The Agent cut her bonds and rubbed her wrists together to get the circulation going. She would need that in order to free the others.

Blair's swollen lips moved, but no sound came out.

You're welcome. The Agent put the wire cutters into Blair's hands and placed them in her lap. She turned to leave, but Blair grasped her arm and, with her other hand, felt the Agent's face. Even with all of the cuts and swollen tissue in Blair's beaten up face, her surprise was evident.

"Lenci!" Karthik cried, his voice cracking. "We've been searching for you *everywhere!*"

The Agent tried to block out the emotions teeming in his voice, but her efforts failed. Her friend's pain echoed down into the depths of her consciousness, threatening to awaken everything that she had laid to rest for both their sakes—for their family's sake.

"What more d—do we have to d—do t—to prove that we're on your side?" he asked.

Nothing because the road ahead cannot include you. You are in way over your head. We all are. The Agent wrenched herself away from Blair and turned to follow the footprints beside which were the grooves from Pete's boots.

"I won't wait for you!" The male Coop agent yelled after her, his tone taking a bitter turn downward. Then he repeated more softly, "I won't wait."

You've spent too much of your life waiting on a girl who doesn't exist anymore.

The Agent silently trudged away through the mud. She had not come all the way Home only to let **B.F.** slip through her fingers. Besides, someone had to save Pete.

* * *

Although Rosa had never been much of a runner in any of her past lives, she found herself sprinting along the outside of the fence of the compound. Daylight was rapidly fading, and she felt some urgency about finding Pete before the darkness gave B.F. more places to hide him.

A kilometer from where she had exited the compound, there was evidence that Pete had perhaps awakened and a struggle had ensued, which was good news. But the grooves made by Pete's heels continued shortly beyond, indicating that he had lost that battle. Rosa wondered what kind of skills B.F. could possibly possess that could overcome Pete's superhuman speed. Super strength, maybe, given how far she had dragged his body.

The tracks went in zigzags, doubling back sometimes, but they eventually veered back into the compound. Rosa's heart sank when she realized that the grooves left by Pete's heels were leading straight to the initiation quarters. Pushing aside the horrific memories that bubbled up within her, Rosa thought of poor Pete, who had intended to return Home without ever laying eyes on the initiation quarters, much less setting foot inside the building.

When she arrived at the area where the initiation quarters had stood, the building was gone. It had not been much before, just a plywood shanty. In its place stood a much larger, more updated structure. It was certainly residential, likely built to accommodate the compound's current overnight staff. Of all things, the doorknob of the front entrance remained the same. There was a note posted above it on the door.

Rosa approached cautiously. She tried to keep her eyes on the note, but they kept wandering back to the brass knob. The knob was embossed with a unique, swirling design that had been imprinted on her palm the first time she'd left the initiation quarters—so tightly had she gripped it.

Rosa didn't want to go, but she began sinking, sinking, sinking. She frantically leapt out of the past's reach and snatched the note from the door.

Remember ME?

She didn't want to remember the inside of the shanty or what had happened there. Images of a man's hands on her body flooded her mind. She could feel them, too, and the hands did not belong to the man who touched her. Well, if she was going to remember that, then she could also remember that the initiation quarters had never been used for *her* initiation.

The Agent crumpled the note and stuffed it into the pocket of her gym shorts. To her right, she saw that the grooves of Pete's heels—after a three meter break—continued moving away from the building.

Rosa sighed with relief at the realization that Pete was not chained to a bed somewhere inside of the building, completely at B.F.'s mercy. B.F. had led Rosa to the initiation quarters, at best, as some kind of sick joke. At worst, she may have been trying to disable Rosa in her search for Pete. If that was the case, Rosa was heartier than B.F. had anticipated.

Even so, Rosa was well aware of the gravity of facing a specially trained opponent who could get inside of her head in such a way. But if B.F. was just another Phib hunting her, why was she delaying the execution with all of these mind games? And what on earth could she want with Pete?

There could be no good answer for that—no answer to Rosa's liking, in any case. She ran on through the mud, following the long grooves out through the fence of the compound, and hoped against hope that Pete would still be alive when she got to him. If he wasn't, she would tear B.F.'s limbs from her body. Well, she figured she might want to do that anyway, for all the trouble B.F. had caused her.

Soon, Rosa found herself on the edge of a shallow basin, only a meter deep and four meters in diameter. It was fringed with trees, but there was no vegetation inside it. The evening light cast a blue glow over the bare ground in the basin. Rosa recognized this area. She had parked the jeep less than ten meters away.

On high alert, the Agent approached the vehicle. The doors were open, but there was no one in the front seat. There was no sign of extra machinery or lights under the car. That was a relief.

Inside, Pete lay across the back seat. In his lap lay the canister that the Agent had taken from SSI on the night that the Cull was supposed to begin. The sight of the canister brought up sad memories. Pushing the past away, the Agent directed her attention to a note that had been attached to Pete's shirt.

*I StolE ThiS JoR You. GivE IT A GO… ThE
CanisteR, NoT ThE MalE.*

It seemed that B.F. had been watching her *very* closely in Lakes. The Agent folded the note and put it in her pocket. Then she squeezed through the space between the front seats and touched Pete's arm. When he didn't wake up, she jabbed him in the chest.

He sprang into action, and she blocked his strikes calmly.

"It's Rosa," she said again and again.

Eventually, he stopped swinging and took a series of deep, shuddering breaths.

"Where is she?" Rosa asked.

"Gone for good, I hope," he said. "I don't even know why I'm still alive. She really seemed to hate me."

Rosa helped him into the front seat and turned on the reading light. There was a pink, glossy kiss mark on his cheek. She smeared it and turned his face toward the mirror so that he could see it.

"I feel violated," he said, hugging himself. After an uncomfortable silence, he added, "and I think my pants are on backwards."

Rosa side-glanced him as she started the engine. "Was she pretty?"

"I guess," he said, slipping out of his pants, "in a deranged and *evil* sort of way."

"Now, we don't know that she's evil just because she knocked you out, dragged you through the mud, and kissed you while you were unconscious." Rosa grinned impishly.

"Not to mention that she separated us as you walked into a potentially very dangerous situation." He zipped up his fly wearily. "But it was really the pants-switching that put it over the top for me. That was really in poor taste."

"Maybe she thought she was being funny. You know, like a joke?"

Pete gave her a scrutinizing glance. "It's not funny. Why are you playing devil's advocate?"

"Don't you see?" Rosa's smile broadened. "Inappropriate sense of humor aside, B.F. tried to warn me when she thought *you* were going to kill me and then she gave us a canister of antipersonnel agent, even when she could have sold it herself. She *must* have a big picture perspective on our situation."

"But that could also be a bad thing," Pete said. "She could be manipulating us into a trap, or she could be using us as pawns to trap someone else."

"That's not the believe-the-best Pete I know," Rosa said, offering him her hand. "Where's your sense of optimism? We've got a big-player Phib feeding us helpful tips. B.F. could be an ally."

Pete squeezed her hand fondly, attempting to mask his anxiety with a smile. Then he tipped his seat back and closed his eyes.

Rosa admired his peacefulness for a moment before asking, "How did you know it was B.F. when she attacked you at the arena?"

"Hm?"

"You warned me that it was B.F."

"I just knew."

"But how? She didn't stop to introduce herself, did she?"

"She makes no secret of it. You'll know her if you ever have the misfortune to lay eyes on her."

Rosa let the matter drop. She had to understand that some memories were not worth revisiting. In any case, she intended to meet B.F. in person in the near future. After all, B.F. had given her the canister and told her to "give it a go." If all went well, a real partnership could form.

"I think B.F. gave us this antipersonnel agent so that I can test out my uncompromisable immunity," she blurted out.

Pete sat up. "What does *that* mean?"

"It means that we need to find a safe place for me to ingest whatever's in the canister."

"It's what's inside of you that matters most," he quoted glumly.

"Yup." Rosa smiled.

"But can't you see this might not benefit you at all?"

"If I do this, B.F. will want to align with us," Rosa told him. "You were medically trained, so you know how not to catch whatever I get, right?"

Pete looked like a dog whose tail had been tied to a skateboard.

Suddenly, Rosa felt self-conscious. "I thought you were excited about my accelerated healing rate. You do think it's true that my ability to regenerate makes me immune to disease, don't you?"

"Undoubtedly, but I don't like tempting fate." He studied her in the dim light. "You have knife wounds. What happened in that arena?"

So, Rosa told him the whole long story, from Horror Frog to Freedom along with the catch and release of the Cooperative FBI agents.

CHAPTER 24

THE DAY AFTER A COOP EXTRACTION UNIT HAD BROUGHT HER TEAM back from Farm And Forest, Theresa sipped on a lukewarm hazelnut macchiato as she waited for a call. Her stomach was sore, perhaps from consuming caffeine without having eaten first. She had been nervous about the call all day and had skipped every meal in favor of pacing her living room. When no call had come, she picked up some coffee from her favorite café and came into HQ to wait in a more secure environment.

The ringing of her flake shot through the silence like a punch to the gut. It was time.

"Cravenly," she said.

"How hard is it to use an auto-car and a cliff to kill people?" B.F. asked. "You were *given* the virus!"

"But Wernicke's a tech genius!" Theresa protested. "She must've found a way to—"

"To make the car fly." B.F. huffed. "I read the report from the car rental agency. If you were aware of the extent of her abilities, you should have done something to mitigate the risk."

Theresa felt ill and not just because she was anxious to placate her WCE contact. Her stomach really, really hurt. Clutching her abdomen, she keeled over. Her macchiato spilled everywhere.

As she lay on the conference room floor, she could hear B.F.'s cold, cruel voice saying, "You failed us."

The line went dead.

Beads of sweat appeared on Theresa's forehead, and she felt like her body was on fire. She called out weakly for help, but her voice was gone. Her stomach flip-flopped until she vomited. A vicious fatigue overcame her, and just as her eyes began to close, she heard the conference room door open. Racky's voice squawked for help, then all went dark.

* * *

When Theresa awoke, Racky and Blair were sitting at her bedside. Blair's face was stitched in multiple places, both of her eyes were blackened, and one of her arms was in a sling. Racky just looked extremely tired.

"Hey, Cravenly," Blair said.

Theresa conjured as much of a smile as she could, despite feeling like her insides had been sent through a meat grinder.

She looked incredulously at Racky. "You saved me?"

Racky gave her a long, hard look. "I'd gone into HQ to get a couple of CFR-67 forms. Almost didn't set foot in the conference room, but Vincent said you'd come in without clocking in. So, I wondered if you'd met some trouble."

"Well, thanks." Theresa looked down at her flake, which was sitting in the bed with her. She had received an anonymous message, which she knew only B.F. could have sent.

That was a warning. Next time will be for real.

"Don't mention it," Racky was saying. "I just can't fathom how that amount of cholera got into one coffee cup. The health department will be all over that."

"Yeah." Theresa tried to keep her breathing normal, but she felt like there was a weight on her chest. The pressure to prove herself to the WCE had become a heavier burden than she could bear.

"You alright, Cravenly?" Blair asked.

"Thanks to Racky's quick thinking," Theresa responded.

"Mmhm." Racky regarded her pensively.

After a quick estimation about whom she'd rather have on her side when everything came crashing down, Theresa decided that she should clear the air. Maybe there'd be some disciplinary action, but there might also be a chance to get more protection if she ended up needing it.

"Look, guys," she said, at last, "about the car—"

Blair waved her hand dismissively. "We already read about the recall on that car model for the deficient command system."

"What?" Theresa's forehead wrinkled. "No, what I wanted to say was that I'm sorry because—"

"No apology necessary," Blair interrupted again. "The rental company has already contacted us to settle things outside of court. The Coop is getting a fat settlement—given to our front company, of course—and the three of us didn't do too shabbily with our individual shares either."

"Oh." Theresa glanced down at her flake again. "I guess it all worked out, then."

"Guess so," Racky said.

Well, that had been her chance. Theresa inwardly shrugged. The failure with the auto-car execution had been a minor hiccup. In any case, B.F. had gotten what she really wanted, which was the canister. Theresa promised herself that, on her next WCE assignment, she would succeed—no matter the cost.

* * *

Rosa and Pete walked up the steps of a dilapidated house in a sleepy little town in Farm And Forest. It was more like well-populated country with houses spaced out at the equivalent of a couple of district blocks.

"You really think no one will disturb us?" Rosa asked.

"Judging from the overgrown yard and the broken down foreclosure sign," Pete said, "I'm going to say that's a safe assumption."

The house was made of deep brown wood and had a wraparound veranda. A large, glass dome sat on top of one room on the second floor, probably a solarium of some kind. A faded notice tacked to the boarded-over front door indicated that the former residents had been escorted out by none other than the military police.

"There's no explanation of what happened here," Rosa said, "but the place has a troubled enough history for the likes of us."

"Troubled has nothing to do with it," Pete replied as he began removing the boards from the doorway. "It's been forgotten, so no one will be by here in the foreseeable future. And *that's* what we want."

She nodded. "And you can burn the house to the ground if I die from the canister."

He looked at her apprehensively.

She crossed her arms. "I'm just saying, to keep the disease from spreading—"

"I'm not really planning for you to die," he said.

"Well, if we're *planning*, then I'm not either," she said. "I just want to be prepared."

"We're about as prepared as a couple of ad-libbing Phibs can be," he said, motioning her through the door.

The house was still furnished. Some of the furniture was overturned, but it was all in rather decent shape. There were pots and dishes in the open concept kitchen, and there was a pile of tools in the middle of the living room floor. The power was down, but with a little tweaking of the electrical lines, it would soon be up and running. Behind the house, there was a lake rimmed with evergreens. The view from the veranda was probably lovely on a nice day, but the eerie layer of fog hovering over the surface of the lake made the Agent uneasy.

"I left my supplies in the jeep," Pete told Rosa when she came in through the back door. "You can get comfortable upstairs, if you want."

"Will do," Rosa said. She trudged up the stairs and past the bedrooms to take a quick peek in the solarium at the end of the hall.

There were a few rows of planters that housed shriveled plants and a couple of dingy porcelain sinks on the left side of the room. It was a dismal little area, but Rosa figured that—if she survived the canister—she could make that solarium into an inhabitable space. She looked up through the dirty glass at the darkening sky. Behind the cloud cover, the stars would soon be twinkling. Rosa got goosebumps just thinking about what a spectacle that would be on a clear night. But business would have to be addressed before spectacles.

She went to the first bedroom off of the staircase. Its carpet was ragged, and the wallpaper was faded. But the queen-sized bed was clean and firm, and the west-facing window let in a decent amount of natural light. It would be the perfect space for her experiment.

There was a thumping in the stairwell, and soon after, Pete entered with a bag of supplies.

"Here we go," he said, pulling the canister out of his bag. "But how are you going to take this? You can't just open it and spray it around in here."

"I was actually wondering if you could depressurize the contents without releasing the—whatever it is—into the air?"

Pete looked at the canister thoughtfully. "Yeah. It would be liquid then."

"And then I could drink it," Rosa said.

"Okay, hold on." He took out a couple of masks and gave one to Rosa.

After they were masked, he pulled out some tools and began working on the top of the canister.

When it was depressurized, he said, "You're *sure* you want to do this?"

"It was B.F.'s one request," Rosa replied, taking the canister from him.

"After luring you Home," he reminded her. "You know, more demands could follow. She doesn't seem like a fair negotiator."

"Well, she's the only lead I have on my son, so it's settled."

He nodded grimly and set up a hanging bag with some kind of liquid in it. "This will keep you hydrated. I'll come in to change it tomorrow. Hopefully, you'll have passed out of the contagious phase by then."

She watched calmly as he set up her IV and turned on the drip.

"The bug was targeted at 4.14s, so it shouldn't be contagious to you," she said.

"Targeted at 4.14s," Pete snorted. "There aren't enough genetic differences across the classes to make the disease *that* rigidly effective. The WCE is full of it from top to bottom."

Rosa smiled. "Well, in that case, thanks for being willing to risk your life for me."

"Anything for a fellow Phib," he said. After some hesitation, he added, "Actually, anything for you—just you."

Her smile widened. "I'll see you on the other side."

"I'm counting on it." He moved to the door and, after taking one last look back at her, he exited.

When the Agent heard the front door close downstairs, she breathed a sigh of relief. At last, Pete was gone. When Rosa did not have to be present for him, the past, present, and future could move about freely such that the big picture came into view.

If the Agent wanted to manipulate the players in this game, she needed to know her true bargaining power. If she really did have uncompromisable immunity, she could walk in many places that she had previously thought inaccessible and make many demands that she had previously thought unreasonable.

"To my son," she said, raising the canister with both hands. "I plan to keep you safe, one day."

She tilted the canister and drank. There was no more than 150 milliliters' worth of liquid in it, and the liquid tasted more like metal than anything else.

After a minute or two, the Agent began to feel very hot. She reached for the bottle of water on her bedside table, and her arm seized up. Then her other arm and both of her legs stiffened as well. Red blotches popped up on her arms, and powerful nausea overtook her. The nausea was so intense that it caused her vision to blur.

"Kiddo," she whispered weakly. Then room went dark.

Her mother and brother and Auntie Preeti and Karthik and Racky were all in the room with her. Or, at least, there were times when she could hear them joking and laughing. She could hear Pete's voice speaking to her as he changed her hanging bag. He told her that she was doing great and to hang in there. But when she opened her eyes, there was never anyone in the room.

As the disease reached its peak, the Agent felt her body growing weaker. It was possible that even the nanobots had limits with respect to their ability to clean up. The Agent sank down, down, down into the depths where there was no light. There was only a dark arena. And the arena was dark because she had taken out the lights. It was her one desperate move in a fight in which she was severely outmatched. But given the chance for a do-over, would a life without light be better than no life at all?

The Agent reached out to replace the lights, but they wouldn't stay up. Her eyes popped open, and she found herself staring at the headstone of Samir Bourghin.

"I'm so sorry," she whispered.

"Don't be sorry," Pete's voice replied as he wiped her sweaty forehead. "You're doing a very courageous thing."

She tried to grasp his hand, but it became a rope. A rope that she wound and wound around her body as she prepared to drag her millstones through the kelp. The kelp grabbed at her with its slimy fingers, dragging her toward a horrid light that was so bright that it forced her eyes shut.

"The shades!" she cried. And it became dark again.

When she opened her eyes, the door was just closing, and there were footsteps descending the stairs. Pete had just left. The Agent's head felt a little clearer than before. Perhaps she was getting better. She tried to sit up, but she couldn't even lift her head. With a disappointed sigh, she closed her eyes again.

Although it was agonizing not to know whether she was asleep or awake at any given moment, the Agent sensed the closeness of her son. She knew that he was not present because she was not yet complete, but he was near to her. It was for him that she had this courage, for him that she would survive, for him that she would move beyond the darkness to live in the light.

The next morning, Pete came back again. When he entered the room, Rosa sat up and smiled at him.

"Hi there!" He grinned from ear-to-ear behind his mask. "Welcome back to the land of the living."

"It's good to be back," she said, her voice gravelly. "Did you bring any food?"

"Hold it, now," he laughed. "You haven't had solid food for three days. We've got to ease you back into it."

Rosa looked at him as if he'd run her through with a spear. "You mean, like start with noodle soup before I have a burger?"

"Well, you wouldn't be getting any beef from me," he replied, "but try clear broth before your noodle soup."

She whimpered as if he'd twisted the spear.

He looked at her amusedly. "Your body just successfully rebounded from enough disease to take out a housing development full of people, but you're upset that you can't have noodles?"

"It's the ultimate comfort food, but I imagine I'll survive," she said sullenly.

"I'm going to make your broth," he chuckled, shaking his head.

Rosa heaved herself out of the bed. She walked on wobbly legs down the stairs to sit on the couch as Pete bustled about the kitchen. Her head was clearer than it had been in recent memory, even from before her illness. Along with the fever, she must have sweated out the regret that had once plagued her.

She reached for the web apparatus, which was sitting on the coffee table in front of her. As she logged in to post an encrypted message for B.F. in a dark web chatroom, she looked up to find Pete staring at her.

"What?" she asked.

He grinned sheepishly. "I was just thinking about that time we were in your kitchen."

"Oh." She smiled. "I've thought about that a lot, too."

CHAPTER 25

for her quick thinking," Karthik said, nodding at his teammate appreciatively. "Her d—decision to swallow that SD card upon our ambush is the reason that the Farm and Forest mission was the success that it was. We n—now have a vast amount of d—detailed intel about the cohort of agents known as the Amphibians."

Blair could barely look at Karthik because of the stitched up gash on his cheek. It was a reminder of her poor judgment with respect to the planning and execution of this mission.

Karthik continued, "Moreover, this was the third close call we've had with Valencia Chang in the past month, besides the false alarm with Arjun Thomas. My projection is that she will remain within the Western States, per her usual escape pattern. We persist in our hope that we will bring her in soon."

He turned off the holoprojector. It whirred wearily as it powered down.

The senior leadership of the Cooperative FBI sat in solemn silence around the conference room table. Director Vincent looked back and forth among the members of the team. They all avoided his gaze.

"I trust Agent Cravenly's recovery is going well?" Vincent asked.

Blair nodded. "She'll be discharged tomorrow morning."

"That's good to hear," he said, flipping through his notes on their presentation. "Just a couple of questions. You said you caught wind of the sale of this biological weapon through an ad on the dark web?"

"Yes, sir," Blair said. "Wernicke was doing a routine sweep of the dark web, searching for leads, when she found the ad in an online forum. From Bourghin's materials, we had gained the understanding that Chang had once been known as Fire Salamander. And that's how we deduced that she was the selling party in the transaction."

"I see." Vincent looked at her with something slightly softer than suspicion. "And then you were caught in an ambush involving *two* other Amphibians?"

"That's correct," Karthik said, his jaw drawn tight. "First by one who then d—delivered us t—to the other."

Vincent huffed. "I think we should take into consideration the possibility that Chang was working with those two Amphibians. Perhaps they banded together to try to get you off her back."

"That's not the way this cohort of agents does things, sir," Racky said. "Bourghin's research indicates that the Amphibians work alone."

"Well, maybe even Bourghin can be wrong," Vincent shrugged, "or his information is outdated. These agents don't exist in a vacuum. They can adapt and learn like any of the rest of us."

"The other Amphibians planned to torture and kill us, but Chang fought on our behalf," Blair said. "They *weren't* working together."

Karthik's face grew tighter, and his hands closed into fists.

"Is there a problem, Agent Wilson?" Vincent asked.

"No, sir," Karthik said. "I just really want t—to bring Ms. Chang home."

"You and the rest of us," Vincent replied. "Well, thank you all for your hard work and dedication on this case. Get your CFR-67s to admin by tomorrow at 1700. Dismissed."

His subordinates bowed their heads slightly and filed out of the room.

Racky shuffled to catch up with Blair. "Happy hour?"

"Yeah, I could use that right about now," Blair replied.

Karthik brushed past them with his flake to his ear.

"Hey, K.!" Racky called. "Can you join us for drinks?"

"I'll take the stairs and meet you in the garage," he replied over his shoulder. Then, into the flake, he said in an empty and strained voice, "Hey Maude, May 17."

"*That's* the wedding date?" Blair said. "Isn't it a little soon?"

Racky sighed. "It's his birthday."

"And Lenci's," Blair added, "if I understand correctly."

"Yeah, he's being as vindictive a bonehead as he can be," Racky said. "Lenci's out there in that big, wide world and she doesn't even know who she is, bless her. She *needs* us."

Blair smiled. "She does. And so does my half-sibling. That's why we've got to do our best work, regardless of Wilson's antics."

"Agent Lee-Smith, may I have a word?" The two women jumped at the director's voice.

"Of course," Blair said.

His face was solemn.

Racky looked between the two of them. "You know, it *just* occurred to me that I forgot my good probes in the lab. I'm intending to clean them this weekend. Might take me a second to collect them. Would you send the elevator back up for me?"

Director Vincent nodded with an air of gratitude, and Racky dismissed herself. When the elevator doors opened, Vincent motioned for Blair to step inside. She did so stiffly, beginning to discern the trajectory of the coming conversation.

Red and green lights passed over them. Then the elevator chimed and began to move downward. When they had descended a couple of floors, the director pulled the emergency brake, and the elevator screeched to a halt.

Thinking it best to get the full story out before Vincent had to drag it from her, Blair began, "Sir, I can explain—"

"I'm sure you can," Vincent replied, "but I don't want to hear what you have to say."

Blair looked at him perplexedly.

"I can tell when my agents are hiding information, Lee-Smith." He looked like a disappointed father. "I imagine you felt you had a very good reason for doing what you did, and there's no denying that you got results. You brought back so much information that it will take a couple of years to sort through. And it's certainly going to fill in a lot of gaps in our knowledge of WCE activities."

The "but" was coming. Blair could hear it in his tone.

"But I can't understand why you still feel like you need to hide parts of your process from me. I have given you so much freedom to work as you see fit on this case."

"There were some risks involved, sir," Blair replied. "I figured, at worst, the consequences would fall on me alone. And at best, you could report this whole thing 'security guaranteed.'"

Vincent's face softened. "Blair, I'm the director. The consequences of what you do will fall on me, as well. A leader is responsible for their team, as you also understand on some level. Wernicke and Wilson were endangered, but I can tell that you took the worst of it. You've got the wounds of an agent who refused to give up information when interrogated. That's certainly a mark of a strong leader. But much of this could have been avoided if you had come to me for additional perspective and resources."

"It won't happen again, sir," Blair said. And she meant it.

Being driven over a cliff and beaten to a pulp was bad enough, but the risk to her team members had been a wake-up call. On the ride back to Corpus with the extraction unit, she had pondered how her tunnel vision about Larva had needlessly endangered the lives of the agents under her supervision.

"You can take your week's suspension to think about practical ways to ensure that it won't," Vincent said. "And when you return, you'll be on a year-long probation. All of your communication devices will be cloned, and you'll report to me *every* week about progress and plans. This will be especially necessary with the addition of your new team."

Blair's brow wrinkled. "Sir?"

Behind his stern gaze, his eyes seemed to sparkle. "You'll be heading up the team investigating the issue of the nanobots, as we now have three different blood samples full of them and no knowledge of the relationships among them. You get the job done, Lee-Smith, which is why I want you leading these teams. But you've got to be completely honest *and* forthright with me on everything. I promise that I'll give your ideas a chance and that if I disagree with you on something, it'll be for your good and the mission's good. Deal?"

She smiled. "Yes, sir."

"Good," he said, disengaging the emergency brake. "Because if you keep key information from me or defy my instructions again, you're gone."

"Yes, sir."

The elevator resumed its descent.

* * *

At 2013, a rental car pulled up in front of Racky's house. Even though Theresa's discharge was scheduled for the next morning, she had snuck out of the hospital in loose street clothing to complete an important mission. In her part of the pre-discharge ward, the nurses only came to check on patients right before lights out. She intended to be back before then.

Racky and Blair were out for drinks, and the way Racky drank, they could be out half the night. So, Theresa had decided to take advantage of the opportunity. She pulled on a pair of gloves as she exited the car.

Leaning heavily on the banister, she labored up the porch steps. She found the spare key under the lawn gnome, then after catching her breath, attempted to unlock the front door.

A white square composed of smaller white squares lit up the air above the doorknob.

"State your purpose," a voice prompted.

Knowing that she could not very well explain to the security system why she was there, Theresa pressed the guest key against the center of the square.

"Spare key identified. Guest entry requested."

Before the system could send a message to Racky to request entry, Theresa terminated the request. The system had never sent a request any of the other times she used Racky's spare key. It seemed that Racky had recently become suspicious of potential houseguests, including Theresa. But that mattered little. Theresa knew that her time as a double agent was coming to an end. She had done her best to prove her loyalty to the WCE, and she would soon need to complete her transition.

She felt certain that Racky was hiding important information from her, something that could—in the right hands—lead to Valencia Chang's demise. That was the only reason Racky would withhold information related to the Chang case, and Theresa expected that obtaining such information would get her back in B.F.'s good graces.

She nudged the pet door with her toe only to find that it was nailed shut, but all was not lost. The garage had a side door without the fancy security trappings. She slowly made her way around to the side of the garage. She tried the door and found that Racky had extended the security interface to cover that area as well. However, she had forgotten to secure the pet door.

Theresa lay on her stomach and lifted the flap of the pet door. Racky's car was inside the garage, probably because she and Blair had ridden in Blair's auto-car. There was a worktable covered in tools and parts of gadgets on the far side of the garage. Under the worktable, there was a kitty bed with a small, gray tabby in it—the infamous

Gustav. His eyes reflected the glow of the streetlights that shone through the side window.

"Hi, kitty," Theresa said softly. "Don't mind me."

The cat meowed in response and began to lick one of his forepaws.

Letting out all of her breath, Theresa stuck one of her arms through the pet door and began feeding the rest of her body through it. She twisted so that her hips would pass through at a diagonal, but even then, it was a tight fit. The bottom hem of her blouse got caught on the edge of the door. She managed to wriggle free, conceding only a small scrap of fabric. Lying on the garage floor, she rested until she'd caught enough breath to get up again.

Gustav hissed at her from the kitty bed.

"Look, Gustav," she said, "I don't really care that you're upset so long as you keep this visit between the two of us."

The cat spat and hopped back and forth with an arched back, but he never left his bed. Taking that as a series of empty threats, Theresa used Racky's champagne-colored jalopy to pull herself to her feet. The lock on the door from the garage to the house wasn't too hard to pick, so Theresa entered easily.

She went straight to Racky's office and retrieved the key to the desk drawer from the flowerpot. Inside of the drawer, there was a funny-looking playback device, something old. It didn't play when she pressed the play button. Probably too old, she figured. The other item in the drawer was a peach-colored journal with a bloody handprint along the spine. She found that to be much more interesting. And inside it, there were messy scribblings about 'Bathsheba', the name with which the Killer had rebranded Fire Salamander—or so B.F. claimed.

After reading a couple of stanzas of the scribblings, Theresa came to the delightful conclusion that she had found Lenci's Song. Never mind the fact that the words never once mentioned an Amphibian. The name 'Bathsheba' was enough.

If Bourghin was to be believed, the bearer of this Song could be the controller of Lenci's thoughts and actions, making this journal of enormous value. Theresa pointed her flake at the journal's front cover. A scan ray shot out of the flake and enveloped the journal.

After a couple of seconds, the flake displayed an error message. The journal couldn't be scanned whole because the pages were too crumpled and there was likely too much bleed through on its extra thin pages. Each page had to be scanned individually.

So, Theresa donned a fingertip scanner and ran her fingertip over each page—first around its borders, then along each line. She was careful to capture not just what was written, but *how* it was written. Any detail could be important, and nothing could be missed. The bitter stench that came off the pages was nauseating, but she stuck to the task because she could not pass up such an incredible opportunity.

It was 2045 when she finally compiled all of the images into a 3-D document that somewhat resembled the original journal. She attached it to a message that she addressed to B.F.

> Maybe this will reestablish your trust in me.

She returned the journal and drawer key to their places. Then she crept to the garage where she squeezed through the pet door. She walked around to the front porch and slid the unhelpful guest key back under the lawn gnome.

On the walk to her car, she felt the ragged edge of her shirt and remembered the scrap of fabric that was still stuck in the pet door. She returned to the garage and plucked the piece of fabric out of the door. When she turned to leave, she found herself face-to-face with Racky.

Racky looked angry but not entirely surprised. "Why are you here, Theresa?"

Theresa thought furiously for an excuse. "I needed to see you in person to talk to you about something important. I knew I was being watched, so I had to leave the hospital."

"I'll bite," Racky said, crossing her arms. "What's so important?"

"You've probably guessed it by now, but the cholera in my coffee was a cleanup act." Well-practiced tears filled Theresa's eyes. "It's really only by accident that I survived. I came to ask for your support for when I petition Vincent for help."

"Whose cleanup act and for what?" Racky asked.

"Oh, Racky, I made a big mistake," Theresa sobbed. "Someone claiming to be from the WCE asked me to scan that box of Bourghin's research—the one you caught me with. And now that they have what they want, they're trying to get rid of me!"

"I *knew* there was something fishy going on with you," Racky said.

There were a thousand questions that she could have asked about what had led Theresa to do something so harebrained, but she didn't ask them.

Instead, with a spark of compassion in her eyes, she said, "And that's the only way you compromised us to the WCE?"

"That's right," Theresa said. "I just scanned the one box and didn't send them anything else. I know it was wrong, Racky, but they offered me so much *money*. And of course, it's only now I realize how good I have it at the Coop."

"Well, your business partners trying to kill you tends to provide you some perspective," Racky agreed. Then she asked, "So, if you were coming here to see me, why did you go inside my house when I wasn't home?"

"I needed a place to wait that was out of sight," Theresa said with wide, innocent eyes. "I couldn't risk sending a request for access through your security system, so I crawled through the pet door. I'm only out here again because I forgot something in my rental car."

Racky sighed. "Alright, well, let's just see what you did while you were 'waiting out of sight.' SecurityFriend!"

SecurityFriend chirped twice, then a holographic screen popped up by the door to the garage.

"Pinpoint movement of warmblooded subjects in the main part of the house between now and 2000 this evening," Racky commanded. "Then play footage backward at seven point five times the speed."

Another couple of chirps ensued, and Theresa watched in horror as her whole mission was played backward at seven and a half times the speed.

Racky paused the recording at the part where Theresa began scanning the journal in her office. "So, you want to run that by me again about how you only ever sent that one box of records to the WCE?"

"I was sending the contents of the journal to Blair," Theresa said, inwardly noting that she'd have to remember to send the attachment to Blair sometime before the next morning.

"Mhm." Racky sucked her teeth. "SecurityFriend, intercept the data that was sent in any message before 2050 from my office. If it was sent by cell waves, pinpoint the tower and send me the info."

SecurityFriend chirped and began her investigation. Before she could finish, the system was hacked, and a new screen enveloped the old one.

A message in flowery script appeared:

I Imagine These Will Be Of Interest To You.

"B.F.'s hacking my masterpiece security system!" Racky exclaimed. "I would know her phantasms anywhere! And I'm too impressed to be agitated!"

SecurityFriend began spitting out image recordings of Theresa tampering with the Peaceful Rental car as well as documents that all created a fairly incriminating record with respect to Theresa's connection to the WCE.

"That B.F. is a *snake*," Theresa said, throwing up her hands. "Okay, look. There's a lot I haven't told you. I *have* been working for the WCE, and I got in way over my head. But I'll tell you what I know. B.F. is a very powerful Phib, and she has her hands in a lot of different pots—"

"Ey, ey, slow down!" Racky said. "Let's just mosey inside and talk about it."

She moved to unlock the garage door when she saw a red dot appear over Theresa's heart. She dove low, hitting Theresa's hips, and knocked her sideways just in time. A bullet hole appeared above them in the garage wall. The shot had come from the second-floor garage apartment on the property behind Racky's place.

Racky pushed Theresa toward the front of the house. There were a couple more shots, but the women hugged the wall and eventually moved out of the shooter's line of sight.

"Thanks," Theresa breathed. "I think I can get to my car from here."

"Wouldn't do that if I didn't want to get blown to kingdom come or driven off a cliff," Racky said. "The WCE seems out for blood."

She made a motion to suggest that someone else could hear them. It was the only way to account for how the sniper knew to fire only after Theresa had begun to tell the unhindered truth.

Theresa sighed. "Well, if they really thought I was going to take the fall for them silently, they had another thing coming. Where's Bambina Extraordinaire?"

"Blair took her in search of the sniper, and they've probably made contact by now," Racky replied. "We suspected you would attract some company."

"Blair's here, too?"

"In all her one-armed and tender-ribbed glory," Racky nodded. "You didn't think I'd come alone, did you?"

"I honestly didn't know you'd be coming at all," Theresa said, her voice taking on a more respectful tone.

When they came around the front of the house, there were two men with guns waiting for them.

"Holy damnation, the WCE is thorough!" Racky remarked.

"We had a feeling Cravenly would blab," one of the men said, "and you've heard too much."

"Well, I wasn't *intending* to hear anything troublesome—if you gentlemen find that pertinent to any current decision-making process," Racky said.

They apparently didn't. Each man aimed at one of the women and cocked his gun. They motioned for the women to enter the house.

"Down on your knees, hands behind your heads," the first man said once they'd entered the living room.

When Theresa saw Racky grab backward for her executioner's gun, she ducked. Both guns went off, and an extra loud shot from a shotgun followed. The men lurched forward and landed facedown on the vinyl flooring. They stayed down.

"About time!" Racky exclaimed.

"I came from a distance," Blair said, coming out of the kitchen with Bambina Extraordinaire cradled in the crook of her good arm. "Guessed right about the location of the sniper, but he was already dead when I got to him—cyanide."

"The WCE is cruel to people who fail them," Theresa explained, touching her back gingerly. There was buckshot embedded in it. "What the *hell* were you aiming at, Lee-Smith?"

"Mostly the guys with the guns," Blair replied with a smirk. "Theresa Cravenly, you'll be in our custody until the completion of an investigation of your espionage activities to be conducted by Internal Affairs."

"Good, get me out of here," Theresa said.

She walked with her colleagues around the block and waited nervously while they swept Blair's auto-car for explosive devices. It was clean. So, she slid into the back seat. Racky followed suit, and Blair sat in the front.

As Racky and Blair called in a special status report, the car began moving toward HQ.

Theresa cleared her throat. "Do either of you have something to record with? After nearly being killed three times, I'm nervous that I won't make it to HQ."

"And now you're concerned with helping the good guys?" Racky huffed.

"No," Theresa said, still smug despite her obvious predicament. "I can't touch B.F., but if I cause her to fail, she'll be at the agency's mercy."

"Imagine that, Cravenly," Blair said coolly. "After all that's happened, our interests are now genuinely aligned."

"At this point, I don't know I'd trust anything you'd say, Theresa," Racky said.

"Trust me or not, you'll act on my words," Theresa told her.

"Why?"

"Because B.F. is the Amphibian who originally delivered Lenci's son to the WCE. She said the boy is still alive and is called by the name Larva. And she knows this because the Assistant Vice recently had Larva transferred to another facility, and B.F. has been assigned to be one of his trainers."

Racky and Blair both started speaking at once, and a barrage of questions ensued.

"Kiddo's a boy?"

"Why is the Assistant Vice having him trained by an Amphibian?"

"What kind of training?"

"Where is the new facility?"

"Why did she have him transferred?"

"Why did she fake his death?"

Theresa held up her hand, and her former coworkers fell silent.

"Last I'll say before I have a plea deal and protection is this: B.F. is not someone to trifle with. She's not exactly the righthand woman to the Assistant Vice, but she is trusted—very well trusted. Anyone who engages her will feel the repercussions for generations."

"I'm willing to take that chance for my half-brother," Blair said.

"Me too," Racky said, "for the boy *and* for Lenci."

"I thought you might," Theresa said. "Now, about that plea deal—"

"Internal Affairs will want a crack at you first," Blair said, pulling out a voice recording device. "Now, start again from the beginning."

"Fine," Theresa said. "But, first, humor me: how did you guys know I was at Racky's house? Did SecurityFriend finally learn to monitor pet doors?"

Racky grinned. "Not yet, but I trained Gustav to dance on his kitty bed when intruders come through one of his pet doors. There's a panic button under his bed that alerted me. You didn't think I'd leave my house vulnerable just because I got a pet, did you?"

"Damn," Theresa said. "I was ratted out by a cat."

CHAPTER 26

Two days after Rosa had completed her experiment with the contents of the canister, she sat in the living room of the dilapidated house, waiting for B.F. to contact her. The encrypted message that Rosa had posted was only for formality's sake. She figured that B.F. must know that the experiment had been a success. In Lakes, B.F. had seemed to watch her every move. So, why the delay?

Pete had tested Rosa's blood to ensure that there were no traces of the disease left. There was nothing, not even antibodies. It was like she had never been ill at all. This was wonderful news, but Rosa found herself quite unable to enjoy her uncompromisable immunity without being able to use it as a bargaining chip for the sake of her son.

A soft hand fell on her shoulder. She looked up to meet Pete's gaze.

"You're thinking about him again," he said sympathetically.

She nodded. "I only know that *a* Phib took him to the Assistant Vice, but I have no leads on who that one is. I just need a way to interrogate them all."

"Well, listen, we'll have plenty of time to scheme and plot about how to make ourselves Phib bait," Pete grinned. "For now, would you join me for some sunshine in the backyard?"

Rosa smiled back. "Sunshine in *Farm And Forest*? This I've got to see."

It was, indeed, a beautiful day. The sun was shining, causing the evergreen-trimmed lake to reflect a bright, shimmering blue. Although the air was crisp, it was unusually warm for that time of year.

Rosa leaned on the veranda's railing and gazed out at the lake. It reminded her—in a still, small way—of the ocean. The ocean was wild, unpredictable, and incredibly powerful while the lake was calm, contained, and quiet. But the light-reflecting properties of both spoke an inner strength to the viewer.

Looking down, Rosa saw a cherry tomato plant growing by the edge of the veranda. Pete had cleared a couple of square meters for a garden. He was kneeling in the dirt, checking the leaves of the butter lettuce he'd planted beside the tomatoes.

"Wow, you must have been busy during my downtime," she said, hurrying down the steps of the veranda. "It's crazy you got those to grow in winter."

Pete fingered the red-tipped lettuce leaves adoringly. "Well, they are naturally hearty that way. They're a good fall and winter vegetable."

Rosa leaned over him to get to the tomato plant, plucked the plumpest, reddest tomato she could find, and popped it into her mouth.

"Oh, those," Pete said, embarrassed.

"What?"

A pink glow appeared in his cheeks. "Those are fast-growing, winter resistant tomatoes."

"Okay," Rosa said. "So?"

"*Genetically engineered* fast-growing, winter resistant tomatoes," Pete clarified. "They were engineered to grow in conditions with little sunlight and occasional frosts, but the change to their genetic structure makes them dangerous to eat raw."

"How dangerous?"

"They can often cause uncontrolled cell growth in the digestive tract—cancer."

Rosa smiled, considering his concern precious. "Well, I guess it's a good thing I've got uncompromisable immunity. Wouldn't want to spend a couple of weeks in the Subclass section at a Farm And Forest cancer ward—if there is such a section."

Pete returned her smile. "Lakes could have had you in and out in a couple days, but the treatments wouldn't have been very pleasant."

After a second, he said, "You really should try the tomatoes cooked in a pasta sauce. *Or*"—he raised his voice excitedly at the thought "—*or* maybe grilled in a salad! They have just the right elasticity with a little pop in the skin and this lovely citrusy, sweet flesh that would go perfectly with goat cheese, arugula, walnuts, and a balsamic dressing."

He appeared almost as satisfied as if he had prepared, plated, and enjoyed the entire dish right then and there.

Rosa gave him a small peck on the cheek. "That was—really something. I might be slightly jealous of that salad."

"Hm," Pete said, pulling her closer. "You only had to say the word."

He kissed her once, twice, three times. From the back of her mind, she recalled something about his conditioning against physical affection.

"But what about your—" was her half-hearted attempt at a warning.

She forgot what she had meant to say because she rather liked his lips and his tongue and the warmth of his body and the tingling thrills that thronged wherever he touched her. She delightedly traced the grooves in his rippling back muscles, then slid her hands around to the front of his body.

Pete shivered in response, and as Rosa was wondering whether the shivers were good or bad, his lips suddenly stiffened. His eyes rolled back in his head, then snapped back to focus on her. His hands became like claws, and his knees buckled, but she managed to get under his arm and steady him.

"It pains me to cut this off here, Pete," she said, "but I can't have you keeling over in the vegetable garden."

"That only happened when we barely knew each other," he said, leaning in to kiss her again. She put her hand on his chest firmly so that he paused.

"It's just the tomatoes," she said playfully. "How will I ever experience the divine pleasure of that grilled tomato salad if you faint on top of the plant?"

The light in his eyes dimmed a little.

"You're right," he sighed, moving toward the steps of the veranda. He sat on the top step and began to massage his hands.

She sat next to him. "You know I really want to be close to you, right?"

A knife wound would likely have been preferable to those words. They apparently stung in a way that Rosa had not intended.

With some effort, Pete raised his gaze to hers, and the corners of his mouth twitched into a brief smile. "I was going to say the same. And I'm sorry."

"Don't be," Rosa replied, holding out her hand. He took it, and she scooted toward him until their hips touched. They enjoyed the view of the lake until the sky turned from blue to pink to orange and back to a blue that grew progressively darker.

When last light was fading, Pete squeezed Rosa's hand. "Shouldn't we head inside?"

"Mm, you're warm," she said, hugging his arm to her body.

He laughed. "Well, my *arm* is warm—thanks to you. But the rest of me is freezing."

Just as he said that, a breeze picked up.

She groaned. "Okay, let's just separate quickly and get it over with."

"As soon as we're inside, both of my arms will be yours."

"You're on," she said. "Count of three?"

"Three, go!" Pete exclaimed, jumping up.

"So inhumane," Rosa grumbled, teeth chattering, as she hastened after him. "What happened to 'respect for all life?'"

They burst into the living room laughing and shivering. Pete snapped on a light, then true to his word, he enveloped Rosa in a big hug.

"See? Both arms," he said.

"Yeah, better," she replied, bringing her arms around his body.

Even though their shivering subsided fairly quickly, they lingered in the embrace. At length, Pete loosened his grip, and Rosa looked up to see a sparkle in his eye.

"No, look now, don't tease me like that," she said. "It gives me false hopes."

"Deferment of your hopes doesn't make them false," Pete said.

Rosa draped her arms around his neck and studied his earnest face. Not unlike her, he had experienced quite a few losses—many of which he didn't speak about. And he was not untainted by treachery and betrayal. It was just that he had somehow managed to hope for more out of life beyond those things. She loved that about him.

"Just one," he said, leaning toward her. "I can handle one."

She savored the kiss for all it was worth and was not sorry when he really drew it out. When they pulled apart, Pete sighed deeply.

"We'll find our way," Rosa told him.

"Yeah," he said, shaking out his right hand, which had begun to tense up. "I'm going to shower."

Rosa made a move for the kitchen. "I'll boil you some water. Hot water's not hooked up yet, remember?"

He turned toward the stairwell as he removed his shirt.

"We're Phibs," he said with a chuckle. "We don't need hot water for a shower."

As he began walking up the stairs, a couple of psychosomatic burn scars appeared across his back. Rosa averted her eyes as though looking upon the evidence of his triggering would make it worse.

"Well, 'need' is such a strong word," she said, trying to sound light-hearted. "I'll, uh, use the boiled water for a bath later."

He must have heard the anxious undertone in her voice because he turned around and came into the kitchen. His gait was confident, but there was something in his manner that seemed injured. His approach was a strange and beautiful event to behold, like watching a runway model with a broken-legged shadow. He was not physically limping, but some inward part of him was.

The most prominent of Pete's scars was not a burn scar but one that appeared to have been made using a sharp implement. Rosa hadn't seen it when she first witnessed the appearance of his scars in his Lakes apartment. In fact, she was sure that the scar hadn't been visible at all that time.

It was now emerging over the Eastern Newt that was tattooed on Pete's right pectoral. The skin raised into a series of pinkish white slits, not uniform but made with the same blade, all originating from the same point—like a handheld fan with ribs of many different widths.

Pete followed her gaze to the scar. "*He* caught me trying to remove my mark. Tried to teach me a lesson, but after all he'd already done to me, the only lesson I really learned was that the mark reaches beyond the top layer."

Rosa could only sort of empathize with him because she only sort of remembered what it was like for someone to teach her that kind of lesson. She felt cold all of a sudden.

Trying to cling to the present, she asked, "Why do they go away?"

"Because I know where to put them," Pete replied.

She *could* empathize with him in that. She also had figured out that putting her problems in appropriate compartments was an effective way to survive, although she had never thought to try it on her own scars. Even if she had wanted to do that, she wouldn't have known where to start. With a trembling hand, she reached toward the fan-like scar.

Pete stepped closer so that her fingertips just touched the fine ends of a couple of the slits. His scarred skin was still warm, reminding her that he was alive under there, beneath the top layer. Then, feeling self-conscious about the tears that came to her eyes, she pulled back and crossed her arms.

"Too bad *he* died on accident," she said, looking away. "I'd kill him on purpose for you."

Pete gently turned her face back toward his. There was an anger lodged beneath his grieved expression, which told her that he could appreciate the sentiment, but he mostly looked tired.

"Good night, Rosa," he said, kissing her on the forehead.

"Good night, Pete."

He folded his shirt lengthwise as he trudged to the staircase. Then he slung it over his shoulder and began his ascent as if his feet were made of lead.

When the water in the shower was running, Rosa let out a deep sigh. She didn't fully understand her feelings toward Pete Bae, but she knew that she longed for him. And since the evening that he had tried to kill her, she had known there was a real possibility that his past would keep him from physical intimacy. But Rosa had hoped that in being her sweet, benign, unphiblike self, she could give him the positive exposure that he needed to overcome his conditioning—to keep him safe from the past.

As much as she wanted that, she came to terms with the fact that it would not be happening that evening. So, she turned her attention to getting a pot of water onto the stove. A hot bath was just what she needed.

While she was waiting for the water to boil, she sat down by her web apparatus. It chimed immediately. The message icon appeared in front of her face. When she touched it, the icon dissolved into a spray of white pixels, and the long-awaited note floated out onto the coffee table.

> Got Your Message. Nice Encrypting Job. Meet And Greet At The Class 3 Cafe On Swan Plaza At 0700. Come Alone. – B.F.

The next morning, Rosa tiptoed downstairs while Pete was still asleep in his room. She drove the jeep to the Class 3 café in Swan Plaza. She tried to remind herself that B.F. likely didn't know her heritages, but the idea of meeting in a Class 3 establishment still bothered her. There was a silver lining, however, in that B.F.'s invitation revealed a key piece of information about *her*: B.F. was apparently Class 3 or could pass for it.

When Rosa entered the Class 3 café, everyone in the place did indeed appear to be some kind of Class 3. No one asked for any documentation to prove her class designation, and she realized it was in her best interest not to go asking around about that.

There was an older woman with feathery white hair who sat in the corner. At the next table, there was a couple sipping on mochas and playing footsy. In front of them was a group of tea-drinking young ladies who looked like they might work at a hair salon. They had nice haircuts, in any case, and trendy jaw makeup. Closest to the door, there was a businessman who had just finished his French roast, no sugar, no cream. He nodded appreciatively at Rosa, then brushed past her to get to the parking lot.

B.F. apparently hadn't arrived yet. Rosa sat down at the table between the older woman and the hair salon ladies. After a couple of minutes, a most striking woman entered the café and paused by the door to take in the room. The woman's hip circumference nearly equaled Rosa's, and she had apparently obtained a couple of enhancements, which she displayed rather proudly through a large cutout near the top of her bright blue, long-sleeved jumpsuit. There wasn't a sports bra well made enough to accommodate such enhancements, so it was unlikely that *she* was B.F.

When the woman saw Rosa staring at her, she smirked. It was the smirk of a winner who never loses, a smirk that Rosa had absolutely seen before—only on the face of someone else. Rosa was chilled to the bone, then she began to sink down, down, down.

The woman in the jumpsuit widened her smirk into a grin. She tucked her chestnut brown hair behind her ear and, as she did so, her sleeve rode up to reveal a tattoo of a bullfrog on the underside of her wrist.

The Agent inwardly kicked herself for not realizing sooner that B.F. stood for Bullfrog—the mark of Arjun Thomas as embodied by Reece Ma, a man whom she'd thought had been murdered and thrown into the bay in Diablo. With all manner of conflicting feelings bubbling up inside her, the Agent found herself without words. She stormed over to the woman and slapped her across the face.

"Ow!" B.F. cried, holding her cheek.

"That's for making me think you were dead!" the Agent said fiercely. Then she slapped her again. "And *that's* for kidnapping Pete and turning his pants backward!"

Suddenly, B.F. pinned the Agent's arms to her sides and leaned her back into a deep, theatrical dip.

"At long last, sister," she whispered, her cherry-fragranced breath hot in the Agent's face.

As her limbs went weak, the Agent was too astonished and angry to be afraid. She couldn't stop thinking about the mark of the Bullfrog. There was nothing in her world that could make sense of this. And yet, in the world of the WCE, many nightmare-worthy scenarios were possible.

"I *thought* you would have developed an immunity," B.F. said, "unless, you aren't who you say you are. I've been there myself recently."

Completely paralyzed by whatever had entered her through her assailant's breath, the Agent had no option but to allow B.F. to drag her into the alley behind the café. As they rounded the corner, however, the Agent noticed the feeling coming back to her limbs. From the way that B.F. had hoisted her over her shoulder and begun to trudge along, the Agent guessed that their road would be a long one. She only had to bide her time.

About two hundred meters down the alleyway, the Agent sensed that her limbs were no longer paralyzed. Immediately, she wrapped herself around her captor and took her to the ground. Without missing a beat, B.F. engaged her, but she seemed half-hearted in the fight. Eventually, she left herself completely unguarded, so the Agent pinned her to the ground and twisted her arm behind her back.

"I've played enough of your games, Reece," the Agent said. "Where's my son?"

"Easy, now," the woman said arching her back to alleviate some of the pressure. "And it's June."

"What?"

"My name is June."

"Seriously?"

No answer.

The Agent continued, "Fine, *June*. Where's my son?"

"I'll tell you," June replied. "But take me somewhere private. Every shadow has ears in this district."

The Agent sighed and pulled her to her feet.

"It really *has* been too long," June said, straightening the waist of her jumpsuit.

The Agent headed for her jeep, dragging June along with her. "You'd better not be stringing me along with this business about my son."

"No, no!" June said, taking hurried tiny steps to keep up. "I really do have information for you."

"Good." The Agent didn't finish the rest of her thought, which included what she would do to June if this whole thing ended up being a lie.

* * *

When they arrived at the dilapidated house, the Agent bounded up the steps of the veranda while June stayed behind in the jeep to adjust her jumpsuit. Pete opened the door just as the Agent turned her key in the lock.

"Where'd you go?" he asked. "I thought you'd—"

He studied her face. "Are you okay? You seem different."

The Agent named Rosa shrugged and adjusted her voice to sound more benign as she said, "No, I feel great! More myself than ever."

June stepped out of the jeep and, as she slowly ascended the steps, Pete's eyes grew wide.

"What is *she* doing here?" he demanded.

June slid her arm around Rosa and massaged her waist with a sultry smile. This elicited a gasp of disgust from Pete and a knowing sigh from Rosa.

"Pete," Rosa said entreatingly, "B.F. is for Bullfrog."

He continued to peer out at them from behind the half-open door. "So I gathered during her treacherous dealings back at Home. What is she doing *here?*"

The Agent patted June's hand, wordlessly explaining that she would handle the situation. June sat down on the steps to wait as Rosa squeezed past Pete and closed the door.

"This wasn't the plan!" Pete said. "*How* could you bring her here?"

He was trembling, probably halfway to a trigger. Rosa gently took hold of his arm. When he finally made eye contact with her, she touched his face.

"June and I—we've got a history from back Home," she told him. "So, can you please just give her a chance?"

"I don't trust her," Pete said, shaking his head.

Rosa laughed softly. "Neither do I. But I know that she loves a good *quid pro quo*, and since I scratched her back with all the canister stuff, it's her turn to scratch mine."

Pete nodded in grim understanding. "She knows where your son is."

"She knows *something*," Rosa replied. "So, if you can survive sitting across the breakfast table from her, we'll reminisce a bit like old friends, then she'll tell me what I want to know and she'll be out of our hair."

"Just breakfast?" Pete's expression showed that he was really trying to adjust his frame of mind about the situation for Rosa's sake.

"June will want to move on afterward, anyway," she said. "Phibs never stay in the same place for long."

"Unless they have a reason to," Pete said with a grin.

"Yes." Rosa kissed him on the cheek and opened the door.

June looked up from the bra strap that she had been adjusting and smiled in practiced shyness.

"That won't work on me," Rosa said. "Get in here, so we can eat."

After smoothing out her jumpsuit, June hopped to her feet and skipped daintily up the steps. She curtseyed to Pete as she walked through the door.

"Kind of you to invite me to stay," she said.

"Not my invitation," he replied, "and you won't be staying."

Casting him an imploring glance, Rosa took June by the arm and led her to the dining table.

"Sit," she said. "I hope you like leftovers."

"Never stopped me before," June said, looking at Pete in such a manner that his cheeks began to glow red. He averted his gaze.

After clinking around the kitchen, Rosa came back with her arms full.

"Lettuce, salsa, cheese, chickpea chorizo, black beans, corn, onions, avocado, corn chips," she said. "Taco salad for breakfast, *bon appetit*."

"*Chickpea chorizo?*" June practically screeched. "You're serving this classic Diablan regional dish without any meat?"

"We don't have any in the house," Rosa said, feeling more self-conscious before June than she would have liked.

June spread her napkin over her lap primly. "You mock your Class 2 as well as your Class 4.14 ancestors. They were all of them lovers of meat—meat as a meal, meat in side dishes, meat in the *vegetables*, for goodness' sake!"

Before Rosa could remind June that plenty of 2s and 4.14s were vegetarian, Pete said, "4.14?"

He looked as if his chair had been pulled out from under him.

June turned to Rosa. "You seemed so close; I assumed he knew."

"I tried to tell him," Rosa sighed. "He didn't want to hear it. Something about rejecting Neo-Eugenic thought."

Pete seemed more surprised than hateful, but the inner turmoil as broadcast on his face seemed greater than the situation warranted—at least in Rosa's opinion. And based on June's judgmental expression, hers also.

"No, I—I'm sorry," Pete stammered. "You tried to tell me. I just spent all that time, uh, mistakenly believing you had Class 3 heritage because of your name and being from Diablo. I shouldn't have assumed."

"Is this going to be a problem?" Rosa asked.

Pete composed himself quickly. "Of course not. It's good to know. Wow, you can't even see the Class 4.14 at all."

"He doesn't mean it how it sounds," Rosa told June.

"If you say so," June replied, "because it sounds like he wouldn't *want* to see 4.14 in you."

"I definitely don't mean it how it sounds!" Pete said, horrified. "I just mean I see you only as I ever have: as human. Sorry, if I offended you."

"It's okay," Rosa said, unable to decide whether to lecture Pete on why no one is ever only human or to overturn the table and have a rage fit.

The celebration of Valencia's cultures was all that she had left of her family. Owning her heritages was the way that they remained with her while they were separated. And because of the threat of the WCE, she knew that she could well be separated from them forever. She hated remaining silent at a potential teaching moment, but she hated overturning furniture like the Killer had always done when angry. Her hand closed around her fork, and she gripped it until her knuckles turned white.

"Humans always have heritages and cultures and loyalties," June said, maneuvering the fork out of Rosa's hand. "Unless you don't, Pete?"

Rosa snatched her fork back. "Anyway, eat up, you two."

She passed the serving bowls around to move the conversation along.

"You spoil me, sister," June said huskily. Then, with a sparkly glance at Pete, she asked, "Are leftovers always this extravagant here, or is she just pulling out all the stops for her dutiful consort?"

Pete's fork clattered onto the table. "I'm sorry. What *exactly* was your relationship back at Home?"

"You didn't tell him that either?" June's eyes glimmered as she crushed tortilla chips over her salad.

Rosa scooped some salsa onto her plate. "Do we have to talk about this right now?"

June smirked. "He'll have to know eventually."

"Fine." Rosa folded her hands in her lap. "It happened after I came out of the arena. They called it an additional phase of enticement training. But now, after all that's happened with—what's inside of me, the possibilities for their true goal seem endless. "

"They just wanted us to have sex," June said cheerfully, "or, that's what I got out of it."

Pete nearly choked on his food.

"Well, it *was* when she was a he," Rosa shrugged.

June put her arm around Rosa's chair. "It was a breach of the isolation protocol to pair us, but the order was clear. And we were a smart match according to the agency tenets. The Agentess was registered as Class 3 from back at SSI, you see, and the project managers at Home had reason to believe I was Class 3 as well."

"Had reason to believe?" Pete echoed.

"Undoubtedly, you heard the rumors of the unfit female who survived the nanobots?" June said. Getting no response, she continued, "But the lesser-known story is that there was also an unfit male from SSI who survived."

"But how?" Pete asked.

"All I know is that I awoke as I was being transported to the dead pile," June said. "I killed the men who carried me. Then I tracked down my counterpart and did the same to him, placing my DNA in the WCE's record to close the loop."

"Even so, I could tell the first time we were—reintroduced." The Agent named Rosa's voice shook as she remembered a little too closely the original emotions connected to the facts. "Arjun, the real one, had been my partner before that, you know."

Pete's eyes grew wide, but he said nothing.

"But I became *more than a partner* to her," June said. "That night, she recognized my breathing pattern immediately and confronted me. I did not deny that I had done what was necessary to survive. From that moment, we were inextricably linked through our shared secret: our defiant existence."

"She recognized your breathing," Pete said. "So, you two had been involved before the WCE, uh, paired you together?"

"No, no," Rosa said. "I—"

"She has a gift!" June said.

"Pattern recognition was one of my main contributors to the agency," Rosa explained. "Just like some people can learn music by heart, I can learn people. Reece and I had sparred occasionally back at the SSI Academy, and Arjun had been my partner on the mission that led us Home. So, I knew their mannerisms like the back of my hand. Before Reece as Arjun even touched me that night, I knew who he was."

Pete looked like his head was reeling. "That and—everything involved—sounds incredibly difficult."

Rosa smiled ruefully. "Well, yes. But being alive when no one else knows that you are is a heavy burden, and to have a comrade in that was priceless. We also saw and experienced the world similarly because we were born of the same parents, in a manner of speaking."

"SSI and the WCE, you see," June told Pete. He looked sick.

"And we've supported each other through a number of difficult situations," Rosa said. "June has even done so at a distance, it seems."

"Disappearing you from every database was more than a notion," June said with a nod.

It was then that Rosa realized just how much June had done for her. All the things that had made her life a little bit easier along the way—these were the interventions of her comrade.

"You really did a lot, didn't you?" she said. "You risked your life bringing me that box in Diablo to help me remember my mission. And it was *you* that kept the SSI alarm system from recognizing me when I broke in to stop the first phase of the Cull. You even hacked the biometric elevator in Lakes and alerted me when you thought Pete had been activated to kill me."

"Someone had to look out for my impetuous sister, and being 'dead,' I was in a uniquely advantageous position to be of service," June said. "Why, it was on your first day in Lakes that I made an appearance at a physical confrontation in Croon A Tune to throw the Cooperative FBI off your scent. I don't know what possessed you to get a profile picture taken in a boutique, but I was luckily able to nip that issue in the bud."

Rosa touched her comrade's hand. "I had no idea the trouble you went to."

June shrugged. "You've always helped out when you've known I needed it. That's what matters most to me."

Pete cleared his throat. "So, the additional phase of enticement training—"

Rosa groaned. "I thought we'd moved on from that."

"Not a chance," Pete said, staring intently at June. "I know that this might be obvious to you two, but it's not to me. If you two were together in *that* way, how and why is June now identifying as female?"

"It *is* a new look for you," Rosa said, passing June an amused glance.

"It's a simple case of shapeshifting, my sister," June told her. "To identify oneself is a privilege reserved for those better born or more serenely developed. But you and I—supreme weapons though we are—know full well that we lack the autonomy to *identify as* anything. Feelings from the inside out are useless against the power of how we are seen. Whether we are seen as male or female, Class 3 or subclass, our survival hinges mainly on being *identified*. I just finally decided to make the systems work for me in every way possible."

"And being identified as female facilitates your survival because—" Rosa began slowly.

"It was most advantageous for me at the time of my erasure," June said. "I returned to SSI to help you, but then I needed to disappear permanently to help myself. A female body was the last place SSI or the WCE or anyone, really, would have looked for me."

She simpered at Pete and said, "I have other useful forms, too—other classes and other genders—but I return to this one often because the masses have found it winsome."

Pete scoffed.

"I see," Rosa said. "So, you're basically passing, even though no one is forcing you to do it."

"Oh, I *know* what you think of passing—in any form of the activity," June said, "but 'forcing' is in the eye of the beholder. There was no gun held to your head at SSI when you went along with Bourghin's plan to register you as a 3.5."

The decision hadn't sat well with Valencia because it felt like a denial of her family and her entire self. She had regretted it ever since.

June smiled understandingly. "You trusted him. And even though *we* are the only ones we can trust now, it is still his motto that we live by."

"Survival is the name of the game," Rosa recited. Then, after briefly reflecting on those words, she said, "So, you've told us why. But *how*?"

"Yes, she conveniently left that out of her answer to my original question," Pete said irritably.

"I was just coming to that," June told him. "The Agentess can attest to the fact that, for reasons as of yet unknown, the euthanasic nanobots that were meant to kill us instead took a liking to our bodies. Hers must have made love to her immune system. As our recent team effort has shown, she appears to be uncompromisably immune, even to novel diseases."

Pete visibly recoiled at the idea of being on a team with June. Rosa reached across the table and squeezed his hand reassuringly.

"*My* nanobots, on the other hand, fused at the very first with my epithelium," June continued. "In essence, I gained the ability to perform cosmetic surgery on myself."

"Yeah, but *that* is not all epithelial tissue," Rosa said, motioning to June's bosom.

"How astute an observation, sister," June replied. "Perhaps, you may remember that I specialized in technology at SSI?"

Rosa nodded, impressed. "So, you reprogrammed the bots and now you can rearrange your body mass at will?"

"Precisely." June turned her attention back to her taco salad. She took a couple of bites. Then, looking up with a glint in her eye, she asked, "Would you like a small demonstration?"

Pete emphatically shook his head "no" as Rosa exclaimed, "Absolutely! Go for it!"

"Very well. I'll make my best effort not to shriek. This process pushes the limits of my pain management." June pulled a flat contraption out of her purse. It was about fifteen centimeters long and seven centimeters wide, and it was made of black plastic. There were glowing buttons with interesting symbols on one of its broad surfaces.

June extended her right hand for her spectators to have a better view, then typed a series of commands on her device. Her hand tensed up and began to shake. In a horrifying yet fascinating spectacle, the skin on her hand became gelatinous and parted to make way for the growing phalanges that were emerging. Flesh and connective tissue came up to join the bone, and the skin soon grew back into place.

"Water, water!" June said with a hint of desperation. "I usually do this in the shower. Need water *now*!"

Rosa dumped a cup of water over her comrade's hand. There was a slimy, peach-colored residue left on the surface of the skin for which Rosa handed June a napkin. Pete looked disgusted.

"And there you have it," June said, holding her hands together for them to see. The fingers on her right hand were about a centimeter longer than those on her left.

"Wow," Rosa breathed. "Where'd you get the building blocks for that?"

"A little loss of bone density here or a little fat or muscle loss there." June shrugged. "I piss out any internal byproducts, so sky's the limit."

The Agent regarded her pensively. "Indeed."

The sky was the limit for physical transformation, but it also seemed that June had managed to train her nanobots to accomplish a variety of tasks—like making her breath into a powerful sedative. The Agent wondered what other applications June had found for her nanobots. And that made her wonder what else June could be hiding about her true reasons for reconnecting with the Agent.

Pete stood and began to clear the table. He piled the dishes into a precariously high tower and hauled them off to the kitchen. When he'd placed them in the sink, he moved silently out the back door—most likely to tend to his garden.

June took the Agent's hand. "I'm sorry I deceived you about my death." She addressed her in Malayalam, one of the languages in which they had communicated to maintain their covers as Class 3 agents at the WCE.

The Agent smiled and answered in Hindi for the fun of it. "Hey, Survival is the name of the game, right? I couldn't begrudge you a chance to win your freedom."

Then, figuring that she had expressed a sufficient amount of good will, she said, "Now, please tell me where my son is."

June dropped her gaze.

"You *do* know where he is, don't you?"

"Yes," June said. "But it might be easier if I show you rather than tell. I'd like to take a shower first, though, if you don't mind."

The Agent pounded the table. "You're stalling, Reece! If you've been lying to me all this time, I will kill you."

"I'm *not* lying," June said indignantly. "And if I'm Reece, you're Valencia. Now, please show me to your shower, so I may attend to my appearance."

"Fine," the Agent said in English. "But I know there's a window in the bathroom. And if you try—"

"You would be welcome to join me, if you are so concerned," June replied.

The Agent scoffed.

"Or you could deign to trust me," June continued. "I came to *you*, remember?"

"Upstairs, first door on the left," the Agent told her. "Hurry up."

"Half a minute, dear sister," June purred.

CHAPTER 28

MORE THAN HALF A MINUTE AND LESS THAN HALF AN HOUR LATER, A man with chestnut brown hair in a French herringbone braid descended the stairs. He was just below average height and very muscular. The Agent stood up from the table, regarding him warily.

The man smirked, and she immediately recognized him. He rubbed the back of his neck in a way that displayed the bullfrog mark on his wrist.

"Apologies for the delay," he said in a friendly tenor voice. "I hooked up your hot water. Can't *abide* a cold shower. And I borrowed some of Pete's clothes. I hope he doesn't mind."

The T-shirt he'd taken was a tad too long for him and so tight that the grooves in his six-pack were visible through the material. The jeans were rolled up about thirteen centimeters, which simply made him look sloppy—much too sloppy for the likes of a Phib. But perhaps that was the ingenuity of the disguise. If the WCE had ever caught wind of June's activity, they certainly would never suspect this guy of being the same person.

"I'm at a loss for words," the Agent told him.

"Well, I suppose we should get introduced," the man said, flourishing his arms. "Identify me!"

"I—uh, Georgie?" the Agent stammered. Then, noticing her comrade's carefully applied jaw makeup, she wondered if she had overstepped her bounds in assuming that the person before her was indeed a man.

So, she added, "Na?"

"*Georgina*? Don't be absurd!" Georgie said with a dramatic eye roll. "Now, if you want to know more about your son, grab a windbreaker or whatever will keep that supple body of yours warm, and let's go for a walk."

A walk? Could it really be that Kiddo had been right there in Farm And Forest the whole time?

"Pete!" Rosa called out the back door. "Georgie and I are just going to step out for a moment. I'll be back in a few."

"Two birds with one stone: kicking the system in the gut and helping you," Pete said, entering the house with his revolver. "If you're going to break your son out of a WCE facility, I'm coming too."

He stopped at the sight of Georgie standing next to Rosa.

"Georgie." Rosa shrugged. "H—he?"

Georgie nodded, so she continued, "He's going to help us break my son out."

"Oh, I don't think we'll be breaking him out," Georgie said hurriedly.

Rosa shook her head. "Nonsense. We'll just find a way in, make a distraction, grab the boy, and get out. I mean, with three Phibs how hard could it be?"

"You'll see," Georgie said. "Come with me."

"In *my* clothes," Pete muttered as he followed the other two out the front door.

It was a perfect, spring-like morning in Farm And Forest. Every puddle along the dirt road reflected the sunlight, and the air was cool and crisp. Georgie led the way with Rosa just behind him, and Pete brought up the rear. About two kilometers from the house, they turned off of the main road and walked into the large expanse of trees. It was more humid beneath the thick canopy, and the air smelled of moist dirt and pine needles.

Rosa found herself overjoyed at the thought of seeing her Kiddo. Finally, after a whole year, she would get to hold him for the first time, to tell him that she would never let anything bad happen to him again.

The Agent pushed the thought away. Although the desire of her heart was finally within reach, she could not let that cloud her judgment. There was most likely a conflict standing between her and her son—a violent conflict for which she, even with the help of two highly skilled fighters, would need to be at her best. Not to mention that, whatever Georgie had up his sleeve, the path ahead was unlikely to be straight and even.

When they came across what appeared to be a community cemetery, Georgie finally spoke. "We're getting close now."

As they continued, the Agent noticed that the clusters of urns placed about the roots of the trees were becoming more and more numerous. It was just like the WCE to set up their secret facility in the woods near an unofficial burial site. Only the bereft would come to this area, and their minds would be occupied with everything other than the WCE's mischief.

At length, Georgie stopped in a small clearing. "Okay. This is it."

Pete drew his gun and moved forward, looking around for their entry point. There was no fence or wall or even a building—just another group of trees with more urns scattered about the roots.

"Where is it?" the Agent asked.

Georgie approached a group of urns, bent, and stood again, holding a very small box. As he did, the Agent's heart sank. This is what he had been hiding from her, the reason why he—as June—had tried to endear himself to her. He was the bearer of bad news.

"No," she whispered as he walked toward her. "It's not true!"

The possibility of seeing her son again had been holding her together, and now that possibility was fading. All of the strength that it had taken to get through the many obstacles of the past year began to drain away. Seeming to have expected this response, Georgie caught the Agent before she could collapse.

"I found him, Sheebs," he whispered, holding her tightly. "I infiltrated the facility where they were keeping him. And I clipped a piece of his hair and put it in this box here, so you'd believe me. I saw firsthand what they were doing to him, the experiments they conducted, infecting him and nursing him back to health only to reinfect him. I couldn't leave him there!"

"No, no," the Agent murmured, covering her ears.

"He did prove remarkably resilient in the face of disease, so I found a way to infect him with a severe case of ebola," Georgie continued. "And when he started manifesting symptoms, the disease traveled through the vents. The facility staff couldn't contain it, so WCE leadership ordered a bomb strike as cleanup."

The Agent let out a loud wail that was somehow both strong and pitiful, anguished and fierce. She jerked herself out of Georgie's arms, ready to run anywhere to escape this awful news. But Pete stepped into her path and put his arms around her. She would have liked to punch his lights out for intruding on her pain, but Rosa would not allow it.

The Agent could not accept that her son was dead. She could not bear the thought of a world without him. She *would* not. So, she did not resist as she felt herself sinking, sinking, sinking. She sank down into the deepest depths where she could remain unbothered in her pain.

Rosa began to sob. It was the only appropriate outlet for pain of such a magnitude.

Georgie was stroking her hair. "I knew about the coming cleanup. So, I stole a hazmat suit and tried to get the boy out through the underground tunnels."

His voice cracked. "I had him slung over my shoulder and I was running with him as fast as I could go. But the bombing started before I could get to the exit. I got knocked out by a blast, and when I came to, there was nothing but rubble around me."

Rosa raised her tearstained face. "You mean, you never saw his body?"

"Well, no," Georgie said. "No one found a body. But that blast blew me backwards a hundred meters into a solid wall! Your son was in my arms, but he was just a tiny little fellow. There's no way he survived the blast."

So, Georgie was the bearer of bad news about a death that he could not confirm. His story lined up suspiciously with the one that the Assistant Vice had wanted the Agent to believe all along.

"When did it happen?" Rosa asked.

"A few weeks ago."

She smiled resolutely. "Then, my son is alive. I sensed him only a few days ago on my sickbed."

Georgie used his sleeve to dab a tear off of Rosa's chin. "Dear sister, our extra help can do many things, but the bots cannot help us to sense the life of another being."

"Not the bots," Rosa said, standing upright. "No, not the bots."

Pete also offered his sleeve to her as tissue, but she declined.

"My son is alive," she repeated.

"None of the WCE's specimens survived," Georgie told her. "They're scrambling with no leads on how to salvage their genetic disease resistance research program, which means that if your son is alive, he's probably not with the WCE anymore."

"All the better," said Rosa. "My boy will find a way to survive in this world. He'll have a better chance without the WCE torturing him."

"Let's hope so," Pete said.

"The WCE aren't the only nasty people in the world," Georgie said.

"Yes, but they're the ones that are the most powerful," Rosa reminded him. "Anyone'd be better than them."

"True," Georgie shrugged. Then he smiled. "Well, sister, why don't you put this grief of yours to good use? You can still make your life worthwhile by obstructing as much of the WCE's efforts as you can while you've got breath in those lungs. Your uncompromisable immunity would be a powerful weapon to use against them."

Rosa nodded pensively. "A way to pass the time until I can pick up the trail again."

She noticed Pete looking between her and Georgie calculatingly.

At last, he said, "In a first, I agree with Georgie. Taking down the organization that separated you from your son sounds like a worthwhile endeavor. And if you take them down, you'll strike a blow to the harmful systems they perpetuate as well."

"They made us fear them, so now we can make them fear us!" Georgie said excitedly. "It is a much more efficient use of time to make our oppressors sweat, tearing down their towers of imperialism. Honestly, sister, that 'kid' business was just dead weight to you."

"Dead weight?" Fire flashed in the Agent's face as she lurched toward Georgie. "Come here, and I'll teach you what dead weight is!"

"You're not angry at me," Georgie said, backing up as she approached. "You're angry about your son. So, channel that into something useful. A little revenge'll get your blood pumping."

Before the Agent could pound Georgie into the ground, Pete stepped between them.

"Not revenge, Rosa," he said. "Purpose—something to fight for, you know? A way to make the world better, even when the world has done its best to make you worse."

"Yeah, purpose!" Georgie echoed, poking his head out from behind Pete.

"Purpose," Rosa repeated quietly, "to make the world better."

She thought of her son and the promise that she had made to him before he was born: that she would keep him safe. The fulfillment of that promise now seemed further away than ever, but maybe her promise could still be fulfilled in making the world safer for him to inhabit.

She looked up and smiled. "Maybe we'll even save some lives."

"You have my full support," Pete said, kissing her cheek.

"And mine." Georgie slipped the box containing Kiddo's lock of hair into Rosa's pocket.

As she felt the tiny box resting against her thigh, the Agent remembered the time that her comrade had delivered a box to her in Diablo. During that conversation, Reece as Arjun told her that to believe he was a double agent was an underestimation of his ability. And now, after his recent stunts at Home and with the canister and the story about her son's death, the Agent saw the potential truth of that statement. But he wasn't the only one who could play that game. She still believed he had information that she wanted, and she planned to get it from him.

Georgie and Pete were still regarding her concernedly. She tucked the past away in a place that was out of the way, yet still accessible, then took their hands.

"Three Phibs against the world," said Rosa.

"*Three* phibs?" Pete exclaimed.

"Well, sure," Rosa said, passing Georgie a carefully cultivated smile of gratitude. "Georgie's practically family to me. And he tried to save my son."

Georgie kissed her hand and smirked at Pete, who could not mask his horror.

"Oh, come on, Pete," Rosa said. "The chances of survival are much better with three Phibs than any one of us would have alone."

9 781737 727538